Bella Vita

ITALIA SERIES
BOOK TWO

MARY BELLE

Bella Vita | Mary Belle

ISBN: 979-8-9885228-2-9

eBook ISBN: 979-8-9885228-3-6

www.marybellebooks.com | info@marybellebooks.com

Edited by Elizabeth Lyons | www.elizabethlyons.com

Cover design by Debbie O'Byrne | www.jetlaunch.net

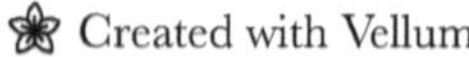 Created with Vellum

For my mom; my love of writing romance stems from your love of reading it, from Wulfgar to Gennaro and beyond.

And for my dad; the ultimate gentleman and the first man I ever loved.

Thank you both for always believing in me, no matter what.

Bella Vita

"Open my heart and you will see graved inside of it, 'Italy'."

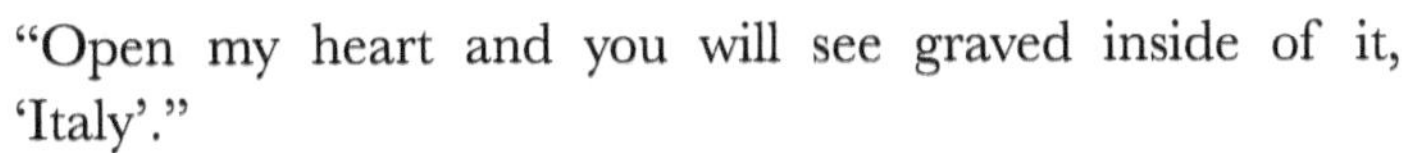

— *Robert Browning* (1812-1889), English Poet & Playwright

Character List

In true Italian-American form, there's a lot of people around here, okay?! Here's a reminder…

The Beletta Family

Rocco (*Papa*), Father

Giovanna (*Gigi or Mama*), Mother

Gennaro, Eldest Brother

Giovanni, Middle Brother

Giuseppe, Youngest Brother

Beletta Family Friends

Pesca Garmo, Parents' Family Friend

Vincenzo Messaro, Gennaro's Best Friend

Salvatore Rosa, Gennaro's Best Friend

Marco Bianci, Gennaro's Rome Polizia Partner

Giustino, Rome Apartment Neighbor & Marco's Uncle

Gina, Rome Apartment Receptionist

Francesca Taglia, Giuseppe's Fiance

Carmine, Owner of Local Osteria

The Luciano Family

Santino, Father

Sophia, Mother

Leonardo (*Lenny*), Brother

Stella, Sister

Jimmy, Brother-in-Law

Mia, Youngest Sibling

Luciano Family Friends

Allie Manten, Mia's Best Friend

Summer

CHAPTER 1

Gennaro

Regret can cause a ripple effect that painstakingly burns through every last part of your heart. Sometimes we regret the things we do, and other times, the things we don't. I sat in the hospital waiting room, with memories of the last two weeks flashing in constant rotation through my mind. As if the ambiance of a medical facility wasn't depressing enough, I found myself bouncing from the worry about an ill parent to the supreme heartache of falling deeply in love with a soulmate who vanished as quickly as she appeared. Add to that the guilt of thinking about her while my father's condition remained unknown, and I felt myself come undone.

Tears pooled in the corners of my eyes, rolling down my cheeks before falling in my lap. I hung my head in my hands, partially hiding my face from Mama, who would have cried instantly had she seen me, and from my brothers, both of whom had their own feelings of regret to navigate.

Life is messy. It tests you repeatedly. And just when you file one lesson away, another often presents itself shortly after. You can either live in a constant state of worry over what's coming next or embrace the challenges and look forward to the growth that stems from them. Mia and I challenged each other to live presently, enjoying each day as it came. And while my heart absolutely ached for her, I knew the most important things to focus on in that moment were my father and my family.

"Mrs. Beletta?" The waiting room was filled with a variety of people, but as Mama stood up, the nurse locked eyes with her, walked over, and motioned for her to sit back down. Calmly, she said, "Your husband had a heart attack."

Mama clutched the rosary beads she'd woven between her fingers until her knuckles turned white, urging the nurse to continue without uttering a word.

The nurse firmly grabbed her hand. "He's stabilized but has a long road ahead of him. An event like this can cause heart damage resulting in chronic congestive heart failure and possibly, eventual total heart failure."

"Meaning he could die?" Her eyes widened and her chest puffed in and out in an effort to hold back tears.

"Possibly, but like I said, he's stable for now. You can go in and see him in a bit."

"He's already awake?"

"He's conscious and in and out of sleep. This kind of episode takes a huge toll on the body so he won't be able to talk much." The nurse answered some more questions with a few tiny attempts at finding shreds of positivity before returning through the double doors. We had to wait a bit before being permitted to see him, and it was clear none of us knew what to say to each other as Mama and I sat alongside my brothers in uncomfortable, disheartening silence.

It was around ten in the evening, and the last few hours

had been an exhausting blur, beginning with Papa unleashing every unfiltered thought he had on Mia after our family dinner. I didn't know what her plan was, given that she left for the airport half a day before she was scheduled. Was she waiting at the airport until her flight tomorrow? Had she found an earlier one?

A large part of me felt that I should make the grand gesture to intercept her so she wouldn't leave on such a negative note, but it didn't seem practical. It didn't feel *right*, no matter how much I wanted our two weeks *not* to be completely tainted by the last smidge of our time together.

Mia was level-headed and mature, and no matter how horribly Papa had spoken to her, she'd understand the severity of the situation if she knew, I was sure of it.

> Gennaro: Did you get to the airport?

Seeing three dots pop up nearly immediately, I assumed that she was still at the airport. Also, there was no hesitation to respond, which helped me avoid overthinking.

> Mia: I did

Her two-word response gave me pause until three more dots popped up, preventing my brain from going into further overdrive.

> Mia: You okay?

> Gennaro: I'm at the hospital

> Gennaro: Not for me

> Gennaro: For Papa

> Mia: What??

Gennaro: He had a heart attack sometime after you left

Mia: I didn't think I could feel worse but now I do

Gennaro: Absolutely not your fault

Gennaro: I wasn't even going to tell you so you wouldn't worry

Mia: Is your family with you?

Gennaro: Yea, we're all here

Mia: Okay. Let me know how he is

Mia: I'm about to board

Mia: There was an earlier red eye

Gennaro: Safe trip

Gennaro: Ti amo

Three dots popped up and disappeared, then popped up and again disappeared.

"Think they've got a bar here?"

"In a hospital? There's something wrong with you, Giovanni, you know that?" I said, squinting my eyes at him and shaking my head.

"So I've been told my whole life," he responded quickly, "but lucky for me, I still don't give a shit. Just trying to lighten the mood."

Giuseppe stared forward from his seat like a zombie, running his hands through his hair with a pained look on his face, incessantly tapping his right foot. "I could use a few drinks myself."

"You can both wait until we see our father," I said,

laying out expectations before either of them thought to start running around town while I picked up the pieces. Mama hadn't shed a tear, always stoic in the moment and releasing pent up emotion somewhere down the line, which meant it would all come streaming out of her soon.

I took the opening I had to check in on her as we waited for clearance to go upstairs to see Papa.

"I know you're not *okay*, but do you want to talk about everything?" I asked, placing her hand in mine and squeezing it gently, a necessary reminder that I was there to support her. She inhaled deeply and exhaled slowly before the tears began falling, as I had predicted.

"I…I can't believe this happened," she stammered.

"Can't believe he had a heart attack?" I tried to clarify.

"All of it. I can't believe what he said to Mia, I can't believe she left, and I can't believe we are here right now," she managed to summarize. "You asked me a lot of questions earlier about my happiness, my life, and my marriage." She wiped away a small tear before continuing. "And you're right, I've never felt particularly *happy*, I've just always forced myself to enjoy what I could."

My heart felt a squeeze of dull pain. I didn't want to cause her sadness or frustration, and I certainly didn't want her to think negative thoughts as Papa lay in a hospital bed above us somewhere. But I also loved her far too much to stand idly by and watch the rest of life whiz past her at warp speed.

She carried on. "You're going after what you want and what you believe in. I've never seen you more comfortable or at ease before Mia arrived. It reminds me of what I dreamed of as a little girl and never quite had for myself. The way Papa and I were forced together removed the *fairy tale* stuff and the years that followed felt a lot more like *busi-*

ness than *romance*." She paused, reflecting. "But we sure did grow to love one another."

She hadn't told me anything I hadn't seen for myself since I'd been old enough to notice. They accomplished an incredible amount together, and they undoubtedly loved each other, but it usually came at a cost. Lack of adoration, affection, and romantic gestures was a steep price to pay as far as I was concerned.

"That's why I never wanted anything with Francesca," I explained. "I didn't have a choice in much of it, but I wasn't going to parade around like it was something I asked for. It actually made me hate the thought of anything having to do with relationships, until…"

"Mia," she interjected.

"Right. My world quite literally stopped."

As if the Universe knew I was hanging on by an emotional string, my phone dinged.

> Mia: My heart physically hurts

> Mia: I miss you already

My hands found their way to my cheeks. I rubbed my eyes, folded them behind my head, and leaned back in the waiting room chair, looking up at the fluorescent ceiling lights, hoping for a temporary distraction. Mama snapped me back to reality.

"Are you planning to see her again?"

"I'd love to, but how?" I shook my head with uncertainty. She'd just told me she missed me, but could this even be anything? The distance was one thing, Papa was another.

"We—and by *we*, I mean *men*—often complicate romantic gestures," she said, matter-of-factly.

The corners of my mouth turned upwards, and I dipped my head in her direction. "Is that right?"

"All I've ever wanted Papa to do was to take me on a date." I could hear the sadness in her voice, and it sent another stabbing pain through my heart.

"He's never taken you on a date?" I was surprised by her admission, but the more I thought about it, I realized in my nearly thirty years, I'd never seen the two of them off the property unless it was for a family event.

She quietly shook her head and looked upwards, scrolling through her life's highlights before responding, "Not a proper one. Maybe one dinner at a restaurant when we first were arranged, but that was all. It's always been work and the property and work some more."

My heart broke for her, and then I felt angry again.

"Don't waste any time being upset about that. It's my life, not yours, and it brought me you and your brothers. You can still be different. You *are* different." She grabbed my hand. "I can tell you, without a doubt, all Mia wants is to know that she's a priority to you."

She lay her head on my shoulder and drifted off to sleep within a few minutes, emotional exhaustion finally taking its toll. I sat contemplating Mama's suggestion about visiting Mia and realized I needed to let Papa know how I felt about all of this. Although I highly doubted he'd *ever* give us his blessing, I'd at least give him the opportunity to.

About an hour later, the nurse quietly nudged us both until our eyes blinked open. "Mrs. Beletta? You can go in to see him now."

Giovanni and Giuseppe waited downstairs while Mama and I rode the elevator until the doors opened to another dimly lit, depressing hallway. We walked the length of it to find Papa's room, entered quietly, and watched as he slowly turned his head in our direction. Almost immediately, a single tear rolled down the side of his face, the likes of which I hadn't seen in my lifetime. I briefly wondered if he was emotional due to his near brush with death, or if it had something to do with Mia, and by default, me. But when he reached out for Mama's hand and pulled her close to his bedside, refusing to let her go and crying fully, I realized both of my assumptions were wrong.

Perhaps the aftereffects of his heart attack had less to do with resulting scar tissue and more to do with softening the existing muscle surrounding it. Maybe nearly losing his life forced him to realize what he had barely appreciated for the majority of it. Maybe the recent trauma inflicted on his heart would push out the trauma of years past, and he'd find room to shower Mama with the romantic gestures she deserved, after all. But his show of emotion was short lived.

He had softened temporarily in response to seeing Mama, but when his eyes narrowed at the sight of me, I quickly realized the judgmental, critical, hard-to-satisfy version of him was still prevalent. A near brush with death had not changed his thought process regarding Mia and me, it appeared.

I powered through, regardless. "Papa, are you in pain?"

"Takes some effort to breathe, but…" He cleared his throat with his arms wrapped around a pillow for chest support. "I'm doing okay," he finished pointedly, tough old bird he is, and while I felt myself moderately tweaked by it, I was empathetic to the fact that he nearly lost his life and was likely processing many emotions, whether he wanted to admit to it or not.

"I'm here in support of you," I reminded him, briefly hesitating before I continued, "but you don't seem happy that I am."

He struggled to catch his breath, and Mama moved in closer to him, holding his hand to support him through it.

Unconditional love. Supporting the person you learned to love over the course of your life, even in spite of the ways they had let you down. It was enviable in a way, but nothing I wanted for myself. Waiting for the possibility of being *without* someone before they showed me proper attention or affection was not a way to live, as far as I was concerned.

Papa finally responded after regaining his breath. "I wouldn't be here if you hadn't brought her to our home."

I felt my body tense up at his admission and slowly inhaled, trying to maintain my composure. Disrespecting my father was something I'd always consistently tried to avoid. This moment was no different, regardless of the fact that he was still disrespecting me and my own adult choices.

He was old school, thick-headed, and completely impossible to get through to in so many ways.

But still, he was my father.

"What do you hate about her so much? That she's an American? Or that she's not Francesca?"

"We had a plan, and…" He hugged the pillow again to brace himself as he coughed, then continued speaking like the obstinate man that he was. "You didn't follow it."

"Rocco, now is not the time," Mama implored, but as was customary, he waved his hand for her to stop talking, the tear he had just shed not even dry on his cheek.

It was the final sign I needed to make the right decision for myself. If Papa had the ability to change, a life-threatening medical complication would be the thing that would do it, wouldn't it? But it was clear as day, he had no interest in trying to understand someone else's perspective.

If he was awake and alert enough to continue acting

like this, he was healthy enough for me to leave him in the care of my mother and brothers. I knew in my heart what I needed to do.

"Papa, there is not one thinkable scenario that warrants the way you spoke to Mia. *She* is the only reason I've ever envisioned myself running our property. *She* brought the beauty, peace, and enjoyment of it to the forefront for me. I love her."

"*Sei pazzo. La conosci a malapena!*" he interrupted,

The irony behind him calling me crazy for feeling this way after barely knowing Mia was lost on him. After all, this was the same man who had arranged my marriage and had his own marriage arranged, to someone *he* barely knew.

"I'm going to go downstairs and have Giovanni and Giuseppe come up." I leaned in to kiss him goodbye on the cheek, and he waved me off in the same manner he did Mama. Shedding my own protective layer to make sure I didn't live with any regrets whatsoever, I continued. "I'm glad you're okay, I really am, but I'm not sure we're ever going to understand each other. I finally began to love our home, our property, and our business, and because I'm not with the person *you* want me to be with, it's not enough. I love you, I'll always love you, I'm thankful for all you've taught me, but I need to follow my own path."

Mama hugged me, an embrace in which I felt completely understood and supported. As always, it made up for the shortcomings that stemmed from my relationship with my father. "Meet you downstairs," she assured me.

At least I had someone in my corner.

Papa and I wanted the same thing—a thriving family business that we were proud of—we just differed on the way to achieve it. So, I decided to control the only part of the process I knew I could. After walking out of his room and stepping onto the elevator, I picked up my phone and opened a text message.

Gennaro: I need your help

Pesca: Don't you always?

If I was going to surprise Mia with a visit in an effort to fix the mess that Papa had left us in, I'd need Pesca to assist.

Local romantic gestures were relatively easy, but coordinating a trip to another country to visit a family I hadn't met yet was something else entirely.

CHAPTER 2

Mia

June, Two weeks later

"Wow, I was expecting to walk into a little more of a shit show." Allie nodded her head slowly with partial approval, assessing both me and my apartment a couple weeks after I returned home, and one day after I texted her for emotional support in the form of a girls' lunch.

After calling from the airport in Rome the night I left Gennaro and filling her in on Papa's choice words, Allie promised to come visit as soon as possible. Given her own marital issues, and as the primary caretaker of her two kids, our reunion was put on a temporary hold. Finally together again, I was excited to spend time with my best friend, but my apartment and life as a whole felt wildly different than it did a few weeks prior.

There was no terrace balcony overlooking Rome, no sliding glass door leading to an infinity pool with a vineyard settled behind it, and most importantly, no handsome man with a glass of wine in one hand and a plate of incredible food in the other reminding me daily all the ways he loved, wanted, and desired me.

Inner Critic: Oooph
Inner Critic: You sound depressed
Mia: Aren't you?
Inner Critic: I mean, North Jersey traffic and New
    York City pollution floating across the Hudson
    River towards us isn't quite as endearing as
    Italy
Mia: So we're both depressed
Inner Critic: You said it, not me

"I'm not sure if that was a compliment or not," I replied, giving Allie a single eyebrow raise.

"Well, my best friend got dicked down for nearly fourteen days by an Italian hottie, probably endured a lack of sleep while doing so, got ripped a new one by the hottie's father before a dramatic early departure for the airport, leaving said father to have a near fatal heart attack, and has been holed up in her apartment since arriving back home, contemplating her life's choices and wondering if the Italian hottie is, in fact, as fabulous as he seems or an asshole like the rest of them. Anything I missed?"

"You did a fantastic job recounting the sporadic vacation texts and emergency airport phone call to recreate an accurate timeline. Very impressive, actually," I half-smiled.

"I *do* pay attention," she reminded me, "even when my own world is spinning like a goddamn tornado."

"Speaking of which, I feel like you need to update me on some things," I reminded her.

Allie shook her head. "Oh no you don't. Don't change the subject just yet. How much have you two spoken since you've been home?"

"Short of texting each other daily and an occasional FaceTime, not much. I'm trying to give him space to deal with the villa and Papa's recovery and don't want to be overbearing."

"Yes, very good, give him some space. They always want what they can't have," she said with an eye roll, clearly jaded by men in general.

"He's not one of those, I know that for sure." I smiled, recalling that the qualities Gennaro possessed were far different from most other men I'd come in contact with. But it didn't seem the right time to gush about them when I could sense Allie was going through it on her end. "Anyway, let's go eat, you pain in my ass."

She blew me an air kiss as we grabbed our purses and headed out. "There's no need for name calling. Are you in withdrawal? Do you have a vibrator?"

I stared at her with my middle finger in the air, a small smile, and a lack of energy for the verbal response it warranted. I was *hangry*, my brain stopped working the moment I was famished, and now she was talking to me about sex toys.

"That's your solution? A vibrator?" I shook my head and closed the door behind us.

"Absolutely. A lack of orgasms can cause distress and anxiety, you know?" She didn't have an indoor voice, but the decibel level she was hitting as we walked the hallways of my building were a bit much, even for her. "I found that on Google a few months ago when I was researching."

"You researched the side effects of not having enough orgasms?" I tried whispering as we waited for the elevator, but she didn't take the hint. Nervous energy had her pushing the "down" button repeatedly, even though it was already lit. As I had detected a few minutes earlier, she had something on her mind and was distracting herself by focusing on me and my "issues."

"Well, yeah," Allie shrugged and then loudly

exclaimed, "when your husband hasn't touched you in months, barely looks at you, and is working *late* more than he ever has, you start to Google a lot of things."

The elevator doors opened, and thankfully no one was in it. When they shut, I asked, "What *else* have you Googled?"

"Oh, I don't know. Signs of cheating, infidelity indicators, couples therapy, difference between mediation and divorce…"

It was the first time she'd stopped the back-and-forth banter since arriving at my place, and I noticed unmistakable dark circles under her eyes.

"You think he's cheating on you?" I asked, pressing the button for the first floor.

She blinked slowly while inhaling deeply, and then tears began rolling down her cheeks. She barreled into me and threw her arms around my waist, squeezing tightly before the doors opened. My own eyes pooled with tears as my heart broke for her. I wasn't at all prepared for where this conversation was headed, but I quickly adjusted. Whatever I had going on with Gennaro was not nearly as important as my best friend struggling through her marriage and contemplating divorce with two kids in tow.

"Looks like we need a liquid lunch," I suggested.

"And fries." She squeezed my hand and managed a small smile.

We drove fifteen minutes down the road to the bar I worked at, planning to Uber home if the need arose.

Did it ever.

After our second martini, we realized there was still more to catch up on and contemplated a third.

> *Inner Critic: You realize it's barely noon on a week-*
> *day, right?*

> *Me: What's the issue?*
> *Inner Critic: If you need me to tell you what the*
> *issue is, you're already drunk*
> *Me: I learned to live in the moment while I was in*
> *Italia*
> *Inner Critic: Okay, but you're home now*
> *Inner Critic: You need to like, I don't know, find a*
> *job or something*
> *Me: Lighten up*
> *Me: You want another martini?*
> *Inner Critic: Fuck it, sure*
> *Inner Critic: Get some potato skins, too*

"Can we get another round, more fries, and some loaded potato skins?" I asked our server. I was in full Italian detox mode, shoving American bar food down my gullet in an effort to ease my mind and soothe both of our hearts.

Allie's situation was profoundly affecting me. How often did we, as single gals, dream of being married one day, assuming in certain ways it would be the answer to all of our "problems"? Meanwhile, the majority of those who *were* married seemed to have their own sets of issues? It was a tale as old as time: learning to enjoy the now rather than pursuing "next destination happiness."

"Okay so, he's working late, you haven't had sex in six months, he isn't helping out at home, you're generally miserable, you feel like you have a useless roommate, and you're trying to keep it together for the kids?" I summarized our first hour of conversation.

"Well that was a depressing sum…summary." She took the first sip of her third martini with red cheeks, a hiccup, and a small stutter.

"Let's focus less on the depressing factors and more on

what we're going to do about it," I suggested. "Have you asked him, point blank?"

"Hey asshole, are you cheating on me while you ignore your family?" She rolled her eyes and shook her head, embarrassed even to say the words out loud. "No, I haven't. I'm just not prepared for the answer."

"Do you think it's something therapy could even help with?" I asked, unsure how much she had researched or how long she had actually been feeling this way.

"To be honest, I have no idea. When he started to *check out*, I think I *checked out* shortly after. It's easier when he isn't around. I'm a better mom when he's not around. I physically dread it when he *does* come home."

True to character and not at all helped by martini number three, I considered my next statement only briefly before it came flying out of my mouth. "If it helps at all, I was never a huge fan of his."

"You don't say." She narrowed her eyes at me and slightly furrowed her brows. "You two have hated each other since high school."

"He cheated on you back then with a freshman, during your senior year, no less. Don't get me started, I want to punch him in his face." While I didn't want to tell her *what* to do, I could at least blame the honest recap of her marriage that was about to come flying off my lips on the martinis, should she take exception to it. "You're too good for him. And I know women often say this to each other without any sort of accurate assessment of our own flaws, but really, yours peak with you never spending money on yourself, surviving on Perdue Dino Nuggets and Kraft Mac & Cheese, and exhausting yourself being the best mother ever. He should feel lucky to have a low-key, easy-to-please woman by his side."

She chugged the rest of her martini and her eyes

started to glaze over, so I signaled for the check. Thankfully none of the staff working were people I'd worked with during shifts before I left for Italy. We weren't embarrassing ourselves by any means, but I didn't need any judgment for weekday drinking.

"Well, he doesn't feel that way…clearly," she retorted.

"How do *you* feel?" I asked, straight-faced, as we got up to walk out. "It sounds like you're feeling sorry for yourself that he's out doing whatever it is you think he's doing. But honestly, if finances and work benefits weren't a consideration, would you even want to still be with him? Do you actually see yourself growing old with him?"

"I haven't thought that far ahead," she shrugged. We walked out the front entrance toward the parking lot, immediately blinded by the midday sun.

As she stumbled past me, I held the door for someone who was heading inside while continuing with my line of questioning. "Well, do it now. Think of one year from now, five years from now, and ten years from now. What do you want that to look like?"

A life coach in the making, clearly, only I didn't get an answer. Instead, I turned around just in time to watch her fall head first into a bush.

And then she threw up.

Thankfully, Allie spared the Uber driver's car, but I quickly realized I'd have to call her husband to let him know she'd be staying with me for the next few hours to sober up. We barely made it up the walkway of my apartment building, into the elevator, and down the hall without injury before noisily managing to get the key in the correct door. She passed out on the couch almost immediately after we got inside.

Damn. Drinking in our mid-twenties could have been an Olympic sport. I had no idea what time it was and was starting to feel dizzy myself but managed to grab her phone from her purse. Unlocking it was easy since she'd had the same passcode since high school. There were eight missed messages from her husband, which I opened because curiosity got the best of me.

> Asshole: How am I supposed to make mac and cheese without milk?

> Asshole: What time do they have to be at dance?

> Asshole: Are you alive??

> Asshole: Wow

> Asshole: Okay

An hour later were two missed calls and the rest of his messages.

> Asshole: They're crying for mommy

> Asshole: I can't listen to this shit anymore

> Asshole: I'm taking them to my parents

What a useless prick.

I dialed him immediately from her phone.

"Look who decided to join the parent party. Having fun in the middle of the week like you're still twenty years old or what?" He wasn't yelling but his attitude was thick and laced with sarcasm, par for the course.

"We *are* having fun, thanks for asking. Shame you can't manage to be a parent for a few hours by yourself, but you'll have to hang tight for a while longer, champ. Allie will be home later." I waited for his smartass remark, and he didn't disappoint.

"Cut the shit, Mia. Tell her to come home now."

"She'll come home when she's ready," I said. Feeling the need to further clarify my sentiments, I followed that with "And don't ever tell me what the fuck to do again" before hanging up.

Every time I saw or talked to him, my blood boiled. They were high school sweethearts, Allie was pregnant by twenty-one, and they were married quickly before her first daughter was born. He was a mechanic but acted like a cop who worked night shifts, coming home whenever he damn well pleased, even if it was in the middle of the night. The only actual connection he had to law enforcement though, was a few misdemeanor charges from bar fights.

I didn't hate many people, but he was one of them. In turn, it was the only thing I didn't "like" about Allie. She was smart and funny with a huge heart, and she could dish out advice like nobody's business. When it came to him, though, she had an incredible lack of self-confidence that simply wouldn't quit. It wasn't quite as hard to understand when we were eighteen and he was the hottest guy in school, but a daily nutritional intake that consisted mostly of beer and cigarettes had not been kind to him.

I planned to tell Allie how I felt about him when she regained consciousness and sobered up. While waiting for that to happen, I continued the Italy-withdrawal stress cleaning I had begun the day prior to avoid taking the nap my body was craving. The Italian playlist poured from my Bluetooth speaker at a low volume, as it had every day since I had returned home, instantly transporting me back. My cheeks flushed envisioning him shirtless around the villa, and my heart began racing thinking of every single place we had, *ahem*, christened.

After a couple of hours scrubbing and organizing, I placed the bottle of cologne Gennaro had mailed me on top of my bedroom dresser, then sat on my bed to text him, because what's a better time to do that than after a few martinis in the middle of a week day?

Mia: How's Papa?

Gennaro: Stable and coming home in a few days

Mia: That's good news, no?

Gennaro: It's better than the alternative for sure

Mia: Oh, also....

Gennaro: Yes?

Mia: I'm craving tomatoes

I threw my phone on the bed, only partially embarrassed by my attempt at sexual humor while simultaneously praying he knew what the hell I was referring to. A few minutes later my phone dinged, and he confirmed, once again, that he was incapable of letting me down.

Gennaro: I'm craving red lace

Gennaro: You can have all the tomatoes you want if you show up here wearing that again

"Italian hottie sending you dirty text messages? And, what's that?" Allie looked like she had run a half marathon with hair matted to the sides of her head, skin flushed as she limped toward my dresser, taking the Acqua dell'Elba bottle in her hands and slowly inhaling. "Holy shit, is this what he smells like?"

I smiled.

"No wonder you're in withdrawal. Christ." She inhaled deeply a second time, eyes slightly rolling back into her skull. "Also, what the hell just happened?"

"We went hard on some martinis, fries, and potato skins and did a lot of catching up," I reminded her.

"I feel like I got hit by a truck," she said, slowly shuffling into the bathroom and closing the door behind her before throwing up one last time.

"Remember when we used to drink twice this amount back in the old days?" I said, remembering some of our bar nights full of dance music, smoke machines, and neon strobe lights.

"I'll puke again thinking about it, so please stop," she said, walking back out and opening my fridge. "God, you're the best. What single chick in her twenties has homemade pizza ready for the toasting at any given moment?"

"One who likes to eat," I reminded her, "and give me that before you burn my place down."

She zombie walked back to the couch, sunk herself into it, and chugged a glass of water. "Thanks for taking care of me. I freaking missed you while you were gone."

Within a few minutes, Allie had three slices of pizza in her belly soaking up vodka remnants along with four Advil and another glass of water, and she was beginning to see the light at the end of the not-in-college-anymore tunnel.

"I missed you, too. Now, don't get mad at me, but…"

"I saw the messages from him, I know what you're going to say," she interjected with a hand in the air before I could finish what I was planning to say. "I need to figure out a plan before I leave him."

"You just saved me a lot of talking," I half smiled, trying to gauge her reaction.

"It's nothing I don't already know or think, I've stalled long enough, and now I need to start taking my own advice." She shoved the last of the pizza crust in her mouth, and while she looked physically pained, I knew she meant what she was saying.

"I'm here for you, whatever you need," I reminded her.

"Can you tell me about your trip now?" she asked, diverting the subject at hand and pulling a blanket up and over her shoulders as she buried herself further into the couch.

"You already know what happened on my trip!" I wasn't sure how much detail she was really asking for, but quickly remembered why she was my best friend. Putting her own issues aside, she wanted to support me the best way she knew how–by letting me relive the best two weeks of my entire life.

She smiled with her eyes closed and urged me to start talking. "I want all the juicy details…from the top. Make me believe in true love again."

I spent the next couple hours recounting every detail, large and small, from meeting Gennaro to the day I left. I fell in love with him all over again, and it appeared that she had fallen in love with him, too.

I couldn't blame her.

"Okay, so which one of his brothers is single?" she asked.

"Are you planning on moving your two daughters to Italy?" I smiled back at her. "Because there is no chance that any of those Beletta boys would ever move away from there."

"Guess I have to get divorced, too, now that you mention it."

"Minor detail," I softly responded, fully aware that she

was peppering her thoughts with sarcasm and humor but was genuinely hurting inside.

Allie exhaled loudly, rubbed her temples, and reluctantly stood up from the couch.

"Time to go back to the crazy house." She hugged me tightly. "I am so incredibly happy for you. It sounds like the real thing, and it feels like the real thing. The minute you start thinking there's no way it could possibly work out the way you want it to, remember there's a reason he showed up in your life to begin with."

"That sounds very *everything happens for a reason* of you," I replied with a slight raise of my eyebrow.

"Yea, yea…just because my life is currently a raging dumpster fire doesn't mean I can't recognize the good in things when they're staring me right in the face." She grabbed her bag, opened the door, and spun back around with a finger pointed at me. "And I'm serious, you better pair me with someone fun in the bridal party."

CHAPTER 3

Gennaro

Family has a way of banding together during hard times. Even with underlying drama and occasional resentment, it seems to be the body's natural response to temporarily shelve those things in an effort to reach a common goal.

We had all taken turns visiting Papa in the hospital over the course of the last two weeks, and Giovanni volunteered to stay there for the last few days while he had time off from the Florence-based law firm where he was employed. With a relatively neutral prognosis, doctors allowed Papa the option to return home and recover, so long as he kept physical exertion to a minimum. It would be tough for him, not being able to assist, but we all agreed it was best for everyone involved. There would be fewer trips to the hospital, he'd be more physically comfortable, and we could all collectively keep an eye on him, thereby forcing him to rest and relax.

Or so we hoped.

Mama, Giuseppe, Pesca, and I were holding it all together in Papa's absence with guests on property and even more checking in weekend after weekend. It had been an unsettling feeling, parking our car and walking up to the main house without hearing the whirs of lawn equipment, the spray of a hose, or much of anything else without him buzzing around but, I could feel a sense of purpose and camaraderie between the rest of us to simply get it all taken care of. With so much work to do, I was pleasantly surprised when Giuseppe picked up an actual clipboard and started rattling off tasks to be completed in an organized fashion.

"I'm impressed by your pen to paper dedication," I told him with a smile.

With a roll of his eyes and a punch in the shoulder, as younger brothers do, he responded, "Yeah, yeah, thanks a lot."

He finally had the ability to shine, recently taking over my spot as Papa's right-hand man. For once, it was nice to show up on my days off from police work in Rome and be directed where I was needed. It took some unnecessary stress away from the usual push-and-pull dynamics when Papa and I worked together. We had put finishing touches on landscaping and pool maintenance, rooms were cleaned for new arrivals, and Mama had the kitchen smelling like a combination of roasted garlic, sautéed onions, basil, and a fresh pop of sweet cherry tomatoes at any given moment.

Papa would be proud, I thought—or maybe not—since he seemed to always have a critique of some kind. I attempted to push away my negative thoughts, regardless of the debacle that landed him in the hospital in the first place. His words had stung, and I wasn't even the one he had unleashed them on. Anger filled me up again as I replayed his verbal attack on Mia in my mind. He was still trying to tell me what to do and who to be, and I tried my best to come back down from it.

Watching my father go through a serious medical

emergency *did* put my brain in constant replay mode of "what ifs," "should haves," and "should not haves." You always think you have longer with the people you're closest to than you actually do, and I wanted to ensure that if and when the time came, I was as supportive as possible, no matter how I felt he had handled the situation with Mia. It was why I kept reiterating that I *did* respect him, but I had to respect *myself* more.

"I can smell your brain cells burning."

I whirled around to see Pesca walking toward me. A big smile on her face, arms open wide, she wrapped me in the bear hug I didn't know I needed. *Honorary aunt strikes again.* "Loaded question, but how are you doing?"

Tilting my head back and looking up at the sky, I tried to describe exactly how I *did* feel. "Confused," I said, shrugging matter-of-factly. "I'm confused and I feel hollow, all while trying to keep it together on the outside."

"That's a lot," she said, looking at me with a bit of worry.

"I mean, I'm here trying to help Mama and Giuseppe, but all I can think about is Mia." I scratched the back of my neck and continued, sitting down with her one-on-one for the first time since requesting her assistance a couple of weeks ago. "I need your help arranging a trip to see her, preferably a surprise. I just don't know when I'd be able to do it, given all that's going on here on top of my regular work schedule."

"We can take care of everything here, Gennaro." Both our heads whipped around to find Mama standing behind us. "Giuseppe has been doing well managing things, Pesca's here for another month, and someone called in for some reinforcements, too."

She nodded toward the entrance to the property, and I turned to watch my best friend Salvatore walk down the driveway with our other best friend, Vincenzo's younger brother, Luca.

What were they doing here?

"I called here yesterday because you hadn't returned any of my messages for weeks," Sal said, narrowing his eyes on me with a smile and only partial judgment. "Pesca briefed me on everything going on." He put an arm around Luca's shoulders and continued, "Luca is in need of some income, and it's time for a job. So, it seemed like a decent plan for him to start now. You can train him, and Giuseppe can manage him while you're gone."

I looked toward Luca with a wrinkled brow, wondering how he got roped into coming. "My brother suggested all of this."

"You look thrilled about that," I joked, which helped loosen him up a bit. "Why do you seem petrified?"

"Uh, well, everyone always told me it's a little intense around here."

"An honest guy," I said. "I respect that. Truth is, though, the intense one is going to be recovering, so there's only so many orders he can bark at you. You'll be directly helping the sweet one, Mama, and the fun, slightly crazy one, my brother, Giuseppe. Think you can handle that?"

He nodded his head while quickly scouring the property, wide eyed.

"It's really not that bad. In fact, I bet you'll end up enjoying it. It's quiet, not many people bother you, and she'll feed you throughout the day," I assured him while nodding towards Mama. I surprised myself with my positive reinforcement and told Sal we'd catch up later over dinner.

Gennaro: Thanks for the little brother loan

Vincenzo: My pleasure

Vincenzo: It's about time he starts doing
something productive

Vincenzo: Dinner tonight?

Gennaro: Yes, I told Sal, too

After a quick thank you to Vin, Sal and Luca headed toward the pool area to meet up with Giuseppe while Pesca, Mama, and I went to the kitchen.

Mama, forever feeding everyone as a method of personal therapy, had the table set for a family of six, with warm bread, cheese, and hand-rolled gnocchi with fresh tomato sauce, a dollop of ricotta, and a drizzle of extra virgin olive oil. I felt myself start to unwind as she poured me a glass of red wine. It was the midday lunch break I needed, both mentally and physically.

"So, when do you think you want to schedule this trip to see Mia?" Pesca asked directly, getting right down to business.

"That's what I need your help with." I paused to think about it. "I have absolutely no idea. Surprising her seems to be the romantic option, but there's a lot of moving pieces involved with that, no?"

"Not when yours truly has a direct hotline to her family," Pesca confidently responded. "Do you have enough time at the precinct to take a week off?"

"I should, but even if I don't, I don't really care. The Polizia di Stato is just going to have to deal with it," I shrugged. "That sounds terrible, doesn't it?"

"Sounds like a man in love," Mama swooned, and it was at that moment I knew I had her full, complete support to chase the woman of my dreams, regardless of whatever family ties were hanging in the balance. It was always her unwavering support and loyalty that helped balance out the unpredictable negativity from Papa. This scenario was no exception.

"And you're sure you'll be okay for a week without me coming back to help out here and there?" Truthfully, I knew they'd be fine, but I needed to confirm it.

"If we have Luca here to help your brother, absolutely. We'll be fine," she responded with the same warm, sweet smile she'd given me since I was little.

"I'm going to reach out to Mia's parents then," Pesca chimed in. I nodded in agreement, a few nerves bubbling in my stomach.

Naturally, I took out my phone to text her so I could get the nerves to dissipate.

> Gennaro: ::picture of tomatoes on the counter::

> Gennaro: Friendly reminder that I still have tomatoes here waiting for you

I was smiling at my own messages now.

"They said they could FaceTime now if you want?" Pesca reported back within minutes.

My face turned hot, and my eyes doubled in size like I was back in grade school, called on to answer a question when I wasn't paying attention.

"Relax, they're normal people. Mia's great but she's not the *Princess of Wales*," Pesca said, playfully rolling her eyes and all but pushing me aside to call them.

I took a few more sips from my glass of wine and glanced at my phone while I waited.

> Mia: Feels a little ill timed to respond to the pomodoros in the manner that I want to

I was acting a lot more confident in the five-thousand-miles-of-separation text than I felt, preparing to speak to the parents of the beautiful woman who had just sent me a half-naked picture of herself.

Down boy.

"Here, I'd love for you to virtually meet Gennaro!" Pesca walked toward me with phone in hand.

Focus.

"Ciao, Santino…Sophia…so nice to meet you." I surveyed their faces for a reaction.

Sophia, much like Mama, was all smiles. Santino, much like Papa, the exact opposite.

Here we go.

"Don't worry, that's Santino's happy face," Pesca joked, breaking the awkward mini silence. I forced a smile and she continued. "Okay, so, we're assuming Mia filled you in on her trip since she arrived home?"

"Yes, she did! We are so thankful for all you did for her," Sophia responded. She was still beaming with happiness, so I could only assume that Mia didn't fill her in on *everything,* specifically the reason she went home slightly early.

"I had a great time with your daughter, and I'd love to

come visit as a surprise, if that's okay with all of you," I interjected.

"Oh my goodness. Absolutely!" Sophia solidified her Mama-like energy, which put a genuine smile on my face, replacing the forced one. "What do you need from us?"

Pesca, still acting as my dating coach, suggested, "Are you going to have the family down for the Fourth of July weekend? Maybe that would be a good time to surprise her. They can spend a few days, and everyone can meet Gennaro. Then the kids can decide what to do after that."

I loved her and was thankful for all she was helping with, but I could have done without the *kids* reference. Pesca must have felt it from me because she hit me with a side-eye and facial expression that said, "Sorry, merely trying to help."

I waved off her apologetic glance, smiled, and counted down the minutes until ending the FaceTime call with parents of the woman I was in love with after only two weeks, had sex with countless times, and had just sent me a lingerie picture, thereby making my pants bulge. The bottle of red wine was unfortunately out of reach, so I answered a few more questions from the lovely Sophia while Santino mostly looked like he wanted to murder me through the screen.

Off to a great start.

Twenty minutes later, the call was complete and my plan was set, even though I'd sprouted a few gray hairs getting to that point.

I'd leave in a couple of weeks and take a red-eye flight from Rome to Newark, New Jersey. Mia's sister would pick me up from the airport since she was a teacher and off for the summer, and we'd drive down to their parents' house together. I secretly hoped she had the same disposition as her mom, but time would tell.

I thanked Pesca profusely for her organization and tenacity, to say the least, feeling better that I had a solid plan in place to see Mia again. I'd worry about her father later, and for now, I'd focus on ensuring she knew exactly how much I still appreciated red lace.

> Gennaro: Sorry for the delay

> Gennaro: Took me a few minutes to pick my jaw up off the floor

Mia: Worth the wait

> Gennaro: Can I call you?

Mia: The answer to that is always yes

"I needed to hear your voice," I reminded her as I felt my body release the tension it was holding onto from the last few days. From her early departure to Papa's heart attack to picking up the pieces at the villa and scheduling a surprise trip I couldn't tell her about, a lot had happened, and we hadn't been able to talk through it besides some text exchanges and an occasional FaceTime.

For two people who had spent nearly two full weeks together, it was an abrupt change and one I didn't entirely appreciate.

"I didn't want to get in the way of anything having to do with your father," Mia quietly responded, "and felt it was best to give you a little space."

"Except as it relates to red lace and tomatoes?" I hoped the smile on my face translated through the phone.

"Precisely. Your father may hate everything about me, but everyone needs a nice garden tomato every now and again, you know?"

My heart involuntarily squeezed.

"My father hates mostly everything, so please don't take any of this personally," I urged her, fully grasping the difficulties associated with the request.

"If my trip there taught me anything, it's that I can't control things in the way I always thought I wanted to. I met you, I'm so grateful for it, and whatever is meant to happen after is what's meant to happen." She sounded like she was reciting a passage from a self-help novel, and I tried hard not to overanalyze her words.

"It was nice meeting you then, Gandhi." I refused to overthink, and leaned on subtle humor to pull us through.

"What's with the Gandhi reference?" I could detect a small chuckle through the phone, but if I knew her well, and I did, she was now analyzing what *I* had said.

"What? You didn't like a generalized response that sounds like an Oprah episode?"

"Okay, okay, I'm trying to play it cool like Allie suggested, but I miss every last thing about you." She exhaled longer and louder than I had ever heard, and it made me want to hop on a plane immediately rather than wait two weeks.

When you fall in love with someone, they take up a large chunk of real estate in your heart. When they hurt, you hurt in return. The truth was, we were both hurting as life swirled around us, not promising either of us a single thing in return.

"Here's the love of your life, five thousand miles away, with some overbearing parents thrown in for added dramatic effect. Now, what are you going to do about it?"

\- Life

What were we going to do about it? Playing it cool hadn't been a part of our vocabulary since the day we met.

"I know Allie means well, but you lit me on *fire* two weeks ago. Do *not* throw ice on it now."

A few seconds felt like minutes before Mia responded, "I'm scared. It feels like an uphill battle between distance and families to get to wherever it is we're meant to be."

Being scared was one thing, acting differently around each other to "play it cool" when we both already dove in headfirst was another. I wanted her to pour fuel on our fire, I wanted the flames to grow taller than I was, engulfing us fully. I wanted to remember why we fell for each other so hard in the first place, and I never wanted to forget what that real, Earth shattering, soul crushing, five-alarm-fire love *felt* like.

"Do you trust me?" I asked, the question now part of our relationship DNA.

I knew she did. She knew she did. But every once in a while, when hesitation and doubt and worry attempted to take over, we had to head back to basics to remember where we were, why we were, and where we wanted to go.

"More than I ever thought possible," she responded without hesitation.

"Good. I just need you to lean in, hang on, and try not to forget what it feels like when we're next to each other. The phone will destroy us if we let it, but we're not going to let that happen. Okay?" I had zero control over my father or Mia's father or much of anything else, but I could control my outlook and emotions as it related to us being together.

If I believed it to be possible. I could help to carry us across an eventual finish line, couldn't I?

That was the goal.

"I needed to hear that," she softly admitted.

"This is just the beginning for us, Mia." I'd have kissed her slowly, deeply, and purposefully if I had her within arm's length, but I didn't. I only had a phone. "I need you to trust that, too."

"I do."

"*Ti amo*," I reminder her, "*sempre*."

She was trying her hardest to believe in it all the same. "Forever," she repeated and confirmed, and this time, her exhale was softer, more relaxed, and more hopeful than before.

A late-night dinner that same evening with Sal and Vincenzo was exactly what I needed in the midst of moderate heartache and family drama. The support of friends could never be underestimated as life continued to take us in a variety of directions, none of which we were particularly prepared for.

Papa would return from the hospital soon, and I'd be counting down the days until I'd have Mia in my arms again, the thought of which would help me navigate the difficulties of having a full-time career, a recovering parent, and a family business where said recovering parent never quite made things easy.

There were no doubts in my mind about us picking up right where we left off emotionally or physically.

I did have a nagging feeling about something else I couldn't quite shake, though.

In a few weeks, I'd discover what it was. And, as it would become clear, it wasn't *only* her father who'd present themselves as a potential problem.

CHAPTER 4

Mia

JULY, TWO WEEKS LATER

A couple of weeks after my soul-bearing liquid lunch with Allie, the Fourth of July weekend had arrived. Red, white, and blue decor hung from homes and store fronts, and I was ready to welcome the impending holiday distraction with open arms and an average of eighty miles per hour down the Garden State Parkway. Gennaro and I continued to text and FaceTime, talking back and forth constantly, which felt good but also left a hollow pit of deep longing. I found myself frequently wishing to be back in Italy, which had a way of leaving me unsatisfied in my "regular" life.

When would I see him again? I told him I trusted him, and I did, so I had to believe that when the time was right, it would happen.

Not having seen my family since before I left for Italy was likely another cause of emptiness. Searching for jobs and interviewing for a variety of positions took up most of my time when I wasn't bartending, and while I loved spending time with them, I hadn't felt ready or willing to answer a barrage of looming questions.

Until now.

Strategy paired with a bit of luck helped me avoid the disaster that's typical holiday weekend travel. I made it to their house late Friday morning, before the majority of holiday travelers would be on the road and after the weekday morning commute debacle. All of those who live at, around, or down the Jersey Shore know the importance of avoiding unnecessary traffic for their mental health and sanity.

I quietly turned my key in an attempt to surprise my mom and dad, which was highly reminiscent of my 3am arrivals back in the day. While I had been to their new home plenty of times prior to my trip to Italy, it was nice to see how settled they had gotten. The house was similar in charm to our old home, with much of the same furniture, wall art, and picture frames but a few modern touches thanks to the newer construction. Somehow, it still smelled like the last house, likely in large part due to espresso, sautéed garlic, meatballs, and fried eggplant.

Speaking of which, I walked into the house somewhere around 11am to my mom layering slices of thin, floured eggplant with fresh mozzarella, a light onion tomato sauce, basil, and grated parmesan cheese. When she looked up from the counter to see me standing there, tears were streaming down her cheeks, which I wasn't expecting.

"Why are you crying?" I asked, embracing her with concern over why she was so emotional. I hadn't seen her in person for a while, but we'd spoken via text, phone, or FaceTime on and off, both while I was away and after I returned home.

"You'll understand when you're a parent one day," she

said, stepping back, scanning me from head to toe. "When your baby travels to another country alone, you worry."

"I'm not a baby anymore, Ma." I smiled, kissed her cheek, and sat on the kitchen counter to catch up as I used to do in the old house, fully planning to keep the tradition alive in the new one.

"You'll *always be* my baby," she smiled. "Too early for wine?"

"It's late enough in Italy, so let's roll with that." We clinked glasses and I filled her in on both Allie and Gennaro, leaving out a majority of the details involving Papa's early send off. Listening intently and offering some words of wisdom for each scenario, she quickly brought me right back to reality.

"So, what's next on the job front?" Ugh. Not now.

"Ma, it's a holiday weekend. The only thing I should be thinking of is when to switch over to beer after this morning wine, cheeseburger or hot dog for dinner, and SPF 15 or 30."

"SPF 30. You'll thank me in a few years." She side-eyed me with a smile but thankfully let the work-related question go.

I had to solidify what my next career move would be in the midst of applying and interviewing, but at that exact moment, all I wanted was my ass in a beach chair with salty air breezing through my hair and ocean waves crashing in front of me.

Ever a mind reader, she interjected my daydream. "Dad is at the club with his friends for lunch, he'll be home later this afternoon. Are you planning to head to the beach?"

My sister and her family would be arriving for dinner, and my brother was planning to drive down the next morning. I decided to take the available free time before the madness began. "Yea, I think I'm going to head there now."

"Enjoy it," she smiled, radiating the warmth that always made me feel right at home. "I'm going to finish cooking. Stay there for a while!"

Had I not been looking forward to it as much as I was, I might have questioned why she all but threw me out of the house. I figured she was just anxious to get dinner prepped.

An hour later I had exactly what I wished for, and for the first time since they had moved, I was grateful that my parents had the determination and desire to downsize. Living closer to the beach had therapeutic effects. While I loved apartment living and being on my own, a two-hour drive south to listen to the exact sounds that noise machines boast to lull people into a slumber now surrounded me. Nature had true healing powers, and the ocean's mind-clearing effects were the New Jersey equivalent of the Tuscan villa I'd recently been introduced to.

I sat quietly for at least a half hour thinking about Gennaro, trying to pinpoint the minute he accidentally changed my life. I'd give anything to return to the start of it and relive our first night together.

It was perfect. And he was as close to perfect as any man could be.

Without a single thing to change—except the distance between us and, well, Papa—I allowed myself to conjure daydreams of us actually being together. Looking out at the vast body of water in front of me, I deeply inhaled the sea air and closed my eyes. Within minutes, I drifted off to sleep.

At some point, my brain waves transported me back to Tuscany. The sounds of the ocean and the seagulls hovering above it were replaced by the rustling of leaves, chirping of birds, and humming of the pool filter. I had a glass of wine in one hand, one leg bent and propped up on a lounge chair. The view of the pool with the vineyard behind it was one I couldn't get enough of, and it was as vivid in the dream as I remembered it being in real life.

My body felt like dead weight in the lounge chair as I continued dreaming. I fought to peel myself out of it to catch a glimpse of Gennaro, but my limbs refused to move. Disappointment tugged at my heart while I remained in a twilight stage of sleep. The sounds of beach waves crashed slowly through the audio portion of my dream, but the Tuscan vineyard scene was all I could see. Still clutching the wine glass, I began to flow from real life to my dream and back again.

I willed myself to stay asleep until I was given the opportunity to see him. I tried yelling his name, but the words caught in my throat. I tried again to use my legs to stand from the lounge chair but felt glued to it.

"Mia?"

I heard a man's voice coming from behind me, but the unrelenting torture of my frozen limbs continued.

Then, a whisper. *"Tu sei la calma nella mia vita."*

I had heard that before, but where?

"Tu sei la calma nella mia vita." This time, the voice was clearer and a bit louder.

"You are the calm in my life," he repeated.

I begged my subconscious to bring his face into focus but was still trapped in my body with an inability to move or see anything other than the pool and vineyard.

"I love you, Mia." The voice was closer now, and I could feel a hand on my shoulder.

Desperately trying to turn my head toward the villa apartments behind me, he continued, "I'm right here."

Right where?

And then, finally spared further torment, my eyes blinked open to reveal beach waves pounding the shore over and over again. Assuming it all to have been part of the dream, I exhaled with a slight smile and moderate disappointment that I wasn't granted a glimpse of his face.

"Mia."

Goosebumps covered my arms and legs as I realized the voice was real this time. I briefly hesitated to turn my head, not wanting to be further disappointed. But when I finally looked up, I was met with all six feet, two inches of the gorgeous Italian man I had accidentally fallen in love with towering over my beach chair. Gennaro's hair was blowing in the ocean breeze, with the most beautiful smile on his face, and the smell of his cologne smacking me in mine.

I was rendered speechless, frozen in place. But as always, he stepped in to lead, holding his hand out to take mine, quickly removing any remaining doubt. My legs quivered like a baby deer as I stood up, and without an ounce of hesitation, he swooped me into him by the curve of my lower back.

His lips traced the length of my face before landing on my neck. "*Cazzo, mi sei mancata.*"

God dammit. I missed him, too.

I felt tears pooling in my eyes with overwhelming emotion. I was elated, moderately confused, and a little anxious, and had many questions to ask him.

The tips of his fingers grazed the sides of my neck before tilting my chin toward his face. He calmed me effortlessly.

"*Bellissima...*"

The moment his lips touched mine, my confusion and anxiety dissipated. The man I fell in love with on a whim in the middle of Italy had flown to surprise me in the

States. He stood before me, my face in his hands, whispering things to me that most women only dream about.

I was living out the fantasies of many.

I was living proof of "If he wanted to, he would."

I was terrifyingly in love with the man standing in front of me.

And I was still completely unaware how much he was about to change the course of my life.

CHAPTER 5

Gennaro

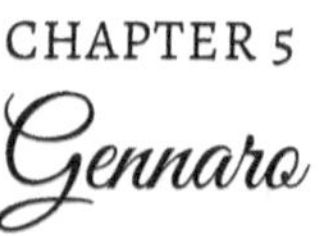

Mia turned around to confirm it was my voice she heard, and with her eyes gazing into mine, a portion of my heart healed itself on the spot.

"What are you *doing* here?" She was equal parts shocked, surprised, and confused, but the soft curve of her smile and the bright whites of her eyes radiated excitement.

Every hour spent in flight and driving was worth it for the look on her face and the electricity burning between us. There was no nervousness or anxiety. In fact, I had zero doubt that reuniting with her would be anything less than perfect. The impact she had on my life in the two weeks I'd spent with her in Italy was so profound that her presence alone made me feel complete.

"I'll tell you everything but for now, I just want to *exist* with you," I told her.

"I knew I missed you, but..." She shook her head slightly, her arms wrapped around my waist as she paused before delivering the rest of her thoughts.

"But?" I held her head in my hands and watched her

eyes flood with tears. When one slid down her cheek, I caught it with the edge of my finger and stopped myself. "Never mind. It doesn't matter."

I breathed her in, brushing my lips over hers, and hovering long enough for her to understand that I missed her just as much. Waves crashed in slow motion around us, and if any beachgoers were watching, we were blissfully unaware. The ocean has a way of making you feel small, and this was no exception. In the grand scheme of things, Mia and I were two small physical blips on a universal radar. The love between us, though, was infinite, all consuming, and blazing like the hottest rays of the sun.

We spent some time looking out towards the water, with Mia perched in between my legs, her back to my chest, leaning into the crook of my neck. I filled her in on life at the villa with a recovering and perpetually moody Papa, as well as Vincenzo's brother helping out while I was gone. She filled me in on Allie, which was tough to hear. I hadn't met her yet, but she seemed like a straight shooter with a solid head on her shoulders—something I greatly appreciated in any friend, let alone the best friend of the woman I was in love with.

"You'll get to meet my sister tonight," she mentioned.

"I already did." She looked up at me with a crooked brow, and I continued. "How do you think I got here?"

"I had no idea. I guess I assumed you rented a car?" I watched her compute all the possible details while attempting to hold back questions. A few seconds later, her attempt became a full-fledged failure. "Wait, do my parents know you're here?"

"I wouldn't have come without telling them," I said, squeezing her a little tighter before she turned around to face me. I continued, "Mr. Luciano doesn't appear to be much more pleasant than Papa. Or did I get that wrong through FaceTime a few weeks ago?"

"Well, that's because you're a guy, and I'm his...*baby*," she rolled her eyes with a smile at the sentiment. "I'll be fifty years old, and both of my parents will still view me that way, I'm sure of it."

"I'd do the same if I was a father." I truly believed it.

"He's kind of tough," she confirmed. "But my brother, Lenny, is actually the one that'll make you rethink your entire trip."

"Protective?" I asked her.

"Overly." She stared up at the sky, likely recounting all the ways they had butted heads in the past. "The last guy I dated was threatened at my cousin's wedding."

"Threatened how?" I laughed. Not in a macho, competitive manner, but because I couldn't quite picture how protective I'd be over a little sister myself.

"Something to the effect of, 'If you break her heart, I'll shoot you in the face and not think twice about it.'"

I smiled and shrugged. "Sounds pretty standard for older brothers."

"How was my sister?" Mia had a curious look on her face.

"Stella said it was more enjoyable sitting in traffic to get to the airport and being yelled at by the parking attendants than it was staying at home with a teething baby, so I think she was good?" I laughed out loud.

"She has an understated way of delivering her sarcastic humor." Mia confirmed my thoughts before explaining more about each of her siblings.

She was close to both her brother and sister but in different ways. She and Lenny had similar attitudes with type-A personalities, and as a result, they often annoyed the hell out of each other.

Mia and Stella, on the other hand, were polar opposites, which removed any semblance of typical sister rivalry. Stella seemed content in her life and supportive of her little sister, and vice versa. The number of times they fought could be counted on one hand, while her brother frequently got under her skin. She suddenly dreaded his arrival the following day, but I attempted to snap her out of it with an entirely genuine "Let's get out of here so I can finally meet your parents."

I had no idea on which planet I was on, now willingly and somewhat eagerly anticipating meeting the parents of the woman I fell in lust and love with on the streets of Rome just over a month prior.

But I went with it.

We packed up her chair, blanket, and shoulder bag and headed toward the car.

"So, what do you think of Jersey beaches?" she asked as we packed the trunk.

"Nicer than I thought they would be," I responded. "Not sure if I'm a Tuscan villa guy or more of an ocean guy, though."

"You're every bit of a Tuscan villa guy," she confidently responded, "and please don't ever forget that, as it's half the reason I fell in love with you."

"Half?! *Gesù Cristo*, what happens if I don't own the property one day?"

"That'll never happen," she said before we headed back to her parents' house. She seemed convinced of it, though I wasn't entirely sure how.

Pulling into the driveway, I could see her dad watering plants, and while I wasn't necessarily nervous to meet him in person, I felt a small pang of dread. It was likely due to the guilt stemming from the way Papa had treated Mia, paired with the number of times she and I had sex in a two-week time span.

After exiting the car, I shifted everything she'd taken to the beach to one hand so I could extend the other to her father. "Mr. Luciano, it's a pleasure to meet you."

He stared at me with the slightest squint before reaching out to shake it. "My name is Santino, but you can continue calling me Mr. Luciano." It was definitely a power play and one I tried my best not to let bother me.

"Beautiful home," I said, nodding my head toward the front of the white brick house with its tan shutters and impeccable landscaping. "We could use some of your gardening skills at the villa."

The corners of his mouth dared to turn upwards. "That villa is my favorite place on Earth. I don't think there's anything I could ever do or provide that would make it any more beautiful than it already is."

It seemed an inopportune time to tell him how wrong he was. That the day Mia stepped foot onto the property, she changed it for the better. A place I used to dread living in, working on, and visiting was now filled with my best memories in life because of her. Add to that, I was at a complete loss for how to live there without her, but I wouldn't change a single, solitary part of the road that led me there.

"Well, I hope you'll visit again soon," I honestly told him.

"That's the plan. Let me help you with that stuff." He appeared to soften ever so slightly as he reached for the cooler about to fall to the ground.

Walking into the kitchen, the familiar smells of garlic and bubbling tomato sauce combined with the sound of a popped cork instantly transported me back home. The enormous embrace from her mom was reminiscent of Mama, too, and it forced a smile from ear to ear.

"Gennaro! I can't believe you're here. Oh my gawd. Have you eaten? Grab a plate. Do you want some wine? How was the flight? I hope you loved the beach!"

"Sophia, maybe give him a second to answer the first question before asking the follow-ups?" Santino said with subtle sarcasm.

"I can always eat. Would love some wine. Flight was great, but my chauffeur was even better. And the beach was absolutely beautiful. Thanks for having me." I made it a point to answer each of her questions on the first try, and I caught the tail end of the look she shot Mia from across the kitchen, a cross between another "Oh my gawd" and possibly a "Does this guy have an uncle?"

"A man who can answer more than one question at a time, what a novelty." Stella had entered stage right and immediately high-fived me. It was clear she'd be my favorite.

She turned towards Mia and continued, "Hate to ruin your night, but Lenny is on his way for dinner."

I heard a low grunt come from Mia's lips. "I thought he was working and wasn't driving down until tomorrow?"

"His sergeant let him go early, and he capitalized on the offer to come and torture you ahead of schedule." Stella smiled with an eye roll before looking at me. "He's harmless, really, it's just more of a stamina game. Keep up with him and his idiotic commentary, and don't let him smell fear. You'll wear him down, naturally."

"I appreciate the strategic advantage," I assured her before swigging a few extra-long sips of red wine. I thrived under pressure in every other scenario in life and refused to let this be any different, especially after what Mia had endured back in Tuscany. It was also something I had anticipated since making this plan. I'd spend a few days at Mia's parent's house, so as to not get in the way of holiday weekend family plans. Then, we'd spend the rest of the week, just the two of us, at her apartment.

All of us sat around the table snacking on cheese, crackers, grapes, small slices of garlic bread, and a tomato mozzarella salad. Had it not been for the hamburgers and hot dogs they planned to pair with the freshly made eggplant parmesan, I might have felt like I was back at home.

"You mean to tell me you don't eat hot dogs or hamburgers in Italy?" Stella was moderately shocked.

"Hot dogs? No. Closest thing we have to a hot dog is dried sausage and soppressata. Hamburgers, yes, but we typically put them on grilled pita bread without cheese."

Mia chimed in, "It's freshly ground beef from the cow that lives in the backyard behind the osteria with home-made mayo and crispy potatoes—all of which is about four thousand times better than anything we eat here."

"You sound like you're in love," Stella quipped.

"You'd be in love with their food, too." Mia quickly responded in defense of herself.

"Yea—wasn't talking about the food, but okay."

Stella continued to solidify her place as my favorite family member while Mia brushed her off due to moderate embarrassment. Mr. and Mrs. Luciano asked how my parents were, as well as Pesca, and I filled them in on all of it. I could see pure adoration in both their eyes as they spoke about their time there. I remembered them visiting previously, but it was years ago, when I was younger and probably a bit of a self-involved loner. I never even both-ered to say hello or have a conversation with them.

"You have the loveliest accent," Sophia declared, "and you speak English so well!"

I could feel the cringe radiate through Mia's entire body next to me, but I kindly reminded her mom that a majority of the tourists both on property at the villa and in Rome spoke English. Growing up, I could understand it and speak it to a degree, but in the last year, I had become particularly fluent.

"We're looking forward to visiting next year for our anniversary," Mr. Luciano interrupted, his own train of thought having nothing to do with my accent or English fluency. We were making some headway into optimistic territory, just in time for the front door to swing open and a burly, tattooed, light-brown-bearded guy to barge through it. I sensed immediately that he would likely *never* take a "favorite family member" spot.

"I'll be right down, I gotta take a shit," Lenny yelled as he took the steps in a few strides. "Can someone bring me a beer?"

My eyebrows must have reacted to the request, because Stella chimed in with her as-usual perfect response. "That goes against family health code regulations. Also, nice to see you, too."

We could all feel his eyes roll. When he finally emerged from his lair and came barreling back downstairs, he said hello to everyone before narrowing his eyes on me.

I was prepared for it, but still, a few pieces of my inner tough guy were longing to be set free. Keeping it under wraps, I extended my hand. "Hey, I'm Gennaro."

"Yea, I know who you are." He looked me up and down, leaving my hand dangling. "What's for dinner?"

He was exactly as advertised, but I refused to let it affect me. In fact, it provided even more of a challenge to do precisely what Stella suggested and not let him wear me down. It wasn't a matter of being scared of him but more so being determined to avoid punching him straight in the face.

"Dinner is ready!" Mia's mom proudly exclaimed, and we all filed out the sliding door to the deck. to find another Italian-American version of Tuscan villa life. The weather was perfect, the birds were chirping, and tree leaves were rustling. The only difference was, the entire property was flanked by other homes, as if no one valued their privacy. Whatever we talked about, neighbors could hear it. I never realized how fortunate we were to have complete privacy at the villa, except, of course, from those who vacationed with us.

Privacy didn't appear to be an issue for Lenny, who spoke as loudly as any forty-two people I'd ever heard. He made Vincenzo seem soft spoken, which was a tall order. "So, what are your intentions with my sister?"

Every single person at the table swung their head toward him with looks ranging from disgust to unease to discomfort. "Did we just teleport back to the middle ages? You're ridiculous." Mia then turned toward me and said, "Don't answer that."

"I asked him a valid question." Lenny looked at me incredulously, waiting for an answer.

"Enough." Mr. Luciano all but blasted him with retinal laser beams, and I was thankful for it.

After Lenny was forced to stand down, the rest of dinner was enjoyable. Mrs. Luciano and Stella seemed to put their stamp of approval on Mia's choice of random-man-found-on-the-streets-of-Rome. Mr. Luciano had moved from Lenny's side toward Sophia's and Stella's side, albeit seeming to stall somewhere in the middle. I considered it a partial win.

I was comfortable there, thinking how well they'd all get along with my family. And then I stopped myself dead in my tracks, trying to understand why I was picturing our families together already.

"What are you thinking about?" Mia leaned toward me as I walked our dishes to the sink, rinsed them, and placed them in the dishwasher.

"He cleans up after himself, too?" Stella interrupted my response. "This is too much. I wasn't aware Italian unicorns existed."

"Oh right, like I don't ever do anything to help," Stella's husband Jimmy chimed in after sneaking through the garage door with their daughter, surprising us all. He was holding an ice cream cake, and when he placed it on the counter, I could see that an Italian flag adorned at the top of it.

"I think you do plenty," Mia chimed in with a bear hug, "especially if that's a welcome home ice cream cake from Dairy Queen."

"You bet your ass it is, sis."

All in all, Mia's family was a tight knit one, seemingly closer than my own, with their own moderate levels of drama and friction. I realized I'd have to side-step the ridiculousness of Lenny over the course of the next two days, took Stella's advice to heart, and outworked him in the stamina department. Eventually, he tired himself out from unnecessary macho commentary and the need to constantly hear himself talk.

I was happy to have met them, but I couldn't wait to spend time with Mia alone. We were sleeping in separate bedrooms like we were little kids, something I wouldn't have ever *not* considered doing. I looked forward to having more conversations with Sophia and Stella, as they were a hell of a lot more approachable than Santino and Lenny.

The intermittent bulge in my pants as I watched Mia walk around in her short pajamas, a towel after a shower, or a swimsuit on the beach with her hair piled on top of her head interrupted my thoughts occasionally, but the mature side of me prevailed.

That is—until the last night of our stay.

I texted her after we said goodnight and went to our separate bedrooms.

Gennaro: I'm down the hall from you but feel further away than I do when I'm back home

Gennaro: Why is that?

Mia: Probably has something to do with the silk shorts I have on

Mia: Or maybe it's the bottom part of my ass that you like to massage that's currently hanging out of them

Gennaro: It's both actually

Mia: Did you brush your teeth?

Gennaro: Of course, what am I? A farm animal?

Mia: I think you should pretend that you didn't

Ah.

Gennaro: Think you can help me find some toothpaste?

Mia: I sure can

Her bedroom door opened, and I waited briefly before heading into the bathroom she had tiptoed into, hiding in the dark like a little kid. I hadn't done this when I was twelve, let alone as a grown man, but it was thrilling, none-theless. I closed the door and locked it, immediately pinning her to the wall behind it. My mouth found the delicate skin of her neck without hesitation while I held her arms firmly above her head. I felt the gentleman in me unravel, leaving the respectful, chivalrous guy who cared about fitting in with her family somewhere down the hall.

Also down the hall was Lenny, apparently, since he was now pounding on my bedroom door.

This fucking guy.

"Go, I'll hide in the shower until I can leave without him seeing me," Mia whispered before lightly biting my bottom lip. It was the smallest of acts, but she knew how much I loved it. I kissed her deeply while squeezing the exact portion of ass cheek that hung out below her sleep shorts, further tortured that I had yet to have her in the way my body craved. Briefly, I realized how ridiculous the whole scenario was, but I did as she suggested and walked out of the bathroom, closing the light behind me, like nothing had happened.

"Ah, there you are," Lenny nodded in my direction. "Where's my sister?"

"Last I saw her she was downstairs grabbing a glass of water," I lied a little too easily, and he assessed me like the law enforcement officer he was, searching for the slightest bit of hesitation on my part.

I didn't give him any, returning my own set of strategic law enforcement skillsets.

He was downstairs in a flash, which allowed Mia enough time to run out of the bedroom undetected. She quickly wrapped her arms around my neck and kissed me one last time to say goodnight. I watched her head back to her room, and as I turned toward my own, proudly assuming we avoided prying eyes, I noticed Stella quietly standing at the top of the steps with her sleeping baby in hand.

"You did good," Stella nodded her head with her lips pursed together. "I, for one, would have voluntarily drowned myself in the ocean to avoid listening to him talk for another minute longer."

"I appreciate your insight. It gave me a slight advantage," I said, smiling.

She squinted slightly, which felt like the final portion of her assessment was complete. Then she nodded one last time. "I only assist those I feel deserve it. I also know my little sister can handle herself without needing me or my big-mouthed brother to threaten you with death should you hurt her."

I thought of responding, but she kept going. "I can tell you're a good guy. I can tell she's head over heels for you. And, most importantly, I can tell you're head over heels for her, too. What I can't figure out is how I'll still find a way to like you if you take her away from me and bring her to Italy to stay."

"We haven't..."

She cut me off with a finger in the air and a slight shake of the head. "I'm not playing mind games or trying to indirectly threaten you. I genuinely don't know how this ends, which I guess means that you both need to live it and see where it takes you, right?"

Vivi il momento. She was absolutely correct.

I nodded my head with whatever remaining energy I had left as she quietly continued down the hall with her sleeping daughter in her arms. After shutting my bedroom door behind me, I collapsed into bed. I was at peace with how things went with her family and looking forward to spending one-on-one time with her, now that my balls had turned a sixth shade of blue.

My phone dinged right after I pulled the blanket up and over the length of my body. Assuming it was Mia with one last goodnight text, I peeled myself from the comfortable position I was in to check.

It wasn't an adoring message from Mia. Instead, it was an enormous paragraph of bullshit from the only person on planet Earth I didn't want to hear from.

Francesca.

CHAPTER 6

Mia

"Aren't you tired of trying to include me in a situation that has nothing to do with me? What's your endgame?"

The usually calm, measured Gennaro went a bit off the rails as he spoke to Francesca on our drive back up the Garden State Parkway North. After about ten minutes of back and forth that seemed to revolve around her blaming Giuseppe for everything and herself for nothing, as usual, he finally ended the conversation. "I'm not there, I can't help, even if I was I wouldn't anyway. Figure it out."

Click.

Watching him dismiss her was still a rewarding experience for me. I didn't dislike many people, but she was certainly on the list, alongside Allie's husband. A woman who had yet to figure out her life after getting impregnated by the wrong Beletta brother, *on purpose*, Francesca was in supreme denial and now appeared to have significant depression with a touch of psychosis. She continued blaming everyone else for her problems without even an ounce of self-awareness of how she could have possibly prevented or fixed any of it.

Helpless. She was simply helpless.

And now, the man who flew five thousand miles from Italy to see me was pissed off because of it. She still managed to affect us from across an ocean. *Infuriating.* I squeezed his thigh as he sat in the passenger's seat next to me and immediately felt a small release. Remembering that it had been nearly a month since I had seen him last, and the few days since he arrived provided no physical interaction beyond a kiss in a dark bathroom, I went into solution mode.

We were heading into Hoboken, situated along the Jersey side of the Hudson River with a perfect view of the New York City skyline, after the time spent at my parents' house. Fireworks would start sometime around 9pm, and we'd be home a little after 10pm. I had a mental assessment of what the later portion of our night would look like, but until then, celebrating America was the game plan.

Speaking of endgames, I wondered what the hell ours was going to be. I loved having him here, but he'd never move, nor would I want him to. Could I move there? My family would lose their ever-loving minds if I did.

Inner Critic: Might as well tell him to leave now
Mia: What is wrong with you?
Inner Critic: Well, you're gonna have sex with him
*   again tonight, aren't you?*
Inner Critic: And every time you're around his
*   Italian meats, you fall even deeper for him*
Inner Critic: So you're setting yourself up for
*   massive disappointment*
Mia: You're so aggravating
Inner Critic: Okay, but am I wrong?
Mia: No, not really

Inner Critic: I'll wait then
Mia: For what?
Inner Critic: An apology
Mia: Fuck off
Inner Critic: Well that was rude, wasn't it?

I rolled my eyes internally before realizing I had driven the last few minutes of the trip on autopilot.

Mia: Okay, I'm going to focus on driving so I don't
    kill us
Inner Critic: Great idea

I pulled into a public lot, playfully fought with Gennaro to pay for parking, and didn't win. We walked hand in hand across a courtyard to the green and lay down on a blanket with a view overlooking the river. Fireworks wouldn't start for a few hours, but we planned to relax and catch up some more while we waited.

Lying on a large blanket in the cool grass as the sun went down and stars came out, I was instantly reminded that wherever he was, my heart followed. We were curled up next to each other, him kissing my neck and forehead as people swirled around us and fireworks lit up the sky—precisely the same way he had described in his letter to me—*spectacular, explosive, a burst of energy, and a brilliant display.*

Gennaro was my safe space. The place I felt most comfortable, most revered, and most desired. He continued to brighten my life like the fireworks above us, just as he did the first night we spent together.

At the end of the show, anticipation radiating between us made it evident that neither of us could wait to get back home. The twenty-minute drive felt like hours, and as we quietly approached my front door, butterflies formed in the pit of my stomach for the first time since I had been in Italy with him.

This was, essentially, the States version of my first night at his apartment in Rome. While I was proud of my new place, it wasn't quite as strikingly beautiful as his, nor did it have an incredible balcony, complete with a view.

Feeling my hesitation and speaking as though he could hear my innermost thoughts, he said, "The only thing I need right now…is you."

Take me now.

I turned the key and opened the door, and before I even had a chance to think of what my next move would be, he made his first.

The gentlemanly persona he adhered to while at my parents' was immediately abandoned in the hallway. There was no apartment tour, no welcome beverage, no time for snacking or small talk.

I locked the door and kicked my shoes off, slowly turning around to meet his gaze, both eyes staring at me intently from above as he breathed in slowly, deeply, measured. I knew him well enough to know he was savoring the moment, refusing to rush any of it, while simultaneously regulating his self-control.

"Old" Mia would start overthinking. I'd wonder if the sex would live up to the standards we set for ourselves back in Italy. I'd wonder how much more attached I'd continue to get after we spent the remainder of the week together. And quite honestly, I'd wonder if I needed a shower after lying in the grass for hours.

"New" Mia stared right back at his bold, brown eyes, glimmering with both intent and desire. There are times in life when even commanding women who know what they want and how they want it need to stand down in the presence of a confident, masculine man who's ready and willing to lead.

This was certainly one of them.

I kept my eyes locked on his long enough to feel the heat between us reach its boiling point. My body craved his, and the way the corners of his mouth curled upward coupled with a singular eyebrow raise confirmed he felt the same. In an instant, both of his hands were pressed against the door on either side of my head as his mouth found mine. It was not sweet, soft, or romantic, nor did I want it to be. In its purest form, it was intensely lustful, passionate, restless.

He was hungry.

And I was ready to be consumed.

"I need you," he whispered to me breathlessly. It didn't happen often, but I was thankful that he said it in English, and I didn't have to ruin the moment with Google translate.

"I need you *inside* of me," I confidently responded in a heavy whisper.

Gennaro pulled me in close enough that I could feel his heart pounding through his chest. "It's my favorite place to be."

He wrapped both arms around my lower back, his lips teasing the skin of my neck before firmly cupping my ass with both hands. The indents his fingers were imprinting in my cheeks seemed like a silent request for me to follow his lead further.

So, I did. I leaned all the way in, and he lifted me all the way up.

Wherever he planned to go, I was following with my legs wrapped around his waist and my arms around his neck. Thankfully, he found my room effortlessly. He carried me to the bed and collapsed on top of me, his mouth desperate for mine while trying to undress me. Unbuttoning my denim shorts with ease, he threw them clear across the room. The lightweight button-down I'd worn over my tube top was next, his impatience shining through as he pulled the top straight down, freeing both tits, leaving the top bunched at my waist. Sitting on his knees, he lifted me up and on top of him, and I returned the undressing favor by pulling his t-shirt over his head.

I forced myself to slow down to appreciate the cuts in his arms, the strength in his chest, and the rolling hills of muscle definition throughout his back. Remains of Acqua dell'Elba Classica were buried deep within his pores, and it was as mind-numbing as the first time I met him.

Gennaro briefly paused for his own quick time-out, this time burying his head in my chest, appreciating the embrace before he began again. Planting both feet on the floor, he unbuttoned his pants. I watched them shimmy down his muscular thighs to his ankles. Kicking them off, he pulled me to meet him at the edge of the bed. Kneeling, I kissed him, our tongues slowly dancing around one other as I slid the waistband of his boxer briefs down his hard, round ass. I pulled the tube top up and over my head as he watched my plush tits with rock hard nipples bounce out of its support.

Skimming both with the sides of his thumbs, he slowly turned me around in front of him. On all fours now as he stood behind me, Gennaro trailed one hand underneath the length of me from my chest to my stomach and around my hips. Urging me to spread my legs further, I felt the tips of his fingers meet the skin of my burning hot slit. He continued tracing the length of me until honing in on my spot. At the first sign of a tremble, he repeated the motion, slowly and robotically, without stopping, until my entire body tensed, his pace quickened, and I let out a loud cry of release.

Hunched over in front of him, my hair matted to the side of my neck, I was briefly frozen in place until his hands grabbed my hips and pulled me closer to him.

Using his knee to spread my legs wider he entered me with one firm hand on my shoulder, guiding himself inside. I let out a moan that could only be described as *"If I ever have to live without this, please, God, take me now."*

As perfect as I remembered it being from our first night together, he filled every part of me, sliding in and out, over and over, with the occasional Italian phrase thrown in, ranging from *"Dio mio,"* to *"fanculo a me"* and beyond. In that moment, I didn't care what it was that he was saying, I only wanted to focus on never forgetting the way he made me feel.

Body, mind, heart, and soul, Gennaro Beletta continued to penetrate every square inch of me.

I'd learned more about myself physically, mentally, and emotionally in the last month than I had in all of my prior years combined. And I had him to thank for it.

Living presently allowed me to trust the intentions of a man who had shown me all of him, which removed any and all doubt. As a result, I was far more confident than ever before.

Confident in myself; confident in my needs, wants, and desires; and confident in what I deserved. I'd never go back to accepting less. And now, I only had to figure out how it'd be possible to spend the rest of my life with him.

In the days following, we acted like a full-blown married couple, not an unofficial vacation hook-up who lived five thousand miles away from one another. I cooked a couple of nights, he cooked once, and went on dates for the others. We did some local exploring so he could experience New York City standards like the Statue of Liberty and Ellis Island, the Empire State Building, the site where the Word Trade Center previously stood, a rooftop brunch, and an overpriced city dinner.

On Long Island, we visited some of my favorite Italy-inspired vineyards, our closest versions of "Tuscan" wine and landscaped beauty. He was excited for and receptive to every destination and experience, even though we both knew none of it compared to the magnificence of his hometown.

From the couch to the bed, we spent plenty of physical time together, and as always, our conversations didn't pale in comparison.

"Where do you picture yourself when you're eighty years old?" he asked me straight faced, then smiled seeing my reaction that teetered between "Uhm, what?" and "I don't know what I'm doing tomorrow, let alone in fifty-plus years."

"Okay let's make it easier," Gennaro quickly adjusted. "Where do you see yourself in a year?" He started rubbing my feet and I not-so-secretly hoped he'd still be rubbing them three hundred and sixty-five days from now.

My eyes tilted upwards toward the ceiling fan, the same way they had in the weeks of depressing withdrawal that followed me home. This time, though, the man I was in love with was skin to skin with me on the same couch, so I had a slightly more positive outlook for what was to come, albeit an unclear one.

"I've always wanted to open an Italian caffè," I blurted with partial regret, "but you're quite literally the only person on planet Earth who knows that."

"Why do you sound embarrassed?" He was taken aback, partially smiling and clearly intrigued.

"Well, for one, ever since meeting you I'm reminded how fake an Italian I actually am," I said. He shook his head and quietly laughed. "And two," I continued, "I'm scared it won't go anywhere."

"Do you have experience working in restaurants?" he asked, reminding me that we sort of skipped over some important life details during our Italian sexcapades.

"I actually went to college for hotel and restaurant management. I stumbled into event planning once I graduated, but I've worked at restaurants since I was seventeen." The highs and lows of the service industry played in my head as I realized running a caffè *in Italy* sounded a whole lot more enjoyable than running one in America.

"Sounds like enough experience to me, but you won't know unless you try, right?" Gennaro had a way of making the simplest thoughts sound like life-changing advice and unwavering support.

"Yea, I guess." I briefly reviewed my next thought before it came barreling out of my mouth. "It's the only thing I'm actually envious of Francesca for. She had a vision and went for it. I remember walking into her store and thinking, 'Wow, it must be nice to live in paradise and manage your own business.'"

"Ehh…" His voice trailed off.

"Ehh, what?" I was being nosy but didn't care.

"It's her family's place, they just put her name on it. She works there, but she doesn't manage it. And to be honest, every time I hear her talk about it, she complains, as she does with everything else." He continued, "To be involved with anything hospitality driven, you need to truly love it. Servicing people day in and day out is a lot to deal with. But, if it's your own place, your own vision, and you have the support you need, it can feel like an extension of your own home."

"Is that why you can't stand working at the villa? Because you never had the support from Papa?" I already knew the answer but was giving him the opportunity to have a mini therapy session.

"Exactly. It's his way, or no way. I've got no voice there, so all I am to him is a machine who gets hard labor done. How do you love something when it's dumbed down to that?"

"I completely understand."

He made a few phone calls back home while I made a simple dinner for our last night together. Caprese pasta is what I called it, with garlic, oil, chopped tomato, and basil as its base with bombs of slightly melted fresh mozzarella throughout. Over dinner he filled me in on the crew at home. Mama, Pesca, Giuseppe, and Luca were holding it all down at the villa. Papa was visibly weaker in ability but still attempting to bark orders at anyone who would poten- tially listen. And Vincenzo, having dealt with his own affair-ridden spouse during the course of the last couple of months, had decided to file for divorce.

Gennaro seemed to long to be back there even amidst the drama and uncertainty of things, and I didn't blame him. I had wished to be back there, perched by the pool, at least once per day for the last few weeks. Now that he had come to visit and we were talking about Italy so frequently, I assumed the longing dread of withdrawal would further torment me. And did it ever.

He was leaving the next morning. I was curled up in a ball next to his chest in bed, and I already missed him. I didn't know when I'd see him again. It was impossible to pick a date since I knew I had to solidify a new job, or more accurately, a steady income, and he wouldn't be able to take off more days anytime soon after using so many to come this week.

Somewhere though, deep in my soul, I knew it wouldn't be too long. I didn't know how, or when, I just knew my heart wouldn't be keen on too much time without him. He was ingrained in me, the very reason that my life felt as complete as it did, even while simultaneously holding so much uncertainty.

The delicate lesson from learning to live in the moment was still present in all that I did. I was determined to do all I could to live for *now* and worry about *later* a little bit less. But, at my core, I simply wanted to spend as much time with him as possible. I was my calmest, most confident self in his presence. My life had a bit more clarity and purpose when we dreamed of our future together, even though the vision was still blurry at best. I yearned for him even as he lay right next to me, and that yearning only deepened as he flew every one of those five thousand miles back home.

I had no idea where our journey was taking us, but I was intent on enjoying all of it. I leaned into the beauty of not having all of the answers all of the time, and we both agreed to see where our next steps together would take us. As I continued finding comfort in the unknown, I began to uncover the answer to his last question.

"Where did I see myself in a year?"

With him.

In Italy.

CHAPTER 7
Gennaro

As I sat on the tarmac, the bright New York morning sun blazing through my window seat, I felt a pit of angst in my stomach.

I absolutely hated leaving her.

Two hours prior, I reluctantly gave her back the long cardigan sweater she left hanging on the bathroom door in her villa. "I think I smelled your perfume right out of it, or else I'm not sure I'd give it back to you," I said as I handed it over.

She smiled, took a graphic t-shirt from her dresser with large letters that spelled out "New Jersey," sprayed it with more perfume, and packed it in my suitcase.

"I'm not sure that'll fit me," I quipped.

"I prefer you shirtless, anyway."

How I went from hating the thought of ever being in a relationship to *this* had me in a bit of a stupor. Peering out the airplane window at the city skyline backdrop had me dreading the flight home and again questioning when exactly I'd be with her again. I truly had no idea how this relationship could work out long-term, and it tore me up to think about it, so I forced myself to stop.

Then, as was always the case, the more I attempted to stay in my own personal bubble with my own personal thoughts, the more I attracted those who wished to try and break me out of it.

"Sir? Sir?" The stewardess repeated until I broke out of my trance. "May I get you anything before we take off?"

I wasn't a frequent flier, but I didn't think tending to passenger needs prior to take off was routine. It was usually quite the opposite: *"Buckle your seatbelt, don't do this, don't do that, and enjoy your flight."*

In any case, I responded with the smallest smile I could muster. *"Sto bene, grazie."* She lingered with a desperate gaze, the kind I was accustomed to from women who found me endearing, even when I was certain I wasn't acting in a way that warranted it. My mind was fixated on Mia, on missing her, on wanting her, on wondering when I'd see her again. So, in retrospect, saying, "I'm good, thanks" was actually a flagrant lie.

I wasn't good. I was unsettled. I was flying thousands of miles home, away from the woman I wanted, the woman who made me believe in true love again, with hope that the Universe would figure out a way for us to be together. I was a doer, not a wait-for-the-Universe-to-help-me-outer. It was another version of living in the moment, without answers, trusting that what was meant to be would be.

The deep breath I slowly released must have been laced with discontent, because my seatmate turned his head ever so slightly to assess my well-being.

"I hope you brought a book or plan to watch a movie. Eight hours in the air is a long time to think about a woman you're flying away from." Filling out the crossword from the daily newspaper, he had a head of thick salt and pepper hair, olive skin that looked like it had been kissed by the sun for at least sixty years, and wore slacks and a short-sleeve button-down with reading glasses on the bridge of his nose.

"How'd you know I'm flying away from a woman?" I asked with a curious smile.

"I was your age once," he said, resting his head back and closing his eyes as if he were recalling some of his favorite memories. "It's always a woman, son. They're either making us question how we could possibly ever live *without* them or making us question why in the hell we chose to live *with* them in the first place. There's hardly an in between."

His delivery style reminded me of Giustino back home, without the sexual innuendos. Before I knew it, we were halfway home and still recollecting our life stories. Vincent was an Italian-American with a successful financial career that contributed to an unsuccessful marriage.

"I thought I was doing right by both of us by going to work and making a ton of money, but one day she told me she was done. 'Done? What do you mean you're done?' I'd never been more surprised by anything in my life. She told me she'd been miserable for ten years, probably even longer, and money didn't mean anything if we didn't have time to enjoy things together." He looked like his heart was breaking all over again as he remembered the conversation.

"Did you try to do anything to save your marriage?" I asked.

"She asked me to do therapy, but I'm not about to talk about my *feelings* with a complete stranger in front of us. No, thanks. I said we could do therapy ourselves, but she insisted it wouldn't work."

"Well that's the point of therapy," I interjected. "You need a third party to help keep you honest and prevent you from interrupting one another. There's three sides to every story: yours, hers, and the truth."

"Are you a therapist?" he asked with a side glance and a moderate amount of judgment.

"No, I just grew up in a household that would have benefitted from consistent communication. And the woman you predicted I was flying away from helped me to realize that. Is your ex-wife still alive?" I was curious to know if she had moved on, because I'd wondered if I could ever see Mama with someone besides Papa.

"She's still my wife. We never divorced, and yes, she's still very much alive." He surprised me with the admission that they hadn't dissolved their marriage. "She moved out on her own. Thankfully we never had any kids, so we didn't have to worry about that part."

"Where are you going in Italy?" I wondered.

"I have some family in Tuscany and a small vacation home, which was the only good that came out of my nonstop working lifestyle." Vincent seemed like a good-hearted guy with the right intentions who, like most of us, learned life lessons as he stumbled through it.

"Which part? My family owns a vacation rental property."

His home was in Pienza, about an hour south of the villa, and much to my surprise, I learned that he had vacationed with us a few years back before deciding which part of Italy he'd purchase a home in. "It was a beautiful property, and I remember your parents well. They were truly in love with their home and property, and so, so proud, with good reason. I remember thinking to myself how much my wife would have loved it, too."

"You didn't bring her with you?"

"It was after we separated," he shrugged. "I invited her to come with me, but she said it was too little, too late. She wanted me to think about these things years sooner and was aggravated that it wasn't until she told me she was done that I even considered taking us on a vacation together."

"Seems like you're in the *how can you possibly live without her* stage," I suggested.

"Oh, I'll be there until I'm six feet under, or until the Universe shows me I'm meant to be with someone else."

I had never spoken to a stranger so effortlessly for so long, but we continued chopping it up throughout the duration of the flight, with occasional nap breaks. Life, relationships, dreams, and aspirations were topics I never discussed with Papa. He never seemed interested, and to be fair, I never appreciated his opinions on any of it anyway. I found the conversation with Vincent refreshing and enjoyed getting insight from someone who had lived a lot of life with plenty of happy moments and his fair share of regrets. He listened to me intently, never interrupting or telling me what to do. He simply supplemented the conversation with his own experience while offering support and positivity.

After eight hours in the air, I determined I'd found the male version of Pesca.

We exchanged numbers after landing and planned to link up in the future for lunch or dinner. I texted Mia to let her know I had landed and Mama to let her know I was on my way home.

Incredibly thankful to Vincent for the one-hundred-and-eighty degree mood shift thanks to the therapy session he didn't even realize we had, I was looking forward to being back at the villa and figuring out next steps with Mia.

Sadly, my optimism and enthusiasm were short lived.

I pulled into the driveway a couple of hours later and the main gate was half open, which was out of the norm. Stepping out of the car to open it fully, I noticed a small pile of cigarettes alongside the cement pillar that held one side of the gate upright. We didn't have smokers in our family, although recent stress factors would surely explain someone taking up the habit. I parked my car down the driveway and walked toward the house, planning to ask Giuseppe about it. Instead, I was distracted by him and Francesca screaming at each other, *again.*

"Yes, this is definitely what I looked forward to coming home to," I said to no one in particular as I surveyed the courtyard. Francesca was whimpering in Mama's arms, and Giuseppe was pacing back and forth, attempting to calm down. My eyes rolled into the back of my head as Francesca looked up to see me standing there.

Like a fly on shit, she swarmed me. "You have to talk to him! He has a problem. He's not supporting me the way he should be, as the mother of his future child." I knew my face relayed the message I felt within, which was nothing short of "This still isn't my problem, nor will it ever be" and a sprinkling of "leave me the fuck alone."

I didn't answer and instead pushed past her to walk into the kitchen. Food from dinner was still sitting on the counter. It was room temperature, which told me they had been arguing for a significant amount of time. I took a wine glass from the cabinet, popped open a fresh bottle of red, and poured a heavy helping. Still on American time, I had plenty of physical energy, but the battle between

Giuseppe and Francesca had a way of unrelentingly draining whatever energy remained.

A half hour of silence, wine, and food helped calm me, until the sound of a door opening behind me caused a bit of stress to return. I turned around to see Pesca.

Thank God.

"So, how was your trip?" she asked with a flicker of excitement in her eyes and a warm smile.

The corners of my mouth curved, and I felt my cheeks flush red, but I thought about my answer before relaying it. "I was about to say I didn't want to come back, but the truth is—I did."

Pesca looked at me quizzically, waiting for a punchline, so I continued.

"I don't love being there. I don't love the city or the States in general actually. I just loved spending a lot of uninterrupted time together. I love being with *her*, but it almost makes me wonder, like, what the *hell* am I doing with the whole situation when the likelihood of us ever actually being together is so slim?"

"Because of the distance?" Pesca asked.

"Yes, exactly. I know I'd never move there, and I can't imagine her ever leaving her family and moving here."

"Never say never, my dear. I moved years ago to be with Michael, and I love the places we lived together so much that I still visit them to this day. In fact, I can't begin to think of my life without having had the experiences we did in those places." As she recollected memories, I could feel the pain and longing in her voice, just as I had listening to Vincent on the plane.

As we sat in a few minutes of comfortable silence, I was grateful, for the first time in a while, to be back. To be sitting in my childhood kitchen, with the comforts of my mother's cooking and an appreciation for someone like

Pesca who checked in on me consistently and anticipated my need to vent before I even realized I needed to. As always, she did it with zero judgment and a large capacity to listen wholeheartedly.

Mama walked into the kitchen with Giuseppe not far behind. Thankfully, Francesca did not follow.

"I can't stand her," he said, shaking his head side to side with his hands balled into fists. "How does someone turn into such a psychopath just because she's pregnant?"

"I'm not sure you can blame that on pregnancy," I responded. Francesca had always been *out there*. She had a generally good heart but carried an aura that screamed, *"I've been devoid of attention my entire life so I'm going to make everyone around me pay for it."*

As I had previously promised myself, I wasn't getting involved in any of their drama. Turning to Mama, I asked, "How is Papa doing?"

"He paces up and down the property, finding things for Luca to do, which we've told Luca to say yes to, and then Giuseppe redirects him."

"Does he know I'm back home today?"

"He does." she said.

I attempted to pry the rest out of her. "Okay...and?"

"Nothing worth repeating." She hung her head and started to clean the dishes in the sink.

My gut reaction was to lash out, but it wasn't right for Mama to be on the receiving end of it. I was disappointed that she hadn't asked how my trip was, or even how Mia was, but as I watched her silently wash dishes, something struck me. She seemed extra tired, deflated, depressed even.

Rather than make our conversation about me, I stood up and grabbed a dish towel to help dry. "How are *you* holding up?"

She broke down on the spot.

Pesca and I walked her to the outside patio for fresh air and sat her on the couch as Mama continued sobbing. After a few minutes, she was composed enough to speak.

"I'm falling apart. I'm worried about Papa. It's hard watching him like this. Giuseppe is doing a good job with the property itself, but Papa does usually handle a lot of administrative things." She nodded towards Pesca and then looked at me. "Even with you two here, it's not the same as Rocco doing it with me. He spent most of his time outside, but he handled all of the back-end tasks, and catching up on those is taking time away from the things I have to do for guests directly. It's way too much to handle on my own."

Pesca reached out her hand to Mama's, which made her weep more loudly. I felt bad that the last month had affected my mother more than I even imagined. But truthfully, a lifetime of putting herself last was finally catching up to her.

I had never been clearer on anything in life.

Mama put everyone else's needs before her own, for years, which is not a sustainable way for anyone to live. Add to that the demands of running a property like this and a lack of true happiness within what should be one's most important relationship and the result was an exhausted woman with little to nothing left to give.

As she and Pesca continued talking, I took the last sip of whatever number glass of wine I was on and began to think about Mia, what I wanted the rest of my life to look like, what I was willing to sacrifice to have it, and what was standing in my way.

A visit to the States as well as living in my apartment in Rome made me truly appreciate what we had in Tuscany. The expansive landscape and cuisine Mama was able to produce from this very kitchen were unmatched. We had a small, collective group of neighbors, including Carmine up the road at the osteria. We even had the convenience of Francesca's store, regardless of how crazy she was. We had almost everything we needed within a short radius. It felt horrible to admit to myself, but even though it was busier without Papa in his normal role, it had the potential to be a bit more enjoyable in many other ways.

Giuseppe was doing a fine job, but I knew him well. He wasn't interested in managing the property fully for an elongated amount of time. Personalities were hard to ignore, and his fared better when he was told what to do. For the first time in many years, I allowed myself to think about what it would look like if I owned the property in the future. Almost immediately, I pictured myself and Mia with children running around, managing it all with plenty of traditions I'd keep and many others I'd change.

Blaming it on the wine, my usually composed self whipped out my phone and texted faster than my brain could compute the severity of the question.

> Gennaro: Would you ever consider moving here?

I hit send and felt a giant lump form in my throat.

Vulnerability was hard work.

My phone lit up with three dots as she crafted a response, and my stomach twisted in knots as I anticipated the delivery of it.

Was this all crazy? Would I sound like a mental case? Did I even care?

Yes. Perhaps. And absolutely not.

My phone dinged.

> Mia: Rome or Tuscany?

Gennaro: Is the answer different for each?

Mia: Yes it is.

Gennaro: Can you put me out of my misery and tell me where you want to live then?

Mia: I want to wake up and walk out of our bedroom onto a terrace with a cup of coffee in my hands

Mia: And then I want to cook in the kitchen while I watch you work outside

Mia:...without a shirt on

Mia: I want to check guests in and serve dinner to them in the courtyard

Mia: And I want one day a week to be our day to do whatever we want with each other

Mia: Clearly I've thought about this in detail

I had a ridiculous smile on my face reading what was the single best response I could have received.

Gennaro: I guess that means you've thought about us getting married then?

I blamed that question on the wine, too.

Three dots appeared and disappeared, appeared and disappeared. Two minutes later, a message came through that would set the tone for the rest of my life.

Mia: Wherever you are, is where I want to be

She was being direct, but I still couldn't quite believe she'd leave her family to live here.

Gennaro: You would really move here?

Mia: Yes, under one condition

Gennaro: What's that?

Mia: We build a separate guest house for my family to visit whenever they can

I was in disbelief at all she was conveying, wondering if she was also drinking wine, but I forged forward to seal the deal.

Gennaro: I'll build it with my own two hands if I have to

My heart fluttered a bit, the lump in my throat more prevalent than ever, but I had never been so sure of anything in my life.

I would propose to Mia here, marry her here, and start a family with her here. So much had to happen before then, but I was clear on what needed to happen next.

She needed to come back to visit.

Soon.

CHAPTER 8

Mia

"Well, I do like him a lot."

Mom was sitting across from me as we ate Sunday morning breakfast in a quintessential Jersey diner. "And, he's definitely handsome."

The nonverbal three-dot pause at the end of her statement caused me mild concern, but she finished her thought while I lathered butter and syrup on my pancakes and stole a few forkfuls of eggs off her plate, as daughters do. "Are you planning to do a long-distance relationship, though? How often will you really be able to see him?"

I chewed on some crispy bacon and quickly flashed back to yesterday's text conversation when Gennaro promised to build them a home on their Tuscan property after I moved there. My brain swirled in what felt like a tornado of excitement, disbelief, and hesitation.

Inner Critic: You're moving to Italy now?
Mia: Don't start
Inner Critic: With what money?
Inner Critic: You're unemployed

*Inner Critic: You've also known this man for a
    month*
Inner Critic: But who am I to remind you of that...
Mia: Yes, who ARE you to remind me of anything
Inner Critic: Well I AM you actually...
*Inner Critic: I was being sarcastic, but you're too
    lovestruck to notice*
Mia: I noticed it plenty
*Inner Critic: But you haven't noticed that moving to
    Italy to be with a guy you've known for a
    month, whose father absolutely hates you, is
    slightly absurd?*
Mia: Pound salt please

She wasn't wrong, but I also wasn't in the mood. So I left the recent conversation with Gennaro out of it when I answered Mom's question to prevent her from worrying, as mothers do.

"I have another interview this week with a new company. If I get it, there's a decent amount of PTO and a significantly higher salary than my last job. I can visit him at least a few times per year."

"And is he planning on visiting you?" Always protective and meaning well, she wanted to ensure I wasn't the one who would be doing all of the work.

~~"He's planning on building your future Tuscan guest home with his bare hands, actually."~~

Let's not give mom a heart attack.

~~"I'm pretty sure he wants to marry me, so I'm sure that includes him visiting, too."~~

Or a panic attack.

"He's done everything he said he was going to, so I'm not worried. You shouldn't be either."

"One day you'll be a mother, and you'll realize

worrying about everything comes with the territory," she responded before stealing some of my pancakes. "Your father seems to like him, though, so that's good."

"Mmhmm." I didn't *mean* to roll my eyes—it happened naturally. My dad and brother had an uncanny way of inserting their opinions about whomever I dated for most of my young adult life, and I'd had just about enough. I appreciated the concern, but the delivery of their messaging was usually piss poor.

"Don't go rolling your eyes, they just love you."

"Ma. I love them, too. But I don't show them love by trying to run their lives for them." I appreciated her attempt at peace-keeping, but she always wanted everyone to get along, even when all parties weren't playing fairly. Watching my brother attempt to intimidate or shake down the newest guy I brought home was quite enough for me.

"Let's move on. Your brother and sister confirmed they're coming with us to Italy next spring for our anniversary, so we'll all be there together."

I hadn't totally forgotten about their anniversary trip, it just seemed incredibly far away. But then, something clicked.

"Are we planning to stay at their villa?" My eyebrows went sky high as I mentally computed what that would mean.

My entire family would be with me at the home of the man I'd fallen in love with. *Check.*

My brother would be allowed to roam free while vocalizing all of his unsolicited opinions. *Check.*

Papa, who hated me and thought I was half an American prostitute, would be socializing with my father. *Check.*

What was I leaving out?

Secretly hoping I'd eventually get married there, too? *Also check.*

It was official, I was losing my mind. There was a fine line between living presently, enjoying the moments as they came, and being certifiably insane. I was the latter. Far gone. Living in a land of mental escapism, a life that couldn't possibly ever be mine.

Or could it?

I sat in a desk chair, opposite a potential employer rifling through my resume in a half-assed manner. This being my sixth interview on what had been a tri-state tour of underwhelming career options, I arrived with higher hopes than I was experiencing a mere half hour in. The manager conducting it had stumbled through the first round of questions without any knowledge of my job history. Beyond that, although administrative level management for more pay and less travel sounded enticing, his expanded description of the job was, in fact, boring as hell.

Spreadsheets, file folders, and freshly printed labels used to make my heart skip a beat. Something about organizing, then reorganizing, and planning everything to death really got my motor running. Problem was, it wasn't a sustainable high, and as I had learned to live more presently, I looked forward to enjoying the satisfaction of slowing down and enjoying things I *loved* to do.

Outside his office window, a plush green tree served as home to at least six different birds chirping in sync. A beautiful blue sky with fluffy white clouds floated above it, and briefly, if for only a half of a second, I envisioned myself back in Tuscany. Since the office was on a higher floor, I couldn't see the parking lot below, cars likely buzzing in and out as disgruntled employees discussed work over rushed lunch breaks or argued with their significant others about coming home late, *again*.

It was a stark reminder about the lack of work life balance here in the States and added another checkmark in the let's-move-to-Italy column.

> *Inner Critic: Don't even do it*
> *Mia: Do what??*
> *Inner Critic: We already know...*
> *Inner Critic: ...you love him and you want to move there*
> *Inner Critic: But do you even remember that you used to enjoy life before him, too?*
> *Mia: Are you trying to tell me you like being here more than you do an entire Tuscan villa with wine and fresh food and an infinity pool, among other things?*
> *Inner Critic: ::silence::*
> *Mia: That's what I thought*

Fifteen minutes and two more rounds of useless questions later, Rick excused himself to "review things" with the Human Resources manager. I lacked the directness to tell him what I already knew to be true—there was no chance in the fiery depths of hell that I'd ever take the job.

Instead, I saw the interview through to the end. When he came back and trailed his fingers up and over the back of the chair I sat in, making contact with my shoulder, my Spidey sense was activated in an effort to determine if his vibes were 1990s Playboy, morally gray dark romance lead character, or most likely to have a collection of women's body parts stored in a freezer at home.

He had given me the creeps since the moment he shook my hand, but I pushed past it in the name of a potentially significant pay raise. It would prove to be my first mistake of the day.

"How soon can you start?" he asked with narrowed eyes that scanned the length of me from head to toe.

The hairs on my arms stood up for the complete opposite reason they had back on the streets of Rome. Rick looked at me like he was trying to figure out what color underwear I was wearing, making the side of my mouth curl up in disgust.

I looked to Inner Critic for some words of wisdom, but it was clear she was hiding. Radio silence. I was on my own.

What a bitch.

"Did I miss an actual job offer somewhere?"

My eyes flickered around the room trying to figure out in what alternate universe a manager asks an employee for a start date without mention of salary or benefits or even a "Congratulations, we think you'd be a great fit."

"Oh, sorry, I assumed you knew I was interested in you based on the number of questions I asked."

The "interested in you" portion of his statement was not lost on me.

"I've always been taught not to assume things," I said with a bit of spice in my voice, aggravated that I'd clearly wasted my time.

His eyes continued to scan the length of me, his mouth curved into a sly smile that channeled his inner Jeffrey Dahmer. My gut fired off warning signs in response.

> *Inner Critic: Why are you even still sitting here?*
> *Mia: What took you so long?*
> *Inner Critic: I was testing your intuition*
> *Inner Critic: Making sure that even though your*

> *heart is in Italy, you're not walking around*
> *America acting like a dumbass*
> Mia: *Very kind of you*
> Inner Critic: *Andiamo, get outta here*

"I'm actually *not* interested in the position after all, but thanks for your time." I stood up and extended my hand to shake his.

"Excuse me?"

"It's just not the place for me," I said, turning on my heels and walking out before he could muster a response.

My face was hot, my stomach rumbled with discomfort, and I desperately longed for fresh air. On my way out, the HR Manager waved me towards her office.

"Honey, we'll need to fill out your onboarding paperwork."

"Thanks so much but I won't be taking the job," I said, filling her in.

She seemed confused and taken aback, but I owed these people nothing. The entire experience solidified, once again, that it was time to think about my long-term future.

I owed *myself* everything.

Did I need financial stability? *Yes.*

Did I need something to call my own and pour myself into for personal fulfillment? *Also, yes.*

Could I work at the bar for now and stockpile money while I figured out what I truly wanted to do with my life? *Yes, thrice times.*

As I rode the elevator down to the first floor, Mom, who was riding the same mental wavelength, texted to check in.

Mom: How'd it go?

Mia: I kindly declined the position

Mom: Another one?

Mia: Sorry, Ma, but I'd prefer bartending over a potential sexual harassment hearing

Mom: I can't tell if you're being dramatic or not

Mia: I'll call you on the way home

Mom: Don't get dead

Mia: That's the plan

The elevator stopped at the second floor, and when I peered up from my phone, a pretty brunette stepped on with a smile as bright as the sun shining through the clouds that day. Dressed in a service uniform from the lobby cafe downstairs, I took note of her name-tag almost immediately.

"Siena."

Stop that, Universe.

"Your name is Siena?"

"Yes!" She was bubbly, radiating a warmth generally hard to find in others.

"Siena, as in the burnt shade of brownish red?" I asked, curious as ever.

"No, as in Siena, Tuscany, Italy. My grandparents were born there."

Of course they were.

The elevator doors opened on the first floor, we walked out together, and she asked if I had ever been.

"I actually got back from vacation a month ago. I was in Tuscany, Rome, Venice, and Florence. It was…" I struggled to find the phrase to relay my obsession. "...life changing."

"Which was your favorite place?"

Wherever Gennaro is.

"Tuscany for sure, but Rome has a special place in my heart, too." My mind wandered as we walked alongside each other, her toward the cafe, me toward the parking lot.

"I can see the love in your eyes as you talk about it," she smiled again. "I hope you get to go back soon."

Me too, girl, me too.

I headed toward the parking lot that was, as accurately as I had predicted, buzzing with stressed out, overworked, and likely underpaid people.

Not until I sat on the hot leather seat—my second mistake of the day—did I fully exhale the breath I was holding.

As I turned the key in the ignition to start both the engine and the air conditioning, Italian love songs streamed from my car speakers. Out of nowhere, I broke down into a full cry.

Was I upset about the job interviews? *No.*

Was I worried about having an income? *Not really. I made more money bartending than any other job I ever had.*

My mom had always been the first one I'd talk to about large-scale life decisions, but for the first time ever, it wasn't her number I dialed as I sat with a huge gaping hole in my soul.

"*Ciao, bella,*" Gennaro crooned into the phone.

Instantly, I calmed, which in turn caused me to get teary eyed all over again. The moment he heard a sniffle, he pressed, "*Stai bene?*"

No, I was not okay.

"The interview today was another disaster. I think it's

best for me to bartend, save as much money as I can, and figure out what I want to do long term."

"What can I do for you?" he asked with his whole heart.

"We could revisit that whole kidnapping thing again if you'd like," I softly muttered into the phone, hoping I sounded as defeated as I felt so maybe he'd take me up on it.

This was not where I wanted to be.

I wanted to be with him.

"Why do I have to kidnap you? Why can't you just… come here?" He must have read my mind through the phone.

The stomach knots returned, but the good kind.

"I'm scared to leave everything behind," I blurted out.

"You're scared to leave your family, and you're scared to leave Allie. What else would you miss?"

Nada.

"Nothing."

"Come here, Mia." His voice sent shock waves through my heart and straight down to my inner thighs.

"Are you asking for me to move there, or do you mean for another vacation?"

"I didn't want you to leave in the first place." My thighs inadvertently pulsed again. "I felt like my life finally started the first night we spent together, and it's been frozen in place since you left. Visiting you reminded me of all we feel for each other, but will either of us be happy if we're thousands of miles apart?"

I paused to breathe it all in, and he mistook my silence for discomfort.

"I'm sorry. I don't mean to put so much pressure on it."

"I don't feel pressured. I…"

I stalled to truly understand what I *was* feeling.

It was fear.

Fear of what my family would think. Fear of what was coming next. Fear of it not working out. Fear of feeling out of place. Fear of the unknown.

But if I had learned anything from my previous trip, it was that pushing past the fear of so many things is what had led me to him in the first place.

Was this where I was meant to be? Was this my *person?* Was I about to have my heart ripped out of my chest? Would I regret all of it?

I had no idea.

But I wouldn't rest until I had the answers.

"What if I plan a trip for October? I'll work at the bar for the next two months and save as much money as possible in the meantime."

"Why can't I pay for it so you can come sooner?"

"Because that'll make me feel worse than I already do without a *real* job, and because you're excruciatingly hot when you're a touch more patient."

"Am I supposed to back off and give you space so you wonder if I really want you in my life?" There was a slight smirk attached to the tone of his voice, and I smiled in response.

"No, actually I hate that. But I do like making my own plans and paying for my own trip, so your Dad, who already thinks I'm a shitty person, doesn't have any more ammunition against me."

"He's walking around here like Benito Mussolini and finds issues with everything he possibly can, related to you or not."

"I know, and I'm sorry, but I still want to do the right thing. So…October?"

"If I can't have you before, then October it is."

We spoke a bit longer until he was satisfied that my

mood had morphed into a positive one and then hung up so he could get to bed. The time change was another thing that slayed me daily because all I wanted at the end of my days was his voice to hear in the comfort of my own bed as I fell asleep.

Music continued blasting through my car speakers while I sat at a red light, and for the first time in hours, I felt a bit of peace. I had a plan and a man who loved me to help make it happen. What else could I ask for?

> *Inner Critic: A family who will understand that you're going there for a second time and will be bartending for income?*
> *Mia: God I hate you*
> *Inner Critic: Go ahead, you know you want to*
> *Mia: I want to what?*
> *Inner Critic: Double cheeseburger, no pickles, four-piece nuggets, small fry, small Diet Coke*
> *Mia: You're right, I do.*
> *Inner Critic: You're welcome*
> *Mia: Thanks, jerk*

I pulled into the McDonald's parking lot to eat my feelings and started my next Italian countdown as I chowed down. I was scared of the unknown, absolutely, but I couldn't ignore the supreme satisfaction that came from knowing I'd be in his arms again in a few months. And whenever I envisioned myself in those arms, it felt exactly where I was meant to be, no matter how scary of an admission it was.

Fall

CHAPTER 9
Gennaro

October, Three Months Later

I couldn't remember the last time I had actually allowed my body to relax. Since the end of Mia's first visit, needing to check in on Papa regularly, and balancing police shifts in Rome with villa work to help ease Mama's load, I had been going non-stop for months.

Now mid-October, I huddled on the outdoor couch underneath string lights, buried in a sweatshirt while a patio heater tried its damnedest to warm me up. With a glass of red wine in one hand and my phone in the other, my body may have stopped moving, but my mind was still racing. It'd been about four months since the day I had met her, and knowing she'd be back with me tomorrow was one reason for that. The other? I heard commotion inside. Giuseppe was rattling off angry Italian curse words, with Francesca's unmistakable whining right behind it.

Barreling through the house like hounds tracing a scent to find me, much to my dismay, they both took separate seats flanking my couch on either side. I sat there without uttering a single word, refusing to take any dramatic bait.

Short-lived silence cut the air like a hot knife before she spoke.

"Are you going to ask me how I'm doing?"

She couldn't actually be talking to me, could she? My eyes moved towards Giuseppe, who was sitting still, rubbing his temples and likely praying to God to deliver him from the seventh circle of hell he found himself living in. When I scanned my line of sight back toward her, I hesitated only briefly before calmly responding.

"Why would I have to ask when I know you're about to tell me *exactly* how you're feeling, like you always do?"

"You say that like it's such a bad thing." She rolled her eyes and shook her head, a standard response, and one I was tired of witnessing.

"I'll answer that," Giuseppe chimed in. "She's nauseous all the time, hates eating, has no energy, doesn't know how to decorate a nursery so she hasn't started, and thinks I don't do anything even though I've asked at least ten times where we want to set up a space for the baby to grow up in. I'm concerned that she's not gaining enough weight, and then she yells at me that I'm a pig who comments on her body. I'm also a useless asshole who doesn't cook for her, even though the forty-two times I've tried to she yells even more and says she can't stomach the smell of anything let alone actually eating anything."

He stared intently at her with what appeared to be complete disdain in his eyes. Defeated, depressed, aggravated, and utterly exhausted, my heart was breaking for my brother, and instinctively, I stood up in his defense before she could try to tear him down even more.

"You two really take whatever ounce of sanity I have left and absolutely demolish it, you know that?" I inhaled, held my breath, and thought briefly about the message I wanted to convey before I continued. "This is my brother. I will always take his side, he's my blood. Unless one day he turns into a giant piece of shit, which I doubt will happen, I'll support him until the end of time." She was snarling at me like a pissed off puppy, and I kept at it.

"You are the most unreasonable human, let alone woman, I've ever known, which immediately makes me and most people want to tune you out. You get mad that I don't listen when you talk, but it's because it's never more than a complaint or an issue you have with something. You want to know why I don't ask how you're doing every time you see me? When have you *ever* asked anyone else how *they* are? You don't. It's selfish behavior, and all of us are over it."

Her eyes glassed over, and I contemplated stopping but couldn't. "You're going to be a mother. Your priorities are completely messed up, and the more you point the finger at him without even an attempt at bettering yourself is yet another reason I'm glad I never actually had a relationship with you."

The words stung as they came out of my mouth, and I wasn't even on the receiving end of them. But it was time. This had gone on long enough. I was done watching my baby brother, who had evolved and leveled up as we all asked him to, continue to get broken down by someone like her.

For once, she was rendered speechless. She stood up, wiped her cheeks, and opened her mouth to speak but stopped herself and simply walked off the patio and into the house.

"Thank you," Giuseppe responded quietly. He sounded more mentally exhausted than even a few minutes ago, but seemed to be breathing a little freer without her presence. "I feel like I don't deserve you to be defending me given the situation, but thank you."

"I said this a while back and it's still true. We were never in a real relationship, so I really don't view it as *my little brother had an affair with my wife*. If anything, I feel bad that you voluntarily got involved with her, because she's a mess."

"...a beautiful mess, at least." He was hopeless.

"Yeah, see, again, I don't view her that way."

"Speaking of, how's Mia?"

"She'll be here tomorrow, actually." I surveyed his wide eyes and large grin. "Surprise."

"How did I not know that?" he asked with equal parts curiosity and disbelief.

"I only told Mama and Pesca–didn't want to deal with anyone else's opinions or input."

"In my next life, I'll be half as strategic, smart, and level-headed as you are."

Little brothers have a way of making you feel like Superman whenever they stop breaking balls long enough.

"In my next life, I'll warn you before you lay down with a crazy redhead."

"Deal."

We stayed on the couch for another hour, long enough for me to hear from Mia that she was at the airport, settled at her gate, and getting ready to board.

"You think you can really have a relationship with Mia? With the distance, I mean?" Giuseppe asked.

"We'll see what happens." I was playing it a lot cooler with him than I did with her, that was for sure.

"How could you have so much to say to Francesca about her and me, but I ask *one* question about you, and it's a four-word answer?" He had a point, and I shrugged in response. "You're scared shitless, aren't you?"

I weaved my fingers together and placed both hands behind my head as a pillow, looking straight up at the stars with a smile on my face and the smallest trace of scared shitless in my heart.

"A little bit maybe," I said. Then, "Okay, fine. Yes, I am. She's the one. Five thousand miles is a lot. I can't ever move there, and I'm not entirely sure she'd *actually* move here."

"Have you talked about it?" It was not lost on me how much I was enjoying some normal conversation with my brother without the drama that always followed him and Francesca wherever they went.

"We have, and we do, all the time. I can't tell if she's nervously joking about coming and us building a house on the property or if she actually wants to."

"You talked that far ahead? Where would you put the house? And how would that work with your job being in Rome?" He was asking solid questions, and I loved him for it, but this was why I usually kept everything close to the chest. I didn't have the desire or the energy to respond to them right now, especially when I didn't necessarily have the answers.

Luckily, a crash from inside the kitchen distracted both of us, and I was able to successfully avoid the rest of the conversation. He leaned forward in an effort to inspect what happened, but I ushered for him to stay seated and relax a bit. It had been a day for him.

Well actually, it had been a long few months.

I left Giuseppe on the couch with a glass of red, the patio heater, and the stars in the sky and headed toward the kitchen.

Shards of glass were strewn about the floor and there was a large red wine puddle, with red splatters surrounding it. I assumed it was Mama bent down behind the island picking up the pieces, but as I approached, Francesca's red hair came into view instead. She was mumbling to herself, words I couldn't make out, and grew silent when she looked up to find me standing there. As though a switch flipped, she licked her bottom lip, subtly nibbled on it, swung her long strands of hair over one shoulder, and stood up straight with both hands resting on the island.

I couldn't quite pinpoint what I felt, but if I was a woman standing across from a man looking at me the same way, I'd have run in the opposite direction. With trouble finding words, I watched her slowly saunter around the island toward me, her nails tracing along the marble countertop.

"*Sei matta.*" I don't know why, of all things to say, I chose to call the crazy person crazy, but it made the most sense given the wild eyes staring back at me.

"*Sono matta di te, Gennaro.*"

For fuck's sake.

"You're crazy about *me?* I've literally given you *no* reason to feel that way." It felt like we were in grade school, and she was mistaking my poor treatment of her for flirting.

"You've always teased me, you've always led me on, and this time has been no exception." She was dead set on her sentiments, confident in her thought process even, and had there been any possibility of her harboring a weapon, I might have feared for my safety.

"Was it the part about me calling you unreasonable earlier that's making you think I secretly want you? Because I can assure you, I don't."

"Pretend all you want. I can see the look on your face when I walk into a room." She was speaking with bated breath, clinging to what I'd say next, but given her absolute detachment from reality, I was at a loss to convey how I felt any more clearly.

"I hate to break it to you, but that look is called

disdain." She continued tracing the edge of the countertop until coming within inches of my face. My blood boiled, my adrenaline pumped, and I actually found myself replaying nearly thirty years of our lives and how few times I had ever actually been nice to her. I wasn't proud of it, of course, but it was the truth.

The fact that anyone in her shoes could think for a second that I had hidden interest in her or us being together was a delusion of epic proportions. But she carried on with her psychosis, whispering in my ear, "*Lei non ti amerà come me.*"

"*She won't love you like I do.*"

My brain finally computed that she was comparing herself to Mia. Too stunned to speak, I stood motionless, staring out the kitchen window with narrow eyes, trying to avoid the full blast eruption that I felt bubbling within. In that moment, I decided to stop trying to give her any benefit of the doubt. When my brother's baby arrived, I'd do whatever I had to in order to support him, but Francesca would be the least of my concerns.

I thought I had made all of this abundantly clear, but her actions were proving otherwise. As I opened my mouth to reiterate it for a final time, she quickly swooped in closer to me, wrapped her arms around my waist, and forcefully attempted to kiss me with a deep thrust of her tongue.

"*Che cazzo!*" We spun around to see Giuseppe standing at the edge of the dining room and kitchen, staring at both of us, his mouth wide open. "What the *fuck* are you doing?"

I looked toward her to explain herself, and can't say I was shocked to see her break down into tears—again. It was her go-to move to avoid any and all ownership of uncomfortable situations as they arose, after all. As I turned my head back toward Giuseppe, I was met with the full impact of his fist to my left eye socket.

Stars twinkled between both of my ears. I fell backward into the island, slipped on the remaining wine still puddled on the floor, and ended up flat on my back with the wind knocked out of me. On paper, I'd beat Giuseppe in any fight on any given day, but his sucker punch took me all the way out.

As I lay there trying to make sense of what had happened, assuming he had left the room, I saw a shadow hover above me and quickly realized he wasn't done. Francesca screamed behind him as he punched me in my sides repeatedly, reminding me of the fights I was used to breaking up in the back alleys of Rome.

Finally, he either grew tired enough to stop or someone forced him to. I couldn't hear anything over the ringing of my ears, my head was pounding, and my left eye was already swollen shut. My brother had absolutely pummeled me—the same brother I had just defended to the absolutely deranged mother of his future child who treated him horribly.

Even when you don't see eye to eye, you assume your family will always have your back. And yet, my brother actually believed I was capable of lying to his face and sleeping with his pregnant, soon-to-be wife. Worse than that, Mia would be here tomorrow, my face was mangled, and I'd have to hope she knew me well enough not to believe whatever Giuseppe would be primed to tell her.

Then, if we made it through that, I'd have to keep Francesca away from her, too.

The last few minutes had made five thousand miles seem like no big deal, but I wasn't about to let it ruin what I had waited the last three months for. More than that,

Giuseppe was about to learn exactly what family loyalty was all about.

His future child's mom trying to seduce me in the kitchen of our parents' home was only the beginning of the impending storm. I was the least of his problems, and as he'd soon find out, the least of his worries.

CHAPTER 10

Mia

I hadn't heard from him since before arriving at Newark International Airport. After sending a message that I was at my gate, three dots had popped up, but nothing more. About nine hours later, having landed in Rome, I was secretly hoping not to be ghosted by the Italian love of my life.

> *Inner Critic: This is why we don't fall in love with*
> *people who live five thousand miles away*
> *Mia: Can't hear you over the sound of the airplane*
> *engines, sorry*

We taxied to the gate, and I picked up my phone for the twentieth time in ten minutes hoping there'd be a message. When there wasn't, I put on my big girl pants and sent one to him.

Mia: Hey, I landed

Mia: Are you still planning to pick me up?

Rather than stare at my phone like a crazy person with a pit of inexplicable dread in my stomach, I shut the screen off, tilted my head back, and closed my eyes. I tried picturing what was in store for me and us in the next few weeks, but all I could see was blank space.

What was going on?

I texted my parents to let them know I had arrived and then, thankfully, by the grace of the Italian gods, he finally sent a message. My cheeks flushed deep red, and the pit of dread disappeared—that is, until I read the entire thing.

> Gennaro: Bentornata amore

> Gennaro: I'm sorry I can't be there to pick you up, but Pesca is waiting for you

> Gennaro: It was a long night and I'm just getting out of the hospital

Papa must have taken a turn while failing to rest and recover at home.

> Mia: Is Papa okay?

> Gennaro: Papa is fine

> Gennaro: It was actually for me

> Gennaro: I needed stitches

> Mia: From what?

> Gennaro: I'll tell you when I see you

> Gennaro: I'm fine, don't worry

"I'm fine." "Don't worry." Why do men continue to use these two phrases and expect us to find comfort in either of them?

I worried less knowing Pesca would fill me in, but I couldn't say the trip was off to the start I hoped for. Seeing her curly black hair as I walked towards the pick-up line gave me mild relief since, like always, she felt like a piece of home. One long embrace later, we heaved my luggage into the back of her car and drove away from the airport.

"I'm going to drop you off at his apartment, okay?"

"Of course, thank you." After a short pause, I continued, "Would you mind telling me why he needed stitches, by the way? And any insight as to why he's barely messaged me since I left home? It's freaking me out a little, and we've got two weeks to enjoy each other before I'm sure I'll need to start making some serious life changes."

She let out a whoosh of air before speaking. "Where to begin?"

The next half hour was crammed with details stemming from Francesca to Giuseppe to Gennaro to Mama to Papa attempting to recover at home. The only person unscathed by drama was Giovanni, holed up in Florence alone, as usual.

"I don't mean to make it sound like you need to be a therapist on vacation, but it's a good thing you're here. You calm him down, and I can tell he needs you around him," Pesca told me.

It simultaneously plastered a smile on my face and pierced a hole in my heart.

He needs me.

"I'm not really looking at this as a *vacation*," I honestly stated. "It's more of a journey into the unknown as it relates to where the hell I'm supposed to be in life."

"Where you are supposed to be *physically*, as in, are you meant to live in Italy? Or in a relationship with him, generally?" She always asked the best questions because she was a thorough, sincere listener.

"I guess a little bit of both. I just…"

"Say it, darling." She always knew when I was holding something back.

"I love him. Clearly. He's a combination of things I didn't believe actually existed in real life. And I keep trying not to think about if I could actually move here or not."

"It's the blessing and curse of having a loving family, Mia," she said, driving in and out of small city alleyways and back roads to get to his apartment as I got progressively more anxious the closer we got. "If you didn't have a family like yours, you'd be able to get up and go anywhere whenever you wanted without the fear of losing anything. But you'd also be alone. Trust me, the latter is not the better option."

I peered out the window, trying to stay fully in the moment without worrying about what came next. For the last few months, I had been so wrapped up in when I'd see him again, how it would be, what would come after, and whether I could ever move here that I'd glossed over the most important part.

For the last four months, we'd communicated consistently. He didn't make any promise he didn't intend to keep. And, miraculously, he never faltered in making me feel as important to him as he did the first night we spent together.

"Your parents are planning to come for their anniversary trip next spring, right? That would be great for everyone to meet each other—as in all of the family members, I mean." Pesca offered the suggestion as a calming measure, but it was anything but.

"I've already played that scenario through my head, and I think the only two people I wouldn't have to worry about are our moms. My brother is a hot head, my dad isn't too far behind sometimes, Giuseppe is clearly emotionally unstable, and Papa, well, who knows what'll happen there. Stella and Giovanni would be perched on a couch somewhere observing human behavior, and hopefully Allie would be there for emotional support, because I would absolutely need it." I sounded like a negative Nancy, but the thought of it all was entirely overwhelming.

I wanted to spend time with him.

That was it.

I didn't need the outside distractions, stress, anxiety, any of it.

"Well, my girl, for the next couple weeks, all you'll have is him. Which, living vicariously through you, is all you need. I know that much." She parked outside of his apartment building, and while I took a few seconds to collect myself, my brain seemed to rapidly slide through moments from the day I first saw him, on this exact street, to the nightclub, walking to the rooftop, arriving back here at this exact building, the incredible night we spent together, and all that followed.

How was it possible that in a few short months, one random meeting had changed my life so significantly? I had no other choice than to fully lean in to wherever it was about to take me, to take him, to take us. Our journey kept leading us along a pathway that made me fall deeper and deeper in love with him. Any residual anxiety I felt from not hearing from him prior to landing completely subsided. I leaned over to hug Pesca goodbye with yet another heart-filled thank you and stepped out of the car, completely embracing the journey ahead of me.

Mia: I'm here

I rolled my suitcase inside of the building and hopped in an elevator with open doors after a sweet older couple with hands entangled held it for me. My heart began beating faster with equal parts nerves and excitement. Peering into the reflection of the metal elevator wall to fix my hair, I wrinkled my nose at the layers of filth I felt on my skin from fourteen hours of travel.

As the elevator doors began to open, I wrongfully assumed I'd have the length of half a hallway to gather myself before knocking on his door. But, as I was still learning, gentlemen didn't operate that way. They didn't receive text messages that their person had arrived and wait on the couch until there was a knock at the door.

I rolled my suitcase off the elevator and lifted my head to find him walking toward me with solid, purposeful strides. One eye was swollen nearly completely shut, the other had deep purple bruises and swelling, and there were some nicks and scratches along his jaw. Tears fell from my eyes at the sight of him, and my heart broke at the brutal violence from his own brother. Leaving my suitcase behind me, I rushed toward him, careful not to add to whatever physical pain he was still experiencing.

We didn't speak, and we didn't have to. One hand found the curve of my lower back and the other the base of my neck, his thumb tilting my jaw toward his. His deep brown eyes scanned every part of my face from my eyes to the bridge of my nose to the bow of my lips. He stopped to assess what his next move would be. I watched him intently staring at me, swallowed the lump in my throat, and licked my bottom lip as I drew in whatever air was left between us. He breathed me in, as he usually did, like he couldn't bear the thought of forgetting the scent that surrounded him.

When he finally exhaled, pulling me in even closer, he traced his lips along the side of my neck before whispering, "God I've missed you."

There was no way to explain how empty my life felt *without* him other than reveling in the complete satisfaction I felt when I was *with* him. My mind went quiet, my senses on overdrive as hot water fell from above us and steam filled the entire bathroom. A trail of clothing decorated the floor from his front door straight through the living room and down the hallway to the bathroom.

When his strong hands touched one part of my body, it set another on fire in response. And when senses were this heightened, the amount of pleasure that could be derived from one touch after another was more than my body felt like it could handle. As water poured down the back of my head and shoulders in a steady stream, Gennaro left no space between us with his muscular thigh nudged between both my legs. His mouth found mine and he kissed me deeply, holding my head exactly where he wanted it, my hips magnetized to him.

He trailed his fingers down my neck slowly and smiled, watching my head fall backward with an unmistakable look of pure satisfaction. Breathing in the steam around me, likely forgetting whatever year we were living in, he pulled me back into him, sucking my bottom lip in between both of his. I could feel myself reach the peak levels of build-up I was willing to accept in his presence and blurted out something along the lines of "Fuck me now, please."

I still questioned whether he pulled an alter ego out of me whenever we were together or there was an otherwise dormant goddess buried within all of the years that came before him. Either way, I was taking full control of every want, need, and desire I had—all of which ended with us completely immersed in each other.

The palm of his hand trailed down the front of my

thigh. He squeezed hard enough for my body to react, a movement that allowed him to swiftly grab the back of my knee and swing it over the side of his leg. It left me wide open and vulnerable, with unbridled lust for whatever he planned to do with me next.

I trusted him, even more than I did our first night together. I didn't second guess anything he did or wanted to do. We were firing on all cylinders, like we always had.

Full steam ahead, we gave in to every single desire.

When his fingers were satisfied with my readiness, Gennaro slowly pulled them out of me. Twirling the bottom of my soaking wet hair, he pulled my head backwards, exposed my neck, and licked the length of it. Always knowing when to make deep eye contact, he did so right before grabbing my hips firmly and spinning me around. With a slight bend to my waist, he rubbed the length of himself along my ass before spreading my legs wider with his knee.

"Are you ready for me?" he asked in a whispered huff over my shoulder.

"Yes," I mumbled gruffly, and all but begged him, "my God, right now."

Gennaro lifted my hips higher to line us up in a perfect position. When I let out an accompanying moan that hung on a few seconds longer than it needed to, he was more than satisfied to hear how much I wanted and needed him to fill me *completely*.

And he did. He filled every inch of my body, my mind, and my heart. He had since the moment I decided to go home with him on a rooftop in Rome. Five thousand miles from home, I had made my sanctuary with him. Wherever he was, I wanted to be.

He pounded in and out of me, with an arm wrapped around my front and the tip of his middle finger rubbing the exact spot he knew would bring me my release. I knew well enough that if he was about to finish, he wouldn't be satisfied if I wasn't finishing, too.

"I'm almost there, baby," I said, helping him out. The kisses his mouth trailed along the back of my shoulder as his fingers and rock-hard dick kept their own rhythm were a masterful display of a man who undeniably knew what he was doing.

I screamed out and let my body melt into his.

Every muscle I had squeezed tightly around him as I struggled to catch my breath. I felt him grasp the sides of my waist as he finished, exhaling a combination of the breath he was holding and the stress he was happy to let go of. As the water relentlessly fell with no regard to the slow-motion movements we were circling, he reached behind me to shut it off. Standing there with flushed skin, soaking wet from shower water and each other's release, he looked at me in a way that made me understand that I was his sanctuary, too.

Whatever he had going on in life always came second to what we felt when we were together. He didn't even have to tell me. I could see it written all over his face. This strong, dominating man melted into a pile of mush whenever he was around me, and with that came power. Not power to hold over his head or take advantage of him. No, it was a power bestowed on those lucky enough to find a person to fall into deep, unconditional love with.

I knew what he needed, I knew what he desired, and I knew what he deserved. An unwavering sense of loyalty to each other, while putting each other's needs before our own, every single time we had the option.

Life before Gennaro seemed gray. The life we wanted together, the one that was paving its way in front of us, was filled with color. He lit me up, he electrified my body, he soothed my previously broken heart, and he stimulated my mind more than I'd ever allow anyone else to.

I was his. He was mine.

There was no denying it.

But could we figure out where to go from here?

Our hearts would be forever connected, but our lives were separated by at least five thousand miles of vast space.

It was the only thing I was doubting. How could we make this work?

Ever a man in charge, one who knew what he wanted and wasn't going to rest until he had it, little did I know that a plan was already in motion to ensure we wouldn't have to doubt it for much longer.

He took charge, like he always had, and soon enough I'd have the answer.

Where *would* we go from here?

CHAPTER 11

Gennaro

I never paid much attention to the living room balcony until Mia's long brown hair blew in the breeze while she was perched in a chair on it. Watching her peer down at the city below, wrapped in a blanket with nothing on underneath, had me already thinking about the next time I'd be buried inside of her. With at least two weeks together, I leaned into whatever patience I could muster, and made her lunch instead.

Two glasses of iced San Pellegrino accompanied one large, shareable plate of thin sliced prosciutto, fresh mozzarella made with my neighbor, Giustino, a few days prior, torn basil, Mama's sun-dried tomatoes and roasted peppers, and a loaf of bread. I stepped onto the balcony next to her, unsure if she was more excited to see me or the food I had prepped.

When she stood, took the plate from me, placed it on the table beside her, and wrapped her arms and blanket around my neck for a hug she refused to loosen, I had my answer.

I inched backward, far enough to bring her face into

view, tilting her chin to mine and asking, "*Amore mia*, are you okay?"

"I've never been happier—and, I've never been more petrified in my entire life," Mia blurted out with her whole heart, as she usually did. "I promise I'll keep on being present and enjoying whatever comes. I didn't want you to think there was anything else bothering me besides that."

"I appreciate it, like I always do. Will you sit back down though so I can stare at you while we eat?"

"I'd love for you to stare at me like half a creep while we eat. Yes, absolutely." She smiled and nudged into me closer, wrapping the blanket around her like a towel as she sipped on her iced sparkling water.

"Thirsty?" I teased.

"Absolutely parched," she replied sarcastically. "Long flights can really dehydrate a girl."

"Anything else that could have dehydrated you a bit?" I asked with a raised eyebrow. She didn't give in.

"If you're referring to leaving me breathless in the shower—which was fantastic by the way—you'd be mistaken."

"How so?" I asked, never quite sure what was going to come out of her banter-filled mouth.

"Because if I can't handle one round of you this morning, how am I going to handle the next couple of weeks?" Her eyes glimmered, her top lip softly biting the bottom one, and she radiated absolute desire.

She wanted me.

I needed her.

And there was no way I'd ever endure a life without her in it.

"I have work until eight, and then I'm taking you back to our rooftop for dinner," I said confidently.

"*Our* rooftop? Did you buy the place while I was back

home?" She smirked with wide eyes, purposefully trying to push my buttons.

"Would you prefer I sit here and ask, 'What do you want for dinner tonight?' like an idiot who can't think ahead, rather than have something already planned for us?"

"Not at all," she pressed her lips together, "but I do like when you get a little mad."

My dick was getting hard as she carried on with this smart mouth of hers, but I *unfortunately* had to leave for work. As I stood up from my chair, her gaze traveled from my eyes to my waist, which was now level with her line of sight.

I attempted to tell her to be ready by 8:30pm for dinner, but she wasn't listening. Licking the bottom of her lip she grabbed the sides of my shorts and pulled them down forcefully.

She didn't care about any of my work obligations, nor did she care about my body parts essentially blowing in the breeze for any and all of my neighbors to see. As her mouth made its way toward me to soothe the hardship it had found its way into, I pulled a portion of the blanket up and over her. Standing there in broad daylight while the woman I craved on a daily basis had her lips wrapped around me underneath it was every ounce of thrill I didn't anticipate I'd receive so quickly.

But that was Mia.

She didn't wait for me to routinely make things about her. She didn't perpetuate a one-sided love. She gave self-lessly, without expectation of anything in return, and because of it, I always wanted to be one step ahead of her. Tonight, we'd revisit the rooftop, but there'd be so much more to it than wining and dining. I was about to remind Mia why the heartbreak she ever endured before me was worth it. That it led her right here to the streets of Rome, the place she was meant to be.

"It's like four months hasn't passed since the last time you were miserable during our shift with her waiting for you at home," my partner Marco chimed in as I sat—pissy as described—in the seat next to him. We weren't on foot patrol, and he had agreed to drive, so I could—fortunately and unfortunately—spend a large majority of my work day thinking about the night ahead of us.

"I need tonight to be absolutely unforgettable, especially since they didn't approve me for more time off."

I realized I was unnecessarily putting pressure on myself and the situation, but it spoke to how much I cared about her. We had limited time together, and I wanted it all to be perfect since it didn't start off the way I wanted with me picking her up at the airport. Add to that the way she left last time, and I wanted nothing but good vibes for the entirety of her visit.

Marco smiled and shook his head. "I love getting short glimpses of *Mr. Confident* emitting some uncertainty. It makes me feel the slightest bit human. Also, you've been employed for like three seconds, how many weeks off did you think you'd get right off the bat?"

"Thanks for taking joy in my struggles asshole," I joked back at him.

The next few hours dragged as I knew they would, but with the clock inching towards eight, anticipation kept building. I found myself longing for the future, coming home to her every night, hoping and praying I'd always figure out a way to make it as exciting as it currently felt.

Then, Mia texted a photo of purple satin. I hesitated

for a few seconds not knowing what she was referencing, but when there wasn't a follow up message, I responded.

Gennaro: Are you doing arts and crafts?

Mia: Something like that

Another photo showed her lying on my bed, long legs sprawled out in front of her with a hand resting on her inner thigh.

Gennaro: Are you trying to get me killed while I'm working and not paying attention?

Mia: No, sir

Mia: I just miss you

Gennaro: Don't even think about touching yourself

Gennaro: I'll be doing that later, more than once

Mia: You're the boss

Gennaro: Tonight I am, yes

Gennaro: See you soon

An hour later I was packed up, showered, dressed, and ready to pick up my woman for what would be an incredible night out together. I called to let her know I was walking toward the apartment building. "Sorry I'm a few minutes late, *amore*. Want to meet me downstairs?"

"Kills you to do one non-gentlemanly thing and not meet me upstairs at the door, doesn't it?"

I could feel her bright smile radiating through the phone as she continued to tease me.

"What nearly killed me was nine hours without you when you're only a few blocks away from me," I recounted. "And what will kill me further is if I don't get to watch you walk off that elevator, looking as beautiful as I know you do, while everyone else stares."

"Hope I don't disappoint you, sir."

"An impossibility. See you in a few minutes, baby girl."

I rounded the corner toward my building, noticing someone pacing in front of it as I approached. They looked toward me, the red, hot blistering end of a cigarette burning with their silhouetted face behind it, then quickly turned, walking away in the opposite direction. With a slight shrug of my shoulders, I walked into the lobby, waved to Gina at the reception desk—still one of Mia's biggest fans—and, just as I had played out in my mind earlier, approached the elevator bank right as the doors split open.

Her gorgeously toned leg stuck out first, and I immediately recognized where the deep purple satin came from in the photo she sent earlier. It was the second dress I had bought her during her last visit, with Gina's help. The jewel tone satin was tight in all of the right places, complete with delicate spaghetti straps—ones I envisioned ripping right off later that night—a high slit on one side and an asymmetrical hem on the other.

She wore her hair down, pin straight, with a delicate gold chain necklace in the shape of a Y that dipped low enough to settle into the curves of her cleavage. Her makeup, as always, made me stop and stare as it subtly enhanced her beauty without detracting from it in any way.

She was more than a vision, she was *my vision* for my entire future.

"*Sei assolutamente bellissima,*" I whispered in her ear after pulling her in closely, my arms wrapped around her waist and lips nuzzled along her neck.

"No one hugs like you do." She didn't release the grip she had around my neck for a few seconds, inhaling my shirt collar and continuing, "or smells like you do."

I audibly laughed and shook my head at the ridiculous fulfillment I felt from being in her presence for barely a minute.

"Do we have time for me to say hi to Gina before dinner?" she asked, her eyes shining almost as brightly as the reflection of purple satin that graced all of her curves.

"Of course."

She kissed me again, deeply, before grabbing my hand and yanking me toward the reception desk. Gina shrieked and catapulted herself from around the desk to embrace Mia like a long-lost friend. As always, it was not lost on me how easily she assimilated into my life. How even though she had to force herself *not* to plan and overthink things, she still had an incredibly light-hearted nature about her with an insatiable desire to enjoy things to the fullest. She added undeniable radiance to my life, the depths of which were still unknown.

After catching up with Gina, I grabbed Mia's hand firmly to leave for the restaurant. As I pushed open the lobby door toward the street, I accidentally knocked into someone camouflaged behind it. Mia tripped up a bit, I turned toward her to ensure she didn't take a tumble down the stairs. Whoever I had almost run over with the door disappeared into thin air. On the ground, though, was another freshly lit cigarette.

My sixth sense began kicking in, but in an effort to not be late for our reservation, I ignored it while we walked to our favorite rooftop restaurant down the street. Riding the elevator with two other couples was reminiscent of the last time we were here together. Passion and desire burned between us then, the same way it did now, with my arm wrapped around her waist and my hand resting on her perfectly round ass. I instinctively pulled her in closer to me, kissing the top of her head and then her lips right after that. When I pulled away, her eyes were still closed, and her mouth slowly stretched into a satisfied smile.

When the elevator doors opened and the other couples walked off in the opposite direction, she looked at me out of the corner of her eye, having assumed we were all headed to our respective tables for individual reservations.

Wrong.

"It's so quiet here tonight," she noticed almost immediately.

I smiled slyly as we walked along the pathway covered in string lights, into the restaurant that was indeed completely empty.

Mia's hesitation was met with curious anticipation as she tightened her grip on my hand. A few moments later, she sucked in all the available air surrounding her, gasping at the sight of a guitar player and singer, both of whom were waiting for us to arrive. When they began to sing and play, she verbally exclaimed, "You did *not…*"

Her mouth wide open, eyes sparkling underneath the complete covering of even more string lights paired with the addition of a few perfectly placed spotlights was worth every single minute planning this complete rooftop takeover. One set lit up the singer and guitarist, and the other set, a bit dimmer, focused on a two-person table set up alongside the railing with full sweeping views of the city.

"I absolutely did."

It wasn't about the money, it wasn't about appearing to be more important than I actually was, it was, quite simply, to have her understand how important she had become to *me*. I thought about Mia constantly. She was the single thing I leaned on to get me through mundane days and hard days, and the person who helped me look forward to the future.

Life felt like it slowed and even sometimes stopped completely when she was with me.

A perfectly quiet rooftop atmosphere with the exception of a beautiful voice behind us crooning Italian love songs was exactly what we both needed.

We wanted life to slow down, to stop and wait for our hearts to catch up. One day, hopefully many years from now, we'd look back on this exact night and know it was where everything changed for good. That it was where we'd set expectations for ourselves and each other that would be the standards we'd abide by until the end of time.

Never take the easy way out.

Never get complacent.

We'd celebrate each other and our accidental love, always.

We'd put each other first, without hesitation, every day from now until the end.

No regrets, no wasted time, just whole hearts and full commitment to each other and our happiness.

Her gorgeous face sitting across from me in an exquisite purple dress was only the beginning of what the rest of this night would bring us both. I didn't think it could get any better, but it absolutely did.

CHAPTER 12
Mia

I've heard that you eventually realize why certain relationships don't work with other people. Most times the heartache, the betrayal, and the disappointment lead you to the one you *are* meant for.

There I sat on the same rooftop in Rome where I originally fell in lust and love with Gennaro Beletta. This time, though, I didn't worry about whether he was an undercover murderer or would bed me with full intention of never speaking to me again. In fact, I wasn't worried about much of anything.

I couldn't get enough of him. I sipped on my red wine, overlooking the railing to the city skyline below and beyond, humming along with the velvety voice of the singer behind us.

"You haven't said much," he quietly mentioned as I peered over the balcony.

He was right, I hadn't, but for once in my life, silence was truly speaking volumes. I was at a complete loss as to how my life had led me here, to him, and to this. Deep down, I knew I deserved it, but isn't that what good-hearted people typically do? Convince ourselves of all the reasons we *don't* deserve the best of things? Or, more accurately, that when good things do happen, the shoe will inevitably drop soon thereafter?

"Stop thinking." He responded to his own question by reading my mind from across the table.

God, I loved him.

My eyes pierced through him with the smallest movement of my head, and I couldn't help but stare. I was peering straight into his soul, wondering what, if anything else, he could have planned.

"I've never experienced love like this," I emptied my heart right out on the table before us. "I've never experienced a man like *you*. I keep trying to remind myself that I'm worthy of it all."

He slid his hands across the table and rested them on top of mine. Weaving his fingers in between my own and holding me firmly in each, he stared back at me until my eyes connected with his. "We both deserve every bit of this and every bit of each other. That's all you need to remember."

"It's been a lesson in ridding myself of shitty memories and experiences I've had in the past and instead, leaning into you fully." I looked up towards the sky, and for the first time all evening I realized how brightly the stars had lit it up. "My life is better with you in it, Gennaro. I don't know how else to say it. I feel complete here. I feel entirely whole when I'm with you. And the only uncertainty I have is how to be a happy person when I'm back home, five thousand miles away from you."

I could see his chest fill with air slowly like he was methodically breathing in order to relax himself. The few seconds it took for him to speak felt like years, but when he finally let the words out, it was worth the wait, though they filled and gutted me at the same time.

"Move here and live with me, Mia."

It wasn't something we *hadn't* talked about before, but in this moment, on this exact rooftop that he had rented out for the two of us, with romantic songs playing as the background chorus of our love story, it felt *real*.

He was looking at me with exactly the same uncertainty I had felt seconds earlier, waiting for my response in the same manner I was trying to piece together the feelings it had evoked.

At the forefront was my initial reaction, my initial desire, my initial *need*.

Him.

I thought a bit longer before answering, because for once, I didn't want to ruin the moment with an interrogation. I was a thinker, educated, intelligent, with depth of soul. With that came questions, many of which tended to kill the excitement and thrill of the unknown.

I stared into his eyes, the browns of which had somehow deepened with want and desire, and without a single question in my mind, responded simply, "Wherever you are is where I need to be."

Without hesitation, he stood up and held his hand out, leading us to the middle of the rooftop. Normally, it would be bustling with diners, but every single table had been removed except ours. The perimeter was dark, the lights above us illuminating a makeshift dance floor. Pulling me in as close as physics would allow, guiding my arms to wrap around his neck, and sliding his two strong hands down the length of me, resting in the arch of my lower back, he swayed back and forth slowly to the beautiful sounds emanating from the singer's lips.

We danced slowly, with silence lingering between us for

minutes until I physically felt something inside of him ignite. Tightening his grip on my back with one hand, the other dipped lower following the curve of my hips to my bottom. The solid strength of his hands engulfed every inch of me as though he were staking claim to my body.

I melted into him, allowing him to lead us wherever he planned to take us. Here, in the moment, or for the future. It didn't matter.

I belonged to him.

He belonged to me.

It became increasingly evident that he would be unable to wait until we returned home to lay stake to his claim. After he walked over to the singer and guitarist, tipped them generously, and rattled off some Italian words that sounded like a resounding "thank you," they immediately began packing up to leave.

Gennaro closed and locked the rooftop terrace doors that led to the inside of the restaurant. He sauntered back confidently to our table, picked up his phone, and typed a message to someone. No more than one minute later, all of the remaining terrace lights were turned off.

As I looked above us, adjusting my eyes to moonlight and city skylights, he appeared inches from me. Breathing rhythmically and heavily, the smell of his cologne was more present than ever. My mouth magnetized toward his, and he wasted not a single second before devouring my lips.

Hearing the deep rumble of his breath as he struggled to maintain his composure sent us both into an animalistic stratosphere. I was glad the restaurant was closed, but the complete and utter disregard for whatever could have been happening around us likely would have prevented me from caring.

Gennaro pushed me toward the railing and spun me

around, the same way he had the night we first met. My arms, outstretched to either side of me, rested on the cool wrought-iron bars as we looked out toward the city. He trailed his fingertips from the tops of my hands, underneath my wrists, up the sides of my arms. When he wrapped both arms around my waist and nuzzled his face in my shoulder, the scruff of his beard raised every last hair on my skin, heightening the sensitivity of every touch that followed.

Eventually, he turned me back around to face him, and my head fell backward. We were standing on a rooftop surrounded by open air, but still, I gasped for more of it. He took advantage of my neck on full display, pushing his boulder of a body further into me. My brain short-circuited, realizing if things didn't work out with him, I was completely ruined for the remainder of my sex life, as there was not another man on planet Earth who looked like him, smelled like him, or felt like him. He trailed his tongue alongside my neck. I audibly moaned, flaming hot blood coursing through my veins while every important body part screamed for him to be touching it, tasting it, or exploring it.

As though he knew *exactly* what he was doing, and at this point I was entirely certain he did, he slid his hand up my thigh, under my dress, tracing the length of me before cupping my warmth with his palm and firmly thrusting a middle finger inside me.

"Do you want me to make you come right now?" he managed to ask me with a breathless, but soulfully deep whisper.

I took the hand that had just been inside me, pulled it toward my mouth, looked directly into his beautiful brown eyes, suddenly darker than I'd ever seen them, and licked myself off his fingers.

There weren't enough words to relay the deep, carnal need I had for him, but I answered him anyway.

"*Fuck* yes, I do."

His eyes rolled into the back of his head before tripping an internal switch.

Dropping to his knees, he widened my stance, lifted my dress higher, pushed the tiny fabric covering me to the side, and ate up every available inch of me.

Stars flashed above me in the sky while his tongue massaged my insides, over and over, and he brought me to a mind-blowing finish. My knees went weak but Gennaro stood quickly enough to support the weight of me, moving toward the seat now resting alongside the wall of the balcony railing, pulling my body with him. I took about ten seconds to collect myself before supreme desire to feel him inside me took over. Unbuckling his belt, I pulled down the zipper of his pants, shimmied them lower, and freed him completely. When his hands firmly grabbed my hips, I knew he was ready to fill me. Hovering above his lap only briefly, I slowly slid myself on top of his throbbing shaft. Our mouths consumed each other as we tried, unsuccessfully, to get even closer to one another.

I guided myself up and down the length of him, slowly at first, and then followed his lead to hit his preferred rhythm. Feeling him try to rein in his finish several times throughout was the incredibly intense connection I craved from him.

I'd love to admit that somewhere between my finish and his—or the aftermath of them both—I stopped to wonder who could possibly have witnessed the entire session that had played out.

But I didn't.

I simply didn't care.

I wanted him. I needed him. And he filled me.

Completely.

Looking out toward the city skyline behind him, I had never felt more convinced that this was where I was meant to be.

My body felt whole when it was intertwined with his.

My heart swelled with contentment and passion as we basked in the afterglow.

As we got ourselves fully dressed and came down from the supreme high we were riding on, dim lights flashed back on.

> *Inner Critic: So, you're a porn star now?*
> *Mia: How'd it look?*
> *Inner Critic: I'm kind of proud actually*
> *Inner Critic: But seriously, get it together*
> *Mia: Proud and jealous?*
> *Inner Critic: I can't be jealous of something I get to benefit from, too*
> *Mia: Okay, don't make it weird*
> *Inner Critic: You're the one banging in public, sister*
> *Inner Critic: Don't pretend you care about things getting weird*
> *Mia: Sorry gotta go*
> *Mia: Hot Italian who loves me is grabbing my hand to take me back to his apartment for another round*
> *Inner Critic: Wouldn't this be four rounds in like a day and a half?*
> *Mia: I stopped counting actually*
> *Inner Critic: Well maybe you should so your vagina doesn't fall off*

"What are you smiling at?" he asked as he pulled me in for another kiss.

"Everything."

"Ready to go?" It was a rhetorical question as he started walking towards the door, but I responded anyway.

"Always ready for you."

"I do have one more stop in mind, actually, if you're not too tired." The elevator doors opened, and if I hadn't been concerned about the state of my lady parts, I probably would have jumped on top of him again.

"Not tired at all."

"Good."

We pressed the lobby button, but the elevator stopped one floor below the rooftop. When the doors opened, no one was there. As they began to close again, the scent of a freshly lit cigarette wafted through. In an instant, Gennaro's foot stopped the door from fully closing. He stuck his head out and looked from side to side.

"Anyone there?" I asked, completely oblivious to any potential issues as I continued to ride my hormonal high.

"All good," he said firmly before allowing the doors to finally close.

When the elevator finally reached the bottom floor, Gennaro took a few steps in front of me, holding my hand but motioning for me to stand behind him. I couldn't understand if he was trying to hide me or protect me from something as he peered out the elevator doors again before deeming it appropriate to walk out.

"Everything okay?" I couldn't help myself. I'd gone a solid couple of hours without asking questions, but I was only human.

"I think so. I'm probably imagining things, but I feel like someone is following me."

"You don't have another hidden wife somewhere, do you?" I laughed out loud as I said it.

He shot me a look that was half eye roll, half smile with a touch of *"You've got to be kidding me."*

"Just a joke. Lightening the mood, you know?" He wrapped his arm around my neck and draped his jacket over my shoulders as the evening air chilled us to the bone without the warmth of the rooftop patio heater.

"One more stop, okay?" He looked to me for the go-ahead.

"I'm going wherever you're taking me."

"*Ti amo*, Mia." He kissed me again as we walked toward wherever we were heading next.

I loved him, more than anything.

And I *would.*

I'd go wherever he wanted to take me.

CHAPTER 13

Gennaro

"According to legend, tossing one coin into the Trevi Fountain means you'll return to The Eternal City (Rome), tossing two coins means you'll return and fall in love, and tossing three coins means you'll return, find love, and marry."

\- The Internet

I walked past this fountain every single workday and never stopped to acknowledge its beauty. Now, with Mia standing in front of it ready to throw some coins over her shoulder and make a wish, I was in full awe of it, her, and how life had led me here.

"You know, technically, you don't have to wish for something. The number of coins you throw in determines if you'll return here, if you'll fall in love, and if you'll marry that person."

"Well that's nice, but I've already returned and I've already fallen in love." She shrugged and turned away from me to assess the beauty of the fountain. "Plus, I wished for something a little different than the standard third one."

"So, you don't want to get married eventually, then?" I smiled with an eye on her to assess her reaction.

"Did I say that?" She kissed me quickly, took my hand in hers, and started walking.

"Where are we going, woman?" I love that she kept me guessing in a fun, light-hearted, didn't *have* to be in charge way but in a liked to *pretend* to be in charge way.

"Back home."

"Already?" It was after 11pm, and while I was absolutely exhausted from Giuseppe's ass kicking, working a full shift, and having enough sex to last a week, I enjoyed exploring around town with her. She was an extension of me, the very presence of which lit me up from the inside out, and I couldn't get enough of her.

"Jet lag is kicking in." She stopped walking and turned to me, cozied in toward my chest, and peered up at me with shiny lips begging to be kissed. "And I've been dreaming of falling asleep next to you for months."

My mouth curved into a smile, my eyes inspected every inch of her face, and my brain attempted to never forget the way her beauty permeated the very depths of my soul. I kissed her slowly, deeply, passionately, hoping to convey all that I felt. "If falling asleep is what you want, falling asleep is what we'll do, *amore*."

She lingered in front of me, eyes closed, lips still longing for more, so I obliged. My mouth trailed the length of her lips and the minimal remnants of gloss left on them. I was never much for public displays of affection, but with Mia, it was different. We carried on within our own bubble, pushing the world around us out every chance we got.

We walked arm in arm back home, approaching the

front of the building at nearly midnight. Living in a heavily visited tourist area came with a decent amount of foot traffic regardless of the time of day. Couples strolled by us hand in hand, either coming home from their night out or heading to their next destination. I found myself on moderate alert for the shadow or silhouette of whomever the person was I had nearly run into a few times, but no one stood out to me.

I opened the front door and stepped to the side, allowing her to walk through first. Feeling the bulge of something under my feet, I looked down to see nearly ten cigarette butts stomped in a pile to the side of the stone staircase.

It didn't take any law enforcement training to deduce someone had been waiting there for a while. Where and who this person was, was the imminent question.

There was no actual cause to believe these run-ins had anything to do with me personally, but it was unsettling. Standing huddled together for warmth by the elevator, no thanks to the unseasonable October evening chill, I pressed the button. After a few seconds, the doors opened to someone dressed in all black, the hood of their oversized sweatshirt hanging over their eyes. Lifting his head slightly to find Mia and I staring back, he stalled briefly before taking off running. I tried, unsuccessfully, to grab the arm of his sweatshirt in an effort to stop him.

I decided against following him and headed into the elevator with Mia instead. Quickened breathing and the concerned look on my face had Mia wondering what was going on.

"There's definitely someone following me," I confirmed my thoughts from earlier.

"Could it be job related since you work so close?" I had given that explanation some thought, but I was a pretty level-headed guy. I rarely got into altercations, even when I apprehended someone. Always respectful, never taking advantage of whatever power I had, I highly doubted anyone would have a reason to seek me out.

"I doubt it," I said, sounding a little aggravated, but not wanting to waste any of my time with her. "I'm sorry, I didn't mean to sound like an asshole."

"If that was you being an asshole, we can get married right now." As always, she effortlessly transformed whatever mood I found myself in to a better one.

"Don't tempt me," I said, pulling her waist toward me as the doors opened to our floor and teasing her with an *almost* kiss before grabbing her hand and leading her to my apartment. Before opening the door, I surveyed her face again and could see how tired she was. "Shower, bed, and a massage to help get you to sleep. That sound good?"

She lightly moaned with her eyes closed, her mouth formed into a sweet, half smile.

"I guess so." I answered for her, kissed her, and led her inside. Twenty minutes later, we both smelled like Acqua dell'Elba Classica and had climbed into bed with minimal clothing. Tapping out at five minutes of rubbing up and down the length of her legs, back, and shoulders, she began lightly snoring and rhythmically breathing, curled up in the little spoon position. With my arm wrapped around her and zero desire to let go, I fell asleep shortly after and didn't open my eyes again until late morning— with only twenty minutes before I had to be at work.

"I'm sorry, you did what on the rooftop?" Marco was open-mouthed, half impressed, and half appalled. "I don't think I can ever eat there again, thanks for that."

I felt my dick harden at the memory and readjusted a bit to push it back down before stepping out of the car. We arrived at a house call within a reasonable timeframe, even after showing up to my shift late. A domestic argument that turned physical between husband and wife landed the man in handcuffs and us with a significant amount of paperwork. The busy work distracted my mind from Mia likely still being half naked in my apartment as well as the black-hooded person who appeared to be following me.

"Okay so let me hear it again from the top," Marco said. "You actually rented out the rooftop so that you could bang her on it?" I shot him a look as I was filling out papers, and he immediately corrected himself. "You know what I mean. *Banging* for, like, people in love who respect each other, or some shit, whatever. You really did that? How much did that cost?"

"Not as much as you think. The owner is a friend of mine from back home," I responded, leaving out the part that he didn't charge me at all. The restaurant owner's father and Papa were childhood best friends. He was heartbroken to hear about his heart attack and having to recover from it and happy to spread some Beletta family joy.

"Incredible. I need a notebook's worth of romance lessons from you." He was complimenting me but also full of shit. He'd never taken the initiative to be overly romantic with anyone.

"I don't think I'd waste time attempting to teach you any of it, but I'm flattered that you're impressed, nonetheless."

"I should probably be offended by that," he said, scratching his head, "but whatever. Do you guys want to come out for some drinks tonight?"

Marco hadn't met Mia yet, and I knew they'd get along, so it sounded like a good idea to me.

> Gennaro: Come stai, bella?

Mia: Doing well handsome, how are you?

> Gennaro: I'll be better in a few hours when I see you again

> Gennaro: Also, the only other person who has ever called me handsome is Mama

Mia: I find that hard to believe

> Gennaro: It's true

> Gennaro: Want to go out for drinks tonight? Marco wants to meet you

Mia: Absolutely

Mia: Wish I had a single friend to bring for him

> Gennaro: He'll find someone within the first five minutes of walking in like he always does

Mia: Can't wait

"We're in," I told Marco. "Where are we going?"

"I mean, is there any other option besides bringing it back to your origin? Savoy, obviously." Marco referenced the night club where Mia and I officially met, before I took her to the rooftop the first time, and he had a point. It would be an incredible feeling to circle back to that first night. Thrilling, even.

Before we finished our shift, I texted Mia to see if she felt comfortable walking a few blocks to the precinct. We'd all have dinner first and then hit the club afterward. She confidently responded with another "absolutely," as I again tried to block out thoughts of who was possibly following me.

> Gennaro: Text me when you leave and when you get here please

Mia: Yes, boss

> Gennaro: You really think I'm bossy?

Mia: No. It's a term of endearment

Mia: I just think you're extremely hot

> Gennaro: Hot or handsome? Now I'm confused

Mia: Do you think I'm hot or beautiful?

> Gennaro: You're both for different reasons

Mia: You just answered your own question, boss

"Oh God, you're doing the face again," Marco said, rolling his eyes as he watched me from across the room.

"Listen, you invited us. If you can't handle it, I urge you to reconsider including us next time," I half joked in response to his ball busting.

"As long as Mia is an effective wing woman, we're good."

I shook my head. "Like you need one. You talk to anything with two legs and a round ass."

"I feel like I should be offended by that, too," he squinted. "Why are we friends again?"

An audible laugh escaped my mouth. "Because you were kind enough to offer me a place to stay when I was in need of one."

"What an asshole I am," he scratched his beard and

continued. "I don't think this has been an even friendship/coworker exchange."

"Let's see if my girl comes through for you tonight," I suggested. "I bet she will."

"You're on."

Mia: I'm on my way

With a towel wrapped around my waist, staring at my reflection in the mirror, I felt anticipation building to see her again. I overly groomed my beard in an effort to calm nerves that came out of nowhere and sprayed my regular cologne from my neck to my chest, adding a few drops of scented oil I had picked up in Florence in an effort to create my very own blend.

The goal? If she walked away from me, she'd still smell like me, and if she smelled like me, any other man attempting to get close to her might think twice about it.

By the time I was finished getting ready, she had texted that she was outside. Marco and I grabbed our things and walked out. I could feel the intense grilling of his stare on us as I forcefully made my way to her, lifting her slightly by the bottom of her ass and simultaneously spun and kissed her before lowering her back to the ground.

"That's lesson one," I said to him as he watched.

"Movie-like twirl and kiss—got it." He rolled his eyes and laughed, hugging Mia hello and introducing himself. "I'm Marco, his work partner and also where he learns all his gentlemanly techniques."

Without missing a beat, she responded, "You know, I often wondered where he learned it all. This makes total sense."

The three of us enjoyed a casual dinner up the street, sipping on wine and sharing a variety of dishes before heading to the Hotel Savoy Discoteca.

"What are you drinking, Mia?" Marco wasted no time attempting to liquor up his wing woman, and the wide smile on her face indicated she didn't mind a bit.

"Pirlo, please," she responded confidently, like she'd been here before, which of course she had. I peered over to the exact seat I was sitting in when I had initially spotted her across the bar and ended up with a goofy ass grin on my face.

Life is wild—a roller coaster actually. Sometimes it's slow, other times completely chaotic, out of control, unpredictable, and thrilling. You have to learn to find joy in the journey without the threat of fear taking over.

I stood there sipping on gin and seltzer, watching Mia and every ounce of her charismatic self, bonding effortlessly with Marco, connecting him with two women standing nearby. Five minutes later, she sauntered over to me.

"Mission accomplished." She grabbed my waistband and pulled me close enough that I could feel the rush of her exasperated breath.

"You okay?" I asked, already knowing the answer.

"I am more than okay, but being his wing woman reminded me of the night we met, and now I want to relive the entire thing." She sucked on my lips, sliding her tongue in to meet mine. We kissed slowly as the patrons moved quickly around us, another slow-motion, world-stopping moment between us. I took her hand and led her to the dance floor–the same one from the first night we met.

The passion of dancing with a stranger was slightly different than dancing with a woman I had fallen madly in love with. The mystery was removed, sure, but excitement and desire were not. I wanted Mia even more than the first time I laid eyes on her. Her arms wrapped high around my neck and our legs weaved between each other, leaving barely enough space for air, let alone anything else. She was suctioned to me, panting heavily, her mouth refusing to detach from mine, pushing into me forcefully as though she couldn't bear the thought of anyone else getting close to me.

"I need you now," I said without hesitation as I felt my dick firm up once again.

"From rooftops to club bathrooms?" she asked curiously.

"I don't give a damn where we go, I just need you now." I felt a little unhinged, like a caged animal dying to be let out, but what else would I expect from the woman who spoke to every love language I had? She was both my kryptonite and my savior. She was the death of me and the strength within me. Thinking of ever being without her left me powerless, but when I envisioned us together, the possibilities were endless.

I became Superman again.

As I grabbed her hand and spun around to find Marco, I bumped into someone who had been standing directly behind me. I looked down to find the same black hooded sweatshirt, wreaking of cigarette smoke. Pushing Mia behind me, I pulled the hood down to see who he was, but much to my surprise, it was actually a woman with scared eyes marred with black circles from fatigue.

"Why are you following me? And, more importantly, who the hell are you?" I asked with limited patience and an authoritative tone.

I could barely hear her voice over the music and nearly convinced myself that what she said wasn't real. But when she repeated it, and I looked to Mia for confirmation, I understood what I had heard to be exactly what she had said.

"I've been trying to figure out how to get a message to your brother," she trembled and finally finished. "Francesca *isn't* pregnant. She never was."

CHAPTER 14

Mia

The color had returned to Gennaro's face shortly after the woman's accusation had drained it completely. An hour later, he and I had returned home, leaving Marco at the bar. The woman, Lina, had explained she was a childhood friend of Francesca's who lived in Rome but was visiting Tuscany at the same time he had returned from the States, which explained the small pile of cigarettes found by the entrance gate.

Lina explained that over the last few months Francesca had been acting off, and when she confronted her about drinking far more than she should have been given her pregnancy, hysterical tears followed the interaction.

"I'm not pregnant! I never was! I don't want Giuseppe, I want Gennaro. I always have." Lina recounted Francesca's admission and answered the lingering question. "Francesca thought she'd be able to guilt you into actually staying married to her and being with her for real, and then she'd pretend to *lose* the baby."

"I always knew she was nuts, but this is next-level psychopath." I couldn't help myself. Far too many times I had tried giving her the benefit of the doubt, but I had nothing left. She was far gone, completely out of touch with reality and human decency. Attempting to seduce an entirely honest and up-front-with-her Gennaro, let alone the mental mindfuckery that she was guiltlessly dragging Giuseppe through, was, simply put, disgusting.

Sitting on Gennaro's couch, we attempted to figure out next moves. He had been relatively quiet, which was a normalcy for most men but atypical for him. Finally, he broke his silence to confirm a thought I had but didn't want to previously admit to thinking. "He bruised my face and ribs in defense of that lying piece of shit. I can't believe it."

I knew a large part of me was tweaked every time Francesca came into the picture in any way, but I could never quite pinpoint why. She seemed like she should have a relatively normal life, with the exception of her arranged marital partner not wanting to be married to her. I tried putting myself in her shoes, understanding what it must have felt like to be in love with someone who wanted nothing to do with you, then watching him fall for someone else so quickly.

I felt for her, truly, but in no possible way were her actions warranted. She was messing with the Beletta family's livelihood, on top of Giuseppe's general sanity. Luckily for me, Gennaro let most of it roll off his back, concerned only with breaking the news to his brother in the best possible way.

"He still thinks I secretly want her, which is an absolutely horrid thought by itself," he said, his face wrinkling. "I can't even imagine he'd sit down long enough with me without trying something, and this time, there won't be any openings for sucker punches."

He was getting riled up prematurely. "Settle down,

killer." I crawled across the couch to plant a kiss on his lips and then sat back suggesting, "Why don't I call him?"

Gennaro's face took the shape of both curiosity and bewilderment. "How would that work?" His brain was stalled, trying to process the suggestion.

"Well, usually you'd have to share someone's phone number with me. I'd dial it and verbally relay the information we were given, which would significantly improve his current life, and in turn, yours." I sat leaning on the back cushions of the couch, the side of my head in the palm of my hand, studying his face. Confusion melted into slight satisfaction when he appeared to visualize the entire conversation unfolding.

"Okay, maybe it *would* go over better if it comes from you first," he shrugged, trying desperately to believe the words coming out of his mouth, "but I don't really like giving you *more* of my family's dysfunction to make sense out of."

"Oh, there's no making much sense out of this anytime soon, but if I can help expedite it with as little physical violence as possible, that'd be my goal."

It was too late to call that night, but when we woke the next morning it was the first thing I did. Gennaro stood in the kitchen, shirtless, brewing espresso in his gray drawstring pants. I didn't know what he was planning to make for breakfast, but I was suddenly starving.

In an attempt to refocus, I took out my phone and dialed Giuseppe.

"*Ciao, sono* Giuseppe." He was out of breath, which likely meant he was already hard at work on the villa property.

"*Ciao* Giuseppe, it's Mia." A couple seconds of silence were followed by a resounding, "Mia! *Come stai?*"

We dabbled in small talk for a few minutes. I reminded him that I was in Rome with Gennaro, and he mildly grunted over the phone.

Men were men—until they acted like little boys.

Suddenly, Mia who acted properly toward the family members of her international boyfriend morphed into Mia from New Jersey.

"Listen, I don't really know how to say this, but I wanted to give you time to digest it before we get there." I waited for a confirmation of some kind and carried on when I heard the smallest of one. "Gennaro and I were out last night, and Francesca's friend Lina found us on the dance floor."

"Okay, and?" He had an attitude with *me* all of a sudden, and it ticked me all the way off.

"Why exactly are you getting aggravated with me?"

Gennaro turned around from the kitchen sink like a tiger ready to pounce, but I shook my head ever so slightly to let him know I was fine. Giuseppe apologized profusely, saying his attitude was directed toward Gennaro. "Well, to be fair, you shouldn't be upset with him either."

"Why's that?"

Ooooph, he wasn't prepared for this.

"Francesca isn't pregnant. And apparently, she never was."

Dead silence.

Actually, the silence was deadlier than dead—like the buried remains of the dead—silence that was weighed down by six feet of soil atop it. I waited long enough until concern for his well-being took over before asking, "Are you going to say anything?"

"How do you know it's true?"

Oy. Hopelessly romantic.

~~"On what planet would someone track us all the way to Rome to tell us this?"~~

Patience, Mia, he's the kind soul of the family.

Inner Critic: Yea right, the kind soul who kicked the
shit out of your boyfriend
Mia: Why don't you go help Giuseppe and leave me
alone since he clearly needs it?
Inner Critic: That's not how this works, girlfriend

~~"How are you the only person in the world who can't see how truly insane your half-ass girlfriend is?"~~

I had to calm down and remember I wasn't dealing with a self-aware Gennaro. I needed to reevaluate my approach.

"Giuseppe. This is good news, isn't it?"

"How is it good news? Just another way for me to be single for the rest of my life."

Oh, he was hopeless *hopeless.*

"Can you actually count on one hand the number of times you and Francesca have *enjoyed* spending time together as opposed to the amount of time you've spent *arguing?*" I hoped for the honest answer, because I knew it would be telling.

While Giuseppe was deep in thought, audibly mumbling in the background, I was instantly reminded why I fell so hard for Gennaro.

His confidence was steadfast, unwavering, and somehow, never arrogant. He knew who he was, what he wanted, and what he'd never settle for. He demanded respect without being abrasive. He exerted an energy that allowed me to revel in the comfort of his security and protection while also supporting every way I wanted to advocate for myself.

He taught me the importance of true self-awareness and reflection, which helped push me further into the poised, self-assured version of myself I had recently uncovered.

I distinctly remembered rumblings back in the day about strong women softening in the presence of a strong man, and I used to doubt it, dislike it even.

No man would soften me enough to mold me.

But now I realized it wasn't about molding anyone. It was about evolving within and through the other. Like vine work, we had woven ourselves in and around each other, growing stronger, together, by the day.

I had never met anyone like Gennaro because there was no one else like him on Earth. He was one of a kind. Exceptionally unique, wholly special, and *all mine.*

"No, I can't actually," Giuseppe said, snapping me out of my Gennaro daydream.

"You can't what?"

"I can't count on one hand the number of times I've enjoyed things with her," he said, letting out an embarrassed muffle of laughter, which I took to be the start of the mental release he needed. After a few more minutes of moderate venting with a side of therapy, we told him we were on our way to the villa.

In the car, Gennaro finally asked, "What did he sound like?"

"He sounds like a little brother who accidentally attempted to beat the shit out of one of the few people who truly cares about him. So maybe go a little easy on him."

He squeezed my hand as we drove toward Tuscany, and for the first time in a while, we listened to music more

than we spoke. To me, it signified a comfort and a famil-
iarity with each other. There was no need for space filling
chatter, and inherently, I think we both knew we'd be
walking into a bit of a shit storm. So, we embraced sweet
silence and the calm that joined it, reveling in the fact that
we were able to spend so much time together.

Three hours later, pulling into the villa drive brought
back a rush of memories, most of which were spectacular.
But my departure night after Papa's undoing ranked
highest in memory, unfortunately.

Knowing Papa was here added to the dark cloud I felt
floating above my head as we pulled into the driveway. Add
to that the uncertainty of what would come from the revelation of Francesca *not* being pregnant and Giuseppe
having done what he did to Gennaro, and we weren't quite
sure what we were walking into.

Hand in hand, we walked in with our heads held high,
as we we'd become accustomed to doing. The kitchen
smelled incredible, a variety of sauces bubbling on the
stove as usual, wine bottles already popped and scattered
across the island counter and voices echoing from the
patio. It appeared everyone had been briefed on
Francesca's gigantic lie, because wine glasses adorned the
patio table with four more bottles scattered amongst the
five adults present.

Giuseppe lay across one couch looking defeated as ever,
Pesca and Mama sat perched in their own chairs giggling
like teenagers, and Giovanni sat on the larger couch, his
arm slung around the neck of a beautiful brunette who
looked as comfortable as comfortable could be.

I was pleasantly surprised, even more so when they saw
Gennaro and me and erupted into excitedly quiet cheers.

"Mia! So, so nice to have you back here!" Mama
exclaimed. Giovanni kissed me on each cheek and intro-

duced us both to his new girlfriend, Dominique. Pesca gave me the same loving hug she normally would, appearing to be even more excited to see Gennaro smiling ear to ear behind me. I waited for Giuseppe to show even an ounce of effort, but he refused to get up. It was unclear whether he was simply embarrassed or had really found issue with Gennaro somehow.

Finally, having reached my limit of being involved with family drama not quite my own, I sat down and generously poured two glasses of wine for Gennaro and me. I felt comfortable among the group of people present with the exception of Giuseppe's silent treatment and only moderately concerned with Papa's whereabouts.

Deciding to focus on the people around me who I felt most comfortable with, after about twenty minutes of conversation I decided I quite enjoyed Dominique and Giovanni together. She matched his quick wit and was an understated beauty who paired well with his under-the-radar good looks. They bantered back and forth effortlessly, and she was one of the first Italian women I had met who didn't make me feel like an oblivious American.

Pesca and Mama filled us in on Papa, and while I dreaded the thought of it, I vowed to make it a point to have a conversation with him. I wasn't sure whether he wanted to see me or not, but it didn't matter. If I was envisioning myself becoming part of this family, and I'd need to ensure I had done all I could to help him see exactly the type of person I was.

At some point during my conversation with Giovanni and Dominique, I noticed Giuseppe had gotten up off the couch and was nowhere to be found. Gennaro had likely realized it at the same time, because he too scanned the area until we heard all hell break loose in the kitchen.

"Here we go!" Giovanni chimed in with a smile. "Get your popcorn."

We all ran inside to find Giuseppe standing over Francesca, who was, not at all surprisingly, whimpering in the corner.

> *Inner Critic: She needs her own critic*
> *Mia: You're already taken don't even think about it*
> *Inner Critic: I can barely put up with your stupidity,*
> *   you think I'd last with her? Absolutely not.*
> *Mia: Thanks, I think?*

"*Ti odio! Sei una bugiarda. Una psicopatica. Sei il peggior tipo di persona!*" I was able to make out the words "deep hatred" as well as something to do with her being a generally horrible person. And, he kept on going.

I didn't blame him, but Gennaro stepped in to pull him backward in an effort to calm down. When Giuseppe started swinging, Gennaro caught his fist in hand and looked at him wide eyed, threatening that if he even thought about hitting him again, Giuseppe would be the one in the hospital this time.

"*Basta!*" I whipped my head around to find Mama standing behind me, yelling louder than every decibel I'd ever heard her speak combined.

"YOU," she said, pointing directly at Francesca and walking in between Gennaro and Giuseppe, who were now separated, frozen at the sounds she was emitting for the first time in their life.

Over the next few minutes, Mama made Papa's disapproval speech toward me seem like a mild dress rehearsal. She laid into Francesca, calling her desperate, deceitful, conniving, jealous, and a disappointment, to name a few. Mama spoke confidently, firmly, and eloquently, and although it was hurtful, it was entirely accurate. Francesca was everything Mama accused her to be and more.

The emotional manipulation stemming from faking a pregnancy was far more than Mama would ever have been able to forgive. "I can't believe I treated you like a daughter. Never again. Get out of my house, and don't ever come back here." She held open the kitchen-to-courtyard door herself. Francesca, hysterically crying and on the verge of hyperventilation, ran toward her parked car.

She had strung everyone along for months and accused Giuseppe of being an inept father-to-be while continually trying to seduce Gennaro, turning brothers on one another, treating me unfairly in response to her supreme jealousy, and taking advantage of Mama's kindness.

Italians hold hard grudges, and this was no exception. On one hand, it was a relief for Giuseppe to know he was not about to bear a child with an emotionally unstable woman, but on the other, how would this change things going forward? Gennaro's and Giuseppe's relationship, the shared land between the families, the arranged marriage, all of it?

Perhaps it was the wine, or maybe it was the pure adrenaline that stemmed from finally speaking a hard truth, boldly and confidently, but Mama wasn't concerned about any of those things in that moment. In fact, she grabbed another bottle, popped out the cork, and walked right back toward the patio.

"More wine if anyone wants to join me," she mumbled, waving the bottle above her head.

And we did. Every last one of us except Giuseppe, who had walked away quietly, hopefully in an effort to regain control of himself.

Inner Critic: So, you're sure you want to be part of

> *a family that could be repeat guests on Jerry*
> *Springer?*
> *Mia: Every family has its issues*
> *Inner Critic: Your family's biggest issue is that*
> *you're up each other's asses*
> *Inner Critic: These Belettas have a lot of things to*
> *work out*
> *Inner Critic: You're really signing on to this*
> *willingly?*

Yes. Yes I was.

They had a lot of baggage and a lot of issues to work through.

Would it be possible?

Giuseppe and Gennaro were not speaking, and Papa was still positioning himself as an outlier, retreating from the family and resurfacing only to instruct people on things to do in an effort to feel like he still had control over the business he was so proud of.

There was certainly a steep hill in front of us, one that everyone would have to decide to climb together. It was too soon to tell if they'd all agree to the journey. I was uneasy, hoping they'd be able to figure out their own family dynamics, let alone accept me as part of it, but I forced myself to focus only on the things within my control.

> *Inner Critic: Can't blame you for trying*
> *Mia: I'm sorry, was that a compliment?*
> *Inner Critic: Just drink your wine, lady*

I sipped on wine with the arm of the man I loved slung around my neck, in my favorite place on Earth.

I reveled in the happiness of the moment in front of me, trying not to worry too much about the future and hoping with every fiber of my being that this *was* meant for me.

Time would tell.

I was certain of it.

Inner Critic: You sure?

We'd find out soon enough.

CHAPTER 15

"She faked an entire pregnancy?" Salvatore was equal parts shocked and appalled but mostly entertained. He threw back the remaining beer in his pint glass and slammed it down on the bar of the osteria. "Carmine, we need some grappa."

Carmine grinned from behind the bar with only minimal concern, used to our antics after all these years. He had watched us go from high school to trade schools or family businesses, bitching about a lot of it with the occasional romance and heartbreak thrown in. When my "situation" with Francesca came into play, he emitted feelings on the matter but never elaborated on them verbally. I appreciated his self-control but silently wondered what he was holding back.

Seven shot glasses were perched in front of Sal, Vincenzo, and me. Carmine held one for himself, raised it, and toasted, "To the young boys that I've watched grow up into *mostly* mature men." He then looked at Sal and laughed. "My wish for you is that you never stop chasing the true joys of life, and more than that, you don't mistake temporary pleasures for long lasting happiness." We paused for a few seconds, digesting the meaning behind his toast before throwing the shot back.

While the guys and I prepped for the next round, Carmine continued talking. "I'm sure I seem like a washed-up old man, but this heart of mine has flourished from the love of a great woman. She pushed me to do things I wouldn't have ever considered. My wife gave me unconditional love without expectation of anything in return except my loyalty and dedication. She was the single greatest choice I've ever made in life. Picking the wrong woman will absolutely change the course of your life, and most times, you won't realize it until it's too late."

We all sat in silence, stunned to hear Carmine utter that many words in a row. Frequenting the osteria after all of these years had brought us close to him as an extended family member, but never particularly yielded heart-to-heart conversations like this one.

"You miss her, don't you?" I asked him, referring to his wife, who had passed away a few years back.

"More and more every day. It hasn't gotten even a little bit easier living life without her," he responded.

"Sounds like a longing I wouldn't ever want to experience," Vincenzo chimed in. "I'd rather be by myself and not have to learn to live without someone who meant that much to me."

"Better to have loved and lost than never to have loved at all," Salvatore responded, looking to Carmine for confirmation of the sentiment.

"You got it." He smiled and then looked toward me. "I need to talk to you alone."

Vin and Sal noticed and kept talking amongst themselves as I slid down the bar to the opposite end. Carmine met me there, leaning over so he could speak quietly. "If I know Francesca well, and I do, she's not going to go quietly into the night with all of this. I've spent years listening to her from the exact seat you're sitting in about how unfair it is that you didn't live up to your part of the 'marriage.' I never said much to her, because she's a lost cause. I could have a better conversation with one of those bottles on the wall over there."

I nodded my head in agreement, and he continued, "I always hated that your parents had agreed to the whole arrangement, because unlike most of the old-school men around here, I believe in actual love. It shaped my life. I've always admired you as a person, as a son, and I want the best for you. I…" He stopped himself mid-sentence to finalize his thoughts before continuing, "I knew within a few seconds that Mia is one of those life altering women."

"I appreciate your support, old man. And for the record, no one I know considers you 'washed up.' Quite the contrary actually. You're an eligible bachelor around these parts."

He smiled and leaned over the bar, his hand on the back of my neck, and whispered, "I already had my love of a lifetime. It's your turn." Then, as he nodded toward the door, my neck whipped around to follow his line of sight. In walked *my* love of a lifetime in dark jeans, an off-the-shoulder cream-colored sweater, high heeled boots, gold hoop earrings, and her long hair swept over one shoulder. The notes of her perfume wafted across the bar as she hugged Vincenzo and Salvatore before laying her gorgeous gray eyes directly on me.

As usual, my pants grew snug, my cheeks flushed, and I felt my heart beat a few thunderous beats in quick succession before returning to their normal pace.

This woman had turned me into a version of myself I

swore I'd never become. Not because I didn't want to but because I convinced myself, repeatedly, it wasn't possible.

I scooped her toward me more forcefully than I planned to, her arms effortlessly wrapped around my neck, our lips magnetized to each other. Lifting her a few inches off the ground by way of the bear hug I held her in, I turned around and kissed her like I either hadn't seen her in years or wouldn't see her again, ever. It was a combination of the two, paired with Carmine's sentiments, that made my love for her and need of her to burst out every seam of my body.

"And to think I almost convinced myself *not* to stop by and bother you," I said, setting her back down on the floor and cradling her head in my hands.

"From now until forever, please know that I *always* want you to bother me," I told her, "especially when you look and smell like this."

"Noted," she smiled before planting her perfect lips on mine one more time to seal the deal. I was nauseatingly in love with this woman.

"Some of us are trying to stomach our food here," Vincenzo half joked, twirling fresh pasta with his fork. Our dinner arrived, and I remembered how hungry I was. Sal sat closest to the door, Vincenzo to his left, Mia next to him, and I scooted in close to her. It was hard to believe that twenty-four hours prior, we had learned of Francesca's non-pregnancy. Here we were, eating and drinking to comfort the depths of our souls as we usually did, even with certain familial relationships hanging in the balance.

It felt like home because it was home, with friends who were family.

When the osteria's front door opened letting in cool October evening air, we all turned to see Giuseppe walk in. The silence was thick until Vin and Sal took the opportunity to bust chops and lighten the mood ever so slightly. "At least you saved yourself from an entire *lifetime* of crazy behavior."

When Giuseppe responded about how crazy behavior correlates to crazy sex—an ill attempt at trying to be relevant around his older brother's friends—I felt even more satisfied with my choice while internally rolling my eyes at his innate immaturity.

Mia's ability to stay calm and level-headed drove me all the way crazy. My body ached for her, my heart pounded in my chest at the thought of her, and my dick relentlessly hardened at the sight of her. I didn't need erratic behavior to fuel my epic desire for her. It happened naturally, in a way that was about to be established as my own norm for the rest of my life.

After catching up with Vin and Sal, Giuseppe hugged Mia hello, ordered a beer from Carmine, and reluctantly sat down next to me, letting an exasperated sigh that felt like relief and uncertainty combined. He'd clearly come here on purpose in an attempt to fix things. "You alright?"

Ten seconds of silence turned into tears trickling down his cheeks and a sincere apology. "*Mi dispiace sinceramente, Gennaro.*"

When I didn't respond right away, he chugged more of his beer and continued. "I need to tell you something."

I turned my head in his direction so he knew that although I was quiet, I *was* listening, and he continued. "I've always been jealous of you." I was surprised by the admission, pulling my head back, squinting my eyes in response. "In some ways, I think, being with Francesca and even thinking I got her pregnant, I felt like I *had* something over you, finally." His face was pained, and while I had seen him cry before, I'd never quite felt discomfort oozing from his pores as I did in that particular moment. "Karma is a real thing though, because look at this mess now. I deserve all of it."

He wasn't telling me anything I didn't already know or feel. It was typical younger sibling behavior, trying to figure out life without living in the shadows of those who came before them. Problem was, rather than try his hand at something completely different, like Giovanni had, he was trying to travel similar roads as me while expecting different outcomes.

Francesca was not the answer, nor the solution. She never would be. "You really don't understand how big your heart is, you know that?"

His sad eyes looked up at me, confused, so I carried on. "You are the core of our family, Giuseppe. If you weren't here, I bet Giovanni would barely ever come home, and I'd either be holed up in Rome avoiding Papa or working alongside him and hating every moment of it. Besides Mama and you, we'd both prefer to be *away from here*."

"Why though? You barely ever even spend time with me," he admitted, more honestly than I cared for him to. It stung.

"I always feel like you think I'm a hard-headed buzz kill," I responded.

"Well, you are both of those things," he shrugged and continued, "but I like you a lot better with her around." He glanced over at Mia and nodded his head in her direction. "I'm not even ready to be married or to be a father. I just want to feel like someone wants me around."

The more he spoke, the more my heart broke, never quite realizing I was acting as the big brother I thought I was *supposed* to be rather than the one my little brother *needed* me to be. I was struck by the fact that it was similar to the way Papa acted.

That ended now.

"I'm sorry I've made you feel like I don't want you around. It's the farthest thing from the truth. I think I've actually tried to protect you from life so much that you haven't had the ability to actually shine." The admission was stark proof of how I'd failed Giuseppe while convincing myself I was doing what was best for him. "I always faulted you for not having direction, but how could you have direction when the rest of us are doing our own thing, escaping each other and this place every chance we get, leaving you here to pick up the pieces?"

He nodded in agreement, so I asked him directly, "What do you want out of life?"

Giuseppe's eyes surveyed me quizzically before darting to the side, pondering an answer. As I waited patiently for his response, I felt an arm wrap around my waist and soft lips suction to my neck. Had I not been having a long overdue heart-to-heart with my brother, I would've had a body-to-body with her in the bathroom she was heading toward.

My big head won this round as Giuseppe finally responded. "I don't want to take for granted all we've been given."

His answer hit me in the depths of my newly discovered soul.

He was right.

We had it all here. Carmine had even hinted at it one of the last times I had visited with Pesca—that those who visited enjoyed the area more than those who had the privilege of growing up here.

Papa was physically ailing, unsure if he'd ever recuperate enough to operate the one thing that meant the most to him. Mama was hanging on by a thread with a majority of her best years hanging in her rearview mirror. Mia was considering upheaving her entire life to start a relatively new one with me, and my brothers and I had wasted years trying to be anywhere but here.

It took a failed arranged marriage, a brush with death, a fake pregnancy, and now the heart of my soulful little brother to make all of this perfectly clear to me. How would we turn our remaining years around to take full advantage of all we had available to us?

I knew exactly what I needed to do. Giuseppe had an innate desire to be wanted, needed, and trusted, and I'd give him the opportunity to be the type of brother that didn't have to linger in the shadows of anyone any longer.

"I need you to help me with something," I told him.

"Anything," he responded without hesitation.

"Anything?"

"As long as I don't have to kill anyone, yes." I mentally noted he wouldn't be my preferred partner for offing someone, should the unlikely need arise.

"No killing necessary," I assured him.

"I'm in then."

CHAPTER 16

Mia

It was only my third morning waking up next to him since returning to Italy, but it felt like the millionth. His arm draped over the dip in my waist as we lay on our sides facing the window with bright rays of sunshine bouncing off our naked skin. His warm breath hit the back of my shoulder in a repetitive pattern, fast asleep and unbothered, solidifying how comfortable we had grown purely existing day to day with each other.

Gennaro and Giuseppe appeared to make amends after a long conversation ended in a big man hug. After another round of grappa shots for all of us and a few more beers for the guys, we walked back home to the villa. Vincenzo and Salvatore slept on living room couches, and I made my way back to Gennaro's room with him since the entire villa was filled with guests.

We were perfectly tipsy but fully functional thanks to a few slices of complimentary pizza that Carmine had given us before we left. Wrongfully assuming climbing into bed meant he was ready to sleep, I watched him reach over to his nightstand and power on a speaker from which the soft sounds of sexy, soulful Italian voices oozed. He dimmed the lamp and crawled back toward the edge of the bed closest to where I was standing. "Are you going to take your coat off?"

He snapped me out of the trance I was in, one that frequently had me in a choke hold as I watched him do regular daily tasks and relatively basic movements. It was the manner he performed them—never wavering in confidence, never second guessing himself or his desires, and still somehow ensuring I was on board with whatever he was planning. "Come here, I'll help you."

I briefly pretended I didn't know why he so often rendered me speechless, but was quickly reminded the moment he pulled his shirt up and over the back of his head. His smooth olive skin blanketed a landscape of muscular peaks and valleys up and over the defined lines of his traps, shoulders, biceps, and chest. The stress of life had given way to defined abs that made me feel slightly inferior. Gennaro had repeatedly told me how much he loved every inch of my body, and still, I occasionally doubted myself in his presence.

As he usually did, in tune with my innermost thoughts, he pulled me toward him by the middle flap of my coat, unknowingly silencing those doubts. "It's insane how God damn gorgeous you are with these clothes on," he said, "but I much prefer the things I'm about to do to every beautiful inch underneath them."

Within seconds, my jacket, pants, and shirt were cast aside as he kneeled on the edge of the bed. I watched him intently survey what felt like every centimeter of my uncovered skin. Delicate parts hidden beneath my bra and underwear were begging for his touch. My hands clung to his shoulders as I stood in front of him while he traced his fingertips from my knees up and over my thighs to my hips, looping his thumbs in the waistband, and pulling them down forcefully.

I thoroughly enjoyed the push and pull of his opposing chivalrous and animalistic need-you-now egos. He never dared to be disrespectful, but when his desires overtook any remaining self-control, his hands, fingers, and mouth had no choice but to act out on them accordingly.

Grabbing me with the strength of no man before him, Gennaro pushed off his knees, and his legs slung over the edge of the bed, situating me on his lap. I straddled him, my fingers weaved in his thick hair, pulling on it firmly enough to tilt his head backward, his parted lips begging to be attached to mine. Nibbling his bottom lip and twisting my tongue around his, a slight moan escaped his beautiful mouth. Unclasping my bra, it quickly joined the rest of my clothes on the floor as he buried his head in my tits, his strong arms wrapped tightly around me.

I pushed him backward as we inched toward the center of the bed. My hands were flat on his chest, supporting my weight, with my nipples dangling right above his mouth and a devilish grin plastered on his face. His tongue circled each of them gently before wrapping his arms around me, my body collapsing right into his. Gently rolling me over to the side, propping his head up with one hand and using the other to push hair out of my face and over my shoulder, he traced my prickled skin all the way to the part of me that was physically throbbing for him.

The strength of his hands and masterful fingers explored every inch of me, alternating from long strokes to deep thrusts to quick, gentle fingertip pulses, which, paired with his mouth on mine, had me muffling my finishing screams into the bed comforter.

In the minute it took me to regain control of my breathing, his pants joined my clothes across the room, and he crawled back on top of me, not breaking eye contact unless he closed them to savor what he was feeling while buried deep inside of me. Watching Gennaro hover above me, powerfully pumping in and out of me as small beads of sweat formed on his forehead, the divots of his muscular frame beginning to glow, I realized that the manliest of men knew how to take control, manhandle a woman's body even, while simultaneously respecting the hell out of it. He did it effortlessly.

He was as obsessed with me as I was with him, and if his full finish where I felt every ounce of his flesh tingle under the touch of my fingertips was any indication, he wouldn't have his fill of me anytime soon.

He was insatiable, and I loved it.

As I lay in bed the morning after, looking at those blinding rays of sun while replaying a compilation reel of our best sexual encounters, he began to stir behind me. I rolled over and nuzzled closer to his chest. He hugged me tight—still half asleep—but alert enough to whisper, "*Tanto la vita è bella.*"

Yes. Life *was* beautiful. The beauty of living presently had brought me to a man who knew how to continuously and relatively effortlessly show me every way it would keep getting better in his presence.

"I think we all need to spend some more time with Papa," Mama suggested over breakfast as fresh *cornetti* dangled from our mouths.

"I just came from his room. He's pleasant as ever," Giovanni declared with an eye roll, still attached at the hip to Dominique, who was all smiles. She looked at him with pure adoration, a new romance blossoming at lightning speed.

These Beletta men know how to get the ladies to fall for them in record time.

"Well that's the thing. How would you feel if you watched everyone running circles around you while wanting to be involved?" she explained. "It's slowly driving him insane and making him even more…"

"Grumpy? Is that possible?" Giuseppe chimed in. "Every time I try to talk to him, he grunts at me and rattles off a new task I should be doing." He sipped on his espresso and shook his head. "I don't think he's told me one thing I've done well since he's been back."

"This place wouldn't be functioning right now without you, all of us see it, even if he doesn't want to admit it." Gennaro confirmed what the rest of us knew to be true, coming off the heart-to-heart during which he pledged to be kinder and more supportive of his brother.

Giovanni added, "Mama, we've all tried. He's not interested in quality time or whatever it is we have to say to him. Unfortunately, it's a lost cause at this point."

"I'll spend some time with him today," I suggested to Mama. I could feel everyone's eyes gaze in my direction but kept mine on her and the small curve of her mouth that told me she appreciated the offer.

"I'll join you, if you'd like?" Maybe it was just to ensure Papa didn't ream me out again, but I appreciated the offer.

"That would be great," I smiled back.

Forty-five minutes later, after cleaning up breakfast and prepping lunch, we walked over to their villa. As we neared the front door and heard pots clanging inside, I felt a pang of nerves attack my midsection. I pushed the discomfort aside, along with my pride, reminding myself I was there to support Mama with her request. Regardless of what state of mind Papa was in or how he'd receive me, I'd sleep better that night knowing I did the right thing, whatever that was.

Mama walked in first, urging me to wait in the small living room. Five minutes and a few hushed whispers from the kitchen later, they walked into the living room with Papa leaning on her for support.

He looked significantly older, with tired eyes and a tired body. Breathing heavily after walking a few short steps from the kitchen made me quickly realize how difficult it was for him to attempt to cook something for himself, let alone perform basic tasks around the property. The supreme displeasure it brought him was disheartening, but the empathy I felt for him was short lived.

Papa's head turned away from me as quickly as his eyes locked on mine. I felt like Gennaro and Giuseppe trying to work through their issues, only Papa wasn't my blood relative, so what in the hell did I think I was going to accomplish?

Inner Critic: He's a tough old bird
Inner Critic: And he ain't ever changing
Mia: People can change
Inner Critic: Not people like him

It frequently plagued me—could I really love this place as much as I thought I did with the patriarch of the family misjudging me entirely and appearing to hate me just the same?

Mama nudged him toward an armchair in the corner, and I leaned forward on the couch in his general direction with plenty of space between us. He continued to peer out the living room window, avoiding eye contact at all costs.

"Hi Papa."

Nothing.

There wasn't the slightest movement of a muscle or rotation of an eyeball in my direction.

"*Fai attenzione quando parla, Rocco.*" I assumed Mama was telling him to pay attention to me—a request he denied—looking at her straight faced before continuing to gaze out the front window like I wasn't even there.

> *Inner Critic: I know his son is the love of your life,*
>   *but this is ridiculous*
> *Mia: ….*
> *Inner Critic: You don't deserve this*
> *Mia: I agree*
> *Inner Critic: Well, thank goodness*
> *Mia: I'm just going to say what I came to say*
> *Inner Critic: Oh dear*

"Papa, I am in love with your son," I said, hesitating slightly to see if he'd react. When he didn't, I continued, "and he's in love with me, too. I'm starting to forget what my life was like before him, and I think I actually prefer it this way, but you're making it a little difficult." I paused again.

Surely, if he were paying attention to me he'd flinch at that sentiment, but he didn't. When I looked at Mama, she was shaking her head in embarrassment. I continued, "Okay, well, point is, I don't want anything from Gennaro or your family that I am not willing to give back in return. I love your home with my whole heart, and I treat it like my own, too. And I feel like that's something you should actually appreciate."

As he continued to ignore me, I felt my patience dwindle.

Inner Critic: Told you

When my phone lit up in my hand and I read the message that came through, I took it as a sign to keep going.

> Gennaro: I love you more than anything

> Gennaro: And I know Papa will learn to love you the same

I smiled and felt some remaining pains of uncertainty fly away.

I could only control myself.

I couldn't control what Papa thought of me, how he reacted to me, or how he'd view me in the future. And I had to stop trying to.

"I feel like you're not giving me a proper chance to show you how much this place means to me—what your son means to me."

Still nothing.

"I'll just say it then. I'm sorry if you feel that we disrespected you in your home, but we love each other. I mean, how do you expect to have grandkids who take over the property years from now, if we don't…"

> *Inner Critic: Why are you making it weird?*
> *Mia: Should I have said "Sorry for banging your*
> *hot son all over your property" instead?!*
> *Inner Critic: Definitely not*
> *Mia: Right, so shut up*

"The point is, I love him. I love your family. I love this property. I love all of it. And I'll treat it accordingly. Gennaro wants me here to do it with him, so if you can't accept it for me, you should try to accept it for him. He loves you and just wants you to understand each other."

Mama sniffled in the corner.

At least someone was paying attention.

I stood up, satisfied with my one-sided dialogue but dissatisfied with his stubbornness. At the last second, I remembered one important detail. "Oh, one more thing." Mama looked at me with a raised eyebrow, unsure what was about to come out of my mouth. "Your sons love this place as much as you do. They just want the freedom to enjoy it as hard as they work on it."

Nothing. Still.

As I waited outside of the front door for Mama, they spoke back and forth inside. It infuriated me even more knowing he purposely hadn't responded to me.

When she walked out, she hugged me tightly. "He *will* learn to love you, exactly as I do." Love emanated from every fiber of her being, and while I highly doubted her sentiment, I enjoyed being in her presence.

Mama reminded me of my own mother, warm, amiable, a peace-keeper, needing nothing more in life than her family and her memories. She was happiest surrounded by the love and laughter of those who meant the most to her, wishing, hoping, and praying daily for good health and genuine happiness for all of us.

Mama could tell the love within me was similar to the love within her own self. In that, she knew at least one of her precious sons would have the ability to live a fulfilled life with a partner in ways she likely longed for during her marriage to Papa.

Would her love and acceptance be enough to offset Papa's judgment and disdain?

The Universe seemingly had plans even greater than the healing of my empty heart when it put me on the same street as Gennaro months ago. Would the Beletta family begin to repair its wounds from the inside out and learn how to truly enjoy, appreciate, and respect each other and their family business as time ticked on?

I hope they would—for them, of course, but selfishly, for me, too.

CHAPTER 17

Gennaro

"He refused to look at me, but I said everything I wanted to say," Mia said, recollecting her time spent with Papa. I certainly wasn't surprised by the admission, but realized the pang of discontent I felt was because I *hoped* he'd magically have a change of heart.

No such luck.

And now, it was my turn to go talk to him, partially due to Mama's request but mostly because he was still my father, whether we agreed or not. It wasn't up to Mia to change him. The last thing I wanted was to see my father, who had essentially been bed ridden for the last four months, and I do what we typically did best—argue. But I felt a bit of discomfort as I considered what I was going to say to him and how he'd respond.

I walked the pathway to his villa alone while Mama and Mia stayed back to clean up lunch and prepare for dinner.

Seated in an armchair in the living room, staring out the window, Papa's head turned in my direction as soon as

I walked into the room. I took it as a good sign, that is until I saw the expression on his face. He had aged more in the last week than I expected. Quite simply, he looked tired.

When his eyes caught mine, I hoped for a smile, but all I could decipher was sadness. He was a man trapped in his own body. A usually active man who wasn't used to relaxing, who was being kept away from the thing he loved most in the world. Standing before him was his son, in love with an American, who had moved to Rome and begun an entirely new career to get away from that same beloved thing.

Why *would* he smile?

For the first time, I felt the slightest bit of guilt for it. Imagine giving your entire self to a family business that none of your three sons had particularly great interest in taking over. But again, as I often forgot to remind myself, Papa never particularly tried his best at making any of it *enjoyable.*

"*Ciao*, Papa." I sat on the couch in front of him.

"*Ciao*," he responded with a small smile. I was pleasantly surprised that he acknowledged me, but still felt uneasy with the trajectory of our conversation.

"How are you feeling?"

Why did I feel so uncomfortable speaking to my own father?

"I'd like to get my energy back so I can start working again, but…" he paused. "I want to apologize to you first."

The world stopped spinning, if only briefly.

He continued, "Not being able to work has given me time, too much time actually, to think." I shifted in my seat to a more comfortable position, taking note of the discoloration in his complexion, the wrinkles in his skin, the thinning of his hair, and his overall shrunken frame. The tall, strong, built-like-an-ox father I grew up with was far too young to look as old as he did. Time trying to recover from the heart attack had not been kind to him, and it was difficult to see.

"I was too hard on you, and I realize how it sucked the joy out of everything we had to do. It's hard work running the property, but I never gave you credit for your work ethic. I could give you any job and know it would get done correctly. I took advantage rather than show you appreciation."

Thankfully, he paused, because his admissions were overwhelming. It was something I always wanted to know, hear, or even feel, but listening to him divulge his every regret as it related to me, my upbringing, and our falling out sounded way too much like a goodbye apology. And I, for one, was not ready to say goodbye to him.

"Papa, you don't have to—"

He stopped me mid-sentence. "Yes, I do. I wasn't ever given a choice on what I wanted to do when I grew up, and I tried to do the same thing to you. I disagreed with you because I never stood up for myself the way you did. I've done the opposite of what a father should do, and should be helping to make your life better than my own. I forced you boys to want to be anywhere but the place I love most in the world."

The unmistakable squeeze in my throat wouldn't let up, but I was able to choke back the few tears forming in the corners of my eyes in order to prevent him from feeling worse than he already did. As I attempted to form words that would somehow heal the many years of parenting regrets he was holding onto, his heart continued to seep through his lips.

"Living with regret is unbearable. Some of what Mia said to me made me realize I've faltered as a father, and especially as a husband. Mama's been left to pick up the slack of my shortcomings, and even though I tried my best to do what felt like the right thing, supporting my family, I missed the mark."

My brain allowed me to formulate words at the same time my heart allowed itself to forgive him for years of built-up resentment. I never hated my father, nor could I say I was ever angry with him. I had simply gone numb to his negativity after so many years of dealing with it. The situation with Mia had been the final straw in my hope of ever trying to change him or his thought process, so I had filed all of this away as a never-going-to-happen notion. But his apologies immediately paved the way for instant forgiveness. He *was* my father, after all, and he had always meant well. He merely lacked the finesse in demonstrating it.

"I *never* thought I'd hear an apology from you," I said, still reeling from the admission. "I *love* our home and our business, but I've always wanted to experience it on my terms, not yours. There's actually nothing I want more than to live and work here." I hesitated before finishing my thought. "With Mia."

A tear trickled down his brown, cracked cheek. "*Perdonami Gennaro, perdonami.*"

"I *do* forgive you. But I also need to know that Mia will feel like an actual part of our family," I requested. "She was just here baring her soul to you, and you refused to even look at her."

"I'm still angry," he shook his head.

"At what?" Equal parts frustration and confusion caused me to raise my voice.

"He's not angry," the door opened behind us and in walked Mama. "He's embarrassed." She handed him a small plate of food and continued, "I know you, Rocco

Beletta, and when you know you're wrong, you get angry instead of apologizing."

"No, no, no…" He attempted to disagree, but Mama interjected.

"No, no, nothing. I can count on one hand the number of times you've apologized to me in over thirty years." Mama was on a mission, straightening pillows, folding blankets, and forcing him to drink some water. "Stop being ridiculous. It isn't 1950 anymore. It's a new time, and our son found someone who loves our home as much as she loves him. I will be so disappointed if you ruin that."

My face bore the sentiment of someone both appreciative and surprised by her demeanor.

"She was as respectful as could be while talking to you before, and you couldn't even dare to look at her. *Disgrazia.*"

"I will apologize to her when I'm ready," he said, appeasing us both with a raised hand.

Mama, seemingly satisfied with his short response, walked out as quickly as she had walked in.

"I hate when she's mad at me." It was another admission I'd never heard him utter, but it was evident that something throughout his physical recovery had allowed him to dig deeply to uncover his feelings and regrets as they related to his relationship with his wife. I felt his energy shift immediately after her visit.

Catching me completely off guard, he asked directly, "Are you planning to propose?"

I swallowed the inevitable lump in my throat, fully knowing the answer but hesitating in admitting it to him. We had made significant strides for the first time in years. Why would this admission derail anything?

He already knew the answer and finished his own thoughts rather than wait for me to respond. "There's a ring I had bought for Mama before we were engaged to be married that I never gave her."

"What did you propose with?" I realized for the first time that I had never seen Mama with a ring on her finger, always assuming she didn't wear one because of the daily cooking and cleaning.

"Nothing. She didn't want anything. Adamantly refused it, actually. It was her own way of protesting our arranged marriage. So, I put it in a drawer and it's been there ever since."

I was astounded. "You have to be the thickest person I've ever met. She said she didn't want it and you took her answer as the final word and moved on? She was scared."

"Scared of what?" It was clear to me that after all the years I'd learned things from my parents, it was my turn to return the favor.

"Scared of everything. She was young—leaving the home she grew up in to be married to a grumpy ass man like yourself." I half smiled, still astonished that he hadn't picked up on this in all of these years. "She was unhappy and didn't want to be told she had to do something against her will. It's exactly the same reason I feel the way I do about the villa. I hate people telling me I have to do something or be someone other than who and what I am. Mama and I are the same in that way."

Papa intently listened and digested what I said. After a short stretch of silence, he slowly stood from his chair and instructed me, "Walk with me to my work shed."

He could walk on his own but was wobbly, so he interlocked one arm with mine as we followed the gravel pathway down a hill toward the chicken coop. From underneath a terracotta flower pot filled with dirt, he retrieved a small key that unlocked the door.

Of course he'd leave something he never wanted

discovered in here. It was the perfect hiding place since he spent a majority of his free time yelling at anyone who ever approached it. Another key for the desk drawer was hidden in an empty wine bottle perched on a shelf above the desk. I smiled as I read the label. "Bottle 1, Beletta Family Vineyard."

"That was the first bottle of wine I ever made with Mama," he recounted with the tiniest bit of water pooling in his eyes.

Papa unlocked the drawer, pulled it open, shuffled around some papers, and found a small black box buried toward the back. I swallowed the lump in my throat as he slowly opened it. A pristine diamond ring stared back at us. One large center stone was flanked on both sides by two smaller stones resting on a thin gold band. It was stunning, like Mama, especially back in the day.

The salt water that had built up in the corners of his eyes was now streaming down his cheeks. I wrapped my arm around his shoulders and hugged him tightly.

Closing the drawer and locking it, he placed the key back in the wine bottle. I wasn't sure what he was planning to do with the ring, but the fact that he had dug it out and allowed himself to reminisce a bit was a big emotional hill for him to climb, harder even than the physical torment he had been dealing with.

Papa had admitted fault and was emitting warmth and sincerity, emotions I'd never seen from him. I knew he felt remorse for the way he treated Mia and I hoped he'd find a way to apologize to her separately. Perhaps most notably, I could feel his complete change in demeanor related to his relationship with Mama. The love she always wanted was buried within him. It was merely lying there dormant as he assumed she'd prefer to be anywhere, with anyone else.

My heart broke for both of them, but I knew I'd do

whatever I could to help change the tides for their remaining years together. I promised Papa a few things as we walked back to his villa, and I'd start on them as soon as I got back to Rome with Mia.

I couldn't tell her about any of them, though.

Not yet anyway.

CHAPTER 18

"Are you properly caring for the health of your vagina?"

She was painstakingly relentless, but I wouldn't expect anything different to come flying out of Allie's mouth after not speaking to her for nearly a week.

"My vagina is more than fine, thank you for your concern."

"Are you sure? Do they have cranberry juice in Italia? Maybe you should preventatively drink some of that," she said, only partially kidding.

"More importantly," I changed the subject, "how are things there? How's the asshole?"

"Still an asshole. Getting worse, actually. If he keeps it up, I'll be taking him to court for full custody." She sounded matter of fact, slightly numb, and not at all sad about it. "I don't want to waste precious time talking about him, though. I swear to Christ if he wasn't the father of my children I'd have thrown him off a major metropolitan bridge by now."

Oh, dear.

"Well, things are getting better here, if you're interested." I attempted to lighten the mood *without* direct references to my lady parts.

"I'm absolutely interested, that's why I keep asking about it." She paused, and I could feel both of our cheesy smiles and loving eye rolls oozing through the phone. "Oh, what are we doing for your birthday when you come home?"

"When I come home? I haven't thought that far ahead, but if you could gift wrap the hot Italian man who can't get enough of me and handcuff him to my bed, that'd be preferred."

"I'll do my best. What's on the agenda for the rest of your time there?" I loved her for asking as she shushed her kids in the background after they'd "mom"-ed her no fewer than twelve times in the last thirty seconds. She had a lot on her plate with nothing light or exciting to keep her spirits up, and while I knew she genuinely cared about the details and wanted me to be excruciatingly happy, I had a hard time divulging it all without feeling guilty. I wanted my best friend to experience every ounce of happiness and fulfillment I had been able to, and with an impending divorce, custody battle, and general downward trend in the good news department, it didn't seem likely any time soon.

"Not sure, actually. We narrowly escaped a whole lot of drama. Oh, actually, I have to catch you up with some of it."

"Do I need popcorn?"

"Popcorn is always a good idea," I assured her, "but you might need something stronger. Francesca was faking her pregnancy, and I spoke to Papa."

"Okay, yea, popcorn isn't going to cut it for me, like, at all." I heard a door open and close behind her.

"Where are the kids?" I asked with only mild concern and little-to-no judgment.

"With asshole's mom in the living room doing arts and crafts. I often wonder how someone so wonderful birthed such a dicknose. She's a literal angel on Earth and he's the walking devil. Ugh, don't get me started. Okay, where were we?"

"Fake pregnancies and mending fences," I reminded her.

"Jerry Springer returns. I hope you're getting royalties from him. How does someone fake a whole pregnancy?" I heard a bottle hit a counter, then a swallow followed by a deep exhale. Mild concern resurfaced.

"What are you drinking?"

"A chai….quila." She paused waiting for my reaction.

"What the hell is that?"

"A leftover cup of chai from Starbs with some tequila splashed in it, obviously." The 'obviously' had a little spice to it, and I didn't want to make her feel any worse than she already did.

"Isn't it, and I mean this lovingly, still morning over there? More importantly, how do those two things taste remotely good together?"

"It absolutely is still morning. Did you miss the part that my soon-to-be ex-mother-in-law is here? If she has a problem with my morning cocktail—or if you do—take it out on the sorry excuse for a man who inspired the need for it."

I was a little more than mildly concerned at this point, but I trusted her to know what she was doing and how she was handling herself. "10-4, roger that, but you didn't answer the last question."

"They don't taste good together at all. We're going for numbing qualities, not flavorful ones."

And then she broke down and cried.

"Jesus, I knew it. Why aren't you talking to me?" I was

desperate for her to string together vulgar words and erratic sentences as an outlet, but she kept resisting it.

"You think I want my dramatic, depressing bullshit to interrupt the happiness you're chasing all the way in Italy? Absolutely not. We both deserve to be happy, but I don't get any happier dumping on you while you're trying to spend time with the love of your life." She was breaking my heart and kept on chipping away at it. "This is my problem. I married an asshole and hoped to change him. Well, assholes don't change their spots, or whatever we hope assholes will do. They keep on keeping on, ruining lives around them. I'm used to it by now and I *will* be fine, I just need a few things to be finalized. I promise I'm good, I just need to occasionally take an edge off, and when I have someone here helping me with my kids, I can do that without any guilt or worry. Now, if you don't tell me all the ways you've ridden his Italian soppressata, we're going to have a problem."

I snorted in accordance with her unabashed humor, reminding me how much I missed her and how much I'd be missing if I moved here. "The Italian soppressata you're referencing is sitting right next to me, so detailing every which way we've hmmm-hmmm'ed would likely be frowned upon."

"Why are women like this?" Gennaro chimed in from the couch cushion next to me, a smile on his face.

"Oh, right, like you and Marco don't detail your encounters the day after when you're driving around?" My eyebrow raised sufficiently, and my head tilted in his direction.

"Marco has refused to eat on the rooftop ever again after I told him about the other night."

Allie could clearly hear Gennaro from the other end.

"Mia, Mia, Mia…*what* did you do on a rooftop in Rome you little—"

"Okay, that's enough." I stood up, mouthed "I'm sorry" and walked outside to the terrace, closing the door behind me.

"I'm still waiting on fake pregnancy and attempting to bury the hatchet details with your future father-in-law, but I'll be damned if you think you're gonna leave out fuckery on a rooftop. Spill it, bitch." She wasn't going to let up, and I knew this was a version of escaping her own problems by diving head-first into the array of shit I was involved in.

"Francesca would have only been four or five-ish months by now, so it wasn't completely out of the question for her not to be showing. In some ass-backward way, she was trying to get closer to Gennaro by finding some way, *any* way, to infiltrate the family again."

"And pretend banging his brother was the best way to do that? Ohhh, she's *sick.*"

"I don't think they pretended to do that, she just pretended to be pregnant." I said, calculating the details in my head.

"Okay, so she was real life banging the brother, hoping for pregnancy by osmosis with the original brother and then…what exactly?"

"I'm not even sure. She's unwell. Mentally unstable, really."

"Let me tell you, if this chick even thinks of offing you, I will go full blown Robert Stack with my own *Unsolved Mysteries* spinoff, find her, and then kill her like Liam Neeson in *Taken.*"

My head shook back and forth, and I looked toward the sky for some relief. When the angels basically LOL'ed in my general direction, I responded, "You've got a shit-load of pent up aggression, you know that?"

"I've got a lot of pent-up sexual energy, too. I'm a mess. The hottest of hot messes. I need to cut off the dead weight hanging from my ankle so I can move on. I want to be a better mother, a better daughter, and a better friend, and I absolutely want to find someone who makes my heart skip a beat and my panties wet like you have."

"Didn't we make a pact years ago to never say the words *moist* and/or *panties*?"

"I'm trying to get a point across here, but anyway, moving on to your father-in-law."

"Oh my god, Allie, he's not my father-in-law," I huffed in response, giving serious thought to pouring my own chai-quila.

"*Yet.* But continue…"

"I went with Gennaro's mom to talk to him."

"No, stop, of all the people there, *you* were the chosen communication starter? The one he called an American whore, incapable of actually loving his son or being an asset to his beloved family, all of whom are miserable in his presence? Ugh. Men. It doesn't matter which country or what age, they all suck."

"Do you want me to talk or not?" She was hilarious in many ways, but she was also getting under my skin, if only mildly. Her silence was code for "Okay, sorry, continue," so I did. "The guy is walking around with years of regret. What do I get from holding a grudge against him besides looking like a piece of shit to the rest of the family?"

"I get it, keep going," she responded. Maybe the chai-quila had kicked in, but she'd finally relaxed a bit.

"Gennaro's mom requested more people to go spend time with him, and it seemed like the right time to show support and do the right thing, I guess. So, I went and spoke to him for a little bit."

"So, how is he now?"

"Who knows, he refused to look at me."

"You're making it really hard for me to be supportive of your kind gestures." She was jaded, oh so jaded, and I completely understood why, but it pierced a hole through my heart to fully realize the gaping one in hers.

She sighed deeply before letting out a little sniffle. "I'm sorry. I need the next chapter of my life to start, and quickly. This area of limbo I'm in ain't it for me. And I miss you." There it was. My best friend needed me, and I felt supreme guilt for not being there for her. "Don't go getting all the sorry feels for me, please. I don't want you coming home to act as my therapist. I just can't wait to see you, whenever that might be."

"I'll be home soon, my girl, and you'll be my first stop, like you always are. Promise me something though?"

"Anything," she responded quickly.

"Not too many of those chai-quilas, okay? At least not in the morning. Don't give him any reason to turn the tables on you."

"Only permitted to overdrink in your company during the middle of the afternoon when greasy bar food is present?"

"Exactly." She could hear the smile through my voice.

"I need to go, but please bookmark the rooftop fuckery recap for me in our next conversation, okay?"

I agreed to do exactly that.

The roller coaster of emotions had come to a slow, steady finish after a half hour on the phone together. When we hung up, I felt a deep longing for my friend, wishing I could step into her shoes to walk the rocky path she was walking and offer up some relief. But I knew she'd never want me to. That's how she was.

"I got myself into this mess, I'm going to get myself out of it. In the meantime, I'll live vicariously through you and your sexcapades." - Allie, probably.

I walked back into the apartment with a sleepy smile plastered on my face to find the Italian sausage she so hilariously kept referring to. Allie was exhausting, albeit entertaining, and now, I wanted to surrender whatever energy I had left in his arms.

Sitting on the couch where I left him, Gennaro looked up from his phone, placed it on the table next to him, and nodded for me to walk over. I crawled up the length of the couch toward him, landing between his legs, resting my weight on his chest, his arms wrapped around me and his lips instantly affixed to mine. "I'm sorry I was out there for so long."

"Don't ever let it happen again." My lip curled up into a smirk, simultaneously turned on by his pretend arrogance.

"Or what?"

"Or I'm withholding the soppressata." I involuntarily snorted, laughing at his and Allie's ridiculousness.

"I miss her," I shook my head.

"I know you do," he said, never missing a beat. "You two are lucky to have each other. She'll be okay, though, stop worrying."

"How are you so sure, sir?" I loved him for caring enough to mention it, but honestly, how did he know she'd be okay? I was struggling to find the same hope for my friend. She had entirely too much on her plate.

"Knowing what I know, she's as strong, determined, and resilient as you are. She'll figure it out, especially with you looking after her like you do." *Swoon*. A man who actually listened and attempted to help out with friend drama rather than running in the complete opposite direction to have beers with the boys instead.

"I love you, you know that?" I couldn't help myself.

"I wouldn't turn down a reminder."

"A reminder of how much I *love* you or a reminder of how much I *want* you?" I tried clarifying.

"I'll take both."

My brain quickly computed a variety of ways to do that, but the doorbell interrupted my short-term plan.

"Are we expecting someone?" I asked him, curiosity fully piqued.

"We are, yes," he said confidently. "Mind going to see who's there?"

I hated surprises but also kind of loved them, and had spent most of my life trying to figure out how both of those things were possible. But here we were—surprises that simultaneously made my stomach hurt with uncertainty and my insides tingle with anticipation. I pushed myself off of him and slowly walked toward the apartment door, looking back to survey his facial expression before opening it. "It's not an assassin or anyone threatening your personal safety, so you can check that off of your mental list."

I smiled at how well he knew me and shook my head. I had briefly pictured Francesca on the other side wielding a knife a la Sharon Stone in *Basic Instinct*. Nevertheless, I trusted the handsome man instructing me to open it, so that's what I did.

On the other side was Gina from the lobby desk downstairs with two shopping bags, one of which had what were quite possibly the most beautiful flowers I had ever seen. Her face lit up like a kid on Christmas morning who'd been given every single thing she had asked for. "Mia, *ciao!* Special delivery."

"Oh my goodness, what is all of this?" I asked her with wide, excited eyes, my heart bursting out of my chest.

"It's a man in love, that's what it is. Here, enjoy it. No explanations necessary." She handed the bags and flowers to me, winked, turned on her heel and walked quickly back to the elevator.

I backpedaled into the apartment and closed the door. When I spun around, all six feet plus two inches of Gennaro was towering over me as I stood barefoot in front of him. "I wanted to surprise you with a few things but also didn't want to spend time *without* you, so I enlisted some help. Open it."

"Right now?"

"Right now." Ugh, I hated when anyone told me what to do—anyone except him.

> *Inner Critic: "Mia, jump to your death off the*
>   *Tower of Pisa for me…"*
> *Inner Critic: You'd do that too!*
> *Inner Critic: What a sucker*
> *Mia: If I was dead, I wouldn't be able to benefit*
>   *from his incredibly satisfying dick, so no, I*
>   *wouldn't do that, actually*
> *Inner Critic: Good point*
> *Mia: I know. You can feel free to throw yourself off*
>   *of it, though*
> *Inner Critic: Well that was rude*

I set the bags on the kitchen island and further inspected the bouquet. Bright yellow sunflowers paired with striking red roses and deep purple stems—the combination of color was breathtaking.

"I asked her to pick out something bright, bold, and unforgettable. Something that reminds me of you," he said softly.

All I could manage in response was a shake of my head. In my entire lifetime, the only flowers I had ever received were from my father or brother. He could have stopped there with the gifts, but he didn't. In the first bag was a satin-wrapped gift box. I opened it to reveal new sets of black and red lingerie. The red one was a set of inter-connected patches of lace-covered satin and string. It would barely cover my lady bits, which was obviously the point. The black was a lace-up bustier with garter belt and stockings to match. I opened my mouth to say something, but he interrupted, "Yes, you're going to look beautiful in both of them."

"You're the boss, right?" I half-joked, looking up at him for a response.

"Only sometimes," he thought about it briefly, "and this just so happens to be one of those times."

The rest of the bag contained massage oils, lotions, and candles, one smelling better than the other. "Guess we're staying in tonight?"

"Yes, I plan to be buried deep inside of you shortly."

> *Inner Critic: To be clear, I'd jump off the leaning*
> *tower of Pisa if he asked me to, too.*
> *Mia: Go play in traffic, I'm busy*
> *Inner Critic: Still being rude, come back when he's*
> *done pleasuring you*

When I regained control of my breath, I opened the second bag.

It was filled to the absolute brim with cheeses, *actual* soppressata, and a variety of other meats, olives, peppers, tomatoes, prepared pasta dishes, a salad, fresh bread, and four different wine bottles.

How this man continued to surprise me was nothing short of the kind of magic provided from quintessential scenes of my favorite romance films.

"I have an important question," I asked him straight-faced.

"Ask away," he responded, sitting on an island stool with his arms propped behind his head, one leg crossed over and propped up on the other.

"Are we supposed to eat, or are we playing with these new gifts first?"

"Gift opener's choice," he nonchalantly responded, fully aware of what all of this was doing to me and riding the wave from the captain's chair. I was happy to let him lead, but when he put the decision in my hands, I didn't falter with my decision.

"In ten minutes, I'm going to need you to walk through the bedroom door with two glasses of wine and very little clothing. I'll take care of the rest from there, deal?"

His mouth twitched. "Red or white?"

"Surprise me," I said almost immediately.

"Are you going to ask which outfit I want you to wear?"

"I'm not." His facial expression relayed a non-verbal *"Okay then."*

He couldn't help himself and curiously asked, "How come?" I shushed his lips with my finger, laid a soft kiss on them, and rubbed the outline of his already hard dick.

"Less questions, more wine, *amore*." I sauntered away with the lingerie bag in my hand, wondering who the hell I was acting this confidently. And then it hit me. I wasn't *acting* at all. He helped to make me feel this way, and the more I was in his presence, the more I learned to lean into every ounce of female power I possessed.

The moment we, as women, stop second-guessing ourselves or convincing ourselves we aren't *enough* is the exact moment we allow ourselves to blossom into all we are capable of being.

My skills blossomed that afternoon. I had traveled five thousand miles to find my most confident self in the bedroom of a beautiful man I met by chance on a side street in Rome.

And I wasn't the least bit embarrassed by the admission.

He reveled in all of it, and so did I.

CHAPTER 19
Gennaro

A black bustier, garter belt, stockings, G-string, and four-inch heels laid on the floor with the image of Mia wearing the absolute shit out of all of it seared into my mind.

"Let's go to Venice tomorrow," I said, *seemingly* out of nowhere.

"What?" It caught her off guard, just like I wanted it to.

"I promised you that the next time you came, I'd go on a gondola with you, didn't I?" Her mental rolodex cycled through a few months of memories, landing on the end of her last trip when she headed to Venice with Pesca—without me—cursing the Rome police department all the way to hell for it.

She rolled onto her side, propped her head in her hand, and traced a line from my shoulder down my chest and toward my waist with the tips of her fingernails. "Actually, yes, you did. Kind of you to remember."

"I didn't just *remember*, I promised you I'd do it." I grabbed her hand and pulled it up and over the side of my waist, rolling onto my side to face her, "and if you weren't fully aware of it by now, I don't break promises."

"You just break *backs*, apparently." She licked her teeth with smoldering eye contact, waiting for my reaction.

"Well, when I walk into a bedroom that smells like tobacco and vanilla with legs like these spread wide open on my own bed, complete with the most perfect pair of tits I've ever seen pushed up and out of a black lace bustier, I sort of lose all sense." I trailed my fingertips up the length of her legs, over her hips, and pulled her closer to me by the small of her back.

Mia wasted not even a second planting her soft, more than supple lips on mine. "A man in control—until he loses it—is the perfect man for me." She traced her tongue along the side of my neck, adding, "And yes, I absolutely want to go to Venice with you tomorrow."

I pushed her flat on her back, pinning both arms above her head, straddling her waist. The muffled breathless moans that escaped her lips as I kissed her told me she was more than ready to go again.

Given the packed itinerary I had for the next two days, I obliged without question.

"What'd you say about losing control, by the way?" I repositioned myself between her legs, tightening my grip on her wrists, sliding my knees to the side to spread her wide open. Her tits were full, nipples at full attention begging to be sucked, and the only sounds she was able to mutter were a variety of deep moans as my mouth made contact with them. "That's what I thought."

The arch of her back was inviting me inside her, and the muscular legs she had wrapped around me solidified the sentiment. I was normally reserved, generally quiet in demeanor, but here, with her, in this moment, I was anything but. I crashed into her over and over again, savoring every bit of warmth and wetness her body offered me.

Was I insatiable? Sometimes—but not because there was a lack of anything. On the contrary, it was everything I ever wanted, desired, and *needed*, which I now refused to ever live without.

"Checking in for one night, Mr. Beletta?" We had arrived in Venice at the Hotel Kette, and I could feel Mia buzzing with excitement.

"Yes." I pulled her in close to me as we waited for our key, kissed her forehead, and squeezed her hand. "And thank you for the early check-in."

"Our pleasure."

Riding the elevator to our room, I began cycling through my *own* rolodex that had led us to Venice four months after we initially met in Rome. Knowing all that was waiting for us felt surreal, like I couldn't wait to live the rest of my life with her in it.

"We can drop our bags, walk around a bit, and then take a gondola ride before it gets dark. That sound good?" I asked, looking at my watch and answering a couple of texts received during check-in.

"You could suggest pretty much anything right now, and I'd agree to it," she rattled off, as though she were in a drunken stupor. Drunk in *love* maybe, but definitely not anything else—yet.

We walked hand in hand along the cobblestone streets, window shopping, taking pictures, and randomly stopping to embrace each other. She kept shaking her head, and I continually asked if she was okay. I knew she was, technically, but wanted to know what she was feeling.

"I don't know how to explain the contentment I feel right now. Like this is exactly where I'm meant to be, on this exact day at this exact time. The Universe just feels *right*. I don't know, I sound like a weirdo, I'm sure."

"No, you don't at all, actually, because I feel the same." I pulled her close, brushing some strands of hair out of her face, weaving my fingers through her hair and gently pulling on it to tilt her chin up to mine. "Let's go fall in love again—on a gondola this time."

I pulled out my phone to locate the nearest Gondolier, typed in a few search terms, and within about fifteen minutes we were climbing on board one. "Celebrating anything special?" the Gondolier asked us, to which I quickly responded, "Finding each other."

"What he said," Mia agreed, scooting closer to me on the bench, cradling her head on the inside of my shoulder, my arm wrapped around her. The weather was perfect—a little cool maybe, but with the coats we were wearing and body heat simmering between us—*perfect.*

We both leaned back, fully committed to enjoying the ride, soaking in every viewpoint Venice had to offer, vowing to remember this exact memory with each other. For her, it was being back here, on a gondola—with me this time. But for me, there was more in store and at stake.

I calmed my mind, focusing on the ripples of the water, the sounds of Italian crooners singing from the bows of their small boats, one across the way belting "*O Sole Mio,*" which echoed down each and every canal. Her hand tightened in mine, and she puckered her lips in my direction, requesting a response from mine. With my hand at the base of her neck, I slowly but deeply kissed her, the tips of our tongues igniting a flame that radiated throughout the rest of us.

It was intimate, sensual, and romantic, but most of all,

it was memorable. I would not soon forget this feeling, floating along a historic canal with the woman I loved.

"I love you so much." It felt like I vomited the words. Not because she didn't already know or hadn't already heard them but because of the nerves that were building behind them.

What was wrong with me?

I didn't get nervous.

Ever.

But I was.

Why?

I knew exactly why.

The Gondoliere slowly approached the dock we left from, and I felt my heart simultaneously roll up in a thick ball in the middle of my throat. "*Grazie mille.*" I tipped him generously, and he thanked me profusely with a wink and a nudge, like he knew exactly what was coming.

Did he?

The world was spinning faster than I'd ever felt it before, my phone buzzing in my pocket. As Mia hugged the Gondolier goodbye like they'd known each other for years, I quickly glanced at it and typed back a few responses.

"You okay, babe?" She held out her hand to mine, and I helped her off the boat and onto the deck.

"Absolutely." It was the second time I had lied to her—the first time purposefully.

I grabbed her hand more firmly than necessary and started walking in the direction of the Piazza San Marco. The scam artists selling flowers dive-bombed me, and I was one, "*a beautiful rose for a beautiful woman,*" away from punching them square in the face.

Finally, we approached the piazza, a giant rectangle of open space flanked by incredible architecture and filled with the speedy feet of tourists, a variety of live music, and the aromas of the many restaurants that spanned the length of it.

My eyes darted to the left, scanning for one singer in particular. My phone buzzed, and as I looked at it quickly, Mia's eyes surveyed the expansive space, amazed by all of it. Suddenly, he appeared.

Dressed in all black, my favorite Italian singer held a microphone, welcoming the crowd for the evening. "Are Gennaro and Mia in the piazza somewhere?"

Her eyes darted from side to side in confusion, likely assuming she was hearing things.

"Gennaro? Mia?" Eros Ramazzotti—a popular Italian singer—asked again into his microphone, and somehow the bustling piazza instantly quieted. If there were ever a time for nerves to subside and me to dive back into the confident, well-spoken man I was, it was now.

I walked toward him with my arm in the air, pulling Mia behind me.

"Where are we going?"

I wanted to answer, but my voice box didn't allow me to. I kept tugging on her hand, hoping she'd continue to follow me.

I knew what and who was waiting, but it was clear she didn't.

Eros saw my arm in the air, smiled at me, and ushered me toward the small platform he was performing on. For the first time, I was thankful that Giovanni worked for the higher ups in Florence, because he single-handedly made all of this happen.

The last month of planning was unfolding in front of my eyes thanks to a client of his who owed him a favor and knew Eros personally. It didn't quite feel real—until she finally saw them come into view.

If it were possible, Mia would have siphoned all the air in the piazza with the size of the breath she inhaled at the sight of each person sitting at the table in front of her.

"No way, not possible," she said, continuing to put one foot in front of the other, her mouth agape and her brain trying to process how it *was* possible, since they were sitting in front of her.

"Mom? Dad? How in the—"

"Mia Luciano," Eros spoke into the microphone softly, "I need you to come up here, *per favore.*"

Her head slowly turned toward me, jaw still frozen in the wide-open position from seeing every member of her family, from her mom to her dad, brother, and sister.

I could barely muster a smile as my body jumped out of its skin, laced with excitement and anticipation of what was next.

"Up here," he said, holding out his hand to her as she stepped on to the stage, her facial expressions relaying that she still hadn't come back down to Earth.

"You, beautiful woman, have found yourself a man that is crazy in love with you. He asked me here to help serenade this moment. So, while I sing this song, the exact one he requested me to, I hope you remember this day, this moment, and the feelings you're feeling right at this moment—forever."

He sat her in a seat next to him and called me up on the platform. "Romantic men are hard to find. This act of love speaks to who you are at your core. We've never met before, but I know you're the type of man that will go above and beyond for his woman for the rest of your life. Yes?"

I nodded.

"The rest is up to you," he said, rolling right into my favorite Italian love song, *"I Belong to You."* I had heard it years ago, and it stayed with me. I wondered how on Earth I'd ever feel the sentiments expressed in it when I was stuck in my previous situation.

I now had my answer. Walking between the two tables, one with Mama, Giovanni and Dominique, Giuseppe, and Pesca, and the other with Mia's family, I stepped onto the platform. Mia's eyes were watering alongside a smile wider than I'd ever seen on her. I turned around to see so many sets of eyes staring me down, waiting for what was next.

The sun had set, lights in the piazza were shining, and the cool air blew through, pushing the warm air from the heat lamps toward us. I felt every sense on high alert, as though I were in slow motion, my heart thundering through my chest cavity.

Turning back toward Mia, I slowly bent down on one knee. Behind me, I heard gasps and clapping from our families as well as complete strangers. Her eyes doubled in size, and for the next few seconds, I heard nothing but the vibration of my own voice in my head.

"I love you, Mia. I've never loved anyone more. I've never wanted anyone more." I stopped to assess her expression, and a few more tears rolled down her cheeks. "My life started the moment I saw you on a street in Rome, and all I want is for it to end, *many years from now*, with you as my *wife*."

I inhaled deeply, fully knowing what she wanted but not entirely convinced whether she could agree to it. If there were ever a time to live presently, to live in the *now*, to live in the *moment*, it was now.

"*Mi vuoi sposare?*"

When she didn't answer right away, I repeated, "Will you marry me?"

Her silence echoed throughout the piazza as we all anticipated her response. My heart continued beating with a force I had never previously felt, and the time that passed between the question and her mouth opening to answer it was crushing me.

No.

This couldn't be happening.

Had I asked her father's permission and emptied my savings account to fly in her entire family only to be met with a "no"? Or, worse yet, continued silence?

As my brain computed every worst-case scenario, I saw Mia peek over my shoulder at someone behind me. The tears rolling down her face turned into a full-blown cry. My head whipped around to see Allie standing there, her hand now resting on my shoulder. No words came out of her mouth, but she was looking directly at Mia with her own set of wide eyes, a nod of her head, and so much love in her heart.

Almost immediately, Mia's demeanor changed from slightly terrified to absolutely certain.

Female friendships are a force to reckon with. They speak to each other without the need for audible words at times. Allie's mere presence provided Mia with the security and self-awareness she needed. I made a mental note to always stay on Allie's good side because, well, *shit*, she was like a fairy godmother for my hopefully soon-to-be wife.

When I looked back toward Mia, the uncertainty on her face had vanished. A smile formed with the curvature of her mouth, her own heart likely beating out of her chest the way mine was.

"How'd you know this was my third wish at the Trevi Fountain?"

"Wild guess, *amore.*"

CHAPTER 20

Mia

I had dreamt of a proposal for most of my young adult life. Restaurant scenarios played out in my head often, and every once in a while, a New Year's Eve ball drop, sporting event, or concert to jazz it up a bit. I did like being the center of attention, baby-of-the-family syndrome and all, but I teetered on wanting it to be grand without being *too* over the top. Nothing cheesy was my only request. Don't show up inside a cake or dressed as a cartoon character and call it a marriage proposal was all I asked of, well, myself, since men hadn't exactly been knocking down my potential-wife doors.

Fast forward to now, in one of the most romantic cities in the entire world, after floating along the Grande Canal on a gondola with the man of my literal dreams. He didn't stop at Venice, because why would he do that? It would be too "regular ol' guy" of him, and Gennaro was anything but regular. He was world-stoppingly handsome, insanely charismatic, incredibly thoughtful, and overwhelmingly generous in all he did. To boot, he was just as obsessed with the thought of spending forever with me as I was with spending it with him.

My brain had a tough time computing the reality of my family sitting in front of me. He had called them? When? Did they know it was for a proposal? I was usually the person planning things and surprising other people. When the tables were turned, I felt supremely uncomfortable not being in the know.

These questions and many others swirled through my brain while a famous Italian singer continued to serenade us. I was taken so off guard, so shocked, completely wordless, and while I knew I absolutely wanted to spend the rest of my life with him, I was also staring at my family a few feet away, wondering how I'd be able to leave them.

My head and heart were at a crossroads. My dreams and the reality of a life-altering choice were in conflict with each other. It left the piazza spinning, to the point where I'd need at least three glasses of champagne to straighten me out. I heard every word of Gennaro's proposal, but my body, as well as my vocal cords, were frozen in time.

Like Ariel in *The Little Mermaid*, I tried opening my mouth to utter something, anything, to the man who was baring his soul to me in front of a large crowd, but that bitch Ursula had stolen our voices. He stared back at me, likely computing what the hell was going through my head.

> *Inner Critic: You're kidding*
> *Inner Critic: I've listened to you obsess over this guy*
> *for four freaking months*
> *Inner Critic: FOUR OF THEM*
> *Inner Critic: And now you're hesitating to*
> *answer him?*
> *Inner Critic: For fuck's sake woman, get it together*

> *Inner Critic: EROS F'IN RAMAZZOTTI IS*
> *SINGING TO YOU RIGHT NOW*
> *Inner Critic: Move over or I'm going to say yes and*
> *marry him myself*
> *Inner Critic: Oh my god, you're embarrassing us*
> *::Allie enters stage left:*
> *Inner Critic: Well, thank God*
> *Inner Critic: Maybe you'll listen to her instead*

Seeing Allie over Gennaro's shoulder unlocked something inside of me. I knew I wanted to marry him, but the uncertainty of what came next as it related to my family was causing my delayed response. In an instant, seeing the person closest to me, who was dealing with so many issues of her own but still had hopped on a plane, leaving her two beautiful kids at home to come here in support of mine and Gennaro's love story, made my next move clear.

She was selfless, yes, but mostly, I knew if she didn't believe in it, or us, or him, specifically, she wouldn't have come at all. Her wide *"What the hell is wrong with you?"* eyes sealed the deal, and I finally came to my senses.

I thought back to the Trevi Fountain, throwing three coins in and hoping that my family would support us in the even that this moment ever actually happened. And here it was—exactly what I had wished for. *"Please let me marry this man and figure out a way to make it work without completely abandoning my family in the process."*

The family I had worried about abandoning was sitting right there, each with their own unique smile plastered on their face. Surely, if they weren't supportive, they wouldn't have come.

I internally shook my head, snapping myself out of the stupor I was in.

Live presently, Mia. Stop thinking so much.

"Yes. A *million times*, yes," I finally responded.

Claps, whistles, and some loud cheers echoed through the piazza. The world continued spinning at warp speed, but somehow, as he stood up and pulled me toward him, my arms wrapping around his neck and my lips begging for his in a way they never had for anyone who'd come before him, I discovered a feeling of peaceful comfort deep inside of me.

I had found my *person.*

The man who emulated the best parts of my dad and brother—with his own incredible set of qualities—qualities I swore I'd never find in any man on Earth.

He spoke to me without speaking at all, holding me in front of throngs of people as we both tuned everyone out, forehead to forehead, our lips still taunting and teasing each other's, grinning from ear to ear.

"This is incredible, you know that?" It was part question, part statement. I wanted to make sure he knew exactly how remarkable he was.

"*You*...are incredible," he replied with no hesitation. "This all pales in comparison." He waved to the back-drop and the musician still singing Italian love songs in our general direction, like it was simply another day for him.

"How the hell did you get my entire family here?"

He held my face in his hands, his thumbs wiping away smeared mascara.

"Let's go ask them," he winked at me, grabbing my hand and walking off the stage in their direction.

I ran to my mother with a bear hug and a new stream of running mascara forming. "How did you guys make this all happen?"

She pulled back, hands to the bottom of my chin, looking intently at my face with a huge smile and her own mascara stains. "Your fiancé is the most organized, determined, romantic man I've ever met."

My fiancé.

Holy shit.

Next up was Dad, his own muted smile flashing across his handsome face. "Congratulations. Quite a dedicated man you found."

"You *almost* sound impressed, Dad."

"Let's not get carried away."

I rolled my eyes, with love. He was predictable in his responses, but he was *here*, which said more than the words rolling off his tongue.

And then, right on cue, I heard, "My little sister is engaged—with no ring. I'm coming to Italy to propose, too, so I can save some money on unnecessary diamonds."

I hadn't even realized there was no ring until Lenny started acting like Lenny.

My sister gave him a side-eye. "Would you stop busting balls for once? Like this guy would organize this entire thing and *not* have a ring somewhere."

Mom smacked him upside the head for good measure, transporting us back to the nineties, if only briefly, while looking at me with the slightest smirk on her face.

A poker player she was not, so I assumed there might be an elaborate plan in motion after all.

The best part? There wasn't one part of me missing, wanting, or needing a ring on my finger.

I was standing in the middle of the Piazza San Marco surrounded by my family, best friend, and the man I had agreed to spend the rest of my life with.

Speaking of my best friend, I scanned the immediate area trying to find her, but two very hot, flirtatious Italian servers had found her first. One handed her a glass of champagne from the tray he was holding, the other delivering his best *fuck me* eyes and rattling off Italian words in succession, none of which she understood.

I walked over and whispered in her ear, "So, Alesandra, what's he saying to you?"

"Hell, if I know, or care for that matter. And why are you calling me by my government name?"

"What better place to call you Alesandra than in the country it was likely derived from?" I hugged her as tightly as humanly possible. "And thank you for—"

"Yea, what in the hell was that?" she cut me off. "The man of your dreams is proposing to you on a stage in Venice with a famous singer serenading you both, and you're *not sure* if you want to marry him? Have I taught you nothing?"

"Oh, sister friend, you've taught me plenty," I shook my head. "I got scared. Marrying him means moving here. Did you forget that part?"

"Of course, I didn't. I'm gonna have hot, steamy, Italian sex with one of these waiters successfully trying to seduce me, have one of his babies, make him pay me some child support, and live at the villa with you and the girls." I studied her face, looking for an ounce of sarcasm.

There was none.

"Speaking of babies, where are yours?" I asked, realizing how much coordination was required for everyone to fly ten hours to surprise me.

"With my mother and loving every minute of it, I am sure. I've been a tightly wound *bitch* lately."

"Mia, *amore*, are you ready for dinner?" Gennaro came up behind me, his arms wrapping around my waist.

"We're going to dinner?" I said, planting a kiss on his perfect lips.

"Why would I ever plan something like this without feeding everyone afterward?"

Love languages. Nobody would be able to tell me they weren't an actual thing ever again.

After a few more family introductions, or, in some cases, reintroductions, we all gathered as a group and followed Gennaro to the restaurant. His hand was interlocked with mine, briefly pausing to kiss my temple a few times on the way. Pesca walked alongside us with her own ear-to-ear smile. "I can't even begin to tell you two how happy I am for you."

We had lots to catch up on.

Gennaro approached the door of a well-lit brick building, the inside warm, cozy, and perfectly inviting after our brisk walk through the canal side streets. A large rectangular table was set up in the back corner, complete with floral centerpieces made up of the same type of flowers he had gifted me the previous day. He knew how to keep with a theme, and it was one of many reasons I had fallen so deeply for him.

Imagine loving a man and wanting to spend your life with him, fully reveling in the fact that he didn't require forty-seven sets of instructions to do basic tasks, or—even better—subtle reminders on how to be romantic.

What a panty dropper.

Inner Critic: I thought we didn't say panties
Mia: You're right, sorry

We all took our seats. The gang was almost all here, except for Papa, who was obviously absent.

"Did you ask Vincenzo and Salvatore to come?" I nudged him with my leg under the table.

"Of course, I did, but Vin couldn't get off work and Sal is back home with Luca running the property." My eyes widened with a straight smile.

"Exactly, we need to get home ASAP tomorrow," he said.

"Where are we staying?" I asked.

He slung his arm around me, fully empathetic to how my brain and mild anxiety worked. By now, whether I was living presently or not, he was aware that his fiancé had questions, lots of them and all the time.

"Everyone here has a room at our hotel tonight. Tomorrow, we'll head back to Tuscany for a family dinner at the villa. Vincenzo and Salvatore are coming to that one."

"You planned every last detail perfectly." I shook my head in disbelief, even though there wasn't a solitary part of me that should have doubted his ability to pull any of this off.

"My future wife sounds surprised by that," he responded with a soft kiss on my lips, "but I'm not sure why."

"Still getting used to the idea of being married to a supreme situation handler. Also, are you broke now?"

"You're going to have to get used to a lot more than that, and no, I'm not. It was time to tap into some of my savings. Now stop worrying." He squeezed my hand, pushed his chair from the table, grabbed a glass, and stood up to toast. "Thank you, all of you, for coming from near and far. Huge thanks especially to Giovanni for helping set up most of it. That flashy attorney career has paid dividends."

The group sent up a "salute" to Gio specifically, and I looked past Gennaro to air kiss in his general direction. I was going to have two more brothers. *Wild.*

"This is a big change for all of us given the distance, but I want you to know," he turned toward my dad, "I will look after and protect her for the rest of my days."

Gennaro then directed his gaze to me. "You, Mia, you've changed my life in the best possible way. People say you'll *know* when you meet the person you're supposed to be with. And I did. I knew it immediately the night we met. I'll leave out all of those details," he paused to shoot a raised eyebrow in Lenny's direction, and we all laughed while Lenny choked on his nausea before he continued. "None of this was an easy process with everything that's happened, but all of you being here solidifies the bond we're about to create together."

My dad stood up, glass in hand with an outstretched arm toward Gennaro. "To Papa, from one father to another, even though he's not here, I'm sure he's proud of the gentleman you are."

As far as my family knew, Papa was not well enough to make the trip. As far as Gennaro and I knew, and according to Giuseppe, whose job it was to get Papa to agree to come, he refused to make the trip.

I wasn't particularly surprised and did my best not to be upset by it.

I could not control anyone's actions other than my own.

The rest of the night was filled with delicious food served family style, reminiscent of our old-school Christmas dinners back in the day, constantly passing large platters of food back and forth down the long table. We didn't even order. The restaurant just kept delivering an assortment of dishes, one after the other, refilling wine glasses without asking, family members playing musical chairs for over two hours, having conversations and getting to know each other.

My heart throbbed with what felt like an overflow of happiness. My favorite people all in one room, in one country, celebrating our love.

It was surreal, something I had always wanted but

never quite pictured unfolding as it had. But that was what I had learned wasn't it? Not to plan, because the more we planned, the more life laughed at us.

I had one job from here on out—continue to lean into Gennaro, trust him, and live wholly, fully, and completely with him by my side.

The rest—Papa specifically—would sort itself out. I knew it would.

It had to.

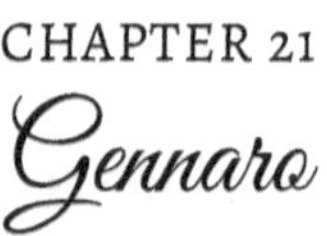

CHAPTER 21

Gennaro

Venice was good to us. I couldn't have asked for more, as every last detail of the proposal I had planned went off without a hitch. It was an incredible feeling, organizing flights for five people, hotel rooms for double that, a gondola ride, a professional singer to serenade us both, and a dinner afterward. Now, all of us were on our way back to Tuscany for another combined family dinner to celebrate.

Mia's family had been easy to talk to, easy to plan with, and way more accommodating than I ever thought they'd be. After visiting during the summer, I had arranged a FaceTime with her parents to fill them in on Mia's October trip, and that's when I dropped the potential marriage bomb. The shock on their faces was more than I bargained for, but thankfully Pesca was close by to help nurse it.

::In case of emergency, break glass::

Except, page Pesca.

She reminded Sophia and Santino that technically, we weren't all strangers. Yes, Mia and I met as strangers, and our feelings and intentions had sped along a fast track, but our families *did* know each other. They had met my parents during Santino and Sophia's previous trip, and had met me this past summer. Pesca's connection helped add an element of comfort that would have been missing had Mia gotten engaged to a total and complete stranger.

We were already becoming an extended family, and *that* was what it was all about for me.

Family.

We were learning to move past the times of regret, the "what ifs?" and the "why mes?" Narrowly escaping the loss of Papa helped to retrain my mind, but truthfully, all I've ever wanted was to enjoy the beautiful place I grew up in, especially now that Mia's family was here, too. This was a place they voluntarily vacationed, so they loved it, and I was fully invested in learning to enjoy it in the same manner. I wanted it to feel like *home* again.

We all pulled into the driveway within fifteen minutes of each other and found Salvatore operating a lawn mower, shirtless, a Peroni in his hand, waving at us like Forrest Gump on the shrimp boat dock.

Christ.

Walking through the courtyard toward the kitchen, I noticed lights on and windows open, which was odd. The only one usually in that kitchen was Mama, and she was with us. The mower sounds had stopped, and as I approached the door to the kitchen, Sal yelled after Mia and me.

"Gennaro! Mia! *Ciao!*" We thanked him for his congratulations and nodded toward the lit-up kitchen, asking who was in it.

"When I told my mama that I'd be here for a few days and why, she wanted to help celebrate," he said. "She's been in there cooking all day so you could come home to a meal and not have to worry about anything. Hope you don't mind."

And friends who became family.

That's what it was *also* about.

"Mind? Why would I ever mind? That's incredible." I shook my head in disbelief, not because I didn't grow up witnessing how much love Mrs. Rosa poured into others but because it further solidified that this was all *really* happening.

Mia and I walked into the kitchen to aromas that rivaled Mama's cooking. Pots were simmering on the stove —one with a simple tomato sauce and another with zucchini risotto. There was a roast of some kind in the oven, fresh bread, salad from the garden, cheeses and meats on the island counter, a fresh pasta pile dusted with semolina flour, and a bowl of freshly made ricotta.

Small, elegant, white floral arrangements were scattered throughout the kitchen, dining room, living room, and outdoor patio alongside tea light candles.

Mia ran to Salvatore's mom and hugged her tightly with a *"Grazie!"* As that happened, the rest of our families came barreling through the door behind us. It was loud and slightly chaotic, bottles of wine popping open one after the other, small plates with cheeses and meats being passed around to sample, with the room's common denominator being genuine, soul radiating happiness.

Mama and Sophia joined Mrs. Rosa to help finish cooking. Santino and Lenny sat on the couch in the living room asking Giovanni about his legal work in Florence. His girl, Dominique, sat alongside Giuseppe and Mia's sister, Stella, as they all got to know each other better. Allie and Mia were chatting feverishly at the dining room table over wine, and Pesca had her arm wrapped around my waist, looking up at me with the adoring eyes of a mother.

"That…was spectacular." She shook her head and squeezed me. "I'm proud of you like I'm the one who gave birth to you."

"A proper proposal according to the Brit's standards? I'm multiculturally appealing, I guess."

"Oh darling, that you are. Mia is a lucky woman as much as you are a lucky man." Pesca sipped on her wine. "I really don't think there are two people on Earth better suited for each other."

"That means more to me than you know," I said, pulling Pesca in for a hug. She may not have given birth to me, but she had been there for a majority of my life's toughest times, always coaching or urging me through them, and it was something I'd never forget. When she was around, it felt like our home was complete. Her being my lifeline to Mia's family was an obvious benefit, but the genuine love between all of them and all of us was the clincher. So much guesswork was removed, and besides Papa not being in attendance, it felt *right*.

A hand rested on my lower back, and I turned around to find Sophia standing behind me, questioning me, *silently*, with slightly raised eyebrows. I nodded and smiled in response, and Pesca looked from her to me with slight concern and moderate curiosity.

"You'll find out right after dinner," I assured Pesca, because she would. Everyone would.

I took a sip of my wine, scanning the room for my fiancé, who was no longer seated at the table with Allie. "Looking for someone, champ?" Allie appeared next to me with a wide grin and her own raised eyebrow, like she was on the hunt to break some balls but knew she was still lovable as she did it.

"You come absolutely as advertised," I said, putting my arm out to wrap her in a hug.

"Oh no you don't. Don't go pretending you're not stealing my best friend and using a hug to smooth over my angst."

My eyes nearly bugged out of my head as I computed how serious her statement was.

When I saw her break into a fit of laughter and then heard Mia directly behind me laughing just the same, I realized they were both messing with me.

"Ah yes, that's funny, isn't it?" I poured more wine and playfully threatened them. "If you two plan to bust balls the entire time you're together, I may lock you both in the walk-in refrigerator."

"He's hot when he gets mad, huh?" Allie zeroed in on Mia, who smiled and winked at me.

"He's hot all of the time, but yes, reaches a different dimension when he's pissy." The banter between the two of them was so epic that it was clear Allie's soon-to-be ex-husband was a self-involved asshole with zero sense of humor.

Women like Mia and Allie were smart, witty, lightning fast with their responses, and they kept you on your toes, so long as you were able to keep your response game at the standard they unknowingly set.

As if on cue, ready for his audition, Vincenzo walked through the door. He hugged the people he knew first and then stood in the middle of the room like the occasionally socially awkward giant teddy bear that he was, waiting to be introduced to the rest.

"*Ciao*, Vincenzo. Let me introduce you to everyone." I started at the far end of the room, introducing him to Mia's family, and then he said a quick hello to Giuseppe, Giovanni, and Dominique. As we walked back, Allie had finally looked up from the personal conversation she was having with Mia, her lips hovered over her wine glass, her sights set on Vincenzo.

The minute he caught her looking at him, realizing an introduction had been omitted, he magically broke out of his reserved shell.

"Gennaro, you missed someone." His head nodded in Allie's direction with a straight face that somehow also bore a few extra emotions.

I hadn't seen Vincenzo around a female in a good long while. He and his ex-wife had finalized their divorce after he found her carrying on an affair with an old flame, and while he was initially heartbroken from it, he now seemed a bit more like the younger Vincenzo I was attached to back in the day.

He was confident, kind, a protector by nature, mildly funny but wildly intelligent, and he loved hard—*really hard.*

If I knew Allie, she wasn't far removed from Mia, which meant she *also* loved hard.

But wasn't it too early to be playing matchmaker? I had to introduce them nonetheless since they'd likely be paired up for the wedding. "Vin, this is Mia's best friend, Allie."

"*Ciao,* Allie." He paused, taking a good long look at her as she returned his hello. After sipping his wine, continued, "How long are you here for?"

The usually boisterous Allie, hardly ever at a loss for words, swallowed a lump in her throat, licked her bottom lip before biting it, and answered relatively quietly, "Just one more day."

"Is she my partner in the wedding?" he asked Mia, which she confirmed from the corner of the kitchen.

"Guess we need to get to know each other then, right?" He hadn't taken his eyes off of her since he said "*Ciao.*"

I didn't think I'd ever seen him speak to someone more

confidently, and the goofy ass grin on my face relayed the sentiment without question.

"Let me get a wine refresh," Allie responded, her eyes glued to him in the same exact way.

"I'll get it for you." He reached out his hand to take her glass, and her eyes rolled damn near into the back of her head before she turned around to Mia and mouthed, "For real?"

The bar was set bone crushingly low for men in the States, it appeared.

Vincenzo walked into the dining room to pour from an already open bottle of red, so Allie took the opportunity to get my blessing.

"He's *not* married, right?"

The corners of my mouth curled into a smile. "Correct."

"Is there any reason I am not allowed to pursue a potentially physical, *consensual*, altercation with him?"

I smiled at her directness. "That sounds like a question better suited for the lawyer of the family, who's currently seated in the living room being interrogated by Mr. Luciano."

She nodded. "Welp, I did my due diligence by asking. The rest is up to the Universe."

Vincenzo had walked back in. Holding out the glass to her, she took it and asked, "Where are we headed?"

"Heated patio outside?" he asked with a lifted eyebrow and a sly smile.

"Are you the heat source?"

"I'm whatever you need me to be." He was *almost* putting whatever skills I had to shame, and I loved to see it.

I twisted my neck toward Mia, who had the same pleasantly surprised and shockingly entertained expression I did. Allie and Vin walked toward the patio, bypassing the crowd in the living room without uttering a word.

Mia walked over to me, wrapped her arms around my waist, and looked up at me, lips puckered. I accepted her invite and kissed them softly.

"You don't think they're headed toward the tomato garden, do you?" she asked with a concerned smile.

The memories from that garden consumed me, and I felt my pants immediately tighten. "Tomatoes *are* good for the prostate, baby. Let's just let them *do* and *be* whatever it is that they need."

"You're the boss."

Sometimes.

Two hours later, most everyone was seated around the fire outside underneath the string lit patio. It was chilly, but the warmth of the fire alongside the heat lamps kept everyone relatively comfortable. I moved inside under the guise of helping the ladies clean up with only two people who knew what was coming next: Sophia and Giovanni.

"You ready?" Giovanni asked me.

"Never been more ready for anything in my life, but where's Giuseppe?"

"Probably still trying to convince Papa to leave his villa, because he doesn't want to let you down." I rolled my eyes at the thought, and Gio continued, "Only you would propose and then, like, keep the anxiety rolling the day after with a follow up proposal, by the way."

There was slight judgment laced in his tone, so I reminded him, "Lots of moving parts to this all, did my best to have it all on the same day, but can't control everything."

"Blah blah, Pope Francis, let's do this."

He handed me a small box that I put in my pocket, and I handed him a bottle of champagne that he tried to hide behind his back as he walked.

Stepping onto the patio, I was graciously met with a breeze of cool, crisp air, and it instantly calmed me. I scanned the area for Mia and found her seated alone in an armchair. Everyone carried on their conversations as I approached, so while I had a small moment of privacy, I pulled her off the chair, lined her up directly in front of my face, and whispered, "I promise to never stop surprising you, okay?"

The whites of her eyes doubled in size as she gazed into mine and around us, trying to figure out what was coming. "If I could have your attention again, thank you again for being with us yesterday. It was all I hoped it would be. As Lenny *graciously* pointed out, though, I didn't propose with a ring."

"What a cheap bastard." Lenny laughed at his own sarcasm, and everyone collectively rolled their eyes in his direction while Santino shot him a look similar to the one Papa used to shoot Giuseppe back in the day.

"I didn't propose with a ring yesterday because I was waiting on a few extra pieces to bring to the jeweler. So…" I bent down on one knee again, the small box in my pocket, looking directly into the eyes of the only woman I'd ever wanted to propose to once, let alone twice. "Mia Luciano, I already know your answer to my original question, but when it came to the ring, I wanted something unique. I wanted the ring you'll wear for the rest of your life to match the beauty you radiate daily. And I wanted it to contain parts of our family history. Papa *did* eventually give us his blessing, even though he's not here right now. Your parents did, too."

I took a breath, opened the box, and made sure to take note of the expression on her face upon seeing the ring. She did not disappoint in the slightest. Her free hand covered her mouth, and her jaw dropped. The center stone was large and clear, one I had bought over a month ago back in Rome. Originally, I planned to set it on a thin diamond band. But after having kept in contact with Mia's parents, her mom had suggested using a couple of the diamonds from her own band to flank the center stone. Then, after I joined Papa in his work shed, having located Mama's original engagement ring, he had suggested doing the same with her two side stones.

"The side stones all belonged to our mothers' engagement rings. It combines the love I have for you, the beauty of our relationship and future life together, and all the good that has come from both of our families. One day, I hope this ring is passed down to a future daughter."

I heard more than one gasp in response to the mention of a daughter, and when I turned from Mia to see who they came from, I realized there weren't many dry eyes on the patio. The only three *not* crying were Santino, Lenny, and Giovanni, which was pretty predictable.

Looking back at Mia, the tears rolling down her face told me everything I needed to know about my choice in ring setting. But as always, in case I needed extra clarification, she was ready to deliver it. "I'm grateful for so many things in life that have led me to you. But mostly, I love that infatuation turned into love. You are everything I could ever need or want."

She inhaled deeply and exhaled slowly in what seemed to be a last-ditch effort to clarify her remaining thoughts. "You could propose a million times, with or without a ring, and I'd say yes each time. But this, and the thought you put behind it, means more to me than anything ever has. I'll absolutely marry you. And yes, I hope we have a beautiful daughter one day we can pass it down to. But mostly, I hope each day that I wear it gives off even a fraction of the happiness and love that I feel in this exact moment. I love you more than I ever thought possible."

Everyone began clapping, but it felt like white noise in the background. Mia was at the forefront of my brain, as she had been the last four months. And as I stood there, her hands in mine, I vowed to never forget where living presently in one single moment had led me.

To her.

One of the best nights of my life had morphed into a journey of self-discovery as I managed to mend fences within my own family and fall in love with hers. My life felt like it was just starting. All of the uncertainty and doubt seemed to vanish.

It was happening.

And now, all we needed to do was plan a wedding.

One wedding, the details of which we'd solidify while living five thousand miles apart as my future wife figured out how she'd uproot her entire life and move to a completely different country.

CHAPTER 22

Mia

I was on a high, floating among the clouds in a way I never had. A whirlwind romance that had started out as pure lust collided with my life's mission to locate the man of my dreams. That same man who proposed in an Italian piazza, flew my entire family in as a surprise, and combined the diamonds from our moms' engagement rings into my own.

Surely the shoe would have to drop at some point, right?

Lenny swung through the kitchen the following morning, literally and figuratively dropping his oversized shoes on the floor. "If you proposed here, does that mean you're getting married here, too?"

I felt the breeze of at least four different heads whipping around to catch my answer. Gennaro swooped in as he usually did with one hand around my waist and a cup of espresso in the other. "Still deciding on all of that, actually. Speaking of which, Mr. & Mrs. Luciano, can we talk to you both?"

My mother stood up like a beaming mom of the bride

ready to spring into action at any given moment while my father stood with slightly less glow and a bit more gloom. He wouldn't have said yes to Gennaro asking for my "hand in marriage," or whatever they asked for these days, if he didn't actually support it. But I knew his facial expressions well, and something was on his mind.

I pulled him aside as we walked toward the patio. "You okay, Dad?"

"Yes, why? I have my *happy* face on again?" he said, shooting an eyebrow toward the ceiling.

"You've had your quintessential *happy* face on the entire time you've been here, like you're forcing enjoyment. What's wrong? He asked you for permission, didn't he?" I studied his face and thought about how much I hated the phrase "He *asked* you for *permission,*" like I was a piece of equipment to borrow or barter.

"He did, not that it would have mattered if I said no. That boy is head over heels for you." He pressed his lips together and nodded his head as if to agree with himself.

"Okay, so what's the problem?"

"It's hitting me now that you'll be moving here." I stopped and turned to face him. He had never cried in front of me, ever, but I could feel cracks forming in his heart, the pain of which was hiding behind his stoic face. "Fathers are supposed to protect their daughters. How am I going to do that when you're thousands of miles away?"

"Dad, I do a pretty good job at protecting my own self, don't I?" I was a problem solver, a get-shit-done girl, so long as it wasn't in response to a weird noise between the hours of 8pm and 6am.

"Respectfully, sir," Gennaro chimed in from behind me, "it'll be my mission in life to keep her safe. I can promise you that."

Chambers of my heart swelled with the rush of blood

that flowed through them. If this man was going to effort-lessly spew one-liners for the rest of my life, I was going to have to increase my inventory of clean underwear.

> *Inner Critic: Down girl*
> *Mia: No, I've found my nirvana*
> *Mia: Crazy hot Italian man who treats both me*
>   *and my family with respect*
> *Mia: What a friggen' concept*
> *Inner Critic: You're the same for him*
> *Mia: Sounds like you're getting soft on me*
> *Inner Critic: The proposal and the ring got me*
> *Inner Critic: I've got nothing negative left to say*
>   *about him*
> *Inner Critic: He's passed every test*
> *Mia: I didn't think this day would come*
> *Inner Critic: Well, you've done well, Young*
>   *Grasshopper*
> *Inner Critic: Now don't fuck it up*

We sat down, huddled around the small patio table, each in our own cushioned wicker chair. It felt like no time had passed since Gennaro had bared his soul to our closest friends and family the night before, presenting me with the most beautiful ring I had ever seen. I glanced down, loving the visual of it, but more than that, the thought process behind its custom design.

He was unreal—the unicorn I had chased my whole life, from the days of Disney princes to TV stars, actors, musicians, and athletes. We all had at least one, the famous person who seemed too good to be true, as close to perfect as one could get. We dreamt of them often, wondering what our lives would be like if we were actually married to them.

Months later, we'd find out they cheated on their wife, verbally threatened someone on set, or passed away from a drug addiction we weren't aware they had. Then, reality would come crashing back into us to solidify the fact that there was no one perfect man out there.

Not that we, as women, were perfect either.

All we could ask was to be perfectly imperfect with the person who was perfect for *us*.

And here was mine, attempting to comfort my parents as they worked to accept the fact that their youngest daughter would be getting married and moving to an entirely different country.

"Thank you both, again, for helping me coordinate all of this. It means so much, and it's not lost on me the amount of trust you need to have in me to go through with it all." Gennaro effortlessly relayed his thoughts and Dad's head nodded, confirming he agreed and appreciated it.

He continued, "Mia and I have talked about this back and forth but haven't solidified what we'll be doing for the wedding. I actually haven't even mentioned this to her, but..." He shifted his weight in the chair, and for the first time in a long time, I could see anxiety sweeping through his body. "What do you all think about having the wedding when you're here next May for your anniversary trip?"

"Why are you nervous to ask that?" my dad questioned him directly, with equal parts concern and curiosity.

"I wouldn't want to overshadow your anniversary cele-bration, but also thought it would be more convenient than flying back and forth an extra time." Gennaro was the anti-man, thinking of things that most women tracked via a mental spreadsheet. It turned me on more than I cared to admit with both of my parents within close proximity.

"I don't think any sane set of parents could think their baby girl getting married to the man of her dreams would in any way, shape, or form overshadow their own anniversary," Mom chimed in. "I think it's a fabulous idea. Santino?"

Dad continued managing his dueling personalities. Was he quiet and calculated because he was getting ready to murder someone and hide the body or because he was containing his emotions in an effort to support us?

Finally, his deeply measured voice broke the silence hanging above us like a thick cloud. "I've never known a man to plan things this much. From the trip this summer to FaceTime asking us about the proposal to the proposal itself down to the ring you designed and this conversation."

My eyes surveyed him for any evidence of how he felt about all he was recounting. Was it appreciated? Respected? Or did he think Gennaro was doing too much? I opened my mouth to ask, questioning people one of my most relentless skillsets, but he answered before I had a chance to speak.

"Most men today, if we can call them that, do the absolute least. I've watched her get her heart broken repeatedly, usually by men who don't deserve her, and it always takes her too long to realize it."

Burn.

Also, who knew my dad was paying that much attention to my dating life?

"You have done everything the opposite of what guys typically do." He paused again before adding, "You have my full blessing in whatever you want to plan. We'll be here to support the both of you, and maybe now Sophia and I can finally buy a small piece of Italian property." His lips curved up in a sly smile when he looked toward my mom, whose expression resembled a deer in headlights.

"Well that escalated quickly, didn't it?" I smiled big,

squeezing Gennaro's hand, processing all that had happened and was about to come.

Proposal. *Check.*

Married in Italy. *Check.*

Eventually moving to Italy. *Check.*

Supportive family. *Check.*

Shoe to drop. *Pending.*

A few hours later, my crew had made their way to the airport, and Gennaro and I were having lunch at the osteria. Pangs of homesickness set in once they left, and as usual, I soothed my discomfort with food. We ordered a variety of pizzas and shared a bottle of house red that Carmine had made himself. In other words, it was strong.

Very strong.

An hour after our arrival, the room was spinning ever so slightly; my cheeks were flushed; and Gennaro, Carmine, and I were giggling like a bunch of little kids listening to farts.

"I still don't know how you landed this one, but I'm glad you did," Carmine nodded toward Gennaro and winked in my direction. "This place has been brighter since she walked through those doors."

At that same exact moment, the door swung wide open, and in walked Pesca. All eyes on her, she stopped dead in her tracks. "Should I leave?"

A few seconds of silence were followed by uncontrollable laughter, to which she replied, "Goodie, liquid lunch is exactly what I needed, too."

One more bottle of red later, wine fatigue had set in for all four of us. Before leaving, Carmine requested Gennaro's help in the cellar to move some barrels. Pesca scooched her seat closer to mine, and with the slightest bit of a tipsy slur, wrapped her arm around my shoulders, looked me dead in the face, and said, "I could not have predicted any of this would have happened, but I'd be lying if I didn't say it has changed this entire family for the better."

"Even with Papa still recovering?" I asked, still reeling from a guilty conscience I knew wasn't warranted.

"Papa would have landed himself in that hospital with or without you," she continued. "That man doesn't know how to take care of himself. He always puts his blinders on, goes to work, and blocks the rest out. He's been skating on thin ice and a prayer for a while now."

"Well, thanks for almost, kind of, sort of making me feel better." I paused. "But mostly, thanks for never judging. From day one, you didn't make me feel any sort of way, you never put any pressure on either of us, never made things uncomfortable. You always supported us. Every time we doubted what we were doing, knowing there was at least one intelligent, rationally thinking adult in the equation kept us hanging on."

She smiled big and squeezed me as the front door opened again. In walked an older man, well-groomed with salt and pepper hair and a short beard to match, dressed in a pea coat and scarf, oozing Macy's catalog vibes, but the Italia edition. I noticed her eyes fixate on him as he removed his coat and scarf and sat a few chairs away from us around the corner of the bar. The only three people in the room, with Gennaro and Carmine still downstairs, he kindly said "hello" to us in an underwhelming American accent.

I deflated, but she perked right up.

"American?" she asked him outright.

What a boss.

"Unfortunately, yes," he smiled. "British?"

"*Fortunately*, yes," she said, smiling right back.

Play on, Pesca.

"Wine?" She held up the remnants of our bottle.

"Don't you want to know my name before you offer me your last glass of wine?" His eyebrow raised at the same time the corner of his mouth formed a smirky smile.

"Not particularly," she zinged him.

"Why is that?"

"Why do I want to get to know someone I'll never see again?" Pesca played a hard game. I was merely a ping-pong match spectator.

"How do you know you'll never see me again?" he asked. I liked this guy. He had Gennaro's confidence with Carmine's good looks and a dry sense of humor that rivaled Giovanni's.

"Well, you're from America and have a ring on your finger. So, you're either married and looking for a midday roll in the hay, separated or divorced and holding out hope she's going to forgive you for something, or it's a decoy and you're hoping it'll attract someone who's into that sort of thing, which I am not."

Shots fired, but he caught the bullets in his teeth.

"You Brits sure are mouthy, aren't you?"

"You have no idea, darling."

They were eating this up as I watched crumbs fall out of both their mouths.

"Vincent!" All three of our heads spun around in the direction of Gennaro's voice, Pesca's eyes nearly popping out of her skull.

"You know each other?" I asked, turning back around to assess Vincent's face. He was seemingly trying to process the same question.

"We sat next to each other on the plane when I flew

back home from visiting you this summer. He has property in Pienza, and I told him we ate here a lot. Is your wife with you?"

My jaw dropped, Pesca's eyes narrowed, Vincent swallowed the lump in his throat, Gennaro stood completely clueless, and Carmine walked in behind him, asking if we'd like more wine.

"I'd prefer some grappa actually," Pesca cooly replied.

Grappa it was.

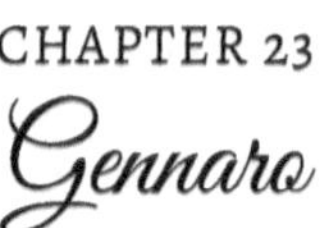

CHAPTER 23

The afternoon took a different turn than I expected after Pesca and Vincent showed up at the osteria. Somewhere between moving barrels and enjoying a few shots of grappa, we learned that Vincent's wife had filed for a divorce, he decided to retire from the world of finance, and he'd moved to his property in Italy, full time.

"You don't have any children?" Pesca asked curiously.

"I don't. My wife always told me she didn't want to raise them alone, so we never tried," he shrugged, some-what dejected.

"She was okay with you making all of the money, but then blamed you for being out of the house as much as you were?" We all looked toward Vincent for his response, the small curvature of his mouth telling us she'd hit the nail on the head.

"It was a tough position to be in. Wanting financial security for both of us but lacking the time to enjoy the stability it brought. Other than a couple weeks of vacation throughout the year, we struggled to spend quality time together. She was always mad at me, so I kept working, even on weekends. It seemed like it was worth it back then for the money, but now I'm not so sure." I don't think Vincent was aware of the therapy session he was about to be part of, but Pesca kept on.

"But now you've retired to a home in Italy, which most people dream of but can't afford. So, the time you spent working as hard as you did for the financial payoff seems worth something, no?" She was onto something, but I could also see how, similarly to Papa, a man diving all-in to his work without spending time and effort on his woman could fall flat.

It's a tale as old as time—work to live and live to work—but at what cost? We all need money to survive, but we also deserve to spend time with our loved ones. Where is an appropriate cut-off?

Truth be told, it's different for everyone.

Pesca had navigated the hardships of a demanding work life balance before her husband had passed away far too early. She'd give anything to have him back, but she was also grateful that his many sacrifices had allowed them to be able to travel, which ultimately introduced her to our family and the villa itself.

Now Vincent, or more accurately his ex-wife, was in her cross hairs as she hashed out the pros and cons of it all. I couldn't remember hearing Pesca speak this much in all of the years I'd known her. Grappa was her weakness, it appeared.

"Apologies darling, I don't mean to go all in on you here, but I'm routinely flabbergasted by men. Here you are, an American in Italy, a ring on your finger but no longer married, retired, and moving here with likely a lot of money in your bank account but even more sadness in your heart. It's depressing."

She continued, but attempted to soften her approach.

"I would do anything to have my husband still alive and here with me, but in his honor and memory, I try my best to appreciate everything his sacrifices brought us. He *loved* traveling, living, experiencing, and while things may not have been perfect when he was here, I'm grateful that I never took him or our life for granted. All relationships require a bit of sacrifice, so long as you both learn to enjoy the times you have in between those sacrifices."

Vincent threw back the rest of his drink and shook his head, unsure where to go from there.

I didn't blame him. Her monologue had me thinking about the hows and whys behind her supporting Mia and me. Would it be easy? No. Would it be worth it? Yes—if we put the effort behind it.

Pesca was tough. She made you think, she didn't sugar-coat anything, and she didn't let you skate on by, especially if she saw potential. I was interested in knowing exactly what she noticed in Vincent, because I knew her asking these questions meant she cared enough to spend the time pressing him.

After a few seconds of uncomfortable silence, Carmine off to the side drying wine glasses, Mia sipping on the remnants of hers, and Pesca smiling coyly at me with a "This is why I don't drink hard liquor" look on her face, Vincent shifted in his seat and shocked us all.

"I've been out of the game for a while, but I'm in the middle of the most romantic country on the planet, so forgive me if I'm reading this wrong." He narrowed his eyes at Pesca, assessing her reaction. "Would you join me for dinner tonight?"

Her mouth softened into a grin, and she turned in his direction, held up her glass, and instantly responded, "I thought you'd never ask."

Love can consume you. Like blood through veins, it courses through your body like an electrical current that has the power to light you up fully or leave you in the deepest, darkest hole when it short circuits.

Mia lit me up when she was around. Two weeks together and my world was brighter, my mind more focused, my spirit simply happier.

She brought joy wherever she went, but her commanding presence and the distinct impact it had on *my* life was undeniable. And now, we were engaged to be married.

I'd get to spend the rest of my days with the one person who truly understood me.

The thought of it, of the person I loved, who loved me back wholly and completely, absolutely consumed me.

After watching Pesca and Vincent expertly flirt with each other before making plans to have dinner, Mia and I stayed one more day at the villa, helping get the place back in order after her family had left. Giovanni and Dominique headed back to Florence, Giuseppe continued to fill Papa's shoes as best he could, and Mama seemed in good spirits, checking in new guests, spending quality time with Papa, and cooking to soothe the stress that accumulated in between.

Back in Rome, Mia and I spent as much time together as my work schedule would allow. Brief mental flashbacks to the times I swore I'd never be the guy to get married or share my life, or home, with a woman made me smile.

How wrong I was.

Continually looking at the clock, counting down the minutes until I could go home to her had me feeling like a lovestruck fool.

"Can you at least promise me that you'll *try* not to be a depressed asshole tomorrow after she leaves?" Marco chimed in from the driver's seat as we patrolled the city. "I've seen this episode before—flying high, until you're not. And you don't even like going out to drink off the sadness anymore because, well, you're whipped."

"Whipped? Or don't have time for bullshit?" I smiled as I pointedly stared at him from the passenger seat.

"Does it matter? I lost my wingman." He shook his head slowly, pressing his lips together with the smallest of smiles. "She better be the best lay of your life to be giving up on the hundreds of other hot tourists lining the dance floors at these bars."

"I'm going to overlook the part where you referred to my fiancé as a 'lay,' but also, what is wrong with you?" I shook my head and smiled, not because I found him funny but because the way he conducted himself as a thirty-four-year-old man was laughable. "We're not getting any younger. Do you plan to chase after tourists until your dick stops working or something?"

"Haven't thought that far ahead yet," he replied with a shrug.

"Well, that's obvious." After another hour of small talk as he planned another night out with one of his single friends, it was finally time to clock out.

Eight hours riding in the car with him as he received half naked pictures from a variety of women and carried on conversations with all of them *at the same time* had me craving the stability of marriage and family life even more than I already did. I enjoyed my "single" time as much as I could, and now it felt good to purposefully share my life with one other person who knew my love languages and spoke to each one effortlessly.

As I turned the key in my apartment door and stepped

inside, I smelled notes of melted butter, caramelized onions, and earthy mushrooms combined with simmering marsala wine evaporating in a skillet as the sauce reduced. Medallions of chicken waited on the side alongside a bowl of freshly made rigatoni pasta. Two empty glasses were waiting to be filled, perched on the island counter next to a small bowl of roasted eggplant tapenade.

Mia twirled around, a wooden spoon in one hand, a pair of tongs in another, wearing an oversized off-the-shoulder sweater. Her hair was pulled back in a ponytail, a pair of her signature gold hoop earrings dangling from her ears, wearing only mascara and lip gloss on her exquisite face. Bluetooth speakers streamed Italian pop music, and the open doors of the balcony terrace allowed fresh air to breeze through.

Perfection.

Sure, I was completely capable of cooking for myself. I did it often. I kept my house clean, organized, and well stocked, too. I was a fully functioning and responsibly mature adult, and I certainly didn't *need* the added touch of a woman.

But the sheer satisfaction it provided to have someone like her doing all of it willingly, happily even, made me beam from the inside out.

It also made my dick hard.

Rock hard.

Marco would be pleased to know there's still at least a little bit of "old" Gennaro buried in here.

"I don't know what's more thrilling," I said, staring at her intently, "the sight of you in my kitchen, looking the way you do and having made all of this, or all of the things I'm going to do to you for dessert." I pulled Mia to me, my mouth delaying any need for food or drink until it had its fill of her first.

Her head fit perfectly between my hands; eyes closed and still holding onto her cooking utensils; the smallest, most satisfyingly happy smile on her face. The feel of our tongues thrashing against each other had yet to get old. Each time we kissed, it was the perfect combination of deep, intense desire and a soft, sensual need for each other. The sheer force of our lips repeatedly colliding into each other felt like a magnetic field with gentle lip sucking and nibbling to balance it out. I could have taken her right at that moment, but not at the cost of a burnt chicken marsala. She pecked my lips, twirling around back to the stove. "Dinner will be ready in ten! Want to pour us some wine?"

Yes, the hell I did.

"Wine, for the love of my life," I said handing her the glass and looking into her gray eyes tinged with a bit of blue and finished my thoughts. "Cheers to us, our next chapter, and a safe trip home for you tomorrow."

"It'll only be my home for a little longer. It feels weird to say that out loud."

I took plates out of the cabinet and situated our place settings at the kitchen island. Fresh rigatoni was topped with medallions of chicken marsala, sauce, and grated Parmigiano Reggiano cheese. Again, whatever issues anyone had with Italian-American cooking were lost on me, because I was salivating at the sight and smell of it all.

We ate and drank, and she filled me in on a conversation she'd had with Allie. "My best friend has given her stamp of approval, by the way."

"Is that right? That means all of the most important people in your life have given us the go ahead, doesn't it?" I smiled.

She took a moment to ponder. "Yes, actually. Even my brother. An amazing feat in itself."

"Same with my family, so we—"

"Not with Papa though," she cut me off mid-sentence. Her bright smile had dulled a bit, but I tilted her chin so she'd look right at me.

"If Papa gave me a ring with diamonds to use in yours, he absolutely approves. He just hasn't given you the apology you deserve yet—but he will." I leaned in and softly planted a kiss on her lips to ensure she believed what I was telling her. When she smiled softly in return, I decided it was time for dessert.

"Let me clean up," I insisted.

"If I help you clean up, it'll get done faster." She eyed me up and down with desire oozing out of every pore. When the dishwasher was filled, the counters were clean, and the leftovers were packed and put in the fridge, Mia had something to give me.

"Sit in that chair over there." She pointed toward the armchair that faced the terrace balcony. "And don't move until I come back."

"Demanding, no?" She smiled with a wink and disappeared down the hallway.

I sat down as instructed, dimmed the lights with the remote, and turned on some slow Italian music, the smell of vanilla and sandalwood wafting from a candle behind me. My head fell back and my eyes closed briefly as I recounted the events of the last two weeks.

I mended fences with my father, arranged a surprise proposal with both of our families, got engaged, and was now supremely looking forward to all the things that would come next. Dreading the thought of Mia leaving the next day, I tried turning my brain off to everything swirling through it and instead focused on why she had me perched in the chair.

Heels hit the hardwood floor of the hallway, and I

immediately perked up. I saw her approaching the chair out of my peripheral vision and closed my eyes again, breathing in the scent of her newly reapplied perfume. Her hand grazed my shoulder as she slowly sauntered around the chair to the front of me. My eyes trailed from the black, four-inch leather heels she wore up and over black thigh-high stockings clasped to a garter belt, my leather jacket overtop her core.

"Well, fuck me," I mumbled my innermost thoughts.

"Yes, we'll get to that." She pushed the ottoman over and sat down, one leg crossed over the other, situated in between my legs. "But first, we're going to play a little game."

"I'll warn you, I'm very competitive." I grinned as my hands went to grab the sides of her hips. She swatted me away before I could make contact.

"I'm counting on that, actually. With every correct answer, I'll take off a piece of clothing…" I couldn't help myself and interjected, my fingers trailing the length of her mesh thigh-high stocking.

"Can we call this clothing?" My dick was hard, my mouth was salivating, and my heart was beginning to pound.

"Okay, fine, I'll remove a piece of *fabric*," she grinned. "Better?"

"Details matter." My eyes trailed the length of her as I bit my lip, wondering what questions I was going to be able to answer with her looking like this.

"Let's begin." She raised an eyebrow and assessed my reaction. "What's my name?"

An involuntary laugh escaped my lips. "Oh. Okay. We're asking easy questions so I can have you naked in record time?"

"Warming you up with an easy one, now answer it."

The way she effortlessly mastered the whole sexy and cute at the same time thing was an unsolved mystery.

"Mia Luciano." I paused, then expanded upon my answer. "Sophia and Santino aren't into middle names and, well, Mia Luciano is a perfect name all on its own, no middle name required."

"Very good." She stood up, unbuttoned the jacket, and let it slowly fall down her shoulders and onto the floor. My jaw joined it before I looked up to find her in a piece of lingerie that rivaled anything I had ever seen in a Victoria's Secret catalog. Small pieces of fabric were expertly connected, barely covering her most intimate body parts. Tiny string ties held together the openings of each nipple-covering as well as the hottest of spots between her thighs.

My mind desperately battled with the swollen club between my own legs, but in an effort to combat premature ejaculation, I distracted myself by asking, "Do I get extra credit for elaborating?"

She leaned over the chair, hands planted on either side of my head, her chest dangling in front of my face, taunting me. Fully aware of every way she was turning me on, her lips curved into a playful smile. "You are permitted to untie a section of your choice."

My gaze followed the outline of her lips as she responded. Blinking slowly, without moving my head, I fixated on her eyes, holding contact as my mouth inched closer to one of her nipples and I used my teeth to pull open the tie.

The look on her face reassured me we were both trying equally hard to maintain composure. Wasn't that the best torture of all? Wanting something so badly you could taste it, literally? I could smell and taste all of her if she'd let me—but she hadn't.

Yet.

With one razor sharp nipple exposed, she sat back down and continued asking questions.

"What's your favorite thing about me?" Her head tilted to one side as she waited for me to respond.

"Isn't the answer to this subjective? How can you determine right versus wrong?" I felt like I was a step ahead of her, but I wasn't, not this time anyway.

"We both know I'm going to end up completely naked, begging for you to take me. These questions are merely a formality." Her eyes had darkened, and her bottom lip was bright red from incessantly biting it. "Now answer it so I can feel your mouth on me again."

Sexy, cute, and occasionally domineering.

If we didn't quickly move forward past the question round, I'd spontaneously combust due to a wicked case of blue balls.

"Your brain," I matter-of-factly responded before leaning forward in my chair, my mouth hovering in front of hers. "You were smart enough to trust me months ago, which led you back here." I untied the second bow covering her other nipple and continued, "You were smart enough to let me fuck you that night—more than once." My hand trailed downward, pushing her legs wide open, heat radiating from her slit as my fingers made contact, untying the last knot. "You were smart enough to come back again and smart enough to agree to marry me, which means you're smart enough to know that as long as we both live, yours will be the only body these hands and this mouth will ever touch again."

I had waited long enough and played her game thoroughly. And, she wasn't in control anymore.

I forcefully pulled her onto my lap with my arms wrapped tightly around her. An instinctual moan, one I grew to anticipate and long for, escaped her. With my lips trailing the delicate and sensitive skin of her neck, she took my thumb into her mouth, licking up and down the length of it, teasing me with a premonition of what she was about to do to me.

That was, if I didn't explode before she had the chance.

"I can't take this anymore." I stood up, one arm still wrapped around her waist, pushed the ottoman halfway across the room with my foot, spun her around and bent her over the chair I'd been sitting in. Unbuckling my belt with a desperate quickness, then unbuttoning my jeans and letting them fall to the floor, I stretched the string of fabric that covered her ass to the side with one hand and slipped the middle and ring fingers of the other inside of her.

She was as warm, wet, and welcoming as I expected her to be. I massaged her G-spot and clit in a perfect rhythm, her moans growing louder and more repetitive with each stroke. As sweat beads formed on the small of her back and down her neck, her skin flushed red and she breathed erratically with more want, need, and desire than anyone ever had as I buried myself deep inside of her.

Mia cried out with the most satisfying sound of pleasure, her long hair draped over her shoulders, her back arched, pushing herself into me in perfect sync with my thrusts as she braced her weight, holding on to the edge of the chair. I held her waist, squeezing it even, allowing myself to reach as deeply inside her as possible, every push and pull a dance between us.

She was everything I ever wanted—and everything I wouldn't be able to live without—now that I had her.

My body craved hers and knew exactly how to devour it.

Devoid of energy but seeing us both through to our respective finishes, I promised to burn the sounds escaping her mouth into my memory. Bringing someone over the edge not once but twice while the length of my dick explored every available nerve inside her had me counting down the minutes until I could have it all again.

Still deep inside her, I kissed along the curve of her shoulder, pushing aside the hair now matted to her neck. Both of us were left panting, desperately in need of cold water, fresh air, a nap, or more accurately, all three.

Mia slid off of me, stood up, and turned around, wrapping her arms around my neck, with whatever parts of her expertly planned outfit had remained intact. "I love you so goddamn much."

I smiled, still breathing heavily, shaking my head at her, and wondering where focused, calculated, unattached Gennaro Beletta had gone.

"What's your favorite thing about *me?*" Turning the questions back around on her, we stood intertwined, skin still stuck to each other, neither of us letting go. After a few seconds of deliberation, I took note of a glimmer in her eye and a coy smile, expecting a string of love- and adoration-filled thoughts to follow.

She looked directly at me, inhaled deeply, threw her head back, grabbing the semi I was now sporting, and whole-heartedly said, "This. I absolutely fucking love this and every single way it's made me feel like the sexiest goddamn woman in the world."

Forever surprising me, she'd responded with an answer I didn't expect but couldn't get enough of.

It was perfect.

And, so was she.

Winter

CHAPTER 24

Mia

BACK IN THE STATES

"Please tell me you were sexed up and down the streets of Rome again before returning home." As usual, Allie wasted no time getting down to the most paramount details once we were finally able to catch up over the phone.

"I was properly sexed in a variety of places prior to returning home, yes, but—"

"Don't you dare ruin the Italian daydreams in my head by asking about the jackass I'm almost divorced from," she cut me off.

"I was actually going to ask you when I'm going to see you next, but now that you're yelling at me, please fill me in on what's obviously brewing."

A few seconds of silence and a deep exhale had me bracing for emotional impact.

"I decided to file for full custody. He's never here anyway, and when he is, he's drunk, high, or both, acting even worse than he does when he's sober. The girls don't even get excited to see him anymore, which was the last straw."

"Sounds good to me. I feel for them, and you, but it's a worse situation growing up with a horrible father than it is growing up without one." I hesitated before delivering my next thought but knew she'd be able to detect my humor. "Plus, now you'll be able to move to Italy with me."

"Don't even act like you're joking! I know you're shitting your American pants thinking about moving there full time. It doesn't matter how dreamy he is." She sipped something, and I felt a pang of anxiety rip through me.

"Relax," said, anticipating my concern. "It's water. Italy ruined me. Wine isn't ever going to taste that good again. Why bother drinking the crap we have here?"

I exhaled. "Well, I get that. It's ruined me for a lot of things."

"American dick isn't the same, is it?"

I almost choked on the lukewarm Folgers coffee I was drinking, another reminder that everything was better in Italy. "You are foul, you know that?"

"Oh please. You're my case in point. Bang the first man you meet, and less than half a year later you're engaged and about to move there. Italian meats are supreme."

"Yes, prosciutto *is* delicious, isn't it?"

"I'm not talking about charcuterie, sister! Speaking of, did Vincenzo ask about me yet?" I couldn't get enough of her and the diarrhea of the mouth that had plagued her for nearly three decades.

"Why are you asking *me* when you two exchanged numbers and have been talking to each other ever since you left?" Radio silence on the other end confirmed my more-than-just-suspicions.

"How'd you know that?!" She sounded shocked, but I

knew the elevated tone of her voice was laced with a wide smile.

"Men talk as much as we do," I assured her.

"Well, maybe the Italian ones do, because the American I've been married to doesn't say much of anything unless he's complaining."

"Might not be fair to lump in all American men with that statement just because you picked a bad apple," I kindly reminded the girl who had a history of attracting every wrong man within a ten- mile radius.

There was a short pause before she responded, "Bad apple? He's an entire crop of rotting apples with worms crawling in and out of their asses."

"Apples have asses?" I inquired, moving off my couch for the first time since I had breakfast four hours ago. Jet lagged beyond belief after arriving back in New Jersey the night before and having slept terribly in an empty bed, I was surprised I even had the energy to be witty.

"For purposes of this example, they sure do," she said, regaining some seriousness, "but for real, why didn't you tell me Gennaro's best friend was a complete stud?"

"Ehh, not really my type, and to be fair, I didn't talk to him all that much the first time I was there. Salvatore is the talkative and friendly one." I rolled back to consider any conversations I'd had with Vincenzo, but there weren't many. I knew he was loyal as all hell and treated Gennaro like his own brother, which made me immediately like and respect him, but he didn't spend much time getting to know me personally. He'd been going through his own divorce, so I didn't exactly blame him for not making it a priority to get to know the woman his best friend was quickly falling in love with.

"You guys are really talking frequently? I kind of love this," I said, grabbing another cup of coffee.

"He might be the only man I've ever known who has mastered the art of keeping in touch without being suffocating or leaving too much time between messages and calls."

"Wait, wait, messages *and* calls? Sounds like Italian soppressata has fallen hard for American…"

"Don't you dare say that word," she forcefully interjected.

"Which word?"

"Any word describing my lady parts. Thank you. Now, moving on."

We spoke for another hour, and I was absolutely elated that Vincenzo had helped take her mind off the issues at hand, inadvertently causing her to stop drinking as much and acting as a catalyst to finalize her divorce and file for full custody. Whether they were meant to be together or not, he was an integral part of the beginning of her next chapter as well as my own, so I was thankful for him and supportive of them.

It made me miss Gennaro even more, and I'd only been without him for about thirty hours.

> *Inner Critic: I don't blame you this time*
> *Mia: Well, thanks*
> *Inner Critic: No problem*
> *Inner Critic: Do I have to keep reminding you to*
>   *shower, though?*

Being back in the States had me desperately trying to understand who I was when I was here. I suddenly felt lost in the place I'd called home my entire life, consistently longing for the enchanting comfort of the Italian countryside mixed with the sexy excitement of the cities surrounding it.

I picked up my phone to text him, but the screen lit up with a picture of us kissing in front of the Trevi Fountain instead. Seeing Gennaro's calls come in was still thrilling, but somehow left me battling the onset of mild depression. I loved him, I wanted him, and I hated thinking of how long it would be until I'd get to be near him again.

"*Ciao, amore,*" I lustfully crooned into the phone.

"Ahhhh, that voice sends me flying," Gennaro responded in a way that twisted my insides into desire-filled knots.

"Please tell me you're about to surprise me and knock on my door."

"*Amore,* I've thought about every possible way I could have gone back with you, and unless we want me to have zero job stability and no money to do anything in life, I can't make that happen yet." Burning hunger in his voice left me breathless. I knew that, at some point, life would get monotonous, predictable, less thrilling, and far less sexy, but until that happened, I planned to lean into every moment that he made me feel like the only woman in the world.

"Worth the wait," I responded honestly, "however long that'll be. Speaking of which, any *idea* how long it'll be?"

"Funny you should ask. I saw Giustino yesterday. Remember Marco's Italian Stallion uncle?"

"How does one forget Giustino?" I asked with a smile on my face.

"Good point. I filled him in on our engagement, and he started pummeling me with questions. 'When is she moving here? How are you planning a wedding when you're in two different countries? She's really going to move away from her family? Is Papa going to be able to be there?' I eventually had to ask him to stop stressing me out, and he changed the subject to asking if you have any single great aunts."

"I do, actually."

"Well save them and yourself by not inviting them." We both laughed and agreed to keep our closest family members away from Giustino and his irresistible lover-boy ways. What did it matter that he was in his eighties? He was unstoppable.

I realized after another hour that we hadn't solidified any answers to Giustino's questions, but given my new way of living life, it didn't bother me much. Gennaro was the man I was going to marry, Italy was the country I was going to move to, and the details would sort themselves out as we navigated it all.

Knowing I'd likely have to wait close to three months to see my man again was the hardest part.

TWO MONTHS LATER, DECEMBER

Target had gleefully taken one hundred of my dollars in exchange for letter balloons that spelled FREEDOM across my living room wall, champagne flutes, cake plates and napkins, baking supplies, and two graphic tees, one that displayed the word "divorced" with a satirical spoof of Webster's Dictionary definition underneath and another that said "Girls Nights are the Best Nights."

Weren't they ever.

We gorged ourselves on homemade pizza, champagne, and dark chocolate cupcakes topped with peanut butter icing, then called an Uber to take us to the closest thing to a "club" for millennials with a dance floor and blissful array of 90s and early 2000s Pop, Hip-Hop, and R&B tunes.

Dressed in jeans and throwback sequined tie-back halters, we sauntered through the double doors of the club feeling like rock stars after being carded by the bouncers. Life was good, even after painstakingly choosing four-inch heels. In retrospect, two women who wanted to deal with absolutely no one should probably have worn something a bit more understated than the "look at us" outfits we were sporting.

Luckily, the champagne had numbed a large number of our body parts, and the adrenaline ripping through our veins underneath neon lights and clouds from the fog machine had us in an unmistakable stupor. We might as well have been the only two in the entire place, because we danced for hours, ignoring everyone around us, taking turns buying drinks, and occasionally sitting down at the bar either to stop sweating or to relieve pressure from the balls of our feet.

Somewhere around midnight, Allie was buried head-first into her phone texting back and forth within the same message. "If that's your ex-husband, I will quite literally throw your phone in the bar well," I told her with unmistakable intent behind each word.

"It's not," she quickly responded, "but I do have to go to the bathroom."

"I'll come with you."

"No, I have to do number two. I'll be fine, wait here." I shot her an aggressive side-eye, my Spidey sense immediately heightening and assuming she was lying about talking to her ex.

"It's not him, seriously, come on," she said, reading my expression. "We're here celebrating my divorce. Why would I waste any more time or money on him than I already have?"

"Okay, fine, but you're holding out on me with something. I can tell." She responded with slightly raised eyebrows and a tight-lipped smile, turned on her heels, and walked toward the bathroom. I had no idea what was going on, but I ordered one last round of vodka sodas from the bar, putting me over my four-drink limit. Since I'd had them over the course of four hours, I'd hoped for the best.

Checking my phone and having no messages or missed calls, I cursed the Italian time difference that kept Gennaro and me in radio silence from 5pm to whenever I opened my eyes the following morning. It was nice waking up to a daily text from him, but I longed to fall asleep to the sound of his voice when I was curled up in bed.

Soon enough, I kept telling myself.

Somewhere between fantasies and daydreams of my soon-to-be Italian-wife life, I felt a body hovering over my shoulder, standing to the side of me while I sat at the bar. Assuming it to be a stranger, I shimmied my stool to the right to gain back some personal space. Someone ordering a drink took it upon himself to occupy the few inches I had allotted as a barrier with his own body. Internally rolling my eyes and immediately recollecting why I often disliked venturing out in public, let alone into packed bars and nightclubs, I prepared myself to ask him to give me some space.

Before I could, Allie rounded the corner of the bar I was facing, her eyes wide like a deer in headlights mid-fall, unsure whether it was about to be taken out by a rifle, bow, or a moving vehicle. Her jaw dropped, and whatever words she wanted to relay to me failed to leave her lips. I leaned my body toward her, squinting, trying to make sense of whatever or whomever she was looking at.

Then it clicked.

My skin, covered in goosebumps a lack of fabric, tingled with anticipation.

"Please, for the love of God, tell me Gennaro is standing behind me."

Her head shook from side to side, which I hoped meant she was dumbfounded by yet another romantic gesture, the likes of which we had never seen from any twenty men we'd wasted time on, combined.

Allie's mouth opened again, words still failing her, so I swiveled on my stool to face the literal and figurative music. "Who's behind…"

Between both of our wide-open mouths, we sucked a fair amount of oxygen out of the room.

"…me?" My eyes met the chest of someone wearing a black coat at the same time I inhaled the unmistakable combination of cigarette smoke and Paco Rabanne cologne.

As I raised my line of sight to meet the gaze of the man standing in front of me, I felt equal parts utter disappointment and immeasurable rage. The last time I saw this face I was throwing lingerie at him in another club's parking lot before drowning myself in the comforting embrace of the McDonald's Value Menu.

"Hi, baby…" My ex, if we could call him that, purring directly into my ear as he bent down to meet the side of my face.

"What the *fuck?*" I immediately put distance between his face and mine, pushing against his chest to regain control of my physical space.

"What's wrong?" He smiled, seemingly in a state of complete oblivion regarding how things had ended between us.

"Why are you here?" I stood up and felt Allie grab my hand.

"Mia, we—" I waved my hand at her as she opened her mouth to speak. I knew she was going to tell me we could leave and not to engage in this conversation. My sober head would have agreed, but my head influenced by my fifth cocktail did not.

"I come here all the time," he winked, causing a ripple effect of loathsome nausea. "Why are *you* here, baby?"

"Jesus Christ, stop calling me that." I waved my credit card at the bartender like a drunken sailor trying to alert his crew to a rogue wave, wanting to pay and leave as quickly as possible. My throat tightened, and the room felt a thousand times smaller than it had a mere few minutes earlier.

Why did I feel so *gross*? And, perhaps more importantly, why do the shitty men we chose in earlier phases of life always find a way to haunt us during our happiest times?

I hated him. I hated all of them.

"Seriously, stop calling her that. She's not your baby. Never been your baby. Never going to be your baby." Allie couldn't help herself. She held my hand tightly, looking in every direction besides than the one he was in. "C'mon, we've gotta go."

She grabbed my wrist and tried pulling me away, but his hand made its way to the bare skin of my waist, holding me firmly in place. His cigarette breath taunted me, his lips brushed across my neck, and he whispered in my ear, "I used to love when you'd wear these shirts when we'd go out."

I'd burn it when I got home.

Inner Critic: Why is he still affecting you so much?
Mia: Because he's a piece of shit?
Inner Critic: You're beyond throwing lingerie in a
    parking lot and crying over losers
Inner Critic: You're damn near Italian queen status
    the way Gennaro treats you

> *Mia: …you're right*
> *Inner Critic: I usually am, not sure why it's taken*
> *so long for you to realize it*

I slowed down long enough to regain my composure, which he mistook for lingering interest while attempting to wrap his arm around my waist and pull me in closer.

"You really need to stop touching me," I reminded him.

"Or what?" His attempt at banter with a sly side smile made my skin crawl.

"What do you mean 'or what'? I told you to stop touching me, which means stop fucking touching me!" I pushed my hand against his chest to put further distance between us, and the bartender came over with my receipt, taking note of my discomfort.

"Are you okay over here?" she asked.

"We're fine. I'm leaving now anyway." I grabbed my purse and turned away from him, but he firmly grabbed my wrist and spun me back around.

Shouting over the music, Allie mouthed to me, wide-eyed, "Mia, we need to go, *now.*"

In the same moment, ignoring every word that had come out of my mouth a few seconds earlier, his lips made full contact with my neck. Instantly, the palm of my hand left a red imprint on the side of his face. "I said to stop *fucking* touching me!"

A small crowd had gathered, reacting to the scene, and the bartender hopped over the bar to put space between us. Out of nowhere, a large body barreled toward him from behind me, landing a punch that undoubtedly broke his nose on contact. As Mike Tyson's stand-in slowly turned around to face me, bar staff tended to the blood dripping out of my ex's nose.

Inner Critic: What the hell is going on here?
Mia: I have no...
Inner Critic: Holy shit
Mia: ...idea
Mia: Holy shit indeed

Thanks to my four-inch heels, I stood eye to eye with the man who had defended my honor.

All six feet two inches of him.

It was my fiancé.

CHAPTER 25
Gennaro

I had thrown Mia off the scent of my Christmas trip by mentioning a possible January visit during one of our phone conversations. Vincenzo and I decided to be both spontaneous and romantic, coordinating a surprise mini-vacation with Mia and Allie, which was simultaneously thrilling and slightly stress-inducing. After sleeping most of the red-eye flight, I woke up in time to watch wheels touch down in Newark Airport, the morning skyline of New York City in my line of sight. Excitement quickly turned to nervousness, since one was never quite certain which direction a five-thousand-mile surprise trip would go.

Allie: The eagle has landed

Vincenzo: What does that mean?

Gennaro: It means we arrived

Allie: I've been tracking your flight

Vincenzo: Are you stalking us?

Allie: If by stalking, you mean picking you up from the airport so you don't have to deal with rude Americans, yes

Vincenzo: So, you're not stalking me then…

Gennaro: Can you two take this weird sexual tension to your own text thread?

Allie: He's the one who got weird first

Allie: Clearly already in love with me

Vincenzo: I did travel nine hours in the air when I don't like planes or heights in general

Vincenzo: Make of that what you will

Allie: In love, like I said

Allie: Let me know when you're through customs

Gennaro: We will

Allie and Vincenzo were surprisingly well matched, as she'd miraculously extracted the lighthearted and fun part of his personality in record time. I hadn't seen him this happy in quite some time. Add to that the serendipitous nature of them both finalizing their divorces in the same year, and there weren't any negatives I could see about them being together. Selfishly, if Vin could manage to sweep Allie off her feet and get her to relocate to our hometown with her two kids, Mia would have her best friend within arm's length.

A perfect scenario, albeit a farfetched one.

For now, though, I'd concentrate on surprising *my* girl.

"So, what's the plan exactly?" I asked Allie as she

aggressively weaved in and out of traffic on whichever overly populated highway we were on.

"I'm dropping you off at my mother's house, but that isn't as bad as it sounds." She continued after eyeing me in the rearview mirror, "because she's at work and then staying with her boyfriend. The house will be empty and it's always fully stocked with food. Not at all the delicious food you're used to, but hey, that's what you get for falling for some Americans. Second-rate food, traffic, and lots of road rage."

She laid on the car horn for five seconds straight, a string of curse words attached to it. Vincenzo smiled in the passenger seat next to her, and if he weren't already convinced she was his soulmate, her bipolar yet hilariously entertaining rant might have sealed the deal.

"Anyway, you'll call an Uber to head over to the bar tonight when I tell you to, okay?"

"Very demanding," Vin replied, the same smile still on his face.

"Oh, you have no idea," Allie replied.

Vincenzo didn't miss a beat. "I don't need to formulate an idea of anything when you quite literally tell me every thought that rolls through your head the moment it begins rolling."

"I feel like I should be offended, but I don't have time for all that."

Time with Allie, although laced with foul language and anxiety-filled outbursts, felt natural and easy. It was similar to what I had experienced with Mia and made it more than evident that the two of them and their personalities were about as genuine as they came.

After dropping us off at her mom's house, we raided the fridge as politely as possible for not knowing the person it belonged to. We then found two couches, clicked on the

TV, turned it to a sports channel broadcasting a week-old soccer game between the U.S. and Italy, and almost instantly fell asleep.

We woke up four hours later when both our phones took turns ringing.

Vincenzo finally answered. "*Ciao...*" he mumbled, half drooling on himself, half hanging off the couch. Jet lag is no joke, and it was sometime in the early hours of the following morning for us as far as body clocks were concerned.

"Yes ma'am," he responded after a solid minute of listening, with a playful salute that Allie couldn't actually see. After hanging up, he relayed the update to me. "We're supposed to Uber over there closer to midnight and avoid the dance floor where they'll apparently be most of the night, until she tells me to approach."

"Sounds like a total chick night we're interrupting," I said with partial sarcasm.

"Well, lucky for us, they seem to be welcoming the interruption," he replied.

A couple of hours, showers, fresh outfits, and a few sprays more than necessary of Italian cologne later, we were on our way. Pockets of anticipation bubbled deep in my stomach as I watched time tick down on the clock of the Uber's dashboard. A line of people had formed outside, but Allie's follow-up text told us to walk to the front and ask for Ryan. Feeling the pointed eyes of each person in line behind us was only slightly more uncomfortable than being asked "Who the hell are you?" after approaching the bouncer.

Thankfully, Ryan emerged from inside the club at the same moment my hand balled into a fist, wanting to punch the second-rate security guard who'd asked the question directly in his face. "Would you relax?" Ryan told the bouncer, pushing him to the side, apologizing on his behalf and explaining that Allie and Mia were good friends of his from way back in elementary school.

The bar reminded me of the night Mia and I met—a mostly dark dance floor brightened by multicolored spotlights suspended from the ceiling. American music—likely from Mia and Allie's college years was blasting through speakers—and the dance floor was crowded enough that it took a minute to spot them.

Dancing with each other like nobody was watching, their sequin shirts glistened underneath the flashing lights above them. Unfortunately for my temper, which had already been activated by the tough guy outside, there *was* someone watching them. A few people, actually, but only one leaning on the bar, his eyes boring a hole into Mia.

Vin and I were under strict orders not to approach them until we got a text from Allie, but I refused to take my eyes off of the creep who refused to take his eyes off Mia. After a few failed text attempts, we contemplated surprising them on the dance floor, but Vin isn't much of a dancer, and he preferred to not ruin his relationship with Allie before it had a chance to begin.

We watched Allie finally step away from Mia after they had ponied up to the bar and quickly followed her to the bathroom.

"Jesus Christ, this is nerve wracking." She grabbed Vin's hand, pulled him behind a partition, and wrapped her arms around his neck, meeting him ninety percent of the way and waiting for him to do the rest. He did not disappoint.

Maybe there *was* something to be said about the romance of Italian culture, because the way he held the bottom half of her body while he kissed her was far more appealing than anything I had witnessed on the dance floor behind me. Snapping out of my stupor and trying not to be a weirdo staring at my friends, I turned back around to find Mia.

It took less than a second to notice a large body hovering behind her, much too close for my liking and, apparently, hers, given the look on her face. "Hey, I'm heading over there now," I told Allie and Vincenzo.

"Hold on, wait for us," Allie responded, walking in front of me and then stopping dead in her tracks, pressing the palm of her hand to my chest to prevent me from continuing forward. "Oh, shit."

"You know him?" I asked, fully aware of what she was reacting to.

"Unfortunately, yes." She let out the deep breath she was holding. "That's her ex. The one who had been cheating on her before she went on her Italian vacation and met you."

My face was frozen in place, my voice monotone. "Okay, and why is he here?"

"What am I, a psychic?" she responded with her quintessential smart-ass tone and Vin laughed, squeezing her waist.

"Well, I'm going to go over there to introduce myself," I said, starting to walk in their direction, but Allie's small frame managed to wiggle in front of me in an effort to reach Mia before I did. As we rounded the corner of the bar, he had closed in on whatever small space remained between the two of them, his lips now suctioned to her neck. In the same moment I wondered why she hadn't pushed him away, Mia lit up the side of his face with the back of her hand. The sound of it could be heard over the thumping bass of the music, and in an instant, bar staff had stepped in trying to separate the two of them.

Fight mode was activated.

I gently moved Allie to the side, and the previously balled-up fist I'd loosened to keep the peace was seconds away from making contact with his nose.

Mission accomplished.

Blood splattered onto my shirt and dripped down the sides of his mouth as he lay on the ground beside us. I wasn't sure whether I'd knocked him unconscious, but I positioned my body in front of Mia, tilted her chin upward, and watched as her eyes took a few seconds to bring me into focus.

Tears immediately streamed down her cheeks.

"No, no, no," I pushed strands of hair behind her neck, "this was not supposed to happen like this." But before I could utter another word, I felt someone's hands pulling my arms behind my body in an effort to restrain me. It was the bouncer from the front door.

"I knew these two were going to be a problem when they walked past the line before." He nodded to another bouncer, motioning for him to take me away. Where to? A police station? There was no way.

Luckily, Ryan came to the rescue, as he had earlier. "What the hell happened?"

Allie chimed in, "This *asshole,*" she emphasized as she pointed toward Mia's ex, still motionless on the floor, "wouldn't leave Mia alone."

"So, you broke his face?" He looked at me wide eyed, seemingly deciding he didn't want to piss me off further. He shook his head back and forth, rolled his eyes, connected his hands as though praying, and looking toward the ceiling. "C'mon, let me get you out of here."

"Where are you taking them?" the other bouncer asked.

"Don't worry about it," he responded, walking us toward the front door of the club, signaling for the DJ to resume the music. Once outside, Ryan turned to us. "Listen, I don't mean to kick you out, but given the circumstances, it's better than a possible physical assault charge. I'm going to tell them you evaded me outside and I couldn't catch up to you."

"Great. I went from a cop in Rome to a perp in America in record time." I shook my head in disbelief.

"No one has any record of your name or identification, so technically you don't exist here. Just go, please." Ryan looked like he needed a vacation. I shook his hand, crossed the street to get out of the area, and Allie got an Uber to pick us up within minutes.

While we waited, I realized I hadn't even properly greeted Mia yet. Arriving at the club, observing from a corner, and knocking her ex-boyfriend out hadn't lent itself to the romantic surprise I had intended. She must have realized the same, because as we waited for the Uber, she asked, "When did the three of you plan this?"

Allie responded for all of us. "We're sneaky, aren't we? Shame that ex-bastard of yours had to ruin it, though."

Mia turned to me, huddling close to my chest for warmth, peering up at me with a smile. "He didn't ruin anything. Thank you for coming. I wouldn't have made it to January." As I kissed her slowly in response, the Uber arrived.

Mia sat in the middle, flanked by Allie and me. Vincenzo was in the front seat next to the driver, who somehow knew he wasn't a small-talk kind of guy. When Vin's screen lit up a few times in a row, Allie incessantly typing on her phone behind him, I assumed they were having their own sidebar conversation.

"Listen, I'm sorry if I ruined the night." I was unsure of what else to say. "It was absolutely not my intention."

"If anyone should be apologizing, it's the dumb-ass we left on the floor of the bar," Allie assured me.

"What she said," Mia chimed in, sounding like she'd be asleep within minutes.

We quietly climbed out of the car, Vin and I following the girls up the stairs to Mia's apartment. Unsure if the physical altercation had us in a depressed state, I tried to move past the deafening silence between the four of us. I hoped it had more to do with it being after midnight and us not being twenty-one anymore. Allie chiseled through any remaining awkwardness the moment we stepped foot in the apartment.

"Okay, listen here, all of you," she said, hoisting herself up on the kitchen island and addressing us like a grade-school teacher, "all of *that*, was not supposed to happen tonight. We were supposed to be dancing until 2am, getting fattening food to soak up the alcohol on the way home, and then getting weird, you know, sexually, in different rooms with music blasting so we didn't get grossed out by each other's sound effects."

"Jesus, you really planned that out, didn't you?" Mia asked as she kicked off her heels and poured four glasses of water.

"That idiot deserves whatever broken facial bones he has right now. Also, screw him for ruining any portion of our night. Gennaro, many thanks for defending my girl's honor, but mostly, thank you both for making the trip all the way over here. It may not have panned out how we envisioned it, but all that means is that it can only get better from this point forward."

"You're very hot when you give speeches, you know that?" Vin chimed in.

"I'm a passionate woman when I need to get laid. I also realize I didn't plan one portion of this well, because your overnight bags are still at my mom's house." She scratched her head while downing the entire cup of water Mia had handed her. Vin playfully added, "As long as we have extra toothbrushes here, it doesn't sound like we're going to need any clothes to sleep."

"Okay great. Mia, you have a t-shirt I can borrow?" Allie said as she dragged Mia down the hallway, seemingly plotting something. After five minutes listening to them laugh over the music playing in Mia's bedroom, they resurfaced. It was hard to believe Mia and I had barely connected since the moment I knocked her ex out cold. Eliminating any confusion or worry that remained, she reappeared in an oversized t-shirt, no pants, barefoot, her hair tied into a messy bun. Smiling at me, she held out her hand and led me into her bedroom.

Within a minute, we could hear the distinct sounds of Allie and Vincenzo checking items off their own to-do list.

We turned the music up a little to drown out the sounds of laughter and the occasional moan while hoping to avoid a noise complaint from a neighbor. Shutting Mia's bedroom door behind me helped the world finally feel like it stopped spinning, if only briefly.

"Please don't think for a second that I'm upset that you punched him like that," she said, stepping closer to me, her mouth inches from mine as she tilted her chin in my direction. "He absolutely deserved it."

Kissing me softly, she opened her eyes slowly and whispered, "I need you, now."

"I'm here," I reminded her that I had no other plans for the next two days, kissed her back, and traced her bottom lip with my tongue before sucking on it.

"No," she said, eliminating any remaining space between us, her arms around my waist, pressing herself against my already throbbing dick. "I need you to fill every inch of me. Now."

Within minutes, we'd drowned out any sounds coming from Allie and Vincenzo.

Was it because they had finished?

We'd never know.

We were too busy recording our own soundtrack.

I woke up the next morning with a cold nose and a warm body. Mia acted as the small spoon, the curve of her bottom situated perfectly in the dip between my waist and thighs. Her head rested on one arm, which had gone numb at least an hour prior, and the other was wrapped tightly around her waist.

My bladder was full, and my stomach relentlessly growled since it was just past lunch time in Italy. I didn't hear any movement in the living room, so I dipped into my academy training and refocused my mind so I wouldn't piss the bed.

With my eyes closed, I began daydreaming about being back in Italy. For the first time since our engagement, I envisioned Mia living at the villa with me. Her in the kitchen with mama, greeting guests as they arrived, helping to set the table for dinner, watching me through the patio doors as I finished cleaning the pool, and putting some final landscaping touches on the outside garden.

Giustino's last round of questions had left me with lots of uncertainty about where we'd live, when she'd move, and what exactly our plan was for after the wedding. I had battled back and forth on the plane ride to the States over whether I could picture Mia working in Rome or working at the villa. According to my daydream, the best choice was the villa. But in that same moment, I realized that where Mia wanted to work was not up to me—it was up to her. A nearly perfect idea struck me right before she started stirring.

I'd look into it as soon as I got back home.

Stretching her legs toward the bottom of the bed frame and crawling back into the same ball she unwound from, I watched her eyes blink open. Her hair fell behind her neck, exposing her shoulder in the exact way I preferred it. I brushed my lips alongside the back of it as a smile formed on her face and my fingertips explored the skin underneath her thin cotton t-shirt.

"If you think I can go another round without getting some sort of personal injury, or, worse, an infection that'll put me out of commission for the next week or two, you are sorely mistaken."

I smiled.

"Sounds like you're the sore one, ma'am." I lifted Mia's shirt up over her waist and head, then rolled her over onto her stomach, pulling the blanket down beneath her ass and straddling the backs of her thighs. She swiped her hair to one side so that her neck, shoulders, back, and arms were exposed. Using a few pumps of the lotion perched at her bedside, I stroked up and down the length of her, using my thumbs to create deeper grooves between each of the tight muscles that lay underneath her delicate skin. The knots that riddled her neck, shoulders, and back told me a massage was exactly what she needed.

As I kneaded, stroked, and scratched various parts of her, I took note of her glowing skin. Fairer than she was back in October, there was now a stark difference between the deep, dark color of her almost black hair with the beige skin that radiated peach undertones. She was a modern-day version of Snow White, with longer hair and perfect curves everywhere.

I still couldn't get enough of her. I didn't want to leave. And, I already dreaded being back in Italy without her.

"I need you to move there and live with me," I blurted out.

"That's the plan, babe," she mumbled into her pillowcase.

"No, like, now," I was floundering. "Well, soon I mean."

"You okay?" She immediately sensed unhinged behavior without having to look at the likely ridiculous expression I was sporting.

"I'm not going to be okay until I get to do this every morning."

I saw her mouth form into another smile. "Did you just promise me daily massages?"

"I'm serious. I don't want to leave here without you." Whatever parts of cool, collected Gennaro Beletta remained from days past seemed to have dwindled. Was I whipped? No, she wasn't demanding that I do anything. Was I obsessed? No, crazy people got obsessed, and I wasn't crazy. Just crazy about her.

She attempted to roll over, so I lifted myself up to allow her room to do so. With Mia on her back, bare chested underneath me, I felt myself harden between her legs.

"What did I tell you?"

"Listen, if you don't want me to get hard at the sight of you, put a shirt back on and go get a different face or something."

I lowered myself to the indent where her neck met her shoulder, softly sucking the area, brushing my chest across her full tits. Her arms wrapped around me tightly as did her legs, like a koala around a tree branch.

"And, if you don't want me inside you again, you've got five seconds to unwrap those legs from my waist." I was smiling, my face still buried in her neck. She laughed softly, and when I didn't feel even an ounce of lessened pressure, I spread her legs wide open, scooped my arms underneath hers to pull her as close as possible, and the stick-straight dick I was working with found her hot and more than inviting slit with ease.

As it always did, relief washed over my entire body once I was buried inside her. Adrenaline and blood pumped through me, but the euphoric feeling of being one with the woman I loved turned me into mush.

I had a hard, muscular exterior, but Mia Luciano knew exactly how to soften all other parts of me. She was both my poison and my antidote. The one thing that could ruin me, but only if I was forced to live without it. Otherwise, she built me stronger, more confident, and more sure of myself than I had ever been—even though the next sentence to stream from my lips scared the shit out of me.

"Move to Italy in January."

"January. As in. a few weeks from now?" She was breathless as I continued pounding in and out of her.

"Yes," I answered in a heavy whisper, my thumb rubbing her throbbing clit until she cried out with a body tensing finish.

Next, it was my turn. I muffled the sounds of my heavy breathing with her pillow. Sticking to each other with sweat and bodily juices combined, I rolled to the side of her after I finished, tilting her chin in my direction.

"Answer me."

She looked up at her ceiling, the smallest of smiles on her face with her lips pensively pressed together. Before she could respond, Allie yelled from the living room. "Mia, someone slipped an envelope under your door."

"What does it say?" she shouted back.

If you plan to watch porn again tonight, please lower the volume of your TV. If you don't watch porn, and that was a regular night of sex for you, please consider sending a pair of noise cancelling headphones my way. Also...bravo.
– Apartment #37

"Guys, we've made it. We're amateur porn stars," Allie said with a pride-filled voice, followed by the sound of a high five between her and Vincenzo. And then, "God, I love Italian men."

Mia rolled over toward my chest and agreed, "I love Italian men, too." I attempted to correct her, but she stopped me with a finger to my lips. "Just one, actually."

"Nice save." I kissed her forehead, swung my legs over the bed, and pulled my boxer briefs on.

"One more thing," she said as she crawled to the edge of the bed, kneeled on it, pulled me close to her, and wrapped her arms around my waist. "How's February 1st?"

"What's the significance of February 1st?" I asked curiously.

"My mom's birthday is at the end of January. I can save some money from one more month of work. I'll celebrate her birthday with the rest of the family. And then, you can take me on my first ever Valentine's Day date."

I had a hard time believing no one had ever taken her on a date for Valentine's Day, but rather than pour salt in an obviously open wound, I responded the best way I knew how.

"I'm going to give you the best Valentine's Day date you've ever been on," I assured her.

She smiled and kissed my chest, her arms still tightly wrapped around me as we heard Allie and Vin rifling through cabinets for food. "Careful. You've already bent me over a private rooftop balcony in Rome. That'll be hard to beat."

I pressed my lips to the top of her head again, my hands traveling from the top of her shoulders down to the bottom of her ass. I cupped both cheeks, closing any open distance between us and likely leaving a handprint indentation in the skin of each.

"Hard, but not impossible," I said, smacking the firm mound of flesh that turned me on every time it was within striking distance. Her lips parted, letting out a moan. If I had no respect for her comfort, I'd have taken her again right then.

But I had all the respect in the world for her, as well as the entire landscape of her beautiful body, so I didn't.

"Let's go make some breakfast before those two accidentally blow up the place."

CHAPTER 26

"At least we know if we ever need a backup career path, we *can* be porn stars," Allie said, lathering butter on the hot Belgian waffle I'd pulled off the iron and placed in front of her, drizzled it with syrup, and slid it over to Vincenzo. "That's kind of cool, no?"

"Probably have to cut down on the Belgian waffles if we're going to pivot like that, but yes, it's always nice to have options," Vincenzo said, planting a kiss on her lips, after which her eyes roll damn near into the back of her head. Witnessing the two of them fall quietly for each other after a little bit of time together in Italy and whatever conversations had ensued after she left was nothing short of amazing.

Allie historically kept her guard up with men. She trusted few, if any, and the soft, sweet, slightly vulnerable side of her fantastic personality was usually overshadowed by her sarcastic, slightly aggressive side in an effort to keep her emotions safeguarded. In the same manner I had almost immediately trusted Gennaro, Allie trusted

Vincenzo. I could see and feel it as I watched the way she interacted with him.

Gennaro and Vin were cut from the same cloth, after all. They were men of stature, protecting those they cared about while letting few people see their softer side. When they did, though, they let you all the way in. I hadn't seen Vincenzo fully open up around me until now. I assumed it was the guys walking around shirtless in their underwear and Allie and I braless in t-shirts and sweats with our hair piled on top of our heads that allowed us to accept each other without judgment.

It had all happened relatively quickly. Gennaro and I became a unit, stumbling through instant lust and love, worried to an extent about what everyone would think. Four months after meeting, we were engaged, and I was moving to Italy in a little over a month. Thinking of it gave me the smallest bit of anxiety, but my mouth blurted out the words before my brain could stop. "I'm moving to Italy in February, Allie."

She finished chewing her waffle, eyes wide as they darted around the kitchen, before sipping orange juice from the glass in front of her. A few seconds of silence remained as I surveyed her face for a reaction. She was my person, the one I bounced my ideas and thoughts off first, no matter how ridiculous, farfetched, or crazy they might have been. When she finally opened her mouth to speak, her reaction surprised me, which wasn't unusual.

"Why wait until February?" She leaned into Vincenzo like they both already knew I was moving there. "The love of your life lives five thousand miles away, and life is short. Go be together."

I looked toward Gennaro, who had a sweet smile on his face but shook his head softly, which I took to mean "Babe, our plan is fine. We're good."

Allie was still reeling from years of emotional neglect from her now ex-husband, and giving whatever energy, emotion, and love she had to her children, she had put herself last for as long as I could remember. Seeing her come alive again, not because of a man's attention but clearly because *this specific man* helped her to remember her value, was priceless.

Vincenzo was to Allie what Gennaro had been to me: a reminder that good, strong, affectionately domineering yet respectful men did exist. They knew when to take charge and when to let their lady shine, how to be supportive without being overbearing, and how to be loyal and committed while still adding the thrill of excitement. She melted in his arms, letting herself fully trust him with her mind, body, and heart.

I knew exactly what I was seeing as I witnessed it unfold at my kitchen island, because it was the same journey I had taken with my now fiancé. Sheer disbelief that someone this perfect could exist in real life. They *weren't* perfect though, and neither were we. All of us were marred and scarred from emotional damage, uncertainty, and self-doubt from previous relationships, our upbringing, or a bit of both. Sometimes we were too outspoken, and oftentimes we were set in our ways, struggling to communicate our needs, wants, and desires without feeling judged.

As time ticked on, for Gennaro and me at least, we learned more and more about each other, anticipated each other's needs, and tied it all together with consistent communication. It was clear that, for the first time in her life, Allie had found the person who would allow her to do the same.

"This is going to go down as one of my happiest moments in life. My best friend, who's usually telling me the guy I'm dating is a giant loser, is urging me to move to

Italy, like, yesterday, throwing all caution to the wind, even if that means moving far away from her."

Vincenzo looked up from his now empty plate, then slowly turned his head in Allie's direction as if waiting for her to respond.

"I'm not opposed to moving to Italy," she said in response.

"Are you two engaged or something?" My eyes damn near popped out of my skull as my mouth curved into the most curious, happy smile.

"*Oh my God*, no," she shrieked, looking at me like I was crazy, which was hilarious given the circumstances. "Only you'd get engaged in four months like a Looney Tune."

> *Inner Critic: I'll take "Best Friends" for $200 Alex*
> *Mia: This is the dictionary definition of insanity...*
> *Inner Critic: What is "Two crazy broads falling in*
> *love with Italian men instantly, picking up their*
> *entire lives and considering moving to a new*
> *country whilst barely looking in the rearview*
> *mirror?"*
> *Mia: Alex Trebek would have told you that you're*
> *correct*
> *Inner Critic: Oh, I know I am*

Allie was smiling, filling four champagne glasses to the brim with Prosecco and drizzling the tiniest bit of orange juice on top. "We've both been married before, and we both have no interest in ever doing it again. I have the girls to think about, of course, but once this divorce is finalized, I won't have to worry about my ex anymore. I can do what I want."

With my eyes still protruding from their sockets, I said, "And Vincenzo is who you're doing!" We all laughed, and I continued, "I'm sure my face does not match what I feel right now. This is incredible. I had no idea you two had talked this much. How many freaking phone conversations have you had?"

"It sounds like Vin's talked to Allie more than he's spoken to everyone else in his life combined," Gennaro joked. "A true American miracle."

"You're not wrong," Vin responded with a smile, cracking his fingers and stretching his arms and neck. "You told me a while back, *'When you know, you know,'* and I do. They don't make them like this over there."

"Like what?" I asked out of sheer curiosity.

He smiled and turned his head to Allie. "*Amore*, what do you want for dinner tonight?"

Allie immediately started mentally rolling through options. No fewer than five seconds passed before she answered, "Potato skins and salad with grilled chicken from the pub down the street. And an ice cream sundae for dessert."

"Are you two sure you're not sisters?" Gennaro asked.

"See? Women who know what they want. It's amazing." Vin said. I couldn't argue with that.

"This wedding is going to be epic," Vin responded.

"Speaking of which," Allie chimed in, "what color am I wearing?"

"Gold, beige, or champagne, and whichever style you want. I truly don't care."

"I love you," she said, walking around the island to hug me tightly.

It was happening. Manifestation was real. Italian men have a way of making dreams come to life, I guess. Or maybe it was downing Prosecco just shy of noon.

"Okay, more importantly, can we really go to the pub for dinner tonight?" She was relentlessly persistent.

"Yes, but can we take a nap beforehand?" I softly begged, my body requiring the relaxation of a thousand naps.

"If by nap, you mean a massage, sure," Gennaro interrupted my thoughts like the mind reader he is.

"Ugh, marry me," I said, walking over to his bar stool and standing in between his legs, my arms around his neck, his around my waist, face buried in my chest.

"Planning on it."

Vincenzo and Allie had made their way over to the couch, ready for their own nap.

"Okay, fellow porn stars, let's keep it down and reconvene later tonight, okay?"

"Yes, boss," Allie responded from the blanket she was buried under and the muscular, olive-skinned, tattooed arms she was wrapped in.

Their contentment in each other's embrace was infectious. Gennaro and I made our way down the hall, back to the bed we had crawled out of just two hours prior.

Sex, eat, sleep, repeat—what a beautiful thing it was.

We discussed our future plans buried underneath the covers, flurries falling outside and the hazy halo of comfort being in true love provided. I'd squeeze every bit of money I could out of the bar I was working at for the entire month of January while figuring out what the hell I needed to do in order to actually reside in Italy.

Moving past those unsexy details, we'd be married on the villa property, the specifics of which Gennaro left for Mama to handle, with my blessing. My mom had already asked to host the bridal shower when she arrived a week before the wedding. Our guest lists were relatively small, consisting of immediate family, Allie, Vincenzo, Salvatore, Pesca, and a handful of others. We'd stay in Gennaro's

Rome apartment, heading to the Villa together on his days off to give Mama and Papa a hand.

The plans were relatively basic, but the love we felt for one another was anything but. I had found the love of my life, with zero doubts about where I wanted to be, so long as I was with him.

Life had aligned alongside the stars, bringing me to Gennaro and ushering us both into our next chapters. Living presently helped me find him, completely unexpected and wholly satisfying. My eyes closed that afternoon and didn't fully reopen until my feet were back on Italian soil.

The two months between the weekend he visited and me flying back to Italy after mom's birthday were a bit murky. One foot in front of the other helped me go to work, make my money, and organize and pack things, little by little, while spending some extra time with my family.

Mom's birthday was bittersweet. It would be the last time we'd all be together until they flew to Italy in May for wedding festivities. It was the perfect dinner, all of us enjoying each other's company, excited for the future. I counted my blessings for them being as supportive as they were, without questioning me, my motives or intentions, or my ability to see a plan through to its best possible outcome. I worked hard in all aspects of life, but especially didn't falter when it came to realizing my own happiness.

After all, if *you* can't prioritize your own happiness, why will anyone else? It was a far cry from being selfish. Discovering the things that brought me joy, contentment, and purpose, then leaning into them while still being a present family member or friend is the key to living a truly fulfilled life. It absolutely has its challenges, but the best things in life don't come easy, especially when relationships are involved. Mastering the balance between self-care and caring for others is a delicate dance, but a necessary one to learn in life. It's what I strive to be great at.

I vowed never to let my family forget how important they are to me, even though I was choosing to move so far away. The night I hugged them goodbye after filling ourselves with freshly fried, crispy chicken cutlets and pasta with broccoli, garlic, and olive oil felt as heavy on my heart as the meal did on my stomach.

I cried uncontrollably, not because I had any doubt about this next chapter, but because, unfortunately, the price you pay for close relationships is the heartbreak you feel when you have to part with them. It was temporary, sure, but it had ripped my heart apart with a jagged edge— one I hoped Italy would be able to stitch back together.

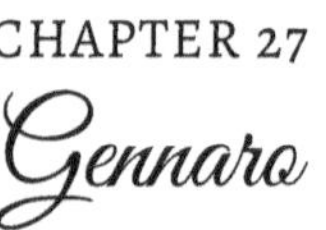

CHAPTER 27

Gennaro

FEBRUARY

A notification came through that Mia's flight had landed at the same time I'd parked, with excitement and anticipation radiating throughout my body. We both thrived in the comfort of predictability at times, appreciating when guesswork was removed from situations, and we were completely enamored with the fact that our lives had melded together.

The moment I saw her long, dark hair, her suitcase rolling behind her, dressed in body skimming yoga pants, a tan hooded sweatshirt, brown boots, and a cream-colored beanie hat, my insides melted like whipped cream in a hot cappuccino.

"*Amore.*"

Her lips found mine immediately with zero hesitation, like we hadn't been apart for nearly two months. "Those were the longest and shortest months of my life," I said, disinterested in letting go.

"Please share your secrets on how it felt at all short," she said, her arms clinging to my neck, refusing to let go.

"I had important things to take care of and have a few surprises for you," I said, stepping back to assess her reaction.

"I'm all yours," she confessed, kissing me softly and gently tugging on my bottom lip with her teeth before pulling away again, completely unaffected by the throngs of people whizzing by us in all directions. "Whatever you want to do and wherever you want to go, tell me."

She sounded more than ready for someone to lead the way, which I happened to excel at. I took her suitcase and led her towards the car.

"We're heading to Tuscany," I surprised her.

"You don't have to work?"

I smiled and stopped walking. "I was going to wait to tell you, but that's your first surprise."

"You're unemployed, and we're going to live out of an Italian refrigerator box?" She blinked twice, mostly kidding but slightly alarmed.

"No, baby." I kissed the top of her head to help her to relax. "I transferred from Rome police to Tuscany police." The curve of her mouth surveyed my face yet again. "I'm going to work with Vincenzo, and you and I, we're going to live at the villa."

Her glowing gray eyes doubled in size. She loved my apartment in Rome, and as I saw her brain computing this new revelation, I assured her, "I kept my apartment as a place to go to when we need a getaway."

Mia released the breath that was trapped in her throat, seeming a bit unsure about the plan.

"Is that okay?" It occurred to me that maybe I should have reviewed this with her prior, but she was busy organizing her own list of to-dos in order to leave the States. I didn't want to add to her plate.

"How will I comfortably live there with Papa? The

villas are all right next to each other. I wouldn't want to feel like I have to avoid him."

"Do you trust me?" I asked her, still my favorite line when life got crazier than we bargained for.

As I hoped the answer would be after packing up and moving five thousand miles to marry me, she said, "More than I ever thought possible."

"Then get in the car so I can show you the second surprise."

Passing time before I could see Mia would normally feel like slow-paced torture, but the amount I wanted to accomplish before she arrived made it move relatively quickly for once. A dinner with Vincenzo at the osteria had not only yielded a homemade wine buzz and planning the surprise trip to visit Mia and Allie but also a decision to transfer police departments from Rome to Tuscany. Having put my paperwork in, I booked the trip to the States and spent the weekends in between preparing an important part of our acreage that many people didn't even know existed.

She was leaving *her* home to join me in *mine*, but I wanted something to be *ours*. Mine and hers, far enough away from the daily stressors of villa life but close enough to help, visit, and enjoy it. I didn't have time to finish renovations completely, but it was more than enough to get my point across.

We pulled past the wrought iron gates at the entrance to our property, and rather than turn right toward the apartments, we continued straight on the white road in front of us. One lane of unpaved dirt brought us a bit further away from the hustle and bustle of the main property where guests checked in. Sounds lessened as we drove past the lone cypress tree overlooking expansive sections of land, including more rolling vineyards and crops. Neighboring properties lined the horizon to the left, but as I climbed one last hill after the road wrapped around to the right, a small house with a terracotta roof, stone-covered front, and stone walkway stared back at us.

Mia's head turned slightly, and while I could feel her assessing my facial expression, I could barely return her gaze. Anticipation simmered in my bones, hoping she'd love what I was about to show her as much as I loved preparing it for her—and us.

From the outside, it was moderately underwhelming. Small in stature with none of the lush landscaping we were used to on the main property. In fact, it had little greenery, shrubbery, or flowers at all. The house itself looked abandoned, because it had been for nearly ten years since my Nonna and Nonno had passed away within a few months of each other.

"What is this place?" she quietly asked.

"Why do you sound afraid of the answer to that?" I smiled and squeezed her hand after putting the car in park.

"Trying my best to *vivi il momento* and all that, but also sort of feel like I'm on candid camera." At least she was honest.

"You said you trust me, *amore*," I reminded her before opening the door and nudging my head toward the house.

Mia walked around the car and weaved her fingers through mine. "Maybe it's the jet lag," she said with a wink.

The breeze blowing on the hilltop was far more prominent than the one we felt back at the villa. Her scent consumed me. After twelve plus hours of travel time, her skin still somehow radiated sweet vanilla. Her hair, another layer of fragrance I was addicted to, felt like home as it enveloped me. And now, here we were, standing in front of the home that was actually ours.

She simply didn't know it yet.

I tugged on Mia's hand before she could attempt to peer through any windows and turned her toward me. "After you left last time, I started searching for houses in Tuscany. Originally, I couldn't imagine us living *on* property, constantly surrounded by family and guests, so I looked for something else worthy of you, and perfect for us, to start our life together. I even visited a few places, but..." I paused to remember the empty feeling in my stomach when I began touring them. "It didn't feel right. It's not where we're supposed to be."

Rotating our stance, with my back to the front door and her facing it, I continued, "A visit with Papa turned into a conversation about you moving here and where we'd be most comfortable. He actually suggested this place, reminding me it even existed. My Nonna and Nonno lived here before they both passed away. It's been vacant for about ten years, but I fixed it up for us."

"They're okay with us being here? Why didn't anyone take it before?" Her eyes displayed a variety of emotions, most of which depicted someone trying to lean in and fully trust the person they loved. But, as I had grown to under-stand deeply, she was a thinker, a question asker, a needs-a-reason-for-everything-er. Regardless of how much more often she lived presently than she had before, Mia still planned for the future and occasionally wanted answers for things.

I love it about her.

"It's far enough away that anyone working on the villa property every day wouldn't find it convenient," I explained. "And yes, Papa and Mama gave more than their blessing. They also gave me free range to fix it up, which I did with the help of my brothers as well as Vincenzo and

Salvatore. But before we go in, turn around and take a look at your front yard."

Her mouth curved upward into a small smile, her arms settled around the small of my waist, and she planted a slow, soft kiss on my lips that solidified the sentiments her eyes attempted to relay earlier. Trust, paired with uncertainty, topped off with excitement, anticipation, and pure, unadulterated love. She was leaning into all of what was before us as much as she possibly could.

When we both turned to take in the front yard view of our future home, the small gasp escaping her lips told me she was as in love with it as I was. We peered out toward hundreds of acres of rolling hills in front of us, all leading to the main property, which, from this far away, appeared to be the size of a Matchbox car. You could make out the pool between the house and the vineyard flanked to its left as well as the garden we christened, the row of guest villas, our family villas, the work shed, and the chicken coop. The white road connected us to the villa where we fell in love, allowing us the perfect distance between our home and the busy atmosphere surrounding it.

"I'm trying to find the right words to tell you how beautiful this is," she said, shaking her head from side to side. "It's incredible. I don't even know what to say."

"Don't say anything until you see the inside," I urged her.

"Inside? What's inside? I assumed it's empty. No?"

"I wouldn't bring you all the way here to show you an empty house," I assured her. "Go inside."

Excitement grew and uncertainty lessened as the minutes ticked by, and even though I knew she'd be blown away when she opened the door, my stomach still bubbled with suspense.

Turning the knob and pushing the door open, her eyes grew as wide as mine did when I first realized how deceptively spacious it was inside. An open foyer with vaulted ceiling boasted tile floors that flowed throughout the entire house. Wooden archways led into rooms on either side of it. On the left was a sitting room with a large, plush, cream-colored couch, a female-approved number of throw pillows, a fireplace, and a tan shag rug. An oversized armchair that could easily fit two adults comfortably flanked the fireplace. On the accent table adjacent to the back of the couch, the first thing you could see when entering the room, were framed pictures of each of our families from the night of our engagement as well as one of Mia and me from the night we met. An envelope also sat with "Mia" written on it, which I nudged her to open.

> Mia,
>
> My great grandparents built this house themselves.
>
> My grandparents raised Papa in it and stayed here long after he moved to the villas.
>
> Mama, my brothers, and I would visit with them often.
>
> And now, it'll become our home, not because of family lineage, but because we'll be living in it together.
>
> My home is wherever you are.
>
> Amore per sempre,
>
> Gennaro

When Mia placed the envelope down, tears streamed

down both sides of her face. She took me in her arms and kissed me deeply, without the need to utter words.

I knew the feeling she was experiencing, because I felt the same, and we continued touring the property.

In the room opposite the foyer was another shag rug, a white desk, and a cream-colored, gold-accented desk chair across from two ivory armchairs, a small coffee table between them. The window in the front of the room served as the backdrop for a sitting bench in front of it. On either side of the window, wall shelving doubled as bookcases.

"I left the detailed decorating for you to handle," I told her, "assuming you'd want to."

Her mouth opened, but her words were jumbled, which I immediately recognized was for the best of reasons. I took Mia's hand in mine and walked her to the back of the house. The kitchen and dining room flowed into each other, with large windows and a pair of glass doors that led to a stone patio, the view beyond which was even more rolling hills. The entire house was surrounded by them, so it didn't matter which window or door you peered out of. Your breath was taken away at every turn.

"Ready to go upstairs?" I asked her.

"There's an upstairs?"

"You missed the entire staircase when you walked in?" I gently asked.

"I think I'm in a state of shock," she said, taking my hand to follow me back through the front of the house and up the stairs.

We surveyed the two small bedrooms upstairs that could double as guest rooms or, eventually, a baby room. Neither was outfitted with much in the way of furniture. Both had windows facing the front of the house, and the views were even more breathtaking thanks to the elevated viewpoint.

Our bedroom suite had the same magnificent view, but faced the back end of the property. A king-size bed was situated to the left directly underneath an ornate crystal chandelier, and to the right, two medium-size closets flanked the door to the bathroom, which was undoubtedly my favorite part of the house. A large soaking tub sat in the middle of the marble tile floor, a waterfall wall perched behind it. It was a feature I splurged on, and received painstaking amounts of installation "help" from Sal and Vincenzo. An oversized gold floor-length mirror sat in the far corner atop a small circular ivory rug, and his and her sinks with marble countertops completed the layout.

"How did you do this in such a short amount of time?"

"I had a vision for it, and Sal, Vincenzo, Giovanni, and Giuseppe were a majority of the muscle behind it." The stories we'd retell among the four of us and anyone willing to listen would be epic. The vulgarity effortlessly flowed as we cleaned, tiled, painted, and assembled what would have taken most professionals double the time to complete. Thankfully, the structure was sound, the foundation originally poured by my great grandfather himself. The memories built into and around this place were vast, but I appreciated that I had spent less time there than at the main property. Plus, enough time had passed since I was last there that it allowed it to feel like it was *ours*.

"So...do you like it?" I asked, already knowing the answer.

She smiled slyly. "*Like* it? I like this about as much as you *liked* red lace lingerie in the pomodoro garden."

"Message received, loud and clear." I kissed the top of her head and filled her in on the final details. "There are a few more things I need to finish before we actually move in, but we can stay in my villa apartment until then."

"Absolutely, we can. I can help Mama around there, too. Whatever she needs," she offered.

I assured her, even though she didn't seem to care, "It'll only be for a couple of weeks."

"For however long, it doesn't matter." I felt her melt in my arms, tired from travel and exhausted from the emotional toll of moving to an entirely different country. I was satisfied, knowing her comfort was the most important thing to me. "Are we going to see everyone up at the villa now?"

"We can, but I have one more surprise for you if you're not too tired," I said, pulling back to assess her facial expression.

"I don't know how you top that, but I will never say no to a surprise from you," she said, planting another kiss on my lips.

"Get back in the car then." I pulled a small piece of fabric from my back pocket. "And put this blindfold on."

"Is this a sex-filled surprise?"

My eyebrow ticked, and while I suddenly wished it were, I knew soon enough I'd have her to myself in every consumable way. There was no need to rush it. "It might turn into one depending on how much you like it," I said, shrugging.

We slowly drove back down the white road, exited the property gates, turned right toward the osteria, and parked in a lot to the side of it. While I had hesitated on this location thanks to its close proximity to Francesca's market, I refused to make our lives inconvenient due solely to her inability to be rational.

I parked in the spot closest to the front door. Mia was blindfolded, her hand in mine. "Are you ready?" I asked.

"I was never ready for any of this, which is the thrilling part, so no…but yes."

"*Andiamo, bella.*"

I opened her door, and rather than head toward the front of the building, we walked farther away from it, to the edge of the last parking spot. Standing behind her, I untied the blindfold. As my arms fell to her sides, clutching the fabric in one hand and wrapping the other around her waist with my chin buried in the crook of her neck, we looked at the building in unison.

A brand-new sign was lit up by the reflection of string lights surrounding it, written in the most beautiful script font I was able to find. "*Vero Caffè.*" She read the sign out loud and stood in silence for a few seconds. "Am I supposed to know what this is?"

"Do you know what *vero* means?" I spun her around to face me.

"Yes. It means *real.*"

"Last summer, I asked you how you pictured the next year of your life," I reminded her.

"…okay." Her face was softer and more entertained than her voice was letting on, but she was still waiting for the punchline, not quite connecting the dots.

"You told me you had always wanted an Italian caffè, but were embarrassed saying it out loud because you felt like a 'fake' Italian."

"Well, compared to you I am, absolutely."

"Mia, I can feel you, smell you, and touch you right now. You're as real as anything could ever be."

I took her hand and started walking toward the building. The front windows, covered with contact paper, allowed for an element of surprise. Pulling the door open, I flicked the light switch to our right, illuminating the entire restaurant. The inside was far more appealing than the outside, which was the sole reason behind her second gasp of the day.

Four crystal chandeliers spanned the width of the restaurant, one hanging over each of the four small stand-alone tables, all adorned with black lace underneath a glass top. Along the back wall was a bar countertop with ten black and gold barstools, a pastry case, and a wood-fired oven in the wall behind it. The walls were painted a warm gray, and thanks to Mama, the tables, counters, and pockets of free space were outfitted with antique gold details. Small bookshelves were affixed to the walls alongside framed black and white photos of the villa. The far-right wall had an arched opening to a hallway that led to the restroom, similar to the osteria. It was dually modern and vintage inspired, with more nods to our relationship journey than the untrained eye would pick up on.

"This is yours, *amore*."

Her eyes again toured the layout, her jaw dropping ever so slightly. "Mine?"

"Carmine from the osteria owns this entire strip. He offered the space to me for lease when the last tenant moved out. Mama and Dominique helped me decorate it." I swept a few strands of hair from her face and held her chin firmly in the palms of my hands. "*Vero Caffè* celebrates everything in my life that has brought me real, true, genuine happiness. And that's you." Tears trickled down her cheeks again. "I've made you cry more times today than I planned to, I'm sorry."

"You are the absolute best thing to ever happen to me," she said, surveying the space again, then forcefully pulling me closer to her by the top of my waist band. "I didn't miss the significance of the black lace table toppers, by the way."

"I didn't think you would," I playfully responded as I

felt the tension of anticipation and uncertainty transform almost instantly to desire.

"I'll accept this on one condition," she warned.

"And what's that?" With a smirk on my face, a pounding in my chest, and a bulge in my pants, I knew exactly where she was going with her request.

"Why are you smiling?"

"Because I know you want me to take you down the hallway to christen the place." With her chin down, her lips pursed, and one eyebrow raised, she shook her head. "No, you pervert."

"Wishful thinking, sorry." I shrugged and waited for her to finish with her actual request. "Only lightening the mood since I like you smiling more than I like you crying."

"They were happy tears. But anyway, I want to put framed photos of our entire family throughout the place— make it feel cozy and traditional but modern and sexy at the same time."

"In other words, you want it to emulate the thing I love about you the most?" I pulled her close to me and kissed her. The softness of her plump, lush lips enveloped mine, and the heat of her sweet breath sucked me into her, like she couldn't quite get enough.

As always, neither could I.

I was relentless in the pursuit of what I wanted, so I tried a second time.

"You sure you don't want to christen the hallway or the bathroom?" I asked.

Instantly responding, "No," she turned around, locked the door behind us, and put her purse on one of the table tops. Inadvertently biting my lip, she pulled me by my waistband again, this time to the leather bench underneath one of the front windows. Nudging me to sit down on it, I did as silently instructed and stretched out my arms to grab the sides of her waist. "I want to ride you right here, so that each time I'm standing at that counter, and looking out this window, I remember exactly who the Universe brought me to answer each and every single wish I've ever had."

She may not have known it, but I had thanked the Universe every single goddamn day since it had brought me to her, too.

Bending down to kiss me, she slowly turned away, shimmied out of her stretchy pants, and dropped them to the floor, lowering her warmth on top of me. In what felt like a drug induced haze, Mia glided up and down the length of me, my arms wrapped around the front of her, and my mouth begging to sample her velvety skin, which was unfortunately covered by the sweatshirt she still had on.

The rest of it was a blur—a soul-crushing burst of a release that I forced to last as long as possible after not seeing her for nearly two months. Our cheeks were red hot alongside dewy, sticky skin that longed for a shower and a bed as much as it longed for a round two.

"You're right," I said.

"About?"

"I'll never be able to step foot in this place without looking at this bench, thinking of this exact moment and every single one prior to it that led us here."

She stood, pulled up her pants, then turned to kneel between my legs. Tired but satisfied eyes stared back at me, as I cupped her face with my hand and she kissed the side of my thumb.

"Want to know the best part?"

"What's that?" I softly responded with a mixture of exhaustion and contentment in my voice.

"I live here now," she smiled, "so we get to do this wherever and however often we want."

"I'm going to need you to remember that you said that two weeks from now," I assured her.

"What's in two weeks?" She asked, completely oblivious to the date.

"Valentine's Day."

CHAPTER 28
Mia

Two weeks later

Windows have a way of squeezing the most dramatic of emotions out of us. Was I partaking in a 90s music video on MTV, or was I staring through a piece of double-paned glass, rain droplets splattering the outside of it, gazing at the parking lot of my brand-new caffè in the middle of Tuscany and hoping the tables would be as filled as they were the day prior for our grand opening?

Carson Daly was nowhere to be found, so I smacked my cheek lightly to remind myself that, yes indeed, I am a living, breathing, human who somehow manifested an entire life's worth of dreams in less than a year.

Meet the love of my life? *Check.*

Move to Italy? *Check.*

Open my own Italian caffè? *Check.*

> *Inner Critic: Technically, he opened it for you*
> *Mia: Technically, kiss my ass*
> *Inner Critic: Alrighty then*
> *Inner Critic: Go make us a breakfast pizza*

Mia: Fine

Creating the menu for *Vero Caffè* had been my favorite part of becoming a restaurant owner and manager overnight. Our hours of operation were Monday through Saturday, 11am through 3pm, brunch and lunch only. Starting small would gauge interest and collect some initial data from guests, which felt far more manageable as a one-woman-ish show. Word spread throughout the town naturally that we were looking for help, and with three new young ladies joining me as part of my staff in addition to Gennaro and his family stepping in when they could, I had enough support to get this new venture off the ground.

A limited menu allowed for quality over quantity. At Gennaro's urging, I didn't hesitate to add my Italian-American flair, fully anticipating the first scathing review that would undoubtedly come from someone wanting genuine, authentic Italian faire.

Vero offered a variety of breakfast pastries, omelets for those vacationing or living in Italy who dared to want protein first thing in the morning, fresh yogurt parfaits, one soup made daily, salad, paninis, and small personal pizzas from the wood-fired oven. To drink, they could choose between still or sparkling waters, iced or hot coffees and teas made American or Italian style, and seltzers flavored with real fruit juices. I looked forward to adding wine and champagne to the menu but hadn't quite cracked the code for Italian liquor licenses.

In due time.

It was a quiet, quaint, modern spot to get work done, meet up with a friend, or have a hot date with a few delicious bites of affordable food.

Speaking of hot dates, Gennaro pulled into the parking lot at the exact moment my music video cameo appearance came to an end. Smoothing my hair, I ran around the counter, grabbed my purse, and sprayed myself with extra perfume, as though this man hadn't woken up next to a slightly cuter version of Shrek the same morning.

> *Inner Critic: Good girl*
> *Inner Critic: Keep the spark alive*
> *Mia: He makes it easy, doesn't he?*

Inner Critic didn't have a chance to answer me. The door swung open, and in walked my uniformed *polizia* with a jacket over what I knew to be a short-sleeved blue uniform shirt tucked into blue cargo pants and finished with black boots. His hair was perfectly combed with a small bit of hair-wax to keep the natural waves in place, and his brown eyes looked alert, like we hadn't spent the entire prior night rolling around in the bed of his child-hood room.

"*Buon San Valentino, amore,*" he said, pulling a small bouquet of flowers from behind his back and placing them on the table next to him.

Why did I keep forgetting about Valentine's Day?

> *Inner Critic: Probably because, historically, it's been*
> *   a horrible day of failed expectations*
> *Mia: Thanks so much for the reminder*
> *Inner Critic: What? You asked.*

"Those are for you," he said, nodding toward the flow-ers, pulling me closely to the hard outline underneath his cargo pants, "and so are these." He was referring to the kisses he slowly planted on my lips that trailed down my neck to the tops of my shoulders.

I rubbed the bulge in his pants and asked, "What about this?"

He exhaled with an inaudible moan. "Yours since the moment you agreed to dance with me in Rome."

"Want to christen the hallway now?" Something about business ownership made me want to drop my pants all over this place.

> Inner Critic: *This is why people don't like eating in public*

"More than anything, but I'm already late for work, and *new guys* aren't supposed to be late." His tongue danced its way around the tip of mine, taunting and teasing me as to what it planned to do later. He finished with the softest of nibbles, eyes locking with mine. "*Ti amo, tanto.* Meet me by the main water fountain at 8pm tonight, okay?"

"What should I wear?" I loved this game we continued to play with each other.

"Doesn't matter," he said with a wink, kissing me one last time before opening the door to leave. "You won't be in it for very long."

My staff arrived early enough to help me minimally decorate for Valentine's Day, adding small vases to each table as well as the bar top, a single red flower in each. Strawberries were drizzled with dark and white chocolate as complimentary treats for each guest. The single version of me vividly remembered the dull pain associated with an entire day's worth of reminders that I was, in fact, epically *alone.* While I wanted to help those in love celebrate, I didn't want to alienate everyone else in the process.

Celebrating my first Valentine's Day in Italy was about to show me, again, exactly what true love was meant to feel like.

With half our tables filled and a few seats at the bar taken, I was busy chopping fresh vegetables for salads and rotating small pizzas in the oven when the jingle of the bell above the door played the symphony of Day Two success.

"Sit anywhere you like!" I yelled, my head in close proximity to the pizza oven, hoping they could hear me.

How very American of me.

When no one answered, I closed the oven and peered over the pastry box to see who had walked in.

There, at the front door of my brand-new caffè, stood Mama, arm interlocked with Papa's, helping to support his weight. He looked even older and more fragile than the last time I had seen him and was trying his hardest to smile. Instinctually, I shuffled quickly around the counter to pull out a seat for him at the nearest available table. He let out a breath that sounded like it hurt as he sat down. I kissed them both and waved to one of the girls to check the pizzas in the oven for a remaining table. "Can I get you something to drink? Eat? I'm so happy you're here."

I surprised myself with that statement but was, in fact, happy to see them and feel their support.

Mama responded, "He requested to come, and wanted to tell you something."

The door swung open before he could get any words out of his mouth. Fire engine red hair took up my peripheral line of vision. In stormed Francesca, a woman on a mission, completely oblivious that Mama and Papa were seated at the table.

"Where is she?" she shouted to anyone willing to listen.

I felt my inner Jersey activate and was thankful to be wearing large gold hoop earrings for added empowerment. "I'm right here. And if you could keep your voice down while people are trying to enjoy themselves, that'd be great. What do you need?"

She whipped around to find me standing beside her, still unaware that Mama and Papa were seated at the table next to me, which wasn't surprising. It wasn't easy to focus on other people when every fiber of your being was spent worrying about yourself.

"I need you to stop ruining my life."

An involuntary laugh escaped my mouth, my eyes wide and bright with absolute bewilderment at her continued irrational behavior.

"I ruined *your* life?" I asked, rhetorically.

The audacity.

"You stole my husband, and now you're stealing my business with this shitty caffè!"

Quickly realizing all conversations had ceased at the remaining dining tables, I pulled her aside and quickly reviewed my response internally before spewing it.

"The delusion that brews between your ears absolutely astounds me. I can't steal something that wasn't yours to begin with. And, respectfully," I said, nodding toward the table Mama and Papa sat at, "the only person who decides who someone is marrying is that person himself. Gennaro never gave you false hope. You never listened to what he repeatedly told you."

Her nose flared as she shifted uncomfortably in her stance, but her silence allowed me to continue. "As for me and my *shitty caffè*, the only people comfortable breaking down others are the ones who are innately broken themselves." I figured there was no better time than the present to get it all off my chest. "You can add this to the list of reasons why Gennaro never actually wanted to marry you. I see right through you. I always have. You don't *love* him. You don't *want* him. You only want the notoriety that comes from being with him. He deserved better, and so did his family."

Francesca was stunned, although I wasn't sure what she expected, walking into *my* business as Gennaro's *actual* fiancé, trying to start with me. I wasn't ever in the mood for it, but with zero doubt on where my relationship stood with him, and now, actually living here, I had even less use for her and the accompanying bullshit.

From behind me, Papa voiced his opinion on the matter. "*Disgrazia.*" I turned to confirm what I assumed, that his eyes were fixated on Francesca and not me.

When she realized it was he who said it, she broke down into tears.

> *Inner Critic: Oy*
> *Inner Critic: Maybe Gennaro could have picked a*
>   *location that isn't walking distance to her store*
> *Mia: Nah, that's okay*
> *Mia: She's gonna have to put her big girl panties on*
>   *and figure it out*
> *Inner Critic: Didn't we have a deal on never using*
>   *the word panties?*
> *Mia: I keep forgetting*
> *Inner Critic: No worries, now finish her*
> *Mia: Combatting asshole tendencies with additional*
>   *asshole tendencies rarely works*
> *Inner Critic: Well, do something, people are*
>   *watching and now they think you actually stole*
>   *her husband*
> *Inner Critic: Maybe Maury Povich has some open-*
>   *ings, too*

"Come here and sit down," I said, motioning to the empty table alongside Mama and Papa. They were pretending not to eavesdrop, but it was nearly impossible given the size of the place. "I never intended that any part of my being here would ruin someone else's life. But I'll never apologize for finding the person I'm meant to be with, who I know for a fact is not the person *you're* supposed to be with."

"How do you just assume that?" Her delusion spanned farther than I thought, but I kept at it, trying to lean on any remaining patience I had.

"Has he ever spent time with you, one on one?" I asked her.

"Yes! Well, at the villa with the family."

"So, no, he hasn't. Has he ever promised to actually be with you?"

She was silent.

"No, he hasn't. Has he wished you the best, even in the absence of himself?"

"Yes, he has."

"Okay, so all he wants is for you to do your own thing, to give up the idea that you'd ever be together, because it's not what he wants or sees for his life. He's actually acted more respectfully than most men, who would be trying to get you in bed with empty promises they didn't intend to keep."

Tears pooled in the corner of her eyes, and after a few deep breaths, she said what most women on this day were known to say. "Valentine's Day reminds me how alone I am. I had him, and then I lost him."

I put my hand on her knee, for the first time finding the smallest glimmer of compassion for her as a fellow woman wanting nothing more than the feeling of all-consuming, unconditional, occasionally suffocating, *true* love. "You can't lose something you never had, but more importantly," I said, making sure she could see the respect in my eyes when I finished my sentiment, "you will not find the love you deserve from someone else until you learn to love yourself in the same manner."

"What do you mean?"

"If you want someone to respect you, respect yourself. If you want someone to appreciate you, learn to appreciate what it feels like to be in your own company. And if you want someone to desire you, lean into all the things that make you the happiest version of you, and then go do them, repeatedly. You'll attract what you put out in the world."

She nodded her head slowly in mild acceptance of what I was telling her. "Right now, all I'm putting out in the world is misery. I'm miserable, and I'm sitting here blaming you for it."

"Yes." I squeezed her hand in agreement. "Want to try something?" When she nodded again, I continued, "Do one thing that makes you feel your happiest, most assured self every day for the next month. I guarantee you, come mid-March, you'll walk back in here with a happy heart, a confident mind, and a completely different outlook on life."

"How are you so sure?"

"It's how life works," Mama interjected. "You have to put into it what you want to get out of it."

In an apparent daze, with a smile and an expression of understanding on her face, she hugged me unexpectedly and quickly apologized to Mama, Papa, and the other customers finishing up their meals that the girls had, thankfully, finished serving them. Then she left. I shook my head, having been wholly unprepared for the encounter and slightly exhausted from it, but mostly grateful to have finally shared some insight with her.

As I walked over to Mama and Papa's table, he patted the chair next to him and placed his hand on top of mine after I took a seat. It took him a while to begin speaking, and when he did, I could feel him holding back a lot of emotion.

"I misjudged you. I'm a thick old man, set in my ways, but mostly, I've always been envious of my son for doing things *his* way and not following the path other people tell him to, like I did. His path led him to you, which as far as the eye can see, is the best decision he'll ever make."

I could feel my throat squeeze under the pressure of suppressed emotion as he continued. "I'm sorry for the things I said and for judging you and your intentions before getting to know you well enough to display them." He paused to refuel and then continued. "I've never known my son to make the wrong choices, and if I know him well, he'll continue choosing you over everything else for the rest of his life." And finally, "My wife was right, as she usually is. I'm sorry it took so long for me to do this." He took Mama's hand in one hand, still resting his other on top of mine, until I stood and helped him up to embrace him in a hug.

I'd imagined and hoped for this apology over the course of the last half a year or so, but hadn't pictured it happening like this. My heart was full, repaired even, from the wounds it endured the night I abruptly left. As I sat at the table of my caffè in the middle of Tuscany with the family I was about to marry into, a few tears streamed down my cheeks. I finally felt like an actual part of the Beletta family.

Most notably, though, I was reminded that the most important relationships we'll ever have begin with ourselves. In order to overflow your cup with goodness, you'll have to turn the faucet on yourself. Only then can others take our lead, adding to the levels of respect, care, compassion, and love we pour into ourselves daily.

I closed the caffè that day with immense gratitude for the lessons life had continually taught me, the relationships it had given me, and all that was still to come. Papa's apology was so emotionally fulfilling, providing even more reason to be surprised when it paled in comparison to what Gennaro had planned for Valentine's Day.

At 8:03pm, I walked from Gennaro's villa apartment to the water fountain outside the row of apartments, expecting to see him standing there—but he wasn't.

My phone lit up with a text.

> Gennaro: Walk around to the opposite side

He continued typing as I scanned the immediate area, trying to figure out where he was stalking my movements from. No sign of anything.

> Gennaro: Find the small candle on the ledge

I did as instructed. A small tea light was perched on the ledge of the fountain, and taped underneath was a small, folded piece of paper. I unfolded it and read the one sentence written on it.

Head to the garden.

> Mia: I've got four-inch heels on, sir

> Gennaro: Respectfully, take them off so we don't end up in the hospital

> Gennaro: And if you're worried about getting your feet dirty, don't

Easy for the guy not walking on gravel to say, but I did as instructed once again. I took a shortcut around the opposite side of the building, walking gingerly along the pebbles and using the grass as an intermittent cushion.

> Gennaro: Nice tactical shortcut skills

> Gennaro: Remember what we did the last time we were on the side of this building?

> Mia: Vividly

I approached the patch of grass he had once laid me down and filled my insides on, and found a gift bag leaning against the stone wall.

> Gennaro: Open it

> Mia: You have a lot of demands tonight

> Mia: Wherever you are

> Gennaro: I'll be inside you soon enough

Jesus Christ.

I untied the ribbon that held the bag closed and pulled it open to find a relatively modest red satin nightgown with lace trim and spaghetti straps.

> Gennaro: Put it on

> Mia: What?

Gennaro: Put it on

Mia: You want me to get naked and change into lingerie in the middle of your parents' property?

Gennaro: Put. It. On.

For shit's sake.

I changed out of the long red sweater dress that hugged my body in all the right places, assuming it was the perfect Valentine's Day outfit. Gennaro had his own ideas, however. Standing there in the relative dark, holding said sweater dress and bra in one hand and my shoes in the other, I awkwardly used whichever free fingers were available to text him again.

Mia: It's on

"I can see that," his voice sounded behind me, causing me to jump straight out of my skin. Adrenaline, blood, and every ounce of wetness that had developed from the tone of his demands were spreading like wildfire through my body as I turned to see him emerge from the bushes like he was part of a covert military operation.

Inner Critic: Black Hawk Down-Your-Pants
Mia: Enough

"Come with me. We're going to shower outside under the stars," he said, stunning me.

"We're *what?*"

"You're asking a lot of questions when you should just be doing what I tell you to do." Somehow Valentine's Day had turned my regular gentleman into a bit of a tough ass, and I was not mad about it.

"Well, it's February and I'm freezing my tits off out here," I reminded him.

He nodded and shrugged, fully understanding my dilemma and pushing me back against the wall, taking each of those aforementioned tits in his strong hands. His mouth found mine effortlessly, like it always did, silently relaying a message of unrelenting desire.

"Do not make me wait for this," I pleaded with him. "Do it right here, right now."

"Abso-fuckin-lutely not."

Walking around the side of the building, past the infamous garden where pomodoros were born during their appropriate season, we continued to the outdoor shower alongside the pool shed. A short pathway leading up to it was lit up with more tea lights, and it was then that I realized there were no other lights illuminated on the rest of the property.

"There are only six villa guests here this weekend, and Mama and Papa took them to the osteria for a 7:30pm dinner. It's only us right now."

He reached into the shower, which was well covered by a wooden door with large, thick slats, and turned the water to its hottest setting. The only openings allowing cool air in were a portion of the roof and a small opening at the bottom.

When the water hit an appropriate temperature, he pulled his sweater up and over his head, and threw it on top of the pile with my other belongings. Staring at me, frigid as I stood in the satin dress he instructed me to wear, he slowly unbuckled his belt. "I'd ask if you're cold, but those tell their own story," he said, lowering his line of sight to my nipples and then back up to regain eye contact. "Do you want to warm up under the water?"

"Yes, I do." He held the door open, watching intently as I began to slip out of my nightgown.

"Don't even think about taking that off," he said, stopping me dead in my tracks, pulling his pants down, standing completely naked a few inches away from me, his dick as rock hard as every other ripple of muscle on his body. Then, he *watched*. Gennaro watched what felt like every single drop of water drip down the length of me, clinging to the fabric as it stuck to my every curve.

Looking me up and down, his eyes assessed me like a road map he was about to take a joyride along. "I want to get down on my knees and finish you with my mouth. I want you to feel the cool air on your skin, that'll be burning hot from this water, and I want that wet fabric to weigh you down, while *I* make you feel like you're flying high at the same exact time."

I didn't respond.

I couldn't.

I walked slowly into the steady stream of hot water and vowed to focus on every sensation he was eagerly waiting to give me, with no more questions, no more thoughts, and no more interruptions. As water streamed down the front of me, sufficiently soaking the nightgown, I turned to face him, my hair on its way to being completely saturated, water pouring down my head and back.

As he predicted, my nipples poked through the fabric damn near begging to be ravaged.

He only watched, standing against the door, devouring the sight of me as the satin hugged my skin. His eyes dipped lower, and he licked his lips at the sight of whatever shape the satin had taken over my lady parts.

"Are you going to make me actually beg for you to touch me?" I asked with whatever breath I could muster.

"I might," he responded quickly in a deep, throaty voice I wasn't sure I had heard from him.

Internally, I rolled my eyes. I loved the build-up. The sensuality of small steps leading up to a grand one was every bit the romance and seduction I had always wanted, perfectly executed by the man I loved and couldn't get enough of. But if he'd made me wait another goddamn second, I would have burst at the seams.

Luckily for me, the only seams that burst were the ones belonging to the red satin nightgown he ripped off my body. In the seconds following, he'd pushed me against one wall of the shower, kneeled between my legs, hoisted one of them over his shoulder, and thrusted his tongue inside me.

Nearly immediately, I matched the rhythm of his mouth with movement from my hips, both of us riding each other in unison, my hands buried in his hair, guiding him like I held the reins of a horse, guaranteeing the pace, pressure, and location of where I wanted him. When I stopped tugging and began twitching, he honed in on all three, refusing to let up on any of them until my moan turned into a semi-muffled scream. He was right—the combination of the elements created an out-of-body experience with each of my senses heightened at the same time.

My legs weak and my knees trembling, I kneeled down between his, both of us still alarmingly naked, covered from view only by pieces of wooden slats, the sky lit up by bright, flickering stars.

My head in his hands, he lifted my chin up. "You just saw two sets of stars at the same time."

"Yes, the *hell* I did," I responded, exhaling deeply and trying to regain whatever energy was left to muster.

"That was our appetizer, *amore*. I have dinner waiting in the kitchen, and a variety of desserts, too."

"Food dessert or sexual dessert?"

"Both."

It wasn't the physical aspect of the date, or the food portion, or the gift portion that already made it the best Valentine's Day I had ever had.

Rather, it was the fact that the night had barely started, and already he had planned details in more depth than any number of previous dates combined.

In essence, it was a reminder that if you found yourself wanting more, longing for more, and in a constant state of disappointment, you weren't with the person meant for you. And the longer you chose to remain with that person, the longer you'd prevent yourself from finding the right one.

Isn't that what everyone deserves? To be loved fully, wholly, and undeniably—utterly consumed by someone who worships them, never giving them reason to doubt it?

That's what love means to me, anyway, and Gennaro was poised to remind me of it from that moment to the early hours of the following morning.

He was right…again.

Best Valentine's Day ever.

Spring

CHAPTER 29

Gennaro

MAY, THREE MONTHS LATER

"Can we go to an Italian strip club?" Allie asked with maximum excitement and zero shame as she earmuffed both daughters against her hips. While that statement was wild enough, I couldn't get over the fact that my fiancé's best friend, her kids, and four suitcases worth of belongings were at the villa to kick off two weeks of wedding events.

"Don't let Giuseppe hear you say that," I said, bending down to reintroduce myself to her girls again. They leaned into their mama's leg with shy smiles, but it wasn't long before I was playing tag with one while the other laughed.

"You get all the girls to fall in love with you easily like this?" Allie said, smiling with only a moderately accusatory tone.

"Hopefully not," Mia chimed in. "Don't want to land myself in jail so early into my hopeful Italian citizenship." After another best friend bear hug, she said, "I can't believe you're here. And this," pointing at Vincenzo, who was walking up the hill from the parking lot, "has been my favorite thing to witness."

It was the first time Vin had seen Allie since December when he and I had visited them. They talked every day, but as far as I knew, while Allie was busy finalizing divorce and custody details, they agreed to save money and simplify their lives, waiting for the wedding to reconnect.

His nose wrinkled, like he was holding back tears as he barreled up the hill to see her. Dropping a shopping bag to the ground, all six feet five inches of him scooped her petite frame into his arms like a rag doll.

"Dare I say her foot just did the Rachel McAdams kickback from *The Notebook*?" Mia whispered to me. Unashamed to admit it, I knew exactly what she was referring to.

After embracing her in a hug and planting a slow, appropriate-as-possible-with-kids-watching kiss on her lips, Vin kneeled down and waved at the girls, who were standing in front of Mia. She nudged them with a "Go ahead!" likely convincing them that although he was as big as King Kong, he was far friendlier—most of the time.

They walked slowly toward him, Velcro-ing themselves to their mom in the process. Vin pulled out two little baby dolls from the bag, one for each of them, watching intently as their smiles grew three times in size. They ripped the dolls out of his hands and ran around the fountain with them while Vin and Allie stood together with content smiles on their faces.

Kids are won over relatively easily, so long as you're a good person, which Vincenzo absolutely is. I could tell Mia liked him more and more every time she was with him. You couldn't deny an appreciation for his large stature, larger heart, and small tolerance for bullshit.

We spent the afternoon by the pool. Vincenzo's stamina for catching two kids simultaneously and repeatedly jumping into said pool did not go unnoticed by Mia.

"I think I'm going to formally induct him into the Allie Boyfriend Hall of Fame," she said loudly enough for me, but not them, to hear. "Not like it's particularly difficult to get in there, since she and I have the rap sheet that we do."

"Burn," I responded with a smile.

"You're not included on that sheet, obviously."

"Nice save." Mia shot me a smile-eye roll combo and walked over to join Allie at the edge of the patio. They dangled their feet into the pool, a floppy straw hat on Allie and oversized sunglasses on Mia, both with a glass of wine in hand.

Mia's phone dinged, signaling the Luciano family was beginning their travel. Scheduled to arrive tomorrow, we'd pick them up from the airport in separate cars. Pesca would bring Santino, Sophia, and their granddaughter back to the villa where they'd watch Allie's girls, too. Mia's brother, sister, and brother-in-law would come with Mia and me and stay in Rome overnight for the bachelor and bachelorette celebration. With a couple rooms reserved at the hotel across the street, there'd be enough sleeping room for all of us.

"Okay, so really no strip clubs?" Allie asked again, this time with Giuseppe within earshot.

"We're hitting the clubs?!"

I know my brother well, that's for sure.

A bottle of champagne popped in the kitchen, which was alarming, given that we'd all been drinking since 4pm and the clock was about to strike 7pm.

"Should I be worried that my date has asked to go to a strip club twice in twenty-four hours?" Vincenzo jokingly asked, nuzzling his mouth into the crook of Allie's neck.

Giuseppe began researching, phone in one hand and champagne in the other, with Mia's brother Lenny providing input whenever asked. The two of them were a bond we didn't see coming, but should have. The brother Lenny always wanted, who was about to bring him to an Italian strip club, was apparently all it took to get on his good side.

Giovanni and Dominique, still going strong, were across the street at the hotel in one room doing Lord knows what, and Mia's sister and brother-in-law were in another, sleeping off their jet lag. Salvatore had arrived and was cracking open champagne bottles in the kitchen, and Marco, my *old* partner, was meeting us out after his shift.

Gang's all here.

The balcony doors were open, allowing everyone to easily mingle from the terrace to the kitchen and back, and while Mia and Sal were talking in the kitchen, I quickly snuck down the hallway into my bedroom to change. I settled on black dress pants, a maroon button down, black leather belt, and dress shoes. A knock sounded at the door and in walked Mia, looking me up and down like she'd prefer to be eating rather than drinking the champagne she was holding.

"One more spray of that cologne and…I don't even know," she not-so-joked.

I sprayed two more.

"I know that look," I said, pulling her closer to me by the waistband of her pants, planting a kiss on her lips, and reminding her, "but dinner is in a half hour, and I need you dressed for that, not naked, unfortunately."

She looked at me, briefly considered what I'd said, and then looked toward the closet. A deep-red satin dress hung, begging to be worn by her. She slowly peeled her clothes off while I watched, the corner of my mouth stretched into a sly grin, my eyes hungrily surveying every last inch of her.

"Don't look at me like that when you're the one telling me I can't be naked."

A thunderous crash came from the kitchen, and I instinctively rolled my eyes but was secretly grateful for the distraction. "Giuseppe or Salvatore?"

"Could even be Lenny," she reminded me.

"Good point." I took a jacket out of the closet and went in for another kiss. "You look insanely beautiful, by the way."

"I'm not even dressed yet."

"I already imagined it in my head," I said, winking at her. "Meet you outside."

I stopped in the bathroom to brush my teeth, then walked toward the kitchen. Whatever had fallen was already cleaned up by the time I got there, so I poured a glass of champagne for myself and headed to the balcony.

"We're leaving for dinner in fifteen minutes," I told anyone listening.

"Okay, thanks, Dad." Impossibly, Giuseppe was even more immature when he drank, but I loved him, nonetheless.

Salvatore whistled, and Lenny, who was standing next to him, looked both mortified and appalled. Their reactions could only mean one thing: Mia looked drop dead gorgeous and was standing behind me.

Turning around felt like a preview of our wedding day. The stretchy satin fabric hugged her hips perfectly, the straight-edge hem hitting a few inches above her knees. Spaghetti straps crossed in the back, and a drapey V-neck lightly skimmed the top of her cleavage. She wore the *Ti Amo* necklace I got her in Florence and thin gold hoops. Gold high-heels with a crystal t-strap completed the look.

I exhaled loudly, scratching my chin, and for the first time in a while had a hard time finding appropriate words.

Sal didn't. "*Gesù Cristo*, Gennaro is definitely getting into a fight tonight."

Allie chimed in next. "Italy looks good on you, my girl, but why aren't you wearing white?"

"Mostly because it's not my wedding day, why?" Mia responded curiously.

"Wrongfully assumed you'd want to stand out as the *bride* for the night," Allie joked.

"I don't want to stand out. I want *him*," Mia said, looking at me, then back at Allie, "and I want to enjoy spending time with the rest of you. That's it."

Allie sipped the last of her champagne with a raised eyebrow. "Should have worn a different dress, sister."

Dinner was perfect, and while I had originally planned to do it in a new location, the owner of the rooftop across the street offered us unmatched menu selections, a complimentary round of drinks, and our own private section with live music. It was also still my favorite ambiance the city had to offer, so there was no need to reinvent the wheel.

That wasn't my style. I was loyal to those who took care of me and did the same in return.

I toasted Mia and thanked our crew for coming. Somewhere in between dessert and far too many espresso martinis, all the cocktails consumed since late afternoon had undeniably started to settle into our systems.

"OH. MY. GOD." Allie sat on the other side of Mia, her mouth wide open as Mia tried to clamp it shut. "*This* is the rooftop you had sex on?!"

The entire restaurant went radio silent, Mia's cheeks

turned red, and I tried my best not to get hot at the thought of it.

"Are you *trying* to make me throw up my highly expensive Italian dinner?" Lenny asked, complete with gagging sounds.

"On that note, are we ready to hit a club now?" I tried changing the subject, but was prevented from doing so.

Salvatore couldn't help himself. "We are absolutely not going anywhere until there's more information shared on this sexual development."

Vincenzo always knew when a situation needed fixing. This one was entertaining, but a bit of a mood killer with my future in-laws talking about sex as it related to their sister, my fiancé. "Gennaro said we're ready to leave, so let's leave." He stood up, urging everyone to follow his lead, and then made Allie and Giuseppe the happiest two people in the place.

"I know a strip club we can go to."

"So, are we supposed to look at the girls or..." Allie was unsure of strip club etiquette but was determined to learn it.

"I have no idea," Mia responded.

Allie tried answering her own question. "Seems rude if we don't, kind of like lesbians if we do, but I'd rather err on the side of not being rude, no?"

I stepped in with an assist. "I can assure you they don't care so long as you give them some money."

"I've got you, babe," Vincenzo said, handing her some bills and sending the mother of two on her way with her new stripper friends. I was slightly amazed that Allie hadn't railroaded him with questions. She didn't care if he knew them personally or any other details that most women would have asked unlimited questions about. When he walked over to her, she kissed him with the passion of ten women, and it was then that I realized she simply trusted him.

"I love this place!" She swung around a makeshift pole between the leather couches we were sitting on, Vincenzo watching with immense pride. Mia's sister and her husband appeared to be falling asleep in the corner, and thankfully, Giuseppe, Salvatore, and Lenny had walked to the front of the club to wait for Giovanni, Dominique, and Marco.

As Mia sat with her legs draped over my lap, sipping on water to hydrate, I couldn't help but laugh. I never voluntarily spent my time at strip clubs. I didn't feel the need to slip my hard-earned money to complete strangers and preferred to go to a local bar instead. But all I needed was to spend my time with her while our friends joined us, and a majority of them were clearly enjoying themselves.

I scratched up and down the length of Mia's leg, slipped her shoes off, and rubbed her feet while it was only the few of us, assuming that Stella, unlike Lenny, was able to handle the sight of me touching her sister.

By the time they all returned to our booth, her shoe had been replaced and Lenny was none the wiser. We said hello to Giovanni and Dominique, and while I caught up with Marco, Mia's multiple glasses of water turned into a need-to-go-now bathroom visit. She motioned to me that she was headed there, to which I delivered a non-verbal "Please let me go with you." A hand in the air, Mia assured me she was fine and would be right back.

Women's bathroom lines in a strip club were short since a majority of the women in the establishment were on stage dancing. Nevertheless, I watched her walk into the restroom and refused to take my eyes off the area until she walked back out of it. A few minutes later, the door opened, her eyes squinted to adjust to the darkness surrounding her, and we locked eyes. Her mouth softened into a smile, but as quickly as it came, it vanished, a large body towering over her from the side.

My line of sight shifted immediately to the arm that had found its way around the small of her waist, attempting to pull her in closely. Anyone paying attention to her body's natural response to pull away—her neck stretched backward and the palms of both hands on his chest to create distance—would realize she was uncomfortable.

He didn't initially take note, but somewhere between the blood and adrenaline spreading rapidly through my veins, my hands instinctively clenched into protective fists. I watched Mia speak to him calmly until he took a step backward, hands in the air.

I intentionally but slowly walked toward them, avoiding any unnecessary altercation that would ruin our night, mostly in an effort to let her shine.

Was I there to protect her? *Always.*

Did I know she was absolutely capable of defusing a situation on her own? *So long as she wasn't dealing with a sociopath, yes.*

As I approached, Mia's smile reappeared, her hand outstretched toward me. I pulled her close with unmistakable eye contact that slowly moved in his direction.

"*Scusami,*" he pardoned himself, walking away without hesitation.

It was time to dance with my fiancé.

I pulled her close by the small of her back, my mouth hovering over her ear, and whispered, "*Vuoi ballare, amore?*"

My mind rewound to the first night I had uttered that

same phrase to her on a dance floor down the street. Now, with music playing loudly in the background, rays of light bouncing off every part of her face illuminating her gray eyes, perfectly pink lips, and neckline, I was reminded how I fell so quickly for her in the first place. Striking beauty combined with a quiet confidence that made jaws drop, both literally and figuratively. When she nodded "yes," I took her hand in mine, gently pulling her through the crowd to a tucked-away spot on the dance floor.

My hands held her waist tightly, as close to me as space would allow, and I softly brushed my lips along the most sensitive part of her neck. Our hearts picked up pace, heat radiated off our skin, and I assumed she felt every last butterfly in her stomach, as I did in my own.

It felt like our first time—*a second time*—and all that was buzzing around us disappeared.

"*Tu sei l'amore della mia vita*," I said, holding her head in my hands, lifting her chin so her mouth would meet mine. "You are the absolute love of my life. Do you realize that?"

Mia smiled shyly, wanting to answer but rendered silent in the middle of a strip club in Rome with all our closest friends and family surrounding us.

"Do you?"

She answered the only way she knew how to in that moment—*with her lips*. They softly brushed up against mine as I breathed her in. Remnants of her perfume surrounded me, the taste of sweet, strawberry lip gloss staining my lips as we continued kissing. We danced slowly, steadily, our mouths never farther away from the other's than necessary. Where I moved, she followed, never breaking stride, never letting me lessen my grasp on her.

Forever was about to begin with the love of my life, and still, somehow, it didn't feel like it would be long enough.

CHAPTER 30

Mia

It took a few days to recover from just one night in Rome with our entire crew, but being back in Tuscany had a way of both reinvigorating and relaxing us. Reconnecting with my parents, and having both our families and closest friends occupying all of the villas with no unknown guests on property, felt like a dream. A vacation destination was my new home.

I could barely recall what day it was, but when I woke up the morning of my shower, sun rays burned through the window, heating up my skin as I lay alone in Gennaro's bed. Finishing touches on our new house had taken longer than expected, but it didn't feel quite right moving in before actually being married, given the family history behind the house. When I rolled over in his villa apartment bed and realized he wasn't next to me, I noticed a small gold gift bag next to his empty pillow.

Inner Critic: So, let me get this straight
Inner Critic: It's not okay to live in the house
together before you're married

*Inner Critic: But sleeping in his villa's bed together
is okay?*
Mia: Shush, you sound like my mom.

Propping myself up on an elbow, I took the envelope from the bag and read the card inside, wrongfully assuming it was from Gennaro.

Mia,
To the ray of sunlight who has changed this family forever...
Ever since you've become a part of Gennaro's life, he has brightened in spirit and lightened in demeanor. I am eternally grateful for your impact on him—and all of us.
My biggest hope for you both is to live a life filled with love, good health, and happiness, never taking each other for granted, and always honestly and genuinely communicating your feelings toward each other.
Enjoy today, your wedding day, and all the days that follow.
And always remember, bright lights allow others to follow their paths with ease and comfort. Thank you for being a beacon of light for this family.
Mama

Tears rolled down my cheeks, staining the paper I was holding. What had happened with Papa made me doubt that I'd ever *really* be accepted into their family. I was a family girl at heart, so how would I be able to marry into one where the patriarch couldn't seem to stand me?

The conversation at the caffè with Papa provided reassurance that he understood how deeply in love I was with his son. It wasn't necessarily the romantic aspect of it, since none of us knew him to be a true believer in any of that, but he seemed to grasp the idea that marrying his son meant being a part of villa life and carrying on Beletta family traditions.

Now, Mama's note in hand, any remaining doubts or worries were removed.

I took the bag with me and headed toward the kitchen to find her.

It looked like white and beige tulle had exploded everywhere. More bodies than I had ever seen in the kitchen at one time were shuffling around each other, focused on the tasks at hand. And Mama, who saw me coming down the steps out of the corner of her eye, yelled at me, lovingly, to get out.

"*Dai, vai via*! Go, go, go!"

My mom quickly ran over to hug me good morning. "We have lots of surprises, my baby. I can't wait!" My sister waved at me from the corner where she was working, blissfully alone in silence, exactly how she liked it. The boys appeared to be moving tables and chairs outside, and I could see Allie and Vincenzo in the pool with the kids, likely on their hundredth catch and release of the day, just shy of 10am.

Parent life.

Then, Gennaro appeared in the doorway. "It's supposed to be a surprise, *amore*."

"I know, but I wanted to thank her for the card she wrote, and I wanted to open the gift with her." His body blocked me from seeing any of what was happening behind him in the kitchen, but Mama heard me and yelled back.

"Sweet girl, those are special gifts for your wedding day, but we can open them together later if you'd like. Now, *vai*, go get ready and get out of here." Mama smiled, swatting the air for me to leave.

Back at the upper level of villa apartments, I sat at one of the patio tables, lying back in the chair, feet propped up, allowing myself to enjoy the kiss of Tuscan sun on my skin. The sounds of birds chirping surrounded me, along with the stream of the waterfall from the main fountain and a couple cars in the distance.

The staff had successfully kept *Vero Caffè* afloat during our time in Rome as well as after we arrived back in Tuscany. I had stopped in at varying times to show my family and Allie, all of them beyond proud and impressed by Gennaro's initiative, vision, and execution, as well as the way I'd made it my own with the menu and decor.

Life had officially come full circle. Relatively accidental manifestations had landed me on the exact street in Rome I was meant to be on to meet the love of my life. And now, I was about to prepare for my bridal shower with our family and closest friends on the property we'd work at and live on for what I assumed would be the rest of our lives.

I couldn't have been happier.

Or so I thought.

Two hours later, after taking my sweet time getting ready—*as instructed*—I benefited from the greatest hair and makeup day of my life.

The blow dry was slow and low for frizz-free hair. The curling iron curled, the flat iron flattened, and the side part fell perfectly to the proper side of my head. It was millennial nirvana, and I hadn't even gotten dressed yet in the outfit I'd been dying to wear since finding it in Rome.

On the same day I had unceremoniously found my wedding gown, in a shop that Gina, the front desk receptionist, had suggested, I also bought my bridal shower dress.

It was not lost on me that a lot of the things women waited their entire life for in regards to getting married were things I either let other people handle or I quickly, effortlessly, and slyly took care of on my own without fanfare. I guess there was something to be said for focusing on the most important part of the marriage: Gennaro and me.

I pulled the nude-colored dress over my head, down the curves of my body. My skin, a glistening bronze thanks to the last couple weeks of warm weather, was a darker contrast to the beige undertones of the dress itself. Trading in my hoop earrings for small, crystal studs, I heard someone behind me.

"Can you wear these instead, please?" I spun around to find Gennaro leaning in the doorway holding a small box with a shy smile on his face, shaking his head like he couldn't be more pleased at the sight in front of him.

"What is it?"

"You'll have to open it and find out, but first, in case I haven't told you enough," he said, spinning me around and looking me over from head to toe, "you take my goddamn breath away."

My eyes rolled automatically with a smile attached, like I still hadn't gotten used to the genuine compliments he'd give me on a daily basis. Opening the small white box he had given me took *my* breath away as I stared at a pair of diamond earrings.

"Are you out of your mind?" I asked him, wide eyed,

mouth agape, wondering briefly if he had a secret life I wasn't aware of that brought in thousands of extra dollars per month.

> *Inner Critic: Oooooh, maybe he's mafia*
> *Inner Critic: Like shoot-you-in-the-head-while-*
> *eating-dinner-with-your-family mafia*
> *Inner Critic: Or blow-up-the-car-your-new-wife-is-*
> *sitting-in mafia*
> *Mia: Were those Godfather movie references on the*
> *day of my bridal shower?*
> *Inner Critic: Perhaps*
> *Mia: Could you not?*
> *Inner Critic: Leave the gun, take the cannoli*
> *Mia: Seriously, stop*

"When it comes to you, apparently yes, I am," he responded. "Just say thank you."

"Thank you."

He kissed me softly. "Let me help you put them on. I've got a bridal shower to get you to."

We walked hand in hand down the stairs into the kitchen, which was now spotless. Two glasses of champagne were perched on the island counter. Handing me one, Gennaro kissed the top of my head, took my hand in his, and led me outside.

Somehow, this family event planning crew had nailed simple yet elegant. One long rectangular table was set with ivory cloths and beige tulle delicately gathered in bunches from one end to the other. Twinkle lights were illuminated underneath with white rose petals sprinkled throughout.

Gold chargers lay underneath gold-trimmed ivory plates and cutlery. Sparkling Pellegrino bubbled in amber water glasses. White floral arrangements spanned the length of the table with small gold frames that held black and white photos of Gennaro and me.

A few speakers hidden subtly throughout the patio landscaping lightly broadcasted what sounded like Gennaro's Italian love song playlist. I knew it well, having listened to it frequently ever since the night we'd met. Across the patio, under white blossoming tree cover, was a giant gold, beige, and tan balloon arch that read "amore". I wasn't convinced this was an actual Italian thing as much as it was a *Mia's American, so let's do some American stuff* type thing, but I loved it, nonetheless.

After taking it all in, I realized I was squeezing Gennaro's hand so hard I was likely cutting off circulation.

"You okay, *amore*?"

Was I ever.

"Truly never been better." I kept looking around. "A little bit overwhelmed that they did all of this for us, I think."

My mom overheard me, wrapped her arms around me from behind, and whispered in my ear, "Wait until your wedding day, my girl."

I turned and returned the squeeze, then did the same with Mama.

"The bride is here! *Finalmente*," Allie chimed in.

I hugged her tightly as her girls ran to me, gold princess wands in hand.

Salvatore's mom, Mrs. Rosa, introduced me to her daughters, Sal's two sisters, and two of her and Mama's friends from up the road. Giovanni's girlfriend happily greeted me next, then sat down next to my sister and started playing with my niece, her own baby fever on clear display. She had solidified herself as a sister-in-law in training based solely on how excited for Gennaro and me she was, and how supportive she had been throughout the entire "road to the wedding."

Last but not least was Pesca, who I caught in my peripheral walking outside from the kitchen, a large platter of roasted, marinated vegetables; fresh cut chunks of cheese and sliced meats; and crusty bread right out of the oven in hand. She winked at me, placed it in the middle of the table set for fourteen, and instructed Gennaro, "All of the men are up at the tables by the villa smoking cigars."

He smiled. "That's it? I'm getting kicked out now that I got the bride here on time?"

"Yes, exactly," she responded. "Someone needs to go make sure they all behave. And Papa was asking for you."

The previous night, before drifting off to sleep, Gennaro and I shared that we hadn't had quality time with our parents since everyone arrived. From the bachelor and bachelorette party to a few days of recovery to now, there hadn't been a time or place that allowed for the six of us to sit down and enjoy each other's company.

"Maybe ask Papa if he wants to have dinner like we talked about?" I urged.

"I'm on it." After a kiss on the lips, he was off up the hill to the villa tables.

I turned to see my sister, the gal historically known for not speaking much at all let alone in a semi-public setting, clinking her champagne glass in an effort to get everyone's attention. "I'd like to say a few words in honor of my sister, but the moms asked to go first."

All guests except Mama, my mom, and my sister sat down. They motioned for me to be seated at the head of the table. With Pesca to my left, Mama began her speech.

"I wrote much of what I wanted to say to Mia in a

letter, but most importantly, for all of you here, I wanted to say what an honor it has been to witness someone with a heart like hers, that has healed and repaired the heart of my son. I believe Gennaro is everything a *good* man should be. As a mother, you always hope your child will end up with someone who completes them, who adds to them, who builds them up, and doesn't detract from them in any way." She paused briefly and began again. "None of this was planned. We were all very surprised and uncertain as old, outdated plans were changed, *refused* even."

A few side-eyes were exchanged through the crowd. I couldn't see them, but I could certainly feel them. Mama continued, "Quickly, I realized my son was creating the life he wanted, and mostly, that he deserves. Nothing has ever made me happier. So, thank you, Mia, for bringing the best out of our family, for being the partner my son wants, and for teaching all of us how important real, true love is. It is the basis of life's greatest relationships, and you've sparked it back into our entire family."

My back was to those sitting behind me, but I could hear sniffling from several before Mama added one more sentiment. "And to Sophia, for sharing your daughter with me, one that I will soon proudly call my own."

My mom hugged Mama tightly, looked out toward our table, and, as I could have predicted, began crying on the spot. "Oh my *gawd*, I'm crying."

"None of us are surprised," my sister reminded her with a smile, "but please keep in mind that we have limited daylight left."

"You sound like your father. Anyway, I'm just so happy," she continued, more tears ensuing, "and, I, uhm, oh my goodness. How do I put this? Mia is the person in our family who brings everyone together. *She's* the party. And…when I think of her not being an hour's drive away, my heart hurts." She paused to collect her thoughts. "I'm sorry, I don't mean to make it sound like I'm upset, but of course I am, my baby is living in a totally different country…"

My sister, wide eyed and standing to the side of my mom, shook her head briefly while likely devising a plan to stop the ship from completely sinking. Finally, she stepped in. "Okay, I'm not much of a talker, but before this one turns the bridal shower into a funeral, this isn't anything we ever envisioned for our family." Taking a breath, the usually stoic Stella had to hold back her own tears.

"Our family is a close one. I've never pictured a life where I didn't see my sister at every event or where I couldn't see a future niece or nephew frequently, if they have one. This is all an adjustment. But the more I've watched her and Gennaro, the more I've realized that most of her memories may be back home with us, but her heart and her future are here with him and all of you."

Stella finished her thoughts with more emotional words than I'd ever heard her string together. "Life is unpredictable, but when you live with the number of balls that my sister does—sorry, can I say that?"

"*Palle!*" Mama threw her support in the ring.

"Thank you, yes, that, when you live with *palle*, things like this happen. You find your soulmate five thousand miles away and you create your own version of happiness. I'm so proud of her, even though it'll tear me apart the minute I get home. Which is what love is all about, I guess. I am happiest when she is happiest, and in my heart, I know this is where my sister belongs…" There wasn't a dry eye in the house. "To Mia's new family and *our* new family. *Salute.*"

For the next couple hours, we sat, ate, drank, and shared stories as families and as friends. Tales of old Italian days as well as stories from Sal's sisters—mainly about how they used to have crushes on Vincenzo and Gennaro, but also how happy they were that he was marrying me, not Francesca.

Thank goodness for that.

Somewhere between too-much-champagne and not-enough-risotto o'clock, Allie appeared to be gearing up to say a few words herself.

Inner Critic: Oh dear

"My best friend found the love of her *fucking* life!"

Inner Critic: Stop her

"And I think I did, too…"

Inner Critic: Why are you still not moving?

"But we haven't done it on a rooftop in Ro—"

Mia: Okay, you're right
Inner Critic: Duh

"Okayyyyy, Prosecco Princess, that's enough." Just then, as luck would have it, the guys came walking down the hill to join us.

Gennaro, with a smile on his face that lit up the outdoors as much as the sun ever could, held my face with both hands, looked me up and down, and asked, "Are you happy?"

"Better than any shower I could have asked for."

"Good. Papa's about to make it even better." He winked, sat me down, held Papa by the arm, and walked him closer to Mama. With a whistle to signal everyone to quiet down, Gennaro spoke first.

"*Grazie mille* to all of you. The love and support surrounding us is so strong, but while I'm so happy to be celebrating *our* love and *our* wedding, Papa has something he'd like to say and do."

Gennaro stepped to the side, and Papa waved his cane to everyone in attendance. Since arriving home from the hospital, his breathing was labored and he sounded at times like it hurt to even talk. Refusing surrender, he stood as tall as his body allowed, thanked those in attendance for being there, nodding to my family and me in particular, before turning to Mama.

Handing his cane to Gennaro, holding on to the edge of her chair to support his weight, Papa slowly crouched down on one knee. Taking her hand in his, he swallowed deeply and surprised all of us, Mama especially.

"*Amore*, I am an imperfect man—impatient, hard-headed, and insensitive. I often wish I could erase so many of our years together to go back and start them all over again, but I can't. All I can do is take control of now and what's left of our future." Gennaro handed him a small box, and a few gasps sounded from the table behind me. Papa opened the box and continued, "Many years ago, I gave you this ring. You refused to wear it, hating that someone had decided our fate to marry. I was too young to grasp the idea of romance, love, affection, or adoration, but as parents often do, I've learned about all of those things from watching our sons. In recent weeks, I've real-ized they've learned all of these things—from you."

A tear streamed down Mama's cheek and landed on the hand Papa was holding. He wiped it away, took the ring from the box, and looked back up at her. "I cannot make up for my shortcomings as a husband for all of these years, but it's important to me that you know I was being the husband I *thought* I had to be for our family. I now realize I wasn't being the husband *you* needed or wanted, and that is what breaks my heart. So even though we are already married, I would like to propose to you again—properly this time."

Her single tear turned to multiple tears, but Mama kept her composure as best she could. "Giovanna Tonelli Beletta, I may have screwed up my first proposal to you as well as many years in between then and now, but I refuse to make any of those mistakes ever again. Will you marry me and let me show you over and over again how much I love, appreciate, adore, and respect you from today until the day I draw my last breath?"

Mama's chest rippled up and down as she attempted to keep her crying to a minimum. Wiping tears from her eyes and holding Papa's face in her hands, she leaned over to kiss him, then slid out of her chair to kneel in front of him.

She wrapped her arms tightly around his neck and stayed there for a good long while. Finally, she sat back and said, "Our marriage brought us our three sons, this beautiful property, and these beautiful people who are here today. No one is perfect, and our life certainly isn't, but no one's is. This is *our* love story, and without it, Mia and Gennaro's would look quite different, too. It has all led us here, regardless of mistakes, and I would not change any of it except one thing."

Papa smiled sweetly. "What's that, *amore*?"

"I will say yes, so long as you take me on a proper date."

"One step ahead of you," he said, reaching into his back pocket and pulling out an envelope.

Inner Critic: Maybe this is where Gennaro gets it?
Mia: ::sniffling::
Inner Critic: Oh Christ, get it together, lady

Mama opened the envelope and pulled out a short note she read aloud. "Meet me at the fountain next Thursday at 8pm. And wear red."

Inner Critic: Those poor pomodoros

Mama cried and kissed Papa some more, and they both stood to enjoy each other's embrace to the fullest. Whether or not Papa had been coached by Gennaro, this simple act of romance seemed to have the power to erase years of disappointment and let down.

That's how women are. So long as you listen to understand us and at least *try* to speak our love languages, a whole lot can be forgiven. Be consistent, be loyal, be thoughtful, and mostly, be present—in our daily lives and in our hearts, throughout the entire journey of life.

Love is more than occasional bouquets, cards, housework, and financial stability.

True love, consuming love, life-altering love, is giving of oneself to another to wholly understand that person— how they *want* to be loved, how they *need* to be loved, and how they *deserve* to be loved.

Gennaro had set his bar high and raised it every day since.

Papa had taken notes and decided that later was better than never.

As for Mama?

She was already planning which shade of red she was going to wear.

A girl after my own heart.

CHAPTER 31

Gennaro

The amount of champagne, Prosecco, and wine that had been consumed in the last two weeks was quite impressive, but not nearly as impressive as watching Papa and Mama make up for forty-plus years of lost romance in the course of a few days.

Papa was intentional with his romantic gestures and displays of affection, kinder than I had ever seen him and more vocal than I had ever heard him. The man who buried himself in home projects and work for years upon years had taken a full one-hundred-and-eighty-degree detour toward being a doting husband, and I hadn't quite figured out if it was the time he spent recovering, witnessing the journey toward our wedding, or a bit of both that allowed for mental clarity. Most importantly, I didn't care, and Mama didn't either. She hadn't kept a score sheet of all the ways he may have disappointed her in the past, and she didn't accept his newfound romantic side only to berate him for years past.

In essence, they had started off with a clean slate, and it was one of my favorite things to watch.

Pesca's, too, apparently.

"Would never have thought I'd witness Papa escorting Mama off property for a date while we sat here and watched," she said to Mia and me as we sipped wine while the sun began its descent. Everyone else was in varying places, and while the excitement of the last week and a half was more than I had cumulatively experienced, it was also a bit exhausting. Sitting in relative silence for the last hour, Mia reading a book with her legs slung over mine and Pesca having walked the property for her daily exercise, was every bit of relaxation we needed.

"Who knew Papa had it in him?" I asked no one in particular.

"Maybe his time with Michael all those years ago rubbed off on him." Each time Pesca spoke of her late husband, she'd briefly close her eyes in what seemed like an attempt to bring his face into focus. She'd smile, inhale deeply with her hand on her chest, then exhale. When her eyes re-opened, it was clear that the residual breakage in her heart had resurfaced. "Which reminds me…"

Opening the small backpack she almost always carried with her, Pesca removed a small white box, handed it to Mia, and looked at me. "I'm handing it to her because she'll be the one wearing it, but it's meant for both of you." She paused, forcing herself to hold back any tears that threatened to squeeze their way out, then continued, "I haven't worn this since the day of his funeral. Michael was the love of my life, every bit as much a gentleman as he was a romantic. I miss him so much, but watching you two fall in love has helped my heart heal quite unexpectedly. I don't have kids of my own to pass it down to, and I'd rather give it to you now as your *something old.*"

Mia removed the top to find a thin, gold chain bracelet

with the letter G. Garmo was her married name, but the nod to Gennaro was not lost on Mia and me.

"Garmo and Gennaro—the G is interchangeable as it relates to our love stories," she said putting her hand on my knee and holding Mia's hand in hers. "I adore you both, and I'm so incredibly proud of you."

Champagne and tears are a common theme in wedding festivities, and tonight was no different. I clasped the bracelet on Mia's wrist and could tell she had no plans of ever removing it.

"We've come a long way since 'the morning after' in Rome, haven't we?" Mia reminded her, and Pesca winked in agreement.

"We sure have, my darling. One more thing, by the way." Mia and I looked to Pesca to fill us in. "I'll be bringing a date to the wedding."

The following morning, the day before the wedding, everyone was buzzing with anticipation. An event planning team had been hired to coordinate details so our families could enjoy themselves, so I didn't know many of the specifics.

Mia had clarified early on that her only requests were good music and good food, which was out of character, since her event planning background seemingly lent itself to a desire to be in control of the details for the "most important day in a woman's life."

In her own words, though, "I want a lifetime of great memories with the man I love over the pressure that one day carries with it. I don't like flowers enough to care which kind we have, and I don't need to weigh in on table-cloths. Just give me delicious food and a refreshing drink, hold me close on the dance floor, and take pictures so I can remember it all."

Strike me with lightning if I didn't hit the future-wife jackpot.

We walked over to the caffè for exercise, alone time, and to check on the staff. Tables were nearly all filled, and one gal was working the oven, another was behind the counter, and the last one was serving customers. Guests seemed happy, the place was clean, my Italian playlist piped through the speakers, and Mia looked happy as could be—until the door opened behind us and Francesca appeared in the doorway.

So much for alone time.

"I come in peace," she said with a hand in the air. "I saw you cross the street and wanted to say congratulations."

Our eyebrows raised in unison, slightly suspicious, but when she motioned toward an empty table, I sat down with her while Mia checked in with the girls. "I meant the *congratulations*, I really did." Staring at me with sad eyes, I wasn't necessarily convinced that she had moved on, but her next words surprised me. "The last time I was here, Mia shared some insight with me. And I wanted to thank her."

Maybe there's hope after all.

Mia sat between us with half a smile conveying moderate skepticism. I was satisfied knowing I no longer had to prove that, as harsh as it sounded, Francesca meant nothing to me. Still, having to deal with her at all was still exhausting.

"What kind of insight?" I asked directly, trying to get to her end goal.

"She told me to focus on one thing every day that brought me fulfillment and contentment, and that by focusing on myself, life would sort of…work itself out."

"How's it working?" Mia asked curiously.

"I've been dating the son of a loyal customer for the last two months, so I'd say it's going pretty well." She blushed, dipped her head, and smiled, avoiding eye contact with me but smiling at and with Mia. "He's amazing, and…" she said, looking directly at me, "no one is forcing him to marry me."

Somehow, I had gotten accidentally roped into girl talk, but if it was leading to the close of an unwanted chapter of my life, I'd follow along accordingly. "You deserve someone who loves every part of you and who chooses to marry you himself. Nothing less," I said. She smiled softly, as I finished with "I mean that."

Francesca's eyes turned glassy. She squeezed my hand and stood up to hug Mia. Women are interesting. Sure, men can have solid relationships with our friends, but we're generally simpler, less chatty, and less emotional. Women? They have the ability to love and hate so deeply, and to switch between the two at an alarmingly fast rate. There was no time or energy left to judge the situation, though, and I was happy that white flags had been waved, insight was shared, and closure followed.

After she left, we stayed until closing time, finally alone after the staff left, with only the sound of music surrounding us.

"Want to practice dancing for our wedding?" I held out my hand, and she looked at it curiously.

"No, I'd rather freestyle for our wedding," she responded, "but I do want to dance with you one last time before I'm a married woman."

"Why one last time before you're married?" I pulled her to my chest, one arm tightly wrapped around her waist, the other holding her hand to my heart.

"Everyone says marriage changes things. So does living

together for years," she said, deep in thought, not doubting her desire to *get* married but definitely hesitating at the thought of what could come—or, more accurately, could change—with it.

"*Amore*," I said, leaning backward so she could see my full face, "I can't promise you what the future holds, but I *can* promise you that I will never, ever become complacent." I pushed some hair away from her face, and she took hold of my hand, kissing the side of my thumb.

We stayed there, staring into the soul of the other, for an undisclosed amount of time. It felt like hours but was surely only minutes, slowly swaying back and forth in each other's embrace, kissing passionately and saying very few words.

When we'd had our fill, life having finally paused long enough for us to gratefully remember all that had occurred to bring us here, we closed the shop and walked back to the villa, starving for dinner.

"And where have you two been?" Allie was sitting down, a glass of wine in one hand, one kid dangling with hope and a prayer over the wall of the fountain and the other splashing from the other side.

"Checked on the restaurant. You missed us?" I said while Mia wrangled the kids.

Grabbing the shirt collar of one before taking an accidental swim in the oversized and glorified bird bath, she kindly asked the other to stop splashing. "If the fountain is empty, the wedding will be canceled, and you won't get to wear your pretty dress."

Worked like a charm.

"Missed you a little, but mostly I'm in withdrawal," Allie answered.

"From your Italian bodyguard of a boyfriend?"

"Perhaps."

"I feel like that's my cue to leave," I interjected before I was enlisted in more girl talk than I was capable of handling in one day. Unfortunately, they both motioned for me to sit down.

"Cheer up, buttercup," Mia urged her. "You're in the most beautiful place on Earth, with healthy kids—so long as they don't dive headfirst into that fountain over there— we've got a Tuscan wedding to go to tomorrow, and you're in love with a groomsman, so you've got a guaranteed wedding hookup."

They both smiled. "Nearly all of our best memories include the path to 'find a man.' We dreamt about it, fanta-sized about it, lived it, regretted it, and kept on with it, at times *painstakingly.*" Her voice took a serious tone out of nowhere, which I assumed was female code for "about to shed some tears." "If I haven't told you yet, I'm *really* freaking proud of you."

I was right about the tears.

"We've been dreaming of this since we're little, we've been there for each other through every single heartache, reminding each other who the hell we accepted way less than we deserved. And now, your decision to come here brought each of us the man we didn't know existed." Allie continued like I wasn't in the vicinity.

Mia pulled a tissue from her purse and handed it to her. She held onto one herself, too. "Maybe the right men *did* exist and *do* exist, but we had to work on ourselves before ever having a chance of finding them," she suggested.

"Men like this don't exist in America, Mia."

"Italy brought out my most confident, independent self," Mia said, reflecting on her own journey, and while I still felt like a fly on the non-existent wall, it was interesting to hear how the woman who accidentally stole my heart came to be. "The man of my dreams was on the right street at the right time. For the first time in my life, I tried to think the least and live the most. A man fell for me, and me for him, and things simply...*worked.*"

She looked to Allie for a response, but when there wasn't one, she continued. "All I'm saying is, maybe the heartbreak and uncertainty prepares us to accept this moment when it presents itself, when it's the right time. Maybe it's less about *where* we find them and more about who we are when they find *us.*"

That's my girl. Being her best self, effortlessly, which was exactly how I found her.

"Okay, I know I just shed some tears in an uncharacteristic display of raw emotion, but this is some Carrie Bradshaw shit you're spewing."

Mia's eyebrow wrinkled and her head shook back and forth. "You're hungry, aren't you?

"Yes, why?"

"Because you turn into an asshole when you're hungry."

It was time for dinner.

All five of us walked into the kitchen. Mama and Sophia were at the stove, and Papa and Santino were talking at the dinner table. Our brothers, sisters, and in-laws were hanging in the living room while Pesca helped Allie prepare plates for the kids.

I was unsure whether calm and casual was normal the night before a wedding but thankful for it, regardless. Everyone was relaxing, sipping on something and excited to enjoy some of Mama's home cooking.

"Help me set the table, soon-to-be groom," Pesca said,

enlisting me to help after corralling Allie's kids at a small table in the corner. "How are you feeling, by the way?"

"Doesn't feel like it's real. It feels like tomorrow's going to be another regular day," I responded. It felt like the calm before the storm—but without a storm in the forecast.

"Good, that's the way it *should* feel."

"You're the boss," I said, reiterating my favorite phrase as it related to her, and one that had stuck since day one. She was my go-to, the backbone of our family even as an extended addition to it, and the love she and Mia shared was just a bonus. As time ticked on and we tackled more and more of what life decided to throw in our direction, I revered her even more.

Two hours and multiple platters of pappardelle with portobello mushroom ragu; bistecca alla fiorentina; a tender, local cut of steak; and roasted, marinated vegetables later, we were more than sufficiently fed, and most of us were ready for bed.

After our siblings had left, while Mia and I helped to clean up in the kitchen, Papa and Mama asked Santino and Sophia to join us in the dining room. The five of us were seated at the table, Papa standing at its head, when Pesca came back through after a change of clothes. "Oh, I'm sorry, don't mean to interrupt."

"You could never interrupt. You're as much a part of this family as anyone at this table, and you should hear this, too," Papa told her. She sat down alongside us.

"Almost a year ago, Mia sat in that chair as I disrespected her, and in turn, your entire family," Papa looked at Santino, not at all easing into the conversation at hand. "I will always wish that I could change what I said that evening, but I can't." Mama held out her hand for him to hold in support.

He took a breath and closed his eyes, lips pinched together to prevent him from crying and continued, "Any parent should be lucky to know their child has found someone to share their life with who loves them deeply. We should also show gratitude by allowing ourselves to learn a thing or two from our children as they grow older. Watching these two fall in love, no matter how tightly I tried to keep my eyes shut at the beginning, has allowed my old, stubborn heart to triple in size."

He paused to take a sip of water. "My sincerest apologies to you, my future daughter. And to Sophia and Santino, many thanks for raising a woman who is strong, intelligent, kind, and more beautiful than my son deserves."

A few laughs around the table lightened the mood perfectly.

"It's important that you know you're part of our family now, too, and with great pride, Gigi and I would like to offer you a piece of our land to do with as you'd like, so you always have a place to call your own here."

Sophia's eyes were the size of our dinner plates, and Santino had already stood up to hug Papa in a way that made it seem they had spoken about this before. I had no knowledge of it, not that it mattered. It was an absolutely perfect plan.

"We can't take land without paying you for it," Santino responded.

"Yes, you can. Spend whatever you'd like to build whatever you'd like on it and make it your own, but the land itself is our gift to you," Papa confirmed.

It felt a little dowry-esque, but if this old-school notion solidified that our families would be joined for life and Mia would have more frequent, convenient access to her parents, I was all for it, especially since I had made a promise to Mia several months ago about this exact thing.

"I'll build it for them with my own two hands…"

Life was connecting a lot of dots.

"Papa, all I've wanted this entire time is for you to know who I really am, and at my core, I'm a family girl. I love mine, and now, I love yours. *I'm sorry* if you ever felt disrespected by our relationship. It was never my intention or purpose, I simply fell in love." Mia wasn't sure whether she should continue, but when the angles of his face softened further, she added, "I know how much this place means to you. I know offering my parents a part of it to make their own is your way of accepting us and welcoming us. And what's most important for you to know is that Gennaro and I would love to take over the business, whenever you no longer want to or are unable to run it."

His neck pulled backward in moderate shock, and his lips parted to draw in a breath, blinking a few times to make sure he heard her correctly.

I jumped in to help.

"I know that deep down, buried in that olive-stained skin of yours, is a fear that one day all these acres won't belong to the Beletta family anymore. But we promise, so long as we and any future children live, it will. Your lifetime of blood, sweat, and, well, not many tears, but blood and sweat, will not be in vain."

A steady stream of tears rolled down the skin of his cheeks. He placed both hands on the table, bracing himself as he absorbed the one thing he had hoped to hear from one of his sons.

Mama stepped in to lighten the moment. "Now would be a good time to open that gift bag I gave you."

The bag was on a dresser in my villa apartment, so I ran over quickly to grab it. Walking back to the dining room across the cobblestone path, through the courtyard, stars brightening the dark sky above me, I flashed back through the last twelve months.

Meeting in Rome.

Two weeks together.

A surprise trip to the States.

A return trip by Mia.

A surprise proposal

A knockout of another trip.

Right back here to a new career, a new caffè, a soon-to-be new home, and a new life forming before my eyes.

Tomorrow, I'd marry the person who accidentally took my breath away a year ago and hadn't stopped since.

She planted a kiss on my lips and propped the bag in her lap. Mama watched from across the table, adding, "The rectangular one is your something blue. It's from me *and* your mom. The smaller box is from Papa and me."

Mia unwrapped the gift to reveal an unmistakable Acqua dell'Elba turquoise blue box. It was my signature scent, but for women, and the perfect full circle moment from the first night we met.

Then she opened the second box.

In it was a medium-sized gold brooch adorned with crystals and pearls. It looked like any old brooch you'd find in an antique or vintage store, but of course, there was history behind it that Mama filled us in on.

"I dreamed of my wedding day since I was a little girl, but when I was set to marry Papa against my will, I was *angry*—at my family, at him, and life itself. I remember my soon-to-be mother-in-law sitting with me at this very table, trying to calm me. She gave me this because it was given to her by her mother-in-law. Each woman that has come before you was arranged in marriage to her husband. You're the first one to have chosen my son on your own.

And while at first, to certain people," she said, looking at Papa with a smile, "it was considered inappropriate and disrespectful, I have always viewed it as courageous. You've allowed my son and our family to live outside of the lines we were used to, and I, for one, am incredibly proud and grateful to be celebrating your love tomorrow."

Mama hugged Mia tightly, and with her hands on her shoulders told her, "You're the fourth generation to wear it on your bouquet the day of your wedding as your *something borrowed*, if you'd like to, because the choice is *yours*. Like you chose my son, the choice is yours and yours alone."

"I'll wear this proudly, of course. And Mama? I'd choose him over and over again, in every lifetime, especially if it meant getting to choose you, too."

CHAPTER 32

Mia

The inner turmoil felt after waking up from a soul-crushingly beautiful dream always ends with us trying to force ourselves back to sleep, doesn't it? If we close our eyes, we'll be able to pick up right where it left off—or so we hope—in an effort to prolong the euphoric feeling that stems from it. The last two times I had woken up on days when I was scheduled to leave Italy, a deeply intense feeling of dread had woven its way through my body.

Today, though, my eyes blinked open, and the only thing I felt was the emptiness in my bed. At the insistence of everyone involved, I was back in my original villa apartment for the night to prevent Gennaro and me from seeing each other until the wedding actually started. But, while my bed was empty, the rest of the apartment was certainly not.

Pots clanged in the kitchen from what I assumed was my mother attempting to brew coffee. The sizzle of melted butter permeated the air, likely from pancakes being cooked by my father. And right outside my door, little feet loudly chased after each other. Allie's apartment was situated to the backside of mine, with a front door adjacent to my side door, allowing bored children to scurry inside their neighbor's house at any given moment.

It was too early for all of this, so I remained in bed for a half hour more, pretending I was still sleeping. I was the bride, after all, and since I hadn't been involved with even one detail besides a general color scheme and couldn't possibly be considered a "Bridezilla" in any way shape or form, I allowed myself to splurge on an extra half hour of relaxation.

Listening to the birds outside my window, the same way I had every morning prior, seemed to calm me. It was the new soundtrack to my life. I had gotten used to the tones of their chirps, the sun shining through my window, the temperatures that varied from the apartments to the kitchen to the pool landing, and everything else this beautiful place had let me experience.

My phone lit up next to me right as I felt myself dozing back to sleep.

Gennaro: Buongiorno amore mia

Mia: Good morning almost husband

Gennaro: There's something hanging outside of your window

Gennaro: Be careful it doesn't spill

My mouth curved into a wide smile, and I hopped out of bed. The stone floor was cool to the touch, but the sun peeking through the curtains tried its hardest to warm it up.

Unlocking the double windows and pushing them outward, I unhooked a small gift bag from underneath the window, inhaling the morning Tuscan air, letting the sun sizzle on my cheeks for a few seconds until I heard an unmistakable voice to my right.

"Hey Belle, *Beauty and the Beast* took place in France, not Italy. And if you start singing the *Bonjour* song, I may have to smack you on your wedding day."

"I'm so glad I chose my sister as my Matron of Honor," I said, smiling at Allie, who was slumped over in a patio chair with sunglasses on.

"Me too. Ain't nobody got the time to be fluffing your dress all day."

"Real nice," I said, sarcastically matching her tone. "I need coffee, and for you to come corral your kids before we have to start getting ready."

She exhaled. "I was hoping your mom would've adopted them as additional grandchildren by now."

"No chance." I smiled, closed the windows, sat on my bed, and opened the card first.

> *Amore,*
>
> *There are not enough words in the English and Italian languages combined to describe what I feel for you.*
>
> *My days are brighter, my heart is fuller, and my life is better—because of you.*
>
> *Da ora per sempre, il mio cuore è tuo.*
>
> *From now until forever, my heart is yours.*
>
> *Gennaro*

I opened the box to find a delicate gold-chain necklace with an exquisite diamond pendant suspended in the middle of it, the shape matching the earrings he had gifted me a few days prior for the shower.

If I could have picked the perfect gift from my soon-to-be husband, this would have been it.

I had my something new.

After an hour of breakfast, good mornings, and relaxing with my family in our villa, it was time to get ready. With hustling and bustling around me, I headed to my room, turned the shower on, waited for steam to cover the mirror, and stepped in. Hot beads of water streamed down my hair and skin, and with my eyes closed, music playing from a speaker from the bedroom, I allowed myself a trip down memory lane.

Things appear when we stop looking for them—isn't that what everyone always says?

I traveled five thousand miles to Italy and quite accidentally found the love of my life. I took a risk by trusting him *and* myself, and it was well worth the reward. From Rome to Tuscany to Florence to Venice and back again, this new life celebrated all the best parts of the Mia Luciano I grew up as while helping me blossom into the future Mia Beletta.

I gently massaged lotion into my clean skin, spraying more than a few sprays of my Acqua dell'Elba on pulse points. A knock at the door sounded, and I wrapped myself in a robe I had received as a gift from my shower before opening it. My mom and sister stood there like little soldiers ready to spring into bridal assistant action.

"The hair and makeup woman is here," Mom said. "Do you care how I get my hair styled?"

"Care how you get your hair styled? You think I'd ever ask you to come thousands of miles to tell you what kind of hair looks best on you?"

"Well, if we're being honest, the Mia who was slightly disgruntled prior to falling in love with a handsome Italian man might have," my sister chimed in.

"Okay, well thank you for that vote of confidence, but that's an outdated version of me."

We rotated through hair and makeup, which didn't take much time at all. I paired a smokey nude eye with a light dusting of highlight and contour; long, dark eyelashes; and a mauve-lined lip my "regular" look with a bit of added drama. My hair was swept to one side with old-Hollywood-type curls draped over my neck, the opposite side pinned up with a small crystal pin.

With a bit of time to waste, mild anxiety began to creep in, as I wasn't sure what to expect as far as setup or game plan, reminding me why I didn't want to be involved with specific wedding details in the first place. I longed to show up and be pleasantly surprised like everyone else, and most importantly, I wanted to spend as much time with Gennaro ahead of time, enjoying things and not stressing over them. I had been granted both wishes.

The other nontraditional component of our wedding —buying a gown without anyone else in attendance— meant that we'd be able to have a surprise viewing, Mom and Stella included. Looking at it hanging in the closet, I flashed back to the day in Rome when I found it. Browsing the aisles of the store Gina sent me to, the relatively plain, nude-colored, cut-out dress I had selected for the shower had immediately caught my eye, but wasn't fancy enough for an actual wedding.

Skimming the aisles for what I *thought* I wanted in a wedding gown—a simple, stretchy-satin mermaid style with a beaded sweetheart neckline—turned into a full-on fashion show for the entire staff. They had me trying on styles of dresses I'd never have considered, in fabrics and shades of white I didn't know existed. It was as much a *Pretty Woman* moment as was our rooftop rendezvous.

I fell in love with a mermaid-style gown on a

mannequin when its sparkle caught my eye from across the store. It was expertly designed and sewn with a glitter tulle underlay, floral embroidery, and a sweetheart neckline with two beaded straps that delicately skimmed each shoulder, creating an open back, and finished with buttons that trailed from my lower back to the curve of my bottom. It took my breath away as soon as I stepped out of the dressing room and caught a glimpse in the side mirror. The faces of each sales associate lit up like they *were* my own family members, and there were a few audible gasps. When I stepped on the platform surrounded by mirrors and overhead lighting to view the gown in its entirety, I knew without a doubt that it was meant for me.

A nod to my inner Jersey girl, with the perfect amount of sparkle bouncing off of the glitter in the tulle, it was balanced by the dull ivory embroidery, an accessible neckline for my *husband* to kiss me across, and a shape that made me feel more confident than I ever had in a dress.

"That gown was made for you, *bella*," the owner of the shop had said as she peeked her head in from a side door, nodding with wide-eyed, chef's-kiss approval.

And that was that—quick, easy, and relatively effortless, just as this entire Italian journey of self- discovery had been.

I called out for my mom, sister, and Allie to come assist with the buttons and veil. When the door opened, Mom cried at the sight of me. My sister nodded slowly, choking back a tear or two, and Allie asked, directly, "How'd you manage to find the hottest dress in all of Italy?"

Accidentally, like I found my husband.

Wearing the "G" bracelet from Pesca, diamond earrings and necklace from Gennaro, the brooch on my bouquet from Mama, and the perfume from Acqua dell'Elba, I had something old, something new, something borrowed, and something blue.

"Santino!" Mom yelled for dad to come see me.

"Is she coming out, or am I coming in?"

"I'll come out, Dad," I responded.

He was standing with his back to the door, dressed in a dark brown suit to compliment my mother's bronze gown. Slowly turning around, he surveyed the length of me, nodding in as much approval as a man could give to a daughter who had moved thousands of miles away and was about to get married. "*Spectacular.*"

He was a man of few words, but usually the right ones.

I smiled, hugged him tightly, planted a kiss on his cheek, and grabbed hold of his arm. My sister, in a flowy, beige halter dress with plentiful cleavage and Allie in a champagne-colored mock turtleneck that perfectly skimmed each curve joined us. My brother and brother-in-law held the back of the line behind three beautiful flower girls, my niece and Allie's daughters dressed in gold.

Someone overseeing wedding details had texted my mom, because she read aloud, "We can head down there now. You ready, baby girl?"

"Never been more ready for anything, actually." I felt it in the deepest part of my soul. The only anxious feeling that remained was that of missing him. I wanted to see his face, and I needed to feel his hands on and around me.

The event crew had laid down a walkway's worth of thin foam, covered in rose petals, allowing for easier foot travel from the villa down the small hill to the backyard. To the left of the pool, bronze-colored chairs were arranged in rows facing the handmade pergola adorned with white and ivory floral, the vineyard as its backdrop.

An event coordinator came to introduce herself, offering standard bridal congratulations and compliments before arranging us in the order we'd proceed down the aisle. As the music started, Dad and I remained at the top of the hill as everyone else began walking the length of the pathway. Instrumental versions of Eros Ramazzotti songs streaming through hidden speakers brought us full circle from our proposal night.

Perched behind a large tree, I watched as the procession began, noticing Pesca standing underneath the pergola and assuming she was organizing the crew.

Lenny escorted my mom down the aisle first, Papa and Mama followed, and then Gennaro, who hugged Pesca tightly when he reached the altar. Allie walked down next, her arms interlocked with Salvatore's on one side and Vincenzo's on the other. She was followed by Stella, surrounded on both sides by Giovanni and Giuseppe. Allie's two daughters held my niece's hands, and they looked like a bunch of drunken sailors that had broken into the cocktail hour stash before the ceremony began. One pulled in one direction and the other in the opposite while my niece tried to find her mother, an occasional cry out for assistance. Eventually, everyone made it to their respective spots, the music changed, and all of our guests stood up.

My father, who hadn't said much up until this point, whispered, "Are you ready?"

"Without a doubt."

We walked the remaining length of the pathway and stopped where the rows of chairs began. Now closer to the action, I scanned the crowd. Plenty of people I had never seen before stared back at me with undeniable smiles, filling my heart with pure joy. There were a few recognizable faces, too—Carmine from the osteria sat next to Gina *and* Giustino from the Rome apartment complex. A man with silver hair sat with an open space next to him, and while he looked familiar, I couldn't pinpoint where from.

As the music changed one last time, Dad motioned for us to begin our walk down the aisle. I hadn't yet made eye contact with Gennaro, avoiding it only to prolong what I knew I'd feel once my eyes met his. Halfway down, I couldn't resist it anymore, and our first glance was every bit as fulfilling as I hoped it would be.

Biting his bottom lip alongside his classic half smile and head shake, his eyes scanned me from head to toe before looking up at the sky, thanking the heavens for having brought us together. When my father and I approached him, they hugged. Dad whispered something in his ear, and Gennaro nodded and smiled in response. I then squeezed my father tightly and planted another kiss on his cheek before he joined my mom in the front row.

"*Sei incredibile, amore mia.*" I definitely *felt* incredible. There was no doubt about that. "And, thank you, for this." Gennaro held up his wrist, adorned with a gold bracelet engraved with our initials. I had bought it in Rome the same day I found my dresses with money I had saved from my last few months bartending. The night prior, I had asked Giuseppe to leave the box along with a short note in Gennaro's room before we had sat down with our parents,

This story, our story, will forever be my favorite one. Thank you for making me believe in true love again. I can't wait to be your wife.

Now, standing in front of him at a makeshift altar, about to *become* his wife, I realized Pesca was standing there with a book in hand. She was the one who was going to marry us.

Relaying the first passage in Italian, she repeated it in English for the American crew. "Welcome to the wedding of Gennaro and Mia, two incredible people, whom I love dearly. When Gennaro asked me months ago to marry them, I was honored. I immediately began thinking about *why* marriage is so important, and what could be done to make a marriage ceremony mean as much as it should to the bride and the groom as well as their families. The more I thought about it, I realized the answer lies in the couple getting married. Any variation of words and promises can be said here today, but the quality of the marriage lies in all the days ahead."

She flipped a page in her notebook and continued, "First, you must choose each other over everyone and everything, from now until the end of time. Second, you must learn the art of true, solid communication, in all its forms: physical, verbal, and emotional. And lastly, recognize that not everyone can give one hundred percent of themselves day in and day out, so, you must promise to always support the other in a way that allows your combined efforts to equal that one hundred percent. If you can remember to do these things daily, you should be able to make it through any conflict, any issue, and any task. Your marriage will strengthen with every passing day in the same manner that your love will deepen alongside it."

My throat tightened as I saw a tear pool in the corner of Gennaro's eye. When it was time for vows, he recited his first.

"Mia, you are the puzzle piece that completes me, a bright light that has transformed darkness, paving the way for my life to finally feel whole. When times are difficult, I promise to never give up on you or us. In both sickness and health, you will be my top priority. And mostly, I vow to enjoy this life we were given together, from now until the end of our days, so that you never forget how thankful I am for you and how much I love you."

He squeezed my hands, and it took all of my effort not to jump the gun for a kiss. When Pesca urged me to begin my own vows, I inhaled slowly and deeply, trying to piece together all of the things I knew I wanted to say to him.

"Little girls tend to dream up their weddings from the day they're old enough to play with dolls and dress-up clothes. In all my days on Earth leading up to this one, I could never have predicted that life itself would feel even more special than those *very* specific dreams of mine. You are calm, confident, intelligent, and passionate, as genuine as you are driven, and as protective as you are nurturing. My heart and soul feel safe with you, and on our wedding day, I promise to never falter in giving you even more of the same love, adoration, and respect that you've shown me every day since the day we met."

Sniffles sounded from the rows behind us, and when we looked to Pesca, we saw streams of tears rolling down her cheeks, too. "Was that okay?" I whispered.

"Oh darling, you nailed it."

An "I now pronounce you husband and wife" and "you may kiss the bride" later, Gennaro pulled me close, cradling my face in his hands, whispering, "*Ti amerò per sempre*," in my ear.

I whispered back, "Forever is not long enough," and we kissed to a round of applause behind us, a chorus of whistles, and the utmost desire to enjoy the rest of the evening the same way we planned to enjoy the rest of our lives— with good music, delicious food, and the company of our favorite people.

String lights criss-crossed high above a makeshift dance floor in the middle of the grass alongside the vineyard's rolling hills. The pool was illuminated with lantern lights, and the white road was subtly lit in the distance by the flight of thousands of lightning bugs. Every which way you turned, you were met with a beautiful view, and I relished in the thought that this was a place I'd be part of forever.

As Gennaro and I forked a few bites of food into our mouths, we sat at our table for two, taking it all in. A small, intimate wedding complete with our favorite people had combined families from two different countries, and a large group of even larger personalities. Somehow, they'd made it a perfect day and night.

During the dance with my father, Santino Luciano *finally* found more than a few words to string together. "I know I'm usually skeptical of much of what you do, but that's mostly because I don't know where you get the drive to do it." He paused for a moment and shook his head in an effort to hold back tears. "You've lived the lives of five adults combined in the twenty-five years you've been on this Earth, simply because you keep choosing to *do* things. I don't say it as often as I should, but I'm proud of you. Really, truly proud of the woman you've become and the choices you've made to get you here."

It was a sentiment I never thought I'd hear, and one I hoped I'd never forget.

"What did you whisper in Gennaro's ear at the altar?" I asked curiously.

"To love you like his wife, and to protect you like my daughter."

My own tears started rolling. "I'll be fine, Dad. I promise."

"I'm not worried, I'm prepared. There *is* a difference."

"Yes, sir," I said, saluting him and preparing to transfer

to party mode after watching Gennaro and Mama have their own dance.

With a glass of champagne in one hand and a man's hand in the other, Pesca walked over to introduce us to her date. "Gennaro, you remember Vincent, of course?" And then I remembered, too. Gennaro's seatmate on the plane, who had magically appeared at the osteria months ago. It turned out he and Pesca had gone out many times since that night, getting to know each other in ways they both deserved. It was a beautiful thing to witness two people, solid at their cores with varying reasons as to why they had been lonely the last few years, find fulfillment within each other.

Vincent offered us congratulations and motioned to Gennaro specifically before saying, "I'm so honored to meet the one you couldn't live *without* who had thrown you for a loop on that plane."

The next few hours burned memories into the heads and hearts of our closest friends and family who were dancing, laughing, and enjoying themselves in unison. Giovanni slow-danced with Dominique in the middle of an upbeat song, looking like he might very well be the next Beletta man to walk down an aisle.

Conversely, Lenny, Giuseppe, Salvatore, and Marco all seemed perfectly content to have no immediate plans to be held down, and fought with Giustino and Carmine to dance with Gina and her daughter.

Allie and Vincenzo huddled in their own little dance floor bubble with the girls until they couldn't keep their eyes open anymore, falling asleep on the patio couches.

"You did it, my girl," Allie said to me as she grabbed my hand on the dance floor and pulled me close for a hug.

"Did what?"

"You stopped waiting for the shoe to drop, and started

living with your whole heart and your invisible balls instead." She smiled at me, shaking her head side to side in disbelief. "And now look at us—a bunch of American broads turned Italian housewives."

"Speak for yourself, I'm a caffè owner."

"You're right. I'm probably just a wedding hookup, but hell if I don't want to go ride that big dick of his right this minute."

"Could you not be vile on the night of my wedding?" I sarcastically responded to the one person I could always count on to be inappropriately hilarious in any situation.

"Oh please, like the two of you are not going to have sex all night and then eat your weight in adrenaline munchies afterwards. *Look* at the way he's staring at you right now," she said, nodding her head in his direction.

With his suit jacket draped over his shoulder, leaning against the shower from the night of Operation-Black-Hawk-Down-Your-Pants, he licked his bottom lip while staring directly at me.

"He did say he had one more surprise for me." I remembered him whispering during our first dance.

"So, what in the hell are you doing here with me?"

"Trying to not be rude," I responded.

"Rudeness has no place getting in the way of a fine Italian gentleman and the consummation of an epic marriage. Now, go."

"Yes, ma'am."

Gennaro and I hugged and kissed everyone goodnight before he held me tightly in his arms and asked, "Ready for your surprise, wife?"

"Abso-fuckin-lutely."

We drove up the white road to our house, which I hadn't stepped foot in since the first day he brought me there.

Tea lights lit up a pathway from the driveway, which was freshly paved all the way to the front door. The house was now surrounded in lush shrubbery and landscaping as far as I could tell from the moonlight. When he ushered me in front of him to open the front door, I nearly choked on air.

More flowers than I had ever seen lined the entire staircase leading to the second floor. A small circular table at the bottom of the steps had a folded piece of paper on it alongside two glasses of champagne.

I will never stop dating you. I will never stop surprising you. And I will never stop loving you.

I turned around to thank him, and his hand was extended to lead me upstairs. Once at the top, I followed the flower-lined pathway to our bedroom. More tea lights lined the tile in the bathroom, leading us to the enormous soaking tub that now had a stone wall perched behind it. A waterfall sounded straight out of a spa. Music streamed through Bluetooth speakers wired into the ceiling. Immediately, my body released whatever tension it had been holding onto from a long, beautiful day of celebration.

"I promised to never stop dating you. So, for our first night as husband and wife, I figured I'd have to live up to, if not improve upon, our night on the rooftop in Rome." His eyes refused to leave mine, I felt my insides twist, and I was already looking forward to every which way he was planning to unravel them.

"Dare I ask how you plan to do that?" I was smiling but still in awe of him.

"You can ask, but I'm not going to answer with words."

"Why not?"

I already knew *why*.

"*Vivi il momento*, Mia Beletta." He inched closer to me, brushing his thumb over my lips in the same manner that always set my insides on fire.

"Vivi…" He turned me around and trailed the length of my shoulder with his mouth.

"Il…" He unbuttoned the back of my dress.

"Momento…" He slipped it down to my ankles, extending his hand to mine, allowing me to step out of it.

The dress itself did not allow for undergarments, which I was sure he was counting on.

I was a married lady, but I could certainly still play the game.

Inching closer to *him* this time, I whispered back.

"Live…" I unbuttoned his shirt and pulled it down over the dips and curves of his arms.

"In…" I unzipped his pants and slid them down to his ankles, removing each of his socks with them.

"The…" I stood back up, face to face with him while dropping my hand to grasp the length of him.

"Moment…" I slipped my hands in his waistband and pulled the last remaining layer of clothing between me and my husband to the floor.

He kissed me with the passion of a thousand men, reminding me that the only one I'd ever need, want, or desire in my life would be him.

"Now get in that bathtub and relax, *amore*," he reminded me, "so afterwards I can show you how a *husband* makes love to his *beautiful wife.*"

And he did—over and over again.

He reminded me of the one decision that had altered the course of my life forever, in the most exhilarating, fulfilling way possible.

He showed me what genuine, true, unbridled love looked and felt like.

He demonstrated the way a real man should treat a woman's body, mind, and heart while still allowing me to shine with my own voice, wants, and needs, never attempting to diminish any of them.

The entire journey had taught me to believe in myself, value myself, and trust myself with unwavering confidence.

I had to discover my best self and find happiness within my own walls before someone else could attempt to add to it.

Had Gennaro changed my life? *Of course he had.*

But it stemmed from a choice *I* made to live presently, to think a little less and do a lot more, and mostly, to stay true to myself, right down to my core.

We lived presently in the most significant of life's moments, all of which had led us here—to the start of an absolutely *beautiful life*—together.

Forever would not be long enough, but it would have to do.

I was his, and he was mine. In this moment, in this lifetime, and in every single one that followed.

Epilogue

PAPA

"We are the sum of all the moments in our lives - all that is ours is in them: we cannot escape it or conceal it." —— Thomas Wolfe

THREE MONTHS LATER

Fatherhood is defined as the state of being a father; a man in relation to his child or children. At its core, though, fatherhood is the art of raising, protecting, and supporting the one or ones you love most in the world.

To some, fatherhood comes easy, naturally, and instinctually, and to others, it's a lifelong struggle. I found myself somewhere in the middle of that, most comfortable teaching skills and building habits.

My boys were always hard workers in one way or another, even though it didn't necessarily align with the family business as they aged. Unfortunately, it took me an entire lifetime to realize that, regardless of how hard you worked and how focused you were, if you didn't stop and *smell the roses*, it would all be for naught.

When you add to that my years spent as a husband—one who focused on providing physically and financially for a loving wife but forgetting to nurture her inner needs—I realized much too late what life was really, truly about: *its moments.*

The last few months had taught me that the one thing I yearned for—my children to proudly take over our family business—would happen when I stopped trying to force it.

A health scare forced me to slow down and self-reflect, which set off a chain of events that allowed for honest communication with the people who meant the most to me.

Why hadn't I been able to see that before?

Why couldn't I adjust my priorities on my own without an illness forcing me to?

The very reason I had initially landed in the hospital was stress from an altercation with the one person who had taught me, albeit indirectly, to live presently.

I had fought it until the bitter end, blind to the lessons laid out in front of me.

Thankfully, though, three months of learning and growth allowed me to witness my family flourish. My sons were more involved than ever, and my wife was the happiest, most content version of herself I had ever seen, especially after I took her on some long-awaited dates.

I was grateful for the lessons and proud of myself for recognizing them, but it *did* feel too little too late.

I had to *hope* she knew how much I adored her, cherished her, and respected her.

I had to *pray* that my boys knew how proud I was of them and their individual accomplishments.

And I had to do it all without ever being able to face them again.

Because I was gone.

An invisible angel, overlooking my beloved property as my wife served her signature dishes, my sons and gracious daughter-in-law helping to manage it all while new guests continued to experience the place I had built with my bare hands and entire heart.

They still had each other, and I was grateful that the last few months before my passing had brought me clarity, understanding, and closure for my wrongs, no matter how late in my life.

The sum of *my* life's moments would live on in my family, even if a large majority of those moments defined what *not* to do. If they could learn from my mistakes and live their lives presently, wholly, and happily, my shortcomings would feel worthwhile.

My ashes had been spread in the plush grass alongside the pool as my last living request. A variety of flowering bushes surrounded the area, only further enhancing the beauty of the rolling hills behind me.

Finally, I was able to enjoy the place I had given my entire life to.

Living in the moment had brought me home.

A home that my family was finally proud to call their own.

Ciao!

Let's stay connected.

Scan the code below with your phone camera to visit my website and subscribe to email updates. You'll be the first to know when new books are available for pre-order!

And, follow me on Instagram, Facebook, and TikTok for some behind the scenes snippets, recipes, teasers, and more. **@mary.belle.books**

Did you love this book? Help me find new readers and leave a review on Amazon and/or Goodreads! After scanning the QR code, click the *Reviews* tab from the dropdown menu.

About the Author

Mary Belle writes relatable romance stories with equal parts steamy scenes and laugh-out-loud *I-want-to-be-friends-with-these-people* banter.

She's an avid supporter of women with a lot to say, as well as the gentlemen—seasoned generously with spice—they're magnetized to along the way.

Mary lives with her husband and daughter in the Hudson Valley of New York, where she celebrates all of life's moments (quite literally all of them) with a good meal. This is her second novel.

www.marybellebooks.com

goodreads.com/mary_belle

instagram.com/mary.belle.books

tiktok.com/@mary.belle.books

facebook.com/mary.belle.books

threads.net/@mary.belle.books

Acknowledgments

I had "write a book" on my Bucket List for over fifteen years. Originally, I planned to write a memoir about being "big boned" (aka "plus-sized"), back before the concept was a bit more mainstream. I quickly realized that even though I'd be spreading body positivity and confidence tips, I didn't want to get that personal, and more than that, I wasn't sure where it would lead me.

Just one book? What would that do for a potential career?

So "write a book" remained a bullet point in my Notes app—until last year when *Vivi il Momento* came to life—and I officially became a romance author. Now, *Bella Vita* is here, I've written two books, and "write a book" has been replaced by "books I want to write." All I need to get them out in the world (besides my incredible support system) is time sweet time.

I have these wonderful people and businesses to thank for helping me get this far.

My husband, Jay—for believing in me while shouting from the rooftops to anyone who will listen, "Hey, my wife wrote a romance novel!" My tour manager, event assistant, heavy lifter, and bodyguard all in one, but most notably, the equal partner every woman hopes for in marriage. You don't "help" me, you just *are* and you just *do*, without any expectations and without ever keeping track of sacrifices made along the way. On my darkest days of self-doubt and overwhelm, you pull me from the holes I retreat into, giving me renewed hope and reminders of how far we've come, all while throwing delicious food at me to keep me happy.

Not one day goes by when I don't count my lucky stars that we made it through our own struggles to get here. I can't wait until we're in our eighties, sitting in rocking chairs on a porch overlooking mountains or a lake, preferably both, and reflecting, "Wow, that was worth it *all*."

My daughter, Marina—for being as patient as humanly possible while I try to balance the joys of parenting, of which there are many, to the stressors of being a parent who works from home, of which there are *also* many. You, like Daddy, love telling anyone who will listen that your mom wrote a book, and I hope that in years far into the future, we'll look back and feel this has all been worth it.

Mostly, I hope you keep leaning into your own incredible imagination and honing your creativity, from playing "pretend" to drawing, coloring, painting, dress-up, makeup, and more. Your smarts combined with your occasional flair for dramatics is a force to be reckoned with. No idea where you get it from, really!

"I love you all the days and I want to keep you forever."

To my parents—who have yet to miss an event, who pass out my business cards to anyone who signals even remote interest in reading, and who have reminded me along the way that this is what I'm meant for. Mares, for all your road trips, beta reading, feedback, and personal cheerleading. Dad, sorry I got her back into reading, and now you're being ignored. LOL.

Rosie & Co.—thank you for spreading the word endlessly, for believing in me, and for always going above and beyond to help us out in any way possible.

To my brother, sister, in-laws, family, and friends, all of

whom wear their MBB apparel with pride—for continuing to show up at events, sharing the books across the world wide web and through word of mouth, and always showing excitement, enthusiasm, and support. I'm so lucky to have you in my corner.

To Alexis and Carmine, especially—for stopping people on the street or beach exclaiming, "My aunt wrote a book!" I hope you never get too old or too cool to help in my marketing efforts. I love you like my own and always will.

To Well Worn Books in Middletown, NY, the first bookstore to ever say "yes" to stock my book, Crossroads Gift Shop in Hopewell Junction, NY., and Barnes & Noble in Poughkeepsie for my first ever B&N signing, thanks for making me feel a little bit more like a "real" author.

D'Amores Tea & Toast in Lavallette, NJ; Hudson Square Boutique in Hopewell Junction, NY; Franco's Deli in Hopewell Junction, NY; Pizza Time in Wappingers Falls, NY; Sabellico Florist in Wappingers Falls, NY; Boutique Wines & Spirits in Fishkill, NY; Sannino Vineyard in Cutchogue, NY; Wanderlux Boutique in Beacon, NY; Ort Farms in Long Valley, NJ; Tiramisu Ristorante in Hopewell Junction, NY; and Board & Brush in Wappingers Falls, NY–thank you for hosting, donating, and/or supporting me through my tour of events. I've met incredible people along the way, thanks to your hospitality!

Jeanne Dorrow of *East Fishkill Living* magazine and Louisa Vilardi, my official photographer, friend, and adopted sister—I could cry every time I think of you putting my family on the cover of a magazine. What an incredible experience it was, allowing me to fall in love with my husband all over again, reminding me of how far we've come, and how lucky we are to be a part of this wonderful community.

Ashli Helm and Tara Boettger—two of my local social media influencers who helped move the needle with initial Amazon book sales from the release date of *Vivi il Momento,* I'm forever grateful for your dedication to the platform that helped introduce me to new readers!

To my beta readers—Nicole, from helping deliver my daughter in the hospital to beta reading my first two books; Lisa, my "#1 Stalker"; and Francesca, one of the first reviews I received from a "stranger" that absolutely blew me away—your positive feedback and constructive critiques helped remind me of the initial joy I felt when writing *Bella Vita,* something authors tend to forget once they're in the thick of editing and have convinced themselves their work is a piece of *crapola.* You renewed my spirit when I needed it most.

Shelby Leigh of Marketing with Shelby—you are a champion for authors and their marketing efforts, and I feel so fortunate to know you and learn from you. Thank you for your endless knowledge and support as well as featuring me on a YouTube video. Anyone interested in poetry should take a look at her books!

Dave Reggina—man oh man, am I glad my solid follow-up (and spreadsheet!) skills landed me on the No Snooze Podcast. You're an epic source of inspiration and motivation for so many and have helped remind me at random times throughout this journey exactly what I'm capable of. I'm patiently waiting to be a guest on your future televised talk show (manifesting it), but will continue enjoying podcast episodes from you and the fabulous Claudio in the meantime. Thanks for being one of the good guys—a gentleman and an incredible Girl Dad who will forever support his baby's dreams. I grew up with my own, which helped land me here, and both you and Jaybird could easily lead the pack for this generation.

Tony and Samantha Pec, my Italian-American support system—I'm grateful that No Snooze Podcast indirectly brought me to both of you and beyond thankful to you for helping me spread the word to our virtual crew, especially Dena Fenza, Italian-American cookbook author, fairy godmother, *Madrina*, and now, special friend. I adore you all.

Jessica Sorentino of the Open Book Podcast—thanks for featuring me as your first ever self-published guest. Here's to both our Italian-American *and* Delaware Blue Hen roots.

Stephanie Madonia—my secret **PR** agent and fellow Italian-American with a heart of gold. We hit it off instantly, didn't we? I can't wait to see what we accomplish together in the future. Thanks for being a ray of sunshine, and quite simply, a beautiful human being, inside and out.

BookTok and Bookstagram—you have the power to absolutely exhaust me some days, but I am entirely grateful for the number of romance readers you've introduced me to. Thank you to my bookish girls for posting, reviewing, and spreading the word for us "baby" authors.

Author friends, whom I can't list fully for fear of accidentally leaving someone out—thank you for the tips, insights, occasional commiserations, and overall support. Let's continue carrying each other and never, ever give up on our dreams.

To my editor and faraway virtual friend Elizabeth Lyons—you continue to be my beacon of light throughout this entire process. When I'm drowning, you pull me right back to the surface. When I doubt myself, you give me renewed hope and motivation. I'm looking forward to meeting *for real* one day soon, but until then, I'll live for our voice notes and audio messages. If anyone reading this has always wanted to write a book, go read *Write the Damn Book*

Already and enroll in every course, workshop, and training Liz offers. And also, thanks for connecting me with fellow foodie and one of my favorite writer friends, Dawn McMullan.

To everyone who holds this novel in their hands— thank you for trusting me with your limited free time—not once, but twice with both *Vivi il Momento* and *Bella Vita*.

"If you can't travel by plane, you might as well travel by page." - Me, I said that.

May you always remember to live in the moment for an absolutely beautiful life…

Grazie mille a tutti.

Thank you all so much.